Her Dark Enchantments

HER DARK ENCHANTMENTS

ROSALYN BRIAR

Her Dark Enchantments
by Rosalyn Briar
Published by Quill & Crow Publishing House

This novel is a work of fiction. All incidents, dialogue, and characters are either products of the author's imagination or used in a fictitious manner. Any resemblance to actual persons, living or dead, or actual events is purely coincidental.

Copyright © 2023 by Rosalyn Briar.

All rights reserved. Published in the United States by Quill & Crow Publishing House, Ohio. No portion of this book may be reproduced in any form without permission from the publisher, except as permitted by U.S. copyright law.

Cover Design by Fay Lane

Interior Art by Nicole Scarano

Printed in the United States of America

ISBN (ebook) 978-1-958228-20-3

ISBN (print) 978-1-958228-08-1

Library of Congress Control Number 2023903672

Publisher's Website: www.quillandcrowpublishinghouse.com

For my soulmate

"What sort of thing is that, that rattles round so merrily?" said the girl, and she took the spindle and wanted to spin too.

— "LITTLE BRIAR-ROSE" BY THE BROTHERS GRIMM

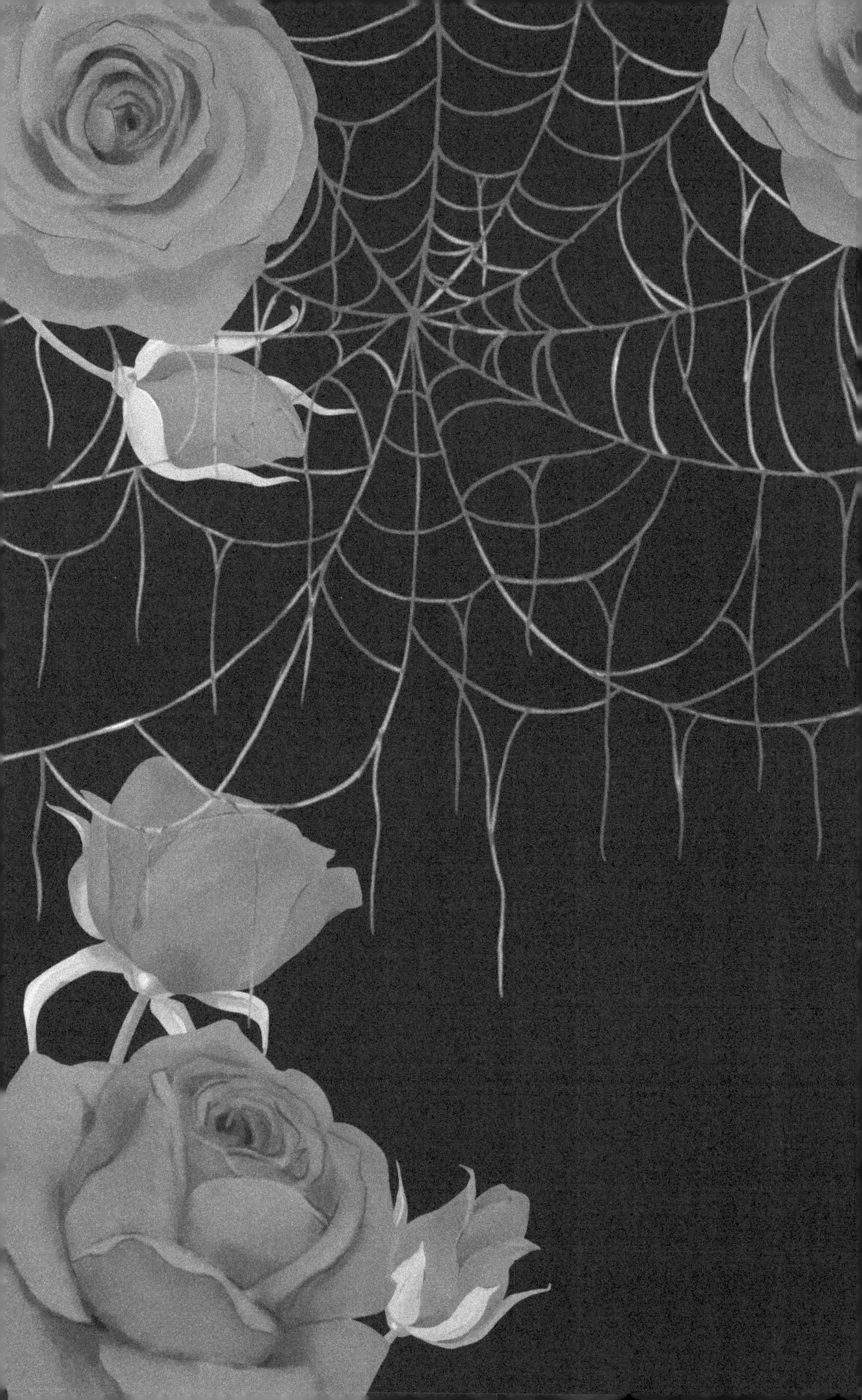

PROLOGUE

Briar Rose

Anger tangled and choked the girl's voice into silence. Furious tears tarnished the view of her three aunts as they exited the strange, elaborate room. It was now her room, and they were not truly her aunts. In only a matter of hours, her entire life had unraveled, its fibers slipping through her fingers. Two unbelievable things had been revealed that morning: she was a princess and her aunts were fairies. Having grown up in a cottage tucked away in the woods, she had only known these sorts of things to exist in fairy tales.

This fairy tale was nothing but a nightmare.

The girl rose under the weight of her velvet gown and tiara, staring into the polished mirror. Her tear-stained cheeks looked anything but regal, and she wished her birthday had never arrived. For the day had ushered in only deceit, confusion, and change. Her entire life had been a lie.

Toying with a silver hairbrush on the vanity, the girl ran her finger over the briar roses etched into the handle. She was named after the flower, according to her aunts, because one had bloomed in the castle gardens on the morning of her birth after a long, harsh winter. The girl felt nothing like a flower with delicate petals. But thorns? Oh yes, she was bristling with those.

Was her life cursed?

She itched at the suffocating fabric of her gown, which threatened to hem her in tight and never let go. Even the stone walls and arches of the chambers narrowed in, ready to swallow her up forever. She wiped at the tears still streaming from her cheeks when a shiny black crow perched on the windowsill. It tilted its head at her before taking flight toward the trees. *Free.*

Jealousy needled at the girl's stomach.

She longed for the freedom of the forest, where her bare feet brushed the soft carpets of moss and warm sunlight dappled across her skin. Where she'd roam for hours in nothing but a light linen dress to collect fruits and nuts. Where she had met *him*. Oh, how her heart ached for the boy. He had not even given her his name, but he had stolen her heart...

She had to escape her gilded prison.

The hinges of the massive door groaned as she tugged on the brass handle. She peeked down the corridor, but both directions looked exactly the same. Choosing to go left, the girl tiptoed along the red runner, past boring and lifeless statues and hideous tapestries, only to reach a dead end. She dared not glance out the arched window, for the crowds of people in the city frightened her, but it offered a swath of light, illuminating the only tapestry she didn't find revolting. It displayed a simple and vibrant woodland scene with wildflowers and forest creatures woven with care.

Something twinkled along its edge. The girl reached out to peel the tapestry back and found a green light gleaming through a gap in the stones as if there was something behind the wall. *Could it be a secret passageway out of this castle? A way out of this life?*

Shuffling feet and bickering voices echoed down the hall and startled the girl. Before her aunts could spot her, she slipped behind the tapestry and pushed against the stone wall. It swung open with magical ease, and she entered an empty and frigid stairwell.

The green glow fluttered like little moths that collected itself into a single orb and bounded up the spiral steps. The girl followed, desperate. It must have been years since anyone had used the tower, she thought, for a thick blanket of dust clung to every tread, and cobwebs fell like curtains from above. She would certainly ruin her hair and gown, but the girl didn't mind. Bewitched, she kept following the light.

At last, the glow dissipated, and she reached a round room edged in darkness. Only a small stream of light filtered through the window, highlighting the dust in the air. A creaking sound made the girl flinch. There in the shadows, a woman rocked in a chair, twirling something with her hands. The wooden thing was round at the top with a long shaft which tapered into a sharp point. Near the woman was a stand wrapped with wool, and on the floor was a heap of gold thread. The girl gasped when the woman pinched at a simple clump of wool and spun it into gleaming gold with the curious wooden thing.

"What is that, ma'am? The thing that spins around so merrily in your hands?"

"Oh, this?" The woman rocked forward and tilted her face into the light, revealing her sallow and sunken skin, rotten smile, and black horns atop her head. "'Tis but a spindle, my darling."

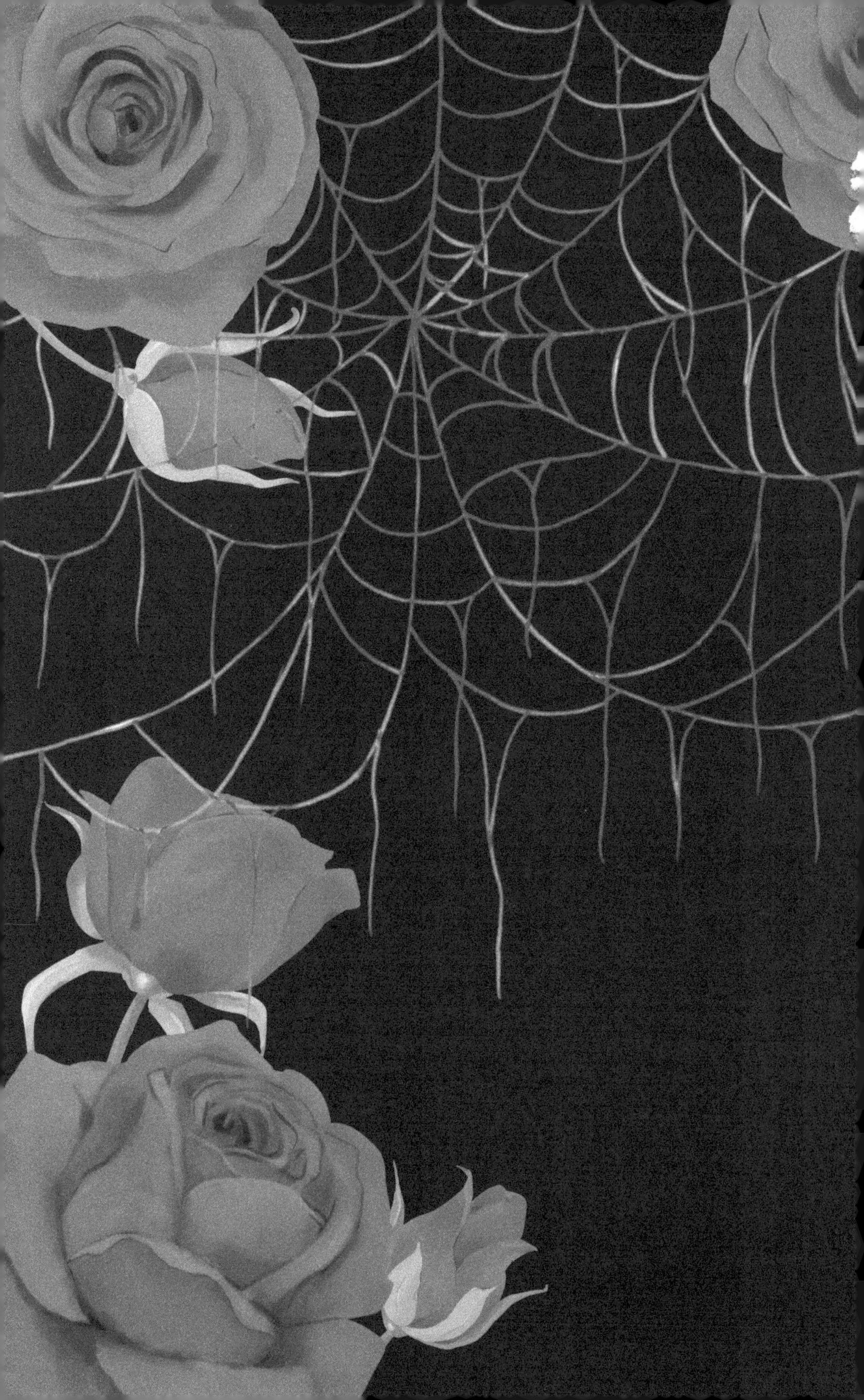

I

Byzarien

Embers danced against the inky night, only to rain upon the soldiers as dead, white ash. The elderwood funeral pyre blazed in rolling flames as Byzarien approached, and the putrid tang stung his nose. The glow erased the mountainous surroundings, as if only the army encampment existed in all the world.

A chant rose above the whistling breeze as the soldiers prayed to the god of war, "As in war, now in death, guide our fallen brother, Lazaire. Let him not be lost along the Darkened Path. Serve him as he served you."

Each soldier tossed a token onto the pyre to ensure the deceased safe passage into the Underworld. While Byzarien waited, the wind of eternal winter bit through the leather and fur of his jacket. He swept his dark hair over the scars on his cheek and squeezed the knucklebones in his grip. He and Lazaire had often gambled into the early hours of the morning with them—when Lazaire was still *himself*, that is.

Byzarien glared, an inferno in his eyes, at the woman standing closest to the pyre. The *witch* had hair darker than volcanic sands, bone-pale skin, and eyes sharp as broken glass. Rumors said she befriended the spiders that spun her midnight gowns. The gloomy fibers clung to her body like a second skin, and the intricate metalwork and beading reflected the flames. Her face remained stoic and empty, with no hint of grief or remorse.

Murderer.

She had mutilated his friend. Byzarien's gut wrenched the more he thought about it. He couldn't properly mourn Lazaire while his insides burned hotter than the pyre itself. When the witch left before the service was over, his hatred deepened. By the time Byzarien reached the pyre, his breaths were erratic, and the knucklebones in his hand were slick with sweat. The flames threatened to lick his scars, and echoes of his family's screams roared from the fire, but nothing would stop him from paying his respects.

After tossing the knucklebones into the flames, he followed the line of soldiers filtering in and out of the Guerrix Temple. Long ago, after a major victory secured the kingdom, the very first Eglantyne soldiers had carved the hollowed-out rock to honor the god of war. The underground temple, though far from home, was sacred to the kingdom and its soldiers.

Ducking inside, Byzarien welcomed the dim glow of candlelight sparkling against the gilded icon of Guerrix. The god of war held two crossed swords, like Byzarien's pendant—a gift from his parents when he joined the army. Age-old murals depicting the gods clung to the walls with chipped and faded pigments, while ghosts of soot rose from every candle niche. Byzarien whispered a prayer to Guerrix, then moved along for the next soldier to do the same.

When most had returned to their quarters for the night, Byzarien and a few others, including his tent-mates, remained. They knelt before the pyre on frost-hardened earth while the Guerrix priest, an old man in red and gold robes, sprinkled oils around it with the swing of his aspergillum.

Rubbing his crossed-sword pendant between his fingertips, Byzarien thought of Lazaire's parents, who'd relied heavily upon their son's salary. Vines of guilt wound around him as he thought of his own struggling family. Even with his stipend, there was never enough—although the fire happened long ago, the deep physical, emotional, and monetary scars still burned strong. The loss of his little brother hovered over him like a ghost.

With strain on his face from the mix of emotions, he prayed even harder. Having grown up in the Pezit Quarter with Lazaire, they had known the only god ever to help poor children like them was Guerrix. *Serve him, and he will serve you.* He stared at his friend's remains as the slowing embers sparkled like the stars he missed so much. The somber sky pressed into his chest like a boulder, and he cursed the god of nightmares and trickery for causing the eternal winter.

When their prayers faded and the flames of the pyre smoldered to ash, Byzarien and his roommates headed to their tent. Dezlan and Xavier held hands as Byzarien ambled behind them. Dezlan's golden-brown hair gleamed in the light of every torch they passed, as did the dark skin of Xavier's shaved head. Xavier lifted Dezlan's hand to press a kiss to it before holding the flap of the tent open for them.

Once inside, Byzarien dropped onto the corner of his straw and wool mattress. Doing the same, Xavier sprawled out his long legs and grinned at Dezlan, who retrieved a jug of ale from his trunk.

"To Lazaire," he said in a raspy voice, and took a swig while nestling against Xavier.

The three men passed the jug around in complete silence. Byzarien's hands shook so violently, he couldn't drink without spilling the contents down his chin.

Byzarien finally broke the silence. "Did you see what he looked like this morning?" He stared at his boots while Lazaire's infected scars, weeping wounds, and graying skin haunted his mind.

"You need to focus on the good memories." Xavier clapped his shoulder.

Ignoring his friend, Byzarien pressed his icy fingers against the scars on his cheek. "*She* didn't even stay for the entire ceremony."

"I noticed that." Dezlan snatched the jug. "But Lazaire certainly enjoyed being her canvas."

Canvas. The word scraped against Byzarien's ears, making him cringe. "You don't really believe that, do you?" He glared back and forth at his friends.

Dezlan passed the jug to Xavier. "He said so many times. He was in love with her."

"He was under her *spell* or something," Byzarien nearly spat.

"It was an honor to be her canvas." Dezlan leaned over and rested his forehead against Byzarien's, swaying a little from the booze. "I say we respect Lazaire's life by believing in his sacrifice."

Before Byzarien could argue, Xavier stood and placated the two with a glare. "You can each believe what you wish about his last two months, but I will remember the good times with Lazaire. I *know* that's what he would want." He scrubbed a hand over his bald head and focused on Byzarien. "And you better watch your tongue, Byz, or someone could think you disagree with the king's orders."

Staring at the floor, Byzarien stroked his hair over his scars and nodded. Xavier was right; every soldier in the Sleepy Wood Company had signed a contract stating that they could become the witch's canvas and that they understood all the risks involved. The witch had used Lazaire as a canvas for enchantments to heal those harmed by fairy curses. *Only magic can conquer magic.* She had saved hundreds upon hundreds of lives—for a heavy price.

He knew she wasn't truly a witch, but the word fit. She was a *fairy*. As in the fairies who curse the trees in the Sleepy Wood. As in the fairies who burned Byzarien's family home so long ago. As in the fairies responsible for his brother's death.

When the jug of ale was dry, the men settled into their beds, heads heavy and spinning. Byzarien barely slept, though, tossing until faint morning light peeked through a rip in the tent. When he glanced at Dezlan and Xavier spooning, burning jealousy coursed through his gut. Not out of desire for either of his friends. No, he was quite delighted for the pair. It was the ache of loneliness he could never snuff, for no one would ever love a man scarred so terribly as he.

Slipping out of bed, Byzarien knelt before the small shrine in the corner. He kissed his crossed-sword pendant, lit a red tapered candle, and prayed before the assorted collection of icons: faux-gilded portraits of the gods and goddesses. The largest and most formidable was, of course, Guerrix. The icon did not contain genuine gold like those in the temple for in the poorer villages, taxes had stripped all precious metals from the effigies. The eternal winter cared not for holy relics. Byzarien prayed for Lazaire. He prayed for his family. He prayed for an end to the damned winter.

Once he finished praying, he massaged olive oil along his itching cheek, torso, hip, and leg with silent movements. Imported from the southern kingdom of Riviere, it was the single luxury he allowed himself, the oil soothing the disfigured skin over half his body. The scars were mountain ridges of anger and shame beneath his fingertips, beginning from his temple down to his foot. Some were raised and red, others thin and papery. *Half monster, half man.* The malformations were a constant reminder of the excruciating bedridden days that prevented him from attending little Benoix's funeral. When he finished his morning ritual, Byzarien tugged a gray tunic over his head, and returned the bottle of oil to his trunk.

While tying his boots, he spotted something shiny tucked under Lazaire's old mattress. He reached for it, his fingers meeting cold metal. Lazaire's dagger. His friend had had no use for it once he became the witch's canvas, for they were exempt from expeditions. Byzarien knew Lazaire would want it in the Underworld, though, so he threw his leather jacket on and slipped into the bleak morning air.

Rows and rows of tents stretched quietly across the field as the brumous sky hugged the mountains with fog. A chill nibbled at the exposed skin of his cheeks and neck as he scanned the horizon for the sun. It was a miniscule touch of brightness, too weak to burn through the endless gray pouring from the Forbidden Mountain.

Boots squelching through the filthy snow slush, he marched toward the pyre to place the dagger upon it. The Guerrix priest would then bury the dagger with Lazaire's ashes, teeth, and bone fragments. However, when Byzarien approached the charred remains, his stomach churned with nausea. Not because of the alcohol the night before. No, because the remains were gone.

The priest of Guerrix rarely collected them until the following evening, giving the soldiers an entire day to mourn and offer prayers. Pushing the bits of ash and logs around with a stick, Byzarien shook his head in disbelief. Even the bone fragments and teeth were missing. The wind whirled only a small amount of ashes around the ground, too little to be a person.

Only one culprit stood out in Byzarien's mind. That witch. Curses spilled from his mouth as he dug around the pyre in a fury. What could she have wanted with the remains? Hadn't she done enough damage? Lazaire needed to be buried properly, so he wouldn't roam the Darkened Path for all eternity. Heaving deep breaths that fogged the air in misty-white plumes, Byzarien brushed the ash from his clothes and set his sights on Captain Abelard's quarters, Lazaire's dagger in hand.

2

Myravelle

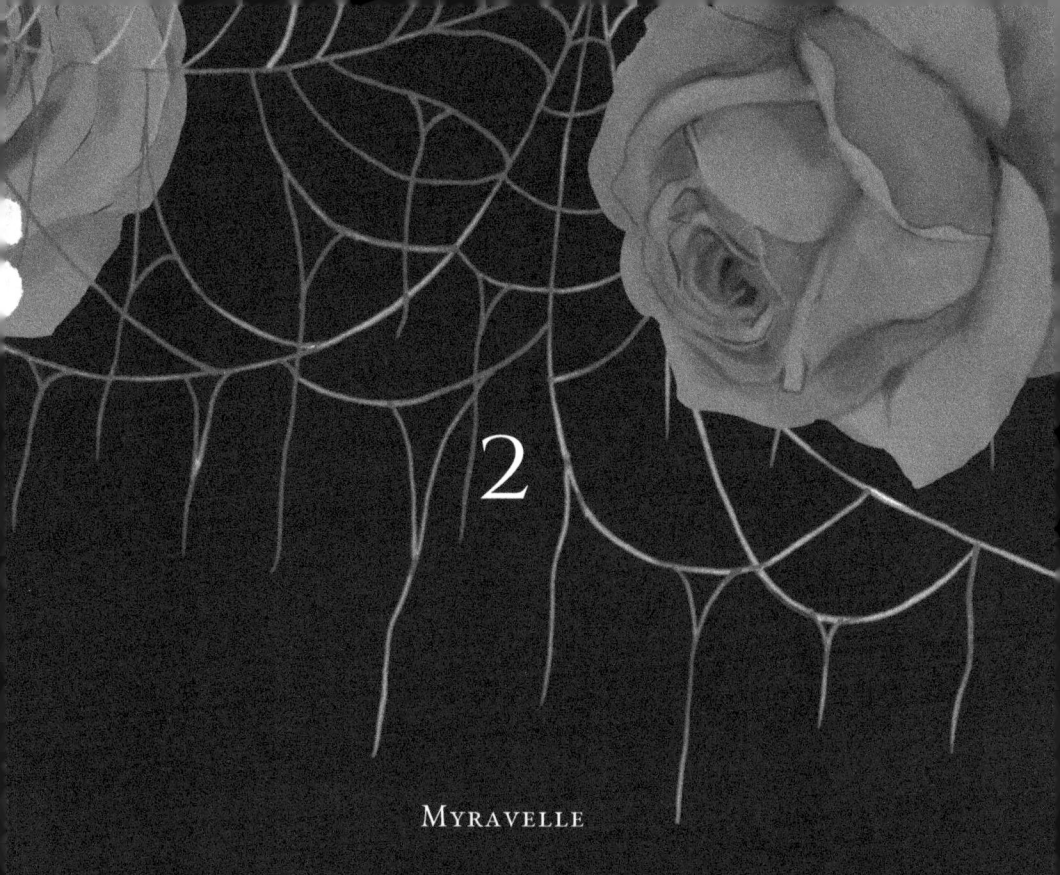

Myravelle sat with her head down, picking fresh earth from black-varnished fingernails during Captain Abelard's scolding. From her peripheral vision, she could still see his rotund frame pacing back and forth. She knew the tired routine was simply to feed his appetite for authority. Abelard, who had been injured during the Shore Wars against the kingdom of O'Leaux years before, was the type of man who used others for personal gain, thinking he had earned that privilege.

Instead of listening, her mind fluttered to a happier time—a time when stars still adorned the night sky, a time when the seasons changed, a time when her mother spun wool while spinning tales.

Abelard punched his desk, causing Myravelle to flinch.

"We are this close," he began, holding his thumb and index finger together in exaggeration, "to defeating the fairies."

Myravelle merely tilted her head, unsure what the captain wished for her to say. Growing up in captivity had made her oblivious to some social cues. She also knew they were, in fact, not *this close* to defeating the fairies, not while any of their enchantments remained upon the Dormrya trees. The soldiers would never get past them unscathed, and too many had already been harmed beyond measure for the sake of the magic wood. Myravelle rolled her tongue between her teeth, for one piece of social etiquette she *had* learned was to not tell the captain or king when they were wrong.

"You must choose another canvas," Captain Abelard said, scratching his graying beard. He had more hair on his chin than on his head. "The king won't tolerate any delay in waking the soldiers after we venture into the woods. We will need your magic more than ever moving forward!"

Not only were the Dormrya trees valuable in their natural, poisonous state, but the fairies' curses created a barrier within the forest, protecting their realm. The Sleepy Wood Company's expeditions were brutal. Though there were horses at the encampment for other travel, they would go wild in the vicinity of a Dormrya, especially a cursed one: bucking, thrashing, even throwing themselves with their riders over cliffs. Therefore, soldiers were forced to go into the woods on foot.

When the men came into contact with the fairy enchantments on the trees, their limbs would fall asleep—if they were lucky. Many unfortunate souls fell into a death-like sleep tormented by Filoux, the god of nightmares. Only Myravelle held the power to wake them, but at a price. A price that carved her up inside.

Her voice came out brittle as broken glass. "Lazaire was number twenty. He was supposed to be my last. I've paid my price!"

Captain Abelard leaned onto his creaky desk and shook his head. "You murdered this one too quickly."

She stifled a sob as the word *murdered* slammed into her chest. "I didn't. Lazaire and I saved more soldiers this past month than ever before."

"The king needs more."

"No." Myravelle crossed her arms and narrowed her eyes.

"Oh, no?" Abelard lifted a feather quill from the inkpot on his desk. "One word to the king and Xylina will be terminated."

Mother. Thorns hooked themselves into Myravelle's throat, and all she could do was shake her head. She seethed a few breaths through her teeth and was about to speak, when a wall of a man barreled inside, dragging a wake of frosty air with him. His dark hair nearly touched the top of the tent, and every muscle in his body was as rigid as the Forbidden Mountain.

An odd sensation stirred inside, like a strand of yarn unspooling from Myravelle's chest and into his. She knew who he was: Lazaire's friend, Byzarien. She sat up straight in her shadowy corner and decided to watch events unfold, knowing she would not be seen.

"What do you think you're doing, soldier?" the captain asked, scowling. "Stand down."

"Where are they?" Byzarien growled, taking a step forward and towering over Abelard.

"Where are what?"

"The remains," he said in a deep, booming voice. "Lazaire's remains. I know that witch took them!" The man brandished a dagger, forcing Abelard to jump back.

"You think bringing a weapon into my quarters is a good idea?" Abelard gasped. "Guards!"

Two soldiers rushed in and held Byzarien back, though they barely reached his shoulders. He thrashed like a horse spooked by Dormrya trees, whipping the guards around like rag dolls. Myravelle caught sight of the scars on the man's right cheek. She recognized the dagger—the man's intentions were not to harm the captain.

"The remains!" Byzarien shouted as the soldiers tried to detain him. "I just want to place the dagger with them. Where is that witch? I know she has them!"

"*Well.*" Myravelle drew out the word as she stood, and all attention turned to her. "Isn't this awkward?" The man's dark eyes widened as she approached, and he stopped flailing under her gaze.

She turned toward Abelard. "Captain, this man does not intend to harm you."

Releasing a dry laugh, the captain squinted at her. "And why should I believe you?"

"He is Lazaire's friend, Byzarien," she said and pointed to the weapon in the man's hands. "And that is Lazaire's dagger."

Abelard gestured to the soldiers, who released the man and exited the tent. "Byzarien, is it?" he asked. "What do you want?"

Myravelle turned to study him, waiting for his reply. *Byzarien*, she thought, *tall and broad, with scars running deeper than his skin.*

"The witch," Byzarien said, the word dripping like venom from his tongue as he pointed to her. "I know she took Lazaire's remains. I must bury them properly!"

Abelard rubbed his temples. "Show him, but we are *not* finished with our conversation."

"Follow me," Myravelle whispered, relieved to distance herself from the captain.

Abelard crossed his arms over his chest. "Serve him."

The soldier copied the gesture and replied, "And he will serve you."

The two stepped into winter's grasp, where the scent of burnt wood stung the air from fires lit at all hours of the day. Smoke stubbornly clung to Myravelle's hair and clothes. Ever since the eternal winter, it had become almost natural to always smell of fire.

She led Byzarien through the winding army encampment, past the Guerrix Temple, and into the ancient forest dusted with snow. There, mushrooms and lichens claimed the corpses of logs, and the skeletal branches of the trees swayed in the wind. Imposing elms, thick oaks, and crooked elders all waited patiently for the spring that would never arrive.

Myravelle was one with the forest as she picked her way through. Fairies were children of the wood, connected to nature by the earth goddess, Terryx. She took graceful steps and swished the beaded skirt of her dress to avoid entanglements. It was as if nature parted for her.

As the two passed a thicket of dried brambles, she glanced back at the giant man, whose boot laces had snagged on thorns. Byzarien glared at Myravelle as he ripped himself from nature's trap, so she spun back around.

"Are you trying to get us killed?" he growled once they had walked for miles. "We're getting close to the fairy curses."

Myravelle scoffed and pulled her fur-lined cloak tighter as she kept walking, for she knew where all the fairy curses were. She could sense them like a light touch of a feather within her bones—but Captain Abelard and King Zylvain were not in the business of *protecting* their soldiers. They simply wanted the rare wood of the Dormrya trees, no matter how many men and women succumbed to their curses.

"What did you do with him, witch?"

Hearing the word again was another knife to her ribs, and Myravelle wrapped her arms around herself. A witch or a *wikkjaz* was a type of being created by the god Enferrix to roam the Darkened Path. According to mythology, they had white claws, bulbous yellow eyes, long black hair traveling like a river...and a penchant for shiny treasures. As necromancers, they would wake only those who could pay with tokens from their death-walk and lead them to the Afterlife. Those without proper funeral rites were fated to blindly roam the Darkened Path for eternity while being tormented by wicked creatures. In hushed tones, soldiers would often sneer the slur about her, but never say it so outright.

Byzarien's heavy breaths drew Myravelle from her thoughts. "Did you use his remains for a potion or spell or something?"

A rush of heat flared beneath her skin and she drew quick breaths, unable to answer his ridiculous question.

Deep in the woods, the pair reached a clearing littered with small stone markers and paper flowers. Leather boots squeaking, the soldier bent down to read the names etched into the rocks.

"This is where I bring them." Myravelle pointed to the one with fresh, loose soil. "Lazaire is here."

Byzarien knelt beside her and ran his finger over the stone of his friend's grave. He lifted one of the paper flowers, which was an intricately designed white rose. "What are these for?"

"They deserved something beautiful."

His dark brows fell hard over his eyes as he glared at her and crushed the rose in his massive hand. "You think paper flowers absolve you for mutilating them?"

She held her head high as tears pricked the corners of her eyes. "I'll leave you to bury the dagger. I'm sure a soldier as *strong* and *brave* as you can find the way back to camp."

Not one to waste opportunities, Myravelle filled her pockets with juniper berries, mushrooms, and pine needles on her journey out of the Sleepy Wood. *Witch. Witch. Witch.* The word battered the grief, shame, and self-loathing further into her heart with every step. Before entering the comfort of her dim and cluttered tent, she stared off toward the mountains, unable to discern their formidable shapes through the dense fog.

Somewhere out there, in a twisted tower of the Eglantyne Castle, Myravelle's mother spun gold for the king.

3

Byzarien

Along with the wind's chilling whisper, a familiar voice echoed through the encampment—a messenger had returned from the kingdom in the late afternoon with news, notes, and gifts for the soldiers. Some eagerly awaited gifts to trade every week, but Byzarien ignored the calls, for his family could never afford presents. He would only use ink and parchment on rare occasions.

He touched his pendant and assumed a position opposite Dezlan by raising his wooden sword. The two sparred in the exercise yard while Xavier ran laps with Zelyx, a fierce woman with cropped blonde hair and muscles that could measure up to even the strongest of men. Though the sky was forever gray, the haze made Byzarien squint while he practiced with his friend. As a small man, Dezlan fought with speed and grace, but Byzarien's long arms could keep him at a distance.

"Are you part bear, Byz?" Dezlan teased between heavy breaths as he zipped around and thrust his sword. "You're huge and even growl like one sometimes."

Byzarien blocked the attack and shoved his friend back with a fist to the chest. "Then are you part hummingbird?"

Dezlan pretended to pout. "Now that's uncalled for."

Byzarien lost himself in exercise, swinging his sword and throwing his tall frame around, when a messenger stepped dangerously close to the fight. The man wore a green uniform, a furry hat, and held a bag sagging with cards and paper-wrapped boxes.

"Byzarien Dumont," the messenger shouted.

When he paused to double-take, Dezlan seized the opportunity and drew his sword near his faux enemy's neck. "Aha! The hummingbird kills the bear!" he said with a grin.

Byzarien rolled his eyes. "Don't gloat." He turned his attention to the messenger. "What did you say?"

"Byzarien Dumont?" The messenger extended a letter.

He snatched the beige envelope and stared at his name, written in his mother's shaky script. Dezlan crowded in to see, joined by Xavier and Zelyx, who had returned from their jog.

"Open it!" Zelyx said as she shook Byzarien's arm.

Byzarien slicked his sweaty hair past the scars on his cheek, his deep voice cracking as his airway constricted. "What could it be? They never write."

Xavier shrugged. "Only one way to find out."

After breaking the tiny clump of wax sealing the envelope, he withdrew the letter. Soldiers exercised and sparred all around them, but Byzarien's awareness fell away as he focused on the writing.

My dearest Byz,

I never like to worry you and wish I could write of happier times. With no break in the eternal winter, we've had no yields on the harvests. Not to mention, jobs are scarce and taxes have drained our coffers.

Unable to pay rent, we have lost our home on Lord Riccard's land and moved to the tenements of Pezit Quarter. It is cramped, and the other tenants are loud and filthy. We hope to marry Beatryz off soon so she can have a better life. Bryda will begin an apprenticeship if we are lucky. Pa has taken up work again at the mine to make ends meet. We are not asking you for more than you already have given, for we are grateful. We simply needed to let you know the situation and where we would be should you come visit. We miss you.

All my love,
Ma

The parchment rippled in unison with Byzarien's trembling. His family needed to get out of the slums. His siblings deserved a chance to have an education. His father's weak lungs couldn't handle another season in the mines. His meager soldier's salary couldn't afford them the life they deserved. The curls of his mother's handwriting swirled in his tears.

"Let's get inside," Dezlan said, placing a hand on Byzarien's back.

His friends escorted him to their tent and sat around him in a tight circle, each reading over the letter in turn.

"Maybe we can scrounge up some coin to get your home back," Zelyx said, leg bouncing. "I can give a little."

"*You* can give a little?" Xavier questioned with a smirk on his face. "You spent all of your money on your last girlfriend."

"Did not!" Z's cheeks and ears flushed scarlet, and she kicked Xavier's leg across the circle. They both giggled, but she cleared her throat and looked at Byzarien. "Seriously, how much do you need?"

He shook his head. "I can't take your money. You have your grandma to think about, Z."

"There's always another option," Dezlan whispered. "A *dangerous* option."

Everyone stared at him, knowing what he meant, but refusing to agree.

"Come on." He rose from the mattress and held out his arms. "None of us are soldiers in the Sleepy Wood Company because we *had it all* growing up. We joined to make money—and there's one sure way to do it."

Securing his own Dormrya tree would not only pay handsomely, but earn Byzarien the rank of lieutenant. A lieutenant's salary was more than enough to support a family. He drew deep breaths to help think more clearly.

"Are you willing to go without a platoon? Without Captain Abelard?" he asked, looking each of his comrades in the eye.

"Yes," Dezlan said. "It's what Lieutenant Eryck did."

"But...the risks," Byzarien reminded him. "Without the captain?"

Lieutenant Eryck had secured a Dormrya tree for the king at a high cost—seven of the ten soldiers who ventured into the Sleepy Wood with him that night succumbed to the fairy curse: a death-like sleep. The witch healed them, but with the heavy price of a man's life. Then, at her next ritual, the witch chose Lazaire as her new canvas.

"I'm in," Zelyx said, placing her hand on Byzarien's shoulder.

Dezlan and Xavier stared at one another for a long moment. "We are, too."

"No." Byzarien stood. "It's too risky. We can't."

"Will you at least consider it?" Zelyx asked.

He shook his head, which brushed the roof of the tent. When he opened his mouth to speak, a woman with ebony skin and dark braids entered along with a gust of wind.

"I thought I'd find you here, Z." The woman's eyes sparkled in Zelyx's direction. "Did you hear the news? Myravelle is holding another ritual tonight."

"No, I didn't know that." Zelyx stood, grinning. "Thanks, Lana."

"We're taking bets in the mess hall now," Lana said, beckoning Zelyx with a tilt of her head.

Byzarien's veins boiled at the mention of bets, and he was certain his face had turned red as the Guerrix priest's robes. Though he enjoyed gambling games such as knucklebones and cards, he couldn't stand the thought of betting on a man's life.

"Lana," Zelyx called before the woman turned away. "You want to get dinner together?"

"You wish," Lana said in a cruel tone, but her wink and lip-bite gave her away.

After Lana left, Zelyx plopped onto Lazaire's old bed. "She loves me!"

Byzarien wilted onto his bed but couldn't focus on the group's conversation about Zelyx's love life. His ears pounded as he thought about the gambling and that another poor soul would become the witch's canvas. Young men and women signed up to become soldiers, wishing to be in battles, see foreign lands, and learn about strategy. Those wishes never came true for the Sleepy Wood Company. The soldiers never saw battle. In fact, they were hardly more than explorers with swords—and leather gloves to protect them from the poisonous wood. They only exercised daily to stay sharp. Touching a fairy curse or getting a splinter of Dormrya wood beneath one's skin was unfortunate, but becoming the canvas meant certain death.

After a while, Byzarien and his friends shuffled to the mess hall for a late dinner. Rumors about an upcoming expedition led by Lieutenant Eryck buzzed around the large tent, for an expedition was the only action some of the soldiers would see. Everyone hoped for a chance to be in Eryck's platoon.

Once they had their trays, Byzarien, Dezlan, Xavier, and Zelyx sat to eat. Zelyx's eyes kept wandering to the corner where Lana counted coins and scribbled into a ledger. Byzarien stirred his beans and added a hefty dose of salt to give them some flavor. Eternal winter was not kind when it came to food. Beans were one of the cheapest imports from Basenfort and, therefore, a large part of a soldier's diet.

Lieutenant Eryck entered the mess hall, and the room fell silent. The man with dusty blond hair and features that looked cut from glass strode toward the back of the hall, where he stood on a table to address the soldiers.

"As you may have heard, Myravelle will perform her canvas ritual tonight," he said. "Which is perfect timing because Captain Abelard and I have been discussing a new expedition into the Sleepy Wood." The mess hall rumbled with chatter.

"I suggest that," Eryck began, and the room hushed, "after you finish dining, you return to your quarters for some leisure and rest prior to the mandatory ritual, which begins at midnight."

After more chatter, Eryck pounded his fists across his chest in a Guerrix pose three times to silence the room. "Serve him!"

"And he will serve you," the entire mess hall replied.

Midnight, Byzarien thought. *A man's life will change completely at midnight.*

4

Myravelle

Twisting the drop spindle, Myravelle admired the carvings upon the whorl. Her mother had skillfully etched each enchantment into the polished Dormrya wood to spin fiber into gold. When the magic faded and the spindle ceased to produce the precious metal, her mother gave it to her to spin ordinary thread. Xylina had forbidden Myravelle from spinning gold, for she feared the king would exploit her daughter for possessing magic. Unfortunately, the king discovered Myravelle's other talents and exploited her anyway.

She often wished to be locked back in the tower with her mother rather than healing hateful soldiers who called her things like *witch* and *wicked fairy*. That was all over—twenty canvases had been the deal King Zylvain made with his dead-fish handshake and gray eyes devoid of concern for the lives he condemned. Lives of those like Lazaire, Henri, Olivier, Guy, Jon, and the other innocent men who lost their chance for a future. She thought about them often, her canvases, as if they were her own pantheon of gods. Gods who sacrificed their lives to save others. Myravelle had no desire to collect any more gods, though. She wanted to rescue her mother and create a new life. Xylina had been cooped up in that tower for far too long. *Would she even recognize the world? Would she recognize me?*

Myravelle nestled her most cherished possession into her trunk with her gowns, mortar and pestle, and other belongings. She left the paper stars hanging across the ceiling, for she could thread new garlands when she and her mother found a home. *Home*—the word warm like a hearth in her chest.

After closing the trunk, she sighed in relief; she would soon see her mother. Earlier that day, she had sent payment with the messenger to fetch a carriage. Maybe they would escape north to the sea. Xylina had always stared out the window past the distant Forbidden Mountain, as if wanting to see the black sand beaches and listen to the crashing waves. Simply reading about the sea in books was never enough to quell her desire to dip her toes into the water.

Myravelle threw on her crushed velvet cloak and secured the rose-shaped clasp when Captain Abelard burst into her tent, making her flinch. She scowled at him for entering uninvited.

"You will perform a ritual tonight."

"No." She gestured to her trunk. "I've paid my mother's price. A carriage will arrive within the hour. I'm done."

Abelard narrowed his beady eyes and shifted his weight onto his good leg. "You're done when *I* say you're done." A sickening smirk exposed crooked teeth.

Myravelle crossed her arms and shook her head.

"Then tell me who's going to heal the sleepers? Hmm?"

"If you stop going into the wood—" she paused to glare at him— "you'd have no sleepers to heal."

"Fine. I'll just send word to the king, and your mother will be executed before your carriage makes it into the city walls."

A void broke open within Myravelle's heart. She struggled to breathe. "You...can't."

"You know I can," he said. "The king isn't done with the Sleepy Wood, so neither are you."

Like little spiders, a chill climbed her spine and tingled across her limbs. A long moment passed while the two of them stared at one another. She was a fool for ever believing she could rescue her mother. The king had never intended to let her go. He would exploit Myravelle and her mother until their bitter deaths. At that moment, she debated running away.

Myravelle would go into the mountains and make a home for herself. There, she would never have to bleed another man to death. There, she would never have to see Captain Abelard or King Zylvain again. There, she would be free. But her mother would still be in the tower, or worse.

I can't leave without Mother.

"Fine," she seethed through clenched teeth.

"Midnight," he said, leaving the tent.

Without a care about cleanliness or organization, she upended the trunk and spread ingredients across the worktable. She wiped the tears hindering her vision and focused on what she would need for yet another ritual. Her fingers swept through dried botanicals, and her rings clinked against amber bottles. Lazaire and the other canvases flashed in her mind with every blink, and she suppressed the urge to vomit at the thought of doing it all over again.

In her collection, Myravelle had the nightshade, acacia, wormwood, sandalwood, rose petals, vanilla, and musk needed for the spell, but she was missing juniper. She had used the last of it to make a batch of contraceptives for some of the women, and a bottle of antiseptic oil for the nurses. They were little gestures to make people like her, but they never were successful. No matter her contributions, she was always the *witch*.

She used juniper to discover a man who could look past her fairy origins and bond with her, which was necessary for her magic to work. She swallowed the lump in her throat. Lazaire had died so quickly, she couldn't imagine any man would want to bond with her again. With a wicker basket and a small torch in-hand, Myravelle wandered into the woods to harvest more juniper. She searched for hours beneath dried thickets, along frozen brooks, and between crooked trees while the light from her torch barely bled through the murky night. It had become harder and harder to forage the longer the eternal winter persisted. Most of her ingredients were imported, but she could still find the long, trailing branches of the evergreen shrub.

Myravelle's bones rattled, not from the chill, but from the proximity of fairy curses. Though sweet and beckoning, the feeling left only emptiness. She wished to follow the sensation into the fairy realm and live among her kind, but she could never, not until her mother was free at her side. Avoiding the curses on a few nearby towering Dormryas, she drew her gardening scissors from her cloak and snipped away at a juniper shrub.

She chuckled at the thought of telling Captain Abelard where the poisonous trees were. Would the king and captain make her sniff them out like a hound searching for prey? Myravelle had seen the damage the fairy curses caused the soldiers and had no intention of watching the catastrophes first-hand. With her guidance, soldiers would fall into death-like sleep at an alarming rate. How many more canvases would she be forced to carve into oblivion?

When she returned from the forest, instead of collapsing onto the mattress, Myravelle found herself tracing the enchantments on the whorl of the drop spindle. The rune her mother used for gilded thread began with a circular base and, from the top, a loop spiraled down toward a lonely star.

Spinning was the one thing that could quell Myravelle's anxieties. It was the one thing that made her feel close to her mother after the years apart—the five wretched years since she had felt her mother's warm embrace. *My little spiderling*, Xylina called her as they spun and sewed together for hours on end.

Myravelle spun into the night, letting her mind go numb as she sang her mother's words:

HER DARK ENCHANTMENTS

. . .

Draft and pinch. Draft and pinch.
Spin. Spin. Spin.
Draft and pinch. Draft and pinch.
Again. Again. Again.

The song was a gentle breeze dancing through the tent, but it only made Myravelle miss her mother more. The timbre of Xylina's voice was always calm and smooth as she sang or recited mythological tales. *The only person lonelier than me*, she thought, *is Mother, tucked away in her tower.* Boots scuffled toward her tent, ruining the enchanting song. Without even looking, she knew Abelard's guards had arrived to escort her to the ritual.

She packed her cauldron, dagger, and ingredients into her basket. As she stepped past the mess of dried flowers at the edge of her table, a particular bloom caught her eye: sweet pea. *Would she dare wish for something she never had?* She plucked the flower from the pile and dropped it into her basket, just in case.

Outside in the snow flurries, two guards led her to the field where everyone awaited her arrival. The crowd of soldiers parted as she glided toward a single table. The wind whipped through her hair and the fur lining of her cloak while she rested her brass cauldron, dagger, and ingredients on the altar. The soldiers' eyes pressed into her skin like spindle tips. Every movement she made was torture.

Myravelle dropped a piece of charcoal into the cauldron and lit it with a trembling hand. Once tendrils of smoke stretched toward the sky, she added acacia for renewal, wormwood and sandalwood for purity, juniper for lust, and nightshade for binding. Some soldiers called it her "love spell," but it was nothing of the sort. Her ritual couldn't create love or lust, but *discovered* it. Having been deprived of her own free will by the king, she would never do that to someone else.

Closing her eyes, she let the aromas heighten her senses. Streams of crackling magic coursed through her body, threatening to undo her. There was always so much darkness she tucked away deep in the caverns of her soul.

For a moment, she thought about her mother. How Myravelle had wanted to spin gold, but Xylina wouldn't allow it. Her mother would never allow her to attempt any sort of magic. *"Your life will be better without it, little spiderling."*

A tear slipped down Myravelle's cheek as her childhood screams invaded her mind, as did the flesh-ripping sounds of her mother's punishments. She would desperately beg to use magic against the guards who whipped Xylina for not producing enough gold. *"I can do it, Mother."*

A gust of frosty air whipped through the field and returned Myravelle to her senses. The soldiers stared at her, waiting. They knelt in silence with their arms crossed over their chests, and the only noise came from the crackling bonfires all around the field.

She sprinkled dried rose petals, vanilla, and musk into her cauldron. The decadent aroma not only pleased her but was meant to attract a lover, for that was the only way she knew to bond with her canvases. She gave them her body, nothing more, and, in return, they gave her their hearts. Her pantheon of gods. Marzel loved to read and write poetry for Myravelle. Henri enjoyed physical fitness so much that even at the end of his days, he would walk with Myravelle in the forest. Olivier was always so shy, but would tell Myravelle stories about his childhood dog. Jon. Cazzius. Pavyl. And the many ill-fated others.

Near the ritual's end, she hesitated. Loneliness clawed into her bones like the cold, and she missed her mother more than ever. So, Myravelle did a foolish thing. She slipped sweet pea into the burning cauldron, hoping to attract a lover *and* a friend: a soulmate.

She bent over the pot and allowed her ragged whispers to set the embers aglow, spells turning the dried ingredients into flames. A pillar of aromatic smoke rose into the air, where it mingled with the ever-cloudy sky, and she gripped the cold hilt of her dagger. As she lifted it to the sky, her magic grew inside, strong and true. Cool, flowing rushes streamed through her veins, all the while boiling currents burned from her heart to collide with a force that made her wail in agony.

She dropped her dagger onto the table and rested her palms against the smooth, worn wood. The pain in her chest spun itself tightly around her heart and tugged outward, connecting to where or to whom she did not know. *Why did it hurt her so? Had she performed the ritual too many times? Had she asked for too much by adding the sweet pea?* She blinked away the tears swirling her vision and met the captain's glare.

Shaking, Myravelle raised the dagger to her palm, where there was a scar in the shape of an ancient rune. This one, a simple circle with a straight line connecting two stars. She had never learned what any of the symbols meant—her mother had never taught her about the fairy enchantments. Nevertheless, Myravelle could see them glowing in her mind when she needed them. It was that raw, untrained magic that had frightened Xylina the most.

With the tip of the dagger, she traced the rune at the center of her palm. The scarred skin broke open with such deep pain, Myravelle gasped. When the shape was complete, she placed her palm face-down above the cauldron, letting the smoke seep into the wound. She made a fist, digging her fingers into the open flesh, and dripped precious rubies of her blood into the cauldron.

It bubbled and sizzled against the coal with a coppery scent, and a fresh burst of smoke rose into the sky, crackling with silver and gold sparks. Myravelle's mouth ran dry, and her legs wobbled. She leaned against the table to gaze up at the smoke while her eyesight betrayed her, wisps of darkness hovering along the edges.

The cloud of smoke and sparks swirled high above the field as the soldiers watched with wide eyes. Bursts of tiny explosions made the smoke grow brighter, like a galaxy of stars. She grew even weaker as the magic churned and spelled the name of her new canvas.

Sparkling letters began to take shape as they burned against the dark sky. They always started randomly: backward, upside-down, and out of order. Then, twisting and twirling the golden letters became clearer and organized themselves into a legible name:

Byzarien Dumont

Her eyelids grew heavy, and her legs finally gave way as any remaining energy slid from her body. She collapsed onto the makeshift altar.

Abelard's voice barked, "Carry her to her tent."

The captain's personal guards grabbed Myravelle by her limbs, though she could barely feel their hands through the pins and needles under her skin.

"I've got her," the largest of them said, and tossed her over his shoulder like a sack.

Everything went dark as a painful sleep dragged Myravelle under its spell.

5

Byzarien

The glittering letters in the night sky were nonsensical. During the ritual, pain had filled Byzarien's chest as something spun around his heart, so tightly he thought it would burst. He tried to discern who had been chosen as the witch's new canvas, while everyone in the crowd turned to him and bowed their heads. A cold sweat glossed his forehead as he stared at Zelyx, Dezlan, and Xavier's haunted faces. He swallowed the bile rising in his throat.

The name in the sky was his own. But, it couldn't be.

He shook his head and took a few steps back, almost tripping over another soldier. His limbs grew so hollow, Dezlan and Xavier had to stand and steady him. Byzarien's eyes darted around in panic, certain there had been a mistake. He glanced at the sky, hoping the letters had changed. They had not, for even in the white smoke left behind, *Byzarien Dumont* was clear.

The captain's guards rushed to the altar where the witch had collapsed—something he had never seen her do before. Captain

Abelard ordered men to carry her away and, after speaking to another group of soldiers, gestured to Byzarien.

He couldn't catch his breath, and darkness crept along the fringes of his peripheral vision like a bruise until everything went black.

"Byz," Xavier said, helping him sit upright on the cold earth.

Feeling weak and dizzy, Byzarien looked around and realized he must have collapsed. Zelyx offered him a canteen of water. As he gulped it down, he noticed everyone was still kneeling for him. The soldiers held their fists across their chests and chanted, "Serve him, serve him, serve him," over and over again. His cheeks flared with embarrassment, and he coaxed his hair to hide his scars.

"Byzarien Dumont," one of Abelard's personal guards said, crossing his arms over his chest. "You have the honor of being Myravelle's next canvas. We will escort you to your tent to pack and take you to her tonight."

Still lightheaded and confused, he let the soldiers help him stand. The crowd parted, and he kept his head down while sleet fell, as if the sky was upset for him. Walking through the rows of tents, an idea sparked. With a quick glance at the two men at his sides, who were squinting against the icy rain, he tore free of their grip and broke into a sprint.

The sleet stung his face, but he kept going. Where? He didn't know. Maybe back to the kingdom to find his family. Or maybe to hide out in the mountains. He knew anything was better than being mutilated to death. Images of men and women trapped in Filoux's death-like sleep flashed in his mind, though. The captain was planning an expedition, and it would be selfish to let everyone suffer.

He slowed when he reached the outskirts of the encampment, and a terribly odd sense of relief washed over him with the icy rain. He was a dead man. He was no longer responsible for his family's happiness. He would no longer live a lonely life without love. He could be reunited in the Underworld with Benoix and Lazaire. Byzarien took a deep, cleansing breath just before it was knocked out of him, and he crashed to the ice-slicked ground. The two guards had tackled him.

"Where do you think you're going?" one of them asked, yanking Byzarien's arms behind his back. "It's an honor to be chosen as Myravelle's canvas."

"I'm...sorry." He panted against the cold air scraping his lungs. "I don't know what came over me."

The men dragged Byzarien toward his tent. He stooped inside and looked around. Without his friends there, the space felt emptier than ever. He wished they were there to encourage him, but he knew everyone would still be in the field, listening to the prayers of the Guerrix Priest. After tossing clothes and personal items into his trunk, he stepped toward the small altar and lifted the icon of the god of war. The other icons of Reverie, Amyor, Enferrix, Cielyx, and Terryx all belonged to either Xavier or Dezlan, but Guerrix was Byzarien's contribution to the shrine.

"What should I do?" he asked the faux-gilded god.

Guerrix stared back with blank and stoic eyes. Byzarien was in this alone. Running was not the answer, for his friends needed him now more than ever. A few tears slipped from his eyes for the family he would never see again...who would be trapped in the slums forever. What could he do? Based on the lifespans of previous canvases, who had been dying by the witch's hand faster and faster, Byzarien only had a month—two at most—to live.

After placing the icon into his trunk, he carried it outside, where the guards seized him by the arms and led him in the direction of the witch's lair. The sleet blew sideways with a choppy wind, nipping at his ears and making it difficult to see. He kept his head down and, in defeat, let the guards drag him through the rows of tents.

With every squelch of his boots, Byzarien's heart sank further and further into despair. *A lamb to the slaughter.* He imagined how the witch would carve him up and bury him in a graveyard with paper flowers—how his family would lose his stipend, forcing them to do unspeakable things to get by. The only consolation was that he might help those suffering from Filoux's curses. *If those I help live on*, he thought, *then maybe a part of me will as well.* At least, that was the idea of the sacrifice.

The soldiers brought Byzarien to an abrupt halt, and he at last opened his eyes, squinting against the freezing rain. He faced the entrance of the witch's tent. Though it was the same standard-issue tarp as the rest, hers had a dark and heavy aura surrounding it. To Byzarien, it seemed to suck in the gloom of the night and hold it within its fibers.

"Myravelle." The soldier to his right projected his voice. "Your canvas is here."

The moments waiting stretched like an eternity as the sleet struck Byzarien's raw nerves.

"You think she's recovered from her little fainting spell?" The second soldier leaned behind Byzarien to whisper to the other. "The canvas will certainly need her to be *conscious*."

The escorts chuckled at the vile joke while Byzarien's stomach twisted, and he bent to dry heave, imagining the horrors that awaited him. One of the escorts patted his back. Then a dim glow of candlelight illuminated his boots, and Byzarien looked up to see the witch holding open the flap of her tent. Her long hair slithered over her shoulder in a loose braid, and she wore a silky black robe and seemingly nothing else, despite the frigid temperature. It skimmed over her skin like black oil and exposed her lean legs.

The witch's glassy, gray eyes flickered to Byzarien for the briefest of moments, before she held her head high and addressed the soldiers. "Bring him in."

Jerking Byzarien upright, the soldiers escorted him into the wide, cluttered tent. As he stumbled inside, his head hit a paper star garland, one of many crisscrossing the ceiling. He gazed upon the witch's worktable, littered with vials, bottles, scissors, a pestle and mortar, with dried botanicals hanging all around. The scents proved rather intoxicating, while warmth radiated from a small coal stove at the center.

Byzarien grimaced, though, when he turned to study the living space. One small bed sat near the center, while a trunk and privacy screen were tucked into the corner.

The witch lifted Byzarien's trunk from his weak hands and placed it next to her own.

She turned and gestured to the soldiers. "Thank you," she said in a smoky whisper. "Goodnight."

The two men left his side, making fear weigh heavier on his pounding chest. *Alone with the witch.* The edges of his sight began to darken again, and he feared he might faint. She took slow and graceful steps forward, while Byzarien avoided looking directly at her.

"You can make yourself comfortable, *Byzarien*," she said, and he hated the sound of his name on her tongue. "Would you like tea or wine?"

"No," he replied, his voice hardly more than a breath.

The witch strolled to her worktable and snuffed the candles, dimming the tent to only the flicker of the lone, dripping candle on her nightstand. She stepped in front of Byzarien, forcing him to look at her. Trying not to show his rising terror, he focused on counting the freckles that dusted her cheeks and nose.

"You've no need to be afraid of me," she said as she focused behind Byzarien's head. She took a deep breath and untied the sash of her silk robe, letting the garment slide open and hang at her elbows. "You may do whatever you want with me."

Byzarien's eyes widened, suddenly very alert. He licked his lips as his entire body flooded with heat, especially his scars. He couldn't help but drink in the sight of her flawless skin, her naked breasts, hips, and thighs intoxicating.

He snapped his gaze away, disgusted with himself. "I don't want to do anything with you."

"It helps...with our bond," she said, closing a bit of distance between them.

"I will not *bond* with you."

"Oh." The witch stitched her brows and adjusted the robe to cover her body.

Byzarien's cheeks finally cooled as he swept his hair over the scars. He frowned at the small bed. "Where do I sleep?"

"With me."

"Not happening," he said and trudged over to a stack of blankets in the corner.

She let him be as he spread one out over the ground and plopped down onto his side. Uncomfortable, but he had slept in far worse places. Thumbing his Guerrix pendant, he prayed everything from the past day had just been a nightmare. A horrible, awful, terrible trick of Filoux's, who had taunted humans for over a century. But it wasn't. He wished again, face strained.

Unable to sleep, he came up with an idea: the one thing he could do to help his family. He waited until the witch's breathing evened out and he knew she was asleep before he crawled across the floor, slipped beneath the tent, and sprinted to his own. There, he found Xavier, Dezlan, and Zelyx drinking. As he caught his breath, they turned to him with tears in their eyes.

"Byz!" Zelyx said. "We're so sorry. Did she hurt you?"

"Not yet. If you haven't changed your minds," he began, looking at each of his friends, "I'm marching into the Sleepy Wood and will have a Dormrya tree before sunrise."

Without hesitation, the group made a plan, readied their supplies, and left the safety of the encampment. Although they had maps of the area, keeping a record of fairy curses had done little to help the Eglantyne soldiers—though they eventually faded, the fairies moved like shadows, carving new enchantments every single day. They were as elusive as the forest was large.

Byzarien led his friends toward the witch's secret graveyard, for that area had recently been safe from fairy enchantments. As they picked through the thick forest, the darkness pressed in on them. The Forbidden Mountain was known to erupt and cause short periods of darkness throughout the ages, but this particular eruption was the longest in documented history. It had been years since anyone had seen the moon or stars above the Eglantyne Kingdom. There was no light filtering through the heavy oaks and tall elms to guide their way.

Each soldier wore gloves to protect their hands, and had an ax and a length of rope on their belt. Even though one Dormrya splinter meant the fate of a fairy curse, the king was desperate for more of the poisonous wood.

Since the beginning of the eternal winter, Eglantyne Kingdom had to rely on crops and goods from other lands. Expenses had piled up, though, and many people fled, causing the economy to further weaken. Trade and diplomacy had grown tense with the nearest kingdoms, O'Leaux to the west and Riviere to the east, and the king worried about war. Things were even shaky with the queen's southern homeland of Basenfort. Securing wood of the Dormrya trees would make the Eglantyne army unstoppable with the destructive weapons they could create.

Once the group had snuck far enough away from camp, they lit their torches. Byzarien treaded lightly when they drew close to the witch's graveyard, so as to not disturb any remains. When a paper flower crunched under his boot, he raised a fist, signaling for them to stop.

"What is it?" Zelyx whispered.

"This is her graveyard," he said, stepping toward one with freshly disturbed soil. "Lazaire."

Zelyx, Dezlan, and Xavier immediately knelt before the small stone marker and prayed with their arms crossed over their chests. Their whispers sent white frost curling into the air, to gods Byzarien wasn't sure still cared for them. Lazaire's death had frayed the fibers of faith he had clung to for so long.

Xavier finished praying first and extended his torch to look around. "This is...horrifying. There are so many," he said, gesturing to the graves before tilting his head. "Are those *real* flowers?"

No one had seen living flowers in years, since the sky had turned an unending gray. Byzarien's mother once kept a modest, yet beautiful rose garden. Her favorites were white, but the eternal winter destroyed them like it had everything else. Zelyx and Dezlan each plucked a flower and held them up, curiosity flickering on their torchlit faces.

"The witch makes paper flowers for them," Byzarien realized.

"That's sort of...*sweet*," Dezlan said, returning the flower to the earth. "In a tragic way."

Byzarien shook his head. "There's nothing sweet about it."

"I don't know." Xavier reached to hold his lover's hand. "It shows she actually cared about them, at least."

"Let's go," Byzarien barked, walking away.

His friends followed, but continued their obnoxious conversation about the witch.

"He always claimed to be happy," Zelyx said, her voice ringing with hope. "I mean...Myravelle is *gorgeous*."

"I knew you were attracted to her," Xavier teased.

"Now, now, I *do* have standards," Zelyx paused to clutch her chest, feigning offense, "standards that Myravelle would definitely meet."

Xavier and Zelyx both howled with laughter while Byzarien grit his teeth at the sound of her name.

"Hey," Dezlan shouted, making the others hush. "Byz obviously doesn't think this is very funny."

"Sorry," Xavier and Zelyx whispered, hanging their heads.

"Let's focus on getting a Dormrya." Byzarien marched ahead, skin still bristling with anger.

"I apologize for the jokes; Z's a bad influence on me," Xavier said once he caught up to Byzarien, then lowered his voice to a gravelly whisper as if he were about to cry. "I don't think I've grasped that you're actually the new canvas. I've just been trying to see the positive in Lazaire's sacrifice because I miss him so much...but I really don't know what we'd do without you."

An aching lump formed in Byzarien's throat; Lazaire's death had taken a toll on the small group of friends. Lazaire had been the charismatic and hilarious ringleader of the "freak show" as he so affectionately called them. Although Byzarien was usually the serious one, he certainly missed laughing with Lazaire.

"Don't worry," he said, clapping Xavier's shoulder. "Lazaire would have been joking right alongside you and Z. I'm just scared."

"You have every right to be." Zelyx, who must have been eavesdropping, marched in line with them. "But he said he loved her and that the enchantments never hurt."

"Again, with this?" Byzarien grumbled. "What if she had him under a spell or something? He probably didn't know what he was saying."

They avoided eye-contact and kept quiet as they walked deeper into the woods, where shadows moved between the trees, and the wind carried whispers. Byzarien didn't know if it was real or a trick of the imagination, but he kept his guard up the entire time, wishing he had the witch's skill of trekking through the forest without a sound.

Most of the soldiers in the Sleepy Wood Company had never actually seen the fairies, which Byzarien thought was lucky. Rumors said they had enchanted swords that seemed to glide through the air and that some fairies could even fly. In recent times, though, the fairies had simply relied on their enchantments to keep them safe, burrowing deep in the forest like rodents.

Through the tangled and naked tree canopy, Byzarien spotted something extremely tall. It was no average tree; it was an ancient Dormrya. He pointed to it, and all of his friends smiled, teeth flashing in the torchlight. They approached the tree with caution, axes at the ready. The bark twisted with odd patterns and whorls while the roots trailed out over the ground. The thick trunk would take all night and all of their strength to chop it down.

When they stood below its massive, skeletal boughs, Dezlan placed his gloved hand upon the trunk and sighed.

"This is our chance," Xavier said, gripping Dezlan's shoulder with a grin.

The air buzzed with their excitement. An image of his family, happy and back in their home bloomed in Byzarien's mind. They searched the trunk high and low for any odd carvings from the fairies.

"Let's chop this beast down," Zelyx said after she circled the entire tree.

Dezlan stepped up first. "The hummingbird versus the beast."

While Dezlan adjusted his gloves and stretched his arms, Byzarien studied the knobby and gnarly roots stretching from the base of the tree. It was hard for him not to compare their patterns to the deformities on his skin. When Dezlan positioned his ax over his shoulder, ready to strike, a circular pattern tucked between the roots caught Byzarien's attention. *Could it be an enchantment?*

"Wait," he shouted, but it was too late.

Dezlan's ax struck the tree—and the tree struck back. An intense blast, crackling with fiery sparks, launched them all back. Byzarien crashed into a tree with a thud, and fell to the ground.

He blinked and rubbed his aching head. A high-pitched sound rang in his ears and the icy air scraped his throat as he caught his breath. Pushing up from the frost-covered earth, he scanned the area for his friends. The torches had all died in the blast, and his eyes needed to adjust to the overwhelming darkness.

When he heard Xavier's wails, Byzarien burst into a sprint to find him. Nearly tripping on logs, bushes, and vines, he found Xavier sobbing over Dezlan. Byzarien's stomach sank so quickly, he thought he would vomit at the sight of his friend, ever so still.

"Is he...dead?" he whispered.

Xavier kept his focus on Dezlan but shook his head. "He's *asleep.*"

The sight of his hummingbird of a friend under the fairy curse sent Byzarien to his knees. It sliced to the core of his emotions, still raw and fragile from losing Lazaire. He pressed his fingers into Dezlan's neck, determining that there was still a pulse. From old myths and new tales of those who had fallen prey to the sleeping curses, he knew that although Dezlan appeared peacefully asleep, he was tortured by nightmares. Those held under the curse for too long were never quite the same when they woke—if they woke at all.

He struggled to breathe through the grief, as if a boulder sat on his chest. It was all his fault. If he hadn't been so desperate, his friends wouldn't have come along. They needed to get Dezlan back to the witch at once. Byzarien's insides curled in on themselves at the thought of needing *her* help.

"Can you carry him?" he asked. "I'll search for Zelyx."

"I...I can't move." Xavier rubbed his legs.

"What?"

"I can't feel my legs," he said. "They must have been hit."

Worry creased Byzarien's brow as his mind raced. "I'll carry Dez to the infirmary, then come back for you."

Xavier leaned over to kiss Dezlan's cheek. Byzarien then cradled his friend in his arms and moved in the direction of the camp, allowing adrenaline to fuel his steps. A few yards away, smoke rose from a smoldering torch. Zelyx was nearby, leaning against a tree with her eyes closed.

"Z!" he shouted, voice rising with a plume of frost. "Are you all right?"

"No. My leg...I can't move it," she said, her voice weaker than he'd ever heard it. When she looked up, her eyes widened at the sight of Dezlan. "Is he..."

"Asleep," Byzarien assured her. "I'm taking him to the witch now, then I'll return for you and Xavier."

"Go."

Byzarien continued with Dezlan, careful to follow the exact path they had taken through the Sleepy Wood. When he reached camp, a soldier who had been outside pissing spotted him.

"What happened?" the man asked, buckling his pants.

"Fairy curses," Byzarien said between heavy breaths. "Tell Captain Abelard to get the witch."

The man bolted in the direction of the captain's quarters while Byzarien jogged to the infirmary, with Dezlan bouncing like a corpse in his arms. When he reached the enormous tent, Byzarien rested Dezlan on a cot and covered him with a blanket.

"I'm going to get Xavier and Zelyx," he whispered to his unconscious friend.

Without waiting for the captain or the witch, Byzarien sprinted into the night to rescue his friends.

6

Myravelle

Myravelle laid awake, staring at the paper constellations hanging from the ceiling, and listened for Byzarien's footsteps to return, but they never did. *Where would he have gone in the middle of the night? Why had he been so repulsed by her?* The rituals had always worked before; the canvases had always been attracted to her and eager to take her to bed.

Had the sweet pea ruined everything?

She slinked out of bed and shuffled to her worktable, where she mindlessly crushed herbs with her pestle and mortar. Worry ground into her skull with every motion. What if changing the ritual formula meant Byzarien would never bond with her? *What would that mean for her magic?* Turning her left palm up, she looked at the deep purple scar in the shape of her rune for harvesting pain—a circle with curves reaching toward a central star. She thought of her first canvas.

Every time the guards had whipped or branded Xylina, Myravelle saw the circle and star runes glow in her mind's eye. With a harrowed face, Xylina begged her never to give in to the magic. Therefore,

Myravelle curated her secret rooftop garden, filled with botanical remedies solely for the purpose of healing her mother.

Then, Myravelle met Pazcal. *Oh, Pazcal.* He had been her first everything—her first kiss, her first love, and—unwittingly—her first canvas. He was the son of a castle steward, on his way to becoming one himself. The two had met when he delivered wool to the tower for Xylina to spin. His blue eyes grew wider than two moons when he saw Myravelle, who blushed under his gaze. Pazcal's golden hair reminded her of the sun, glittering beyond her reach. She couldn't help but reach out and touch it. They began seeing one another more and more. Lonely and naïve, Myravelle all too eagerly gave him her heart.

I will save you from this place, he promised her.

One evening, she and Pazcal made love under the stars, tantalized by her garden's herbal aromas. Myravelle knew Xylina was too preoccupied spinning gold to notice her absence. But they had spent too much time on the rooftop, lost in one another. When the young lovers finally snuck down the winding stone steps, Myravelle discovered her mother slumped in her chair, asleep.

Not just any sleep, a death-like sleep.

Myravelle shook her mother's shoulders, to no avail. Xylina's fingertip was bleeding, and the drop spindle on the floor revealed why. What scared Myravelle most was not knowing whether her mother had pricked her finger by accident or design.

She screamed Pazcal's name, hoping he hadn't gotten too far down the spiral stairs. When he slipped back into the room, Myravelle saw a glowing and crackling rune hovering over his heart, as bright as his golden hair. She instinctively knew what to do—as she had always felt the pull of fairy magic inside—and Pazcal, *sweet Pazcal*, had been all too willing to help.

Myravelle carved the rune into his chest, starting with the circle, then the curves and, at last, the star. She winced, worried she was harming the man she loved, but he enjoyed it. His eyes rolled, and he moaned just as loudly as he had on the rooftop—and it was Myravelle who harnessed all of his pain. She cried out in agony, but kept going. A matching glowing rune then appeared on her palm. After she sliced into her skin, she rested her hand against Pazcal's chest, and the healing force grew inside her like a raging fire. It burned and boiled every corner of her being, and Myravelle gasped against the torment. She wanted to make it stop. She wanted to give up, but she didn't. She needed to save her mother.

With tears streaming down her cheeks, Myravelle placed her hands upon Xylina's eyes. A gust of wind rustled her hair, but she continued to focus her energy into her mother. When Xylina woke, her eyes grew wide, but not at her daughter. Myravelle followed Xylina's gaze to find Pazcal's father and a castle guard in the doorway. Both men looked back and forth at Pazcal's chest and Myravelle's dagger. Blood soaked the room.

Xylina grabbed her daughter's hand and cursed under her breath at the rune. "What have you done?"

Myraville blinked the memory away with her tears. She had no idea then that saving her mother's life would lead to her own being filled with nothing but death, darkness, and despair. That her first love would become her first canvas.

"Pazcal." His name left her lips in a breathy whisper for the first time in years, drawing her back into the drafty and cluttered tent in the army encampment.

She dropped the pestle into the mortar and wiped the tears from her cheeks. Knowing she wouldn't be able to sleep, Myravelle decided to spin yarn on her mother's drop spindle to settle her nerves. *Draft, pinch, spin, park, and repeat.* All the while, she stared at the tent flap, wishing she had never changed the ritual. What was she thinking with the sweet pea? Her heart couldn't bear to be broken again.

After about an hour of mindless spinning, Myravelle flinched when Abelard barreled into her tent.

"The...infirmary," he said, out of breath. "Now!"

"Why?"

"There are injured soldiers."

Myravelle huffed and followed the captain out into the blustery wind. They walked in silence along a familiar path toward the infirmary. The cold air stung Myravelle's eyes as she gazed out at the mountains, thinking about her mother somewhere in the distance. She cursed herself for failing Xylina...and cursed the king for his lies.

They entered the wide tent lined with cots and tables of medical supplies. The usual sterile scent mixed with a hint of copper stung Myravelle's nose. Near the exit, there was a nurse attending to a sickly pale soldier, but they did not concern her. Myravelle's gaze narrowed in on the tall man with dark hair and scars. Her eyes dipped to the leather gloves he was wearing; she should have suspected Byzarien was up to no good when he'd snuck out. He towered over an unconscious soldier. There were two others lying on cots who appeared to have deadened limbs from the fairy curses, but were at least awake and lucid.

She recognized the group: Lazaire's friends. Byzarien, of course, along with Zelyx, Dezlan, and Xavier. She knew little things about each from listening to Lazaire's ramblings. Like how Dezlan and Xavier were romantic partners, and Zelyx burned through women faster than Desirien, god of lust. Myravelle also knew Byzarien wasn't the only one who called her a witch. These soldiers loathed her, yet there they were, requiring her help. *The irony*, she thought.

"She's here," Abelard announced, startling the soldiers and Myravelle alike.

Byzarien, Zelyx, and Xavier turned to them. An unreadable expression contorted Byzarien's face when Myravelle made eye contact with him. His light skin was flushed and damp, possibly from exertion, but the intense fire in his eyes sent a shiver down her spine.

"Help them," Abelard said, gesturing for Myravelle to move.

She approached Zelyx first and examined the woman's leg. Myravelle removed her boot and pinched her toes. "Do you feel this?" she asked.

Zelyx shook her head.

Myravelle tapped the middle of her shin. "This?"

"No."

After continuing the tests, it was clear that Zelyx had no feeling from her hip down. Myravelle moved on to Xavier, who was awkwardly leaning between the cots to hold Dezlan's limp hand. Something resembling pity struck Myravelle's heart as she watched the man cry over his unconscious partner. Pazcal's lifeless and drained body haunted her.

Myravelle shook the thought away and tested Xavier, discovering he had lost feeling in both legs. Next was Dezlan, the man trapped like an insect in a web of death-like sleep filled with terrors most humans could not imagine.

"Can you wake him?" Byzarien said, standing on the opposite side of the cot.

"I don't know."

"Please," Xavier said, his voice choked by desperation. "Will you try?"

Myravelle pushed Dezlan's light brown hair from his forehead, placed her hands upon his face, and closed her eyes. She tried to reach inside and wake him, but her chest and arms grew hollow, and her veins turned to ice. A dark, oily tide of magic rose inside, but she pushed it down. Her own pain always wanted to lash out, but it scared her like it had scared Xylina. *Never give into the darkness*, her mother would say.

Behind her lids, Myravelle's eyes danced along the burning shapes of runes, and her hands tingled with the desire to hold a blade, to carve the shapes into skin. To heal soldiers, she needed to draw pain from a source. She needed Byzarien to be her canvas.

"I can't," she whispered, stepping back with trembling limbs. "I need to harness magic from Byzarien."

Abelard turned to Byzarien. "Take her back to rest, and do not leave her side. She must be ready to work tomorrow."

"Yes, sir."

Byzarien gave his friends tearful goodbyes and escorted Myravelle to her tent. In order not to topple over, she wrapped her arm around his muscular torso. The man stiffened, but said not a word the entire way. She thought about asking him what he had been thinking. She even thought about scolding him. She did not, though, for Myravelle understood desperation more than most.

When they entered the tent, she let go, and Byzarien rested on his small blanket on the floor. The attempt to heal Dezlan had drained her energy, and she collapsed onto her bed to let sleep embrace her in its inky arms.

※

The scent of olive oil wafted into Myravelle's nose and drew her from the depths of sleep after only a few hours. She opened her eyes to find Byzarien without his tunic, slathering his skin with the expensive oil. Scars in the shape of licking flames covered the entire right side of his body. Myravelle was surprised how extensive they were as they curled toward his spine, and it hurt her heart to think about the trauma he must have endured. Her eyes danced their way from his shoulder all the way down to his hip. She flushed, as if she could feel the heat of the flames radiating from him.

When the odd sensation of yarn unspooling from her chest returned, her breath caught. She wanted nothing more than to reach out and touch his scars but, after his escape from her the night before, she decided against it.

She sat up in her bed and stretched, startling Byzarien. He threw on his tunic and re-corked his bottle of oil. Sliding out of bed and kneeling beside him on the floor, Myravelle studied his strong jaw and full lips up close. He leaned away from her, avoiding eye-contact.

"Olive oil is certainly great for moisture." She raised her hand near Byzarien's cheek, but when his skin flared red, she retracted it. "But I can make you something to help with the itching."

"I want nothing from you except help for my friends." He put the bottle into his trunk and grabbed his leather jacket.

She should have been hurt but deep in the caverns of her soul, she knew she never deserved anything but hatred. The fact that Pazcal and her other canvases ever cherished her at all was miraculous. She rolled her tongue between her teeth and cursed herself for ever thinking she could change the ritual to find a soulmate. As Byzarien shrugged into his jacket and stepped toward the tent flap, Myravelle stood on weak legs.

"Where are you going?"

When Byzarien turned around, his head hit a paper star garland. He ripped it down. "To the infirmary."

She stared at her stars crumpled upon the floor. "We must perform the enchantment before I can try to help them."

"So, you can carve me up like Lazaire?" He dropped his chin to his chest and sucked in a deep breath.

A rush of cold sank toward Myravelle's stomach at the thought of Pazcal, Lazaire, and all her other canvases. Gray and drained. Empty insect carcasses strung along a web. *Her web.* She opened her mouth but couldn't form words.

Byzarien turned toward her, heavy brows furrowed. "And what do you mean by *try*?"

She felt so small under his intense gaze. "Well, since we didn't bond, I'm not sure if it will work."

"*Bond*," he said, disdain dripping from his lips. "Did you even love Lazaire?"

She whispered the truth. "No." She hadn't given her heart to anyone since Pazcal. She couldn't.

Byzarien released a sharp and humorless laugh, then turned to leave.

"But," she began, making him pause, "I did care for him, and the rest of them, in my own way."

"You have an interesting definition for the word 'care.' I don't mutilate the people I care about."

She wrapped her arms around herself, containing a shiver.

"You are a spider," Byzarien said, stepping close and glaring down at her. "A black widow. You drain and drain and drain until there is nothing left. All you do is hurt people."

"You'll see." She gestured in the direction of the infirmary. "It won't hurt."

He huffed and stepped outside. She watched him walk away, his dark head of hair hanging down as it fought the heavy snow pattering against the tops of the tents. With worry creasing her features, she draped herself in her crushed velvet cloak and snatched her dagger from the table before setting off toward the infirmary.

This canvas would be her last. She felt it in her bones.

7

Byzarien

"So, are you no longer a virgin?" Zelyx asked.

Wisps of rage flickered from Byzarien's chest and up his cheeks at the question. He bit his tongue while his friends snickered in their cots. If his hands hadn't been shaking, he would have chucked a bottle of antiseptic at them. He couldn't believe Zelyx had the audacity to ask whether he had slept with the witch.

He wanted to feel nothing but disgusted at the thought, but flashes of her naked body tormented him and roused other feelings. He cursed himself for finding the witch beautiful, if that was what he could call it. More like *haunting*. She hovered in his mind like the moon glowing behind the clouds.

Xavier choked down his laughter and touched Byzarien's arm. "She's just joking, Byz. You don't have to tell us anything."

"Nothing happened," he finally spat. "How can you joke about this? I'm going to end up just like Lazaire."

Both Xavier and Zelyx fell silent. He knew they were coping with their twisted humor, but Byzarien only wanted to lash out at his friends. Cold air nipped his neck, and he turned when the witch entered the infirmary. She glided toward them with her head held high and a dagger in her grip. He grew lightheaded and swayed. Catching himself on the edge of Xavier's cot, he sucked in gasps of air.

"Byz?" Zelyx said, rubbing his back. "You don't have to do this!"

"I do." He flopped into the chair between the cots and avoided eye contact with the witch.

She stepped close and knelt before him. "I promise this will not hurt."

"Just get it over with," he whispered.

The witch cleared her throat. "I'm afraid I only have the strength to help one of you."

"Only one of us?" Xavier said. "What about Dezlan?"

The witch shook her head and caught Byzarien in her gossamer gaze for a brief moment before she stared at the floor. *The bond*, he thought, a tidal wave of nausea and guilt crashing into him.

"Well, Z should go first then." Xavier awkwardly leaned between the cots to stroke Dezlan's cheek. "Because I'm not leaving his side, anyway."

Zelyx tilted her head, making her short blonde locks fall over one eye. "Are you sure?"

Xavier gave her a smug grin. "Ladies first."

She narrowed her eyes and threw her pillow at his face. "I'm no *lady*."

He laughed and shook his head. "We know, but that doesn't change the fact that I'll stay with Dezlan. You should go first anyway, before Lana loses interest and moves on from...whatever game it is the two of you are playing."

"Byz, give me back my pillow," Zelyx said, glaring at Xavier.

He did, and she promptly chucked it at Xavier again. The two laughed and continued teasing one another. Byzarien, though, shook against the ice building in his veins. He wanted to get the *enchant-*

ment over with, but his bickering friends were prolonging the inevitable.

"I'll start with Zelyx," Myravelle interrupted as she stared at the floor. "Her injury is less severe, so it will require less magic from me."

"Fine," Zelyx said and stuck her tongue out at Xavier.

With his leg bouncing wildly, Byzarien took deep breaths to fight the lightheadedness. The witch stepped closer and twirled the dagger in her fingers, making his heart jump into his throat.

"Byzarien," she whispered his name like a midnight breeze, sending chills over his skin. "Remove your tunic."

"What?" His fingers clutched at the fabric. "Why?"

"For the enchantment."

"Just cut my arm or something."

"It's not that simple."

"Why not?" he asked. "You carved Lazaire's entire body."

"I carve where my magic tells me to," she said and bit her bottom lip. "The enchantment...well, it's glowing on your chest."

Byzarien thumbed the hem of his tunic and shifted his gaze around the infirmary, which was mostly empty aside from a few patients and nurses at the opposite end.

"If you're nervous about your scars, don't be," Xavier said. "Z and I have seen them before."

He tried to ignore the heat in his cheeks as he gritted his teeth. When he slipped off his tunic, to his surprise, the witch didn't stare at the scars—her gaze lingered just above his heart. Her gray eyes glowed with stardust as she studied his chest. He swallowed when she leaned even closer, and her midnight hair tickled his skin. She smelled of smoky vanilla and rose petals mixed with a tantalizing medley of herbs.

"May I?" she asked, raising the dagger.

Byzarien nodded.

The witch rested the cold blade against his chest. He squeezed his eyes shut and waited for the pain. It never arrived. Instead, waves of warmth and bliss came from her dagger. First, she carved a circle, then dragged the blade inward to create curves reaching for the center. Each one felt better than the last, and Byzarien lost himself in the euphoria. His body fell slack, and he stifled a moan when she carved the central star. It was the greatest pleasure he had ever felt. When the sensation ended, he opened his eyes to find the witch licking the blood from the blade. Her wicked tongue danced along the metal.

She raised the dagger to her palm, carving into an old scar. When she finished, she placed her palm against Byzarien's chest. As their blood swirled together with every beat of his heart, more intense waves of pleasure tingled through him. Tiny fires and explosions of euphoria burst through his mind and body. The witch's haunting silver eyes were the only things Byzarien could see. She was beautiful. Yes. *Myravelle* was beautiful.

When she removed her hand, Byzarien grabbed it. "Don't stop," he said, pulling her in for a kiss.

Myravelle's lips felt like silk and tasted of chamomile and jasmine tea. The tightness that had cinched itself around Byzarien's heart the night before now unspooled into her. He relaxed completely into the kiss and tangled his fingers through Myravelle's hair to draw her closer. Desperation shot through him like lightning when she squirmed away.

His brows furrowed. "Come back."

"Shh." She placed a finger over her full lips and pushed him back into his chair. "I must help Zelyx now."

The lusty mist began to lift as he remembered where they were. His cheeks burned the rest of the fog away when he realized his friends were staring at him.

"So, how did it feel?" Xavier asked, his voice rising with a smirk.

"It...didn't *hurt*," he squeaked.

The witch stepped toward Zelyx, who had a sinister grin on her face. Byzarien wanted nothing more than to die at that moment. He threw his tunic back on, not caring when the blood seeped from his wound and into the fabric.

"May I?" Myravelle asked Zelyx as she gestured to her blanket.

"Please do," she said with a giggle and a wink. "And can you make me feel like him?"

The edge of Myravelle's lip curled up slightly. Byzarien wondered if she ever fully smiled. He swept his hair over his cheek and avoided Zelyx's teasing gaze. Myravelle placed her hands on the dead leg and closed her eyes.

Wisps of crackling magic filled the air and darted toward her hands. An unsettling static buzzed through the air of the infirmary. Myravelle's entire body began to tremble, and she winced. Byzarien stood next to her, unsure how to help. All the shimmering light disappeared into Zelyx's leg, and Myravelle wailed in agony. The nurses and other patients either cringed or covered their ears at the sound.

Myravelle stumbled back, and Byzarien caught her by the elbows. When he checked, her eyes rolled, and she fell slack in his arms.

"What happened?" Xavier asked from behind. "Z, are you all right?"

"It...worked," Zelyx said, lifting her leg from the cot. "It worked!"

Byzarien stood shocked, with Myravelle's body slumped against him, and watched his friend stand. Zelyx was a bit wobbly at first but regained her balance with a huge smile.

"It's a little tingly still, but it worked!" she said, staring at Xavier. "That means she can help you and Dezlan!" Xavier and Zelyx finally glanced at Myravelle, and their celebratory smiles faded.

"I, uh," Byzarien started, shifting her limp body into a cradle-carry, "I think she needs rest."

Zelyx's white-blonde eyebrows narrowed as she studied Myravelle. "Have either of you ever seen her leave the infirmary like this?"

"No," Xavier whispered. "What happened?"

"Lazaire said she healed an entire tent of sleeping soldiers in one day after the last failed expedition." Zelyx looked at Byzarien. "Why is she so weak?"

His heart pounded against his ribs, and he feared he knew the answer. Was it because he didn't *bond* with her? He pushed it from his mind and shook his head. "I don't know, but I'll take her back to her tent."

After saying goodbye to his friends, who shared mixed emotions about Zelyx's repaired mobility, Byzarien tucked the dagger into his waist belt and carried Myravelle to her tent. The air was bitter, and the mountains hid behind a curtain of gray clouds. Soldiers stared as Byzarien passed with the unconscious healer in his arms. Whispers rose above the tents and blended with the wind and snow.

Once in the warmth of the tent, Byzarien rested Myravelle on her bed. Her lips were tinged blue, and her skin was raised with goosebumps. He drew a knit blanket and a heavy fur up to her shoulders before adding more coal to the stove. When he turned toward the worktable to find some tea to brew, Captain Abelard stood in the entrance with one boot on the star garland Byzarien had ripped down.

"I heard Myravelle was unconscious." The captain stared at the sleeping woman with a scowl. Byzarien couldn't believe the rumors had made their way to him so quickly. "What happened?" Abelard asked, taking a few strides into the center of the tent.

Something tugged at Byzarien to step between the captain and Myravelle, though he didn't understand why he suddenly felt protective.

"I don't know, sir," he answered with a shrug. "She healed Zelyx's leg, then collapsed."

"Find me when she wakes up," the captain said and crossed his arms over his chest. "Serve him."

Byzarien copied the gesture. "And he will serve you."

The flap whipped in the wind after the captain left, so Byzarien secured it and turned toward Myravelle. What she had done to him in the infirmary had felt incredible, and his stonewall guard had begun to slip away. Touching his lips, he realized they still tingled from the kiss. *Stop.* He cursed himself. *It wasn't real—it was just her wicked magic.*

He tensed all the muscles in his body and decided to stay angry. It was his armor. He focused on how the witch couldn't save his other friends. He focused on how she had embarrassed him. He focused on how she had killed Lazaire. He focused on anger.

He could handle anger.

8

Myravelle

The thick gravity of sleep and coiling vines of nightmares did their best to hold Myravelle hostage. She fought to peel open her eyes, which felt sewn shut. Dreams of unspeakable things faded, but left haunting whispers. She struggled against the pull to slip back under sleep's spell.

"Myravelle," a deep and smooth voice echoed through the darkness. "Myravelle?"

It was bliss to her ears. Though groggy, she remembered how Byzarien had only called her *witch* until then. The rise and fall of her name on his lips was like a song lulling her from peril. She waited for him to say it once more before opening her eyes.

Byzarien sat on the corner of her mattress, which sank under his tall frame, holding out a steaming mug of chamomile tea.

She shifted to sit against the pillows and accepted the mug, allowing its warmth to seep into her hands. "Thank you," she said in a painful, scratchy voice.

"You were screaming," he said. "I had to wake you."

Shuddering, Myravelle grasped bits and pieces of the nightmare and tried to push them away. *Mother's pricked finger. Pazcal's carved up body. Her past canvases rising from their graves, their bone fragments held together by thorny vines.* Filoux's illusions not only caused distress during the night, they would hover in the shadows of one's mind throughout the day, waiting for a moment of weakness to torture the individual all over again.

"Are you all right?"

Myravelle sipped the tea, a balm to her sore throat. "What happened?"

"You collapsed."

Her stomach sank as she rested the mug on the bedside table. "What about Zelyx's leg?"

"Healed but tingly." He coaxed his dark hair to cover his scars. "Can you tell me what went wrong?"

"What do you mean?"

"Why couldn't you do more? Why couldn't you help Xavier and Dezlan, too?"

"I'm too weak, I told you," she said. "We need a stronger bond for the magic to work properly."

"Bond with you?" He huffed. "You didn't tell me what would happen; you embarrassed me in front of my friends!"

"All of *that*," she began, tilting her head, "could have taken place here, but you are quite stubborn."

"But you knew I would be..."

"Aroused?" she finished for him, watching his neck and cheeks flush. "Yes."

He stood and paced around the tent. "I should go inform the captain that you are well."

"What?" she gasped, eyes going wide. "H-He knows?"

When he nodded, a metallic iciness swept through Myravelle's insides. *What would he tell the king?*

"Don't go to him yet," she begged in a crumbling voice. "We can help Xavier first! I'm sure I can heal his legs."

"Are you joking?" Byzarien's brows pinched together. "Look at you!"

Myravelle hadn't realized she was shaking. Her limbs reminded her of a soldier who had lost too much blood. She was so cold and weak. Something was terribly wrong.

"It's the bond," she said. "If we could just—"

"I am not having sex with you."

"No, no, no," she said, reaching for his arm. Even when her other canvases had grown too weak for sex, their connection remained strong in other ways. Was sex just the easiest avenue to gaining their affection and trust? Byzarien was different, therefore, bonding with him could be different too. "Maybe it doesn't have to be *physical*. Please, sit and, um, tell me about yourself. We can bond about our lives."

"You want to know about my life?" he asked, narrowing his eyes and tilting his head. "And bond over our *shared experiences* or something?"

"It could work."

Byzarien laughed, humorless. "I don't know what type of luxurious life you had at the castle, but I grew up with nothing. Nothing besides my family—and they are suffering! The Fairy Raids took everything from us, including," he paused to scrunch his face and swallow hard, "my little brother." He leaned so close to Myravelle's face she could see the fury swimming in his deep brown eyes. "Becoming your canvas destroyed any chance of getting my family out of the slums. Like I said, you are a spider. Even after I'm gone, your web will kill my family. You don't care about anyone."

Though Myravelle pitied him, anger flared up in her chest and burned any compassion away. "How dare you judge me?" she hissed, slipping out of bed.

Without looking at Byzarien, Myravelle grabbed her cloak and left the tent. She walked for a few hours, to nowhere in particular, with only rage to fuel her exhausted body and keep her upright.

She weaved her trail just inside the border of the woods to avoid being spotted by Captain Abelard and because she couldn't bring herself to visit her secret graveyard. A sourness rose in her throat at the mere thought. *You are a spider.* Byzarien's words echoed in her ears. The only thing keeping the brittle fragments of her soul together was her mother. As much as Myravelle wanted to sink into the earth and become one with the soil and roots, she had to keep working. Xylina deserved freedom.

Deciding to forage for roots, mushrooms, and pine needles in the snowy woods, Myravelle's mind turned to Byzarien's family. They had lost a member to the fires—a little boy even. Were they really trapped in the slums? Is that why he'd joined the lowest division of the king's army, only meant for those escaping the horrors of poverty or abuse?

Byzarien and Lazaire had known one another since childhood, but Lazaire had rarely talked about his past. He had always preferred to live in the moment, clinging to Myravelle like a lifeline from the first orgasmic slip of her blade. He had known she was killing him with pleasure, and that's why he'd loved her so. *Don't feel sorry for me*, Lazaire had often said. *There are worse ways to go.*

Although Byzarien had only done so in anger, he *had* opened up to her. Whether or not he meant to, he had given her a glimpse behind those thick stone walls as to what made him *him*. She thought maybe it was her turn to spill a secret or two. Wasn't that what *friends* did? Like her, Byzarien's every thought and action were for his family. Maybe they weren't so different, healer and soldier.

Myravelle twisted her silver rings as she paced the forest floor, hardened with frost. Her finger stroked over a ring of silver and rose quartz, the goddess of love Amyor's symbol. It had been a gift from Pazcal—a promise neither of them could keep. Aside from Pazcal, none of her canvases knew anything about her past...but she had never changed the ritual formula either. Since he deeply cared about his family, maybe Byzarien would understand the love she had for her mother. A friend. She wanted a friend.

Adjusting her cloak, Myravelle snuck back to the army encampment and, like a shadow, slipped between the tents until she arrived at her own. She found Byzarien lying on his makeshift bed, and he made no movement indicating he sensed her return.

She snatched her mother's drop spindle from the worktable and chucked it at his broad back to gain his attention. The tool was well-polished, and of no real risk to Byzarien. "Ouch!" He sat up and grabbed the spindle. "Why'd you do that?"

"Beware of splinters." She perched herself on the corner of her mattress. "That's made from Dormrya wood." Byzarien dropped the spindle like a venomous snake and glared at her. "You told me about your life," she said, picking at her nails, painted black because they were always burnt or stained anyway. "So, I've decided to tell you about mine."

He sucked in a deep breath. "Fine."

"Firstly, I want to say how deeply sorry I am about your little brother; my heart breaks for your family," she said. "What was his name?"

Shaking his head, Byzarien scoffed and turned his glassy eyes toward the star-lined ceiling.

"Fine. I was raised in the castle," she began, "but you were wrong to assume my life was luxurious. I was born in the loneliest and tallest tower, where my mother remains captive to this day."

He leaned forward a little, brows furrowed. "Captive? Why?"

"Magic." Myravelle lifted the spindle from the floor and twirled it with her fingers. "My mother spun gold for the king, but he didn't want the secret that he had enslaved a pregnant fairy to get out. So, he locked her away and hid her from the world." Byzarien shook his head, but Myravelle pressed on. "She grew so feverish during labor, Mother crawled up the spiral stairs to the rooftop for fresh air and gave birth to me under the night sky. She said that, in that moment, the stars fell for me, soaking into my skin, eyes, and hair. She read it as an omen that I possessed more magic than any fairy in existence." She stared at the paper stars lining the tarp ceiling above her, glistening through her tears. "She raised me in the tower's small room but forbade me from performing enchantments."

"Why?"

"She worried that, if the king learned of my gifts, he would lock me away and exploit my magic for the rest of my life too."

He gestured to the surrounding space. "But you are not locked away."

With a tilt of her head, she said, "Oh, but I am. My mother is my everything. She held me when I was frightened. She taught me how to spin and to garden. She told me stories of gods and heroes. She's a gentle soul and I would do anything to save her...even disobey her."

She recited the story of how she learned healing magic in order to save her mother from eternal sleep. But her tale was like a flat stone skimming across water, for she skipped bits and pieces to hide anything to do with Pazcal. A few tears meant only for her first love slipped down her cheeks, regardless. "My mother remains in that tower; therefore, I do," she said. "Her safety depends on me. If you think I want to do this, slowly killing canvases to wake sleeping soldiers, you're wrong."

"I don't believe the king would do such a thing," Byzarien said. "I mean, he is a great man."

Myravelle shook her head. "You're blinded by duty."

"And spinning gold? Is that even possible?"

"You've seen what I can do with the human body, but you can't wrap your mind around something as simple as gilded thread?"

"If she has been spinning all of this gold for the king, then why—"

"Then why is there such misery and despair in the kingdom, especially within the *slums*?" Myravelle leaned close to search Byzarien's eyes, hidden behind his dark hair. "Because he has been using the gold for something else."

"For what?"

"I would love to know."

He pushed his giant frame to rise from the floor. "That's a

wonderful bedtime story, Myravelle, filled with nonsense," he said. "Why didn't the fairies ever try to rescue you? Why didn't your mother use her magic to just run away?"

"I don't know," she said, hanging her head.

"It doesn't make sense." The truth in his words shivered through her, but she couldn't make sense of the fairies and what happened to her mother without crumbling to dust.

"Either way, we have people to help." She sighed. "When I get enough rest, will you return to the infirmary with me?" Byzarien groaned as he retrieved his oil and nightshirt from the trunk, and his cheeks bloomed with crimson splotches when he faced her. "I can do the...*enchantment* here, if that would be more comfortable for you." He nodded and avoided eye contact. "How does it look, your chest?" Myravelle glided forward, reaching for him.

He avoided her touch and stepped behind the privacy screen. "It's fine."

"I can stitch your wound and make something proper to soothe your sc—"

"I said it before: I want nothing from you."

Myravelle swallowed the splinters in her throat and moved to her worktable, where she opened a drawer and switched her mother's old spindle for a new, unused one she had saved for an emergency. A golden and glittering rune appeared on the polished whorl of the spindle, and she engraved it with the tip of her dagger. She had watched her mother do it so many times that the act was as natural as breathing; a circle with a spiral looping down the center toward a star at the base.

As she prepared the roving onto a distaff and sat on her stool to begin, Byzarien rested on the floor with his back to her. Myravelle spun her dangerous threads in silence for hours, watching the rise and fall of the man's breaths.

9

Byzarien

When the first light of dawn bled into the tent, Byzarien stretched to fight soreness in his neck and hip. He rolled to look at the welcoming bed, only to discover it empty. Sitting up to scratch his scars, he wondered where Myravelle could have gone so early.

The star garland crumpled upon the floor caught his attention, and a touch of sickness swam in his belly. After a deep yawn, he stood and grabbed the string of stars. With the little pins holding all of Myravelle's constellations together, he returned the garland to its home, only slightly higher this time, though, so he wouldn't hit his head. It was a beautiful sight, Myravelle's tent, with the paper stars hanging down like medallions, the scent of herbs and dried flowers wafting in the air, the embroidered pillows scattered about, and a multitude of candles on nearly every flat surface. It may have been odd and cluttered, but it was beautiful.

He returned to the floor palette and rubbed his temples. They were supposed to heal Xavier...and a rush of hot tingling coursed through his body at the mere thought of Myravelle's blade. The way her velvety voice tantalized his ears. The way her stormy eyes held him captive. Byzarien pressed his palm against the wound on his chest, if he could call it a *wound*. A normal cut so deep should have bled more and hurt to touch, but it felt good and eased his aches from sleeping on the ground.

Myravelle slipped into the tent, making Byzarien flinch. Her freckled cheeks had been bitten red by the cold, and her long wavy locks had been tousled by the wind.

As she removed her cloak, revealing a dark gown with sickle moons and stars adorning the netting of her skirts and sleeves, Myravelle glanced at him. "Ready?"

He nodded, still under some sort of charm caused by her sudden and wild appearance.

"Remove your tunic and get on the bed."

Byzarien did as he was told, slowing every movement so as not to appear eager. With nimble fingers, Myravelle braided her hair and secured it with a black satin ribbon before perching herself on the edge of the mattress.

His tongue finally deciding to work, Byzarien asked, "Where were you?"

"What?"

"This morning, where were you?" He reclined onto Myravelle's bed, his heart thrumming in a chaotic tempo.

"I was getting fresh air," she said and lifted the dagger. "Ready?" He nodded, unable to keep his breaths under control. "This will feel even better than before," she said, tilting her head.

When his eyes met hers, there was no hint of humor. Realizing she was telling the truth, he took a pillow and placed it over his groin. Myravelle leaned over Byzarien's chest with her blade hovering just above his skin.

Loud explosions and shouts rumbled from outside, making them jump out of bed.

"What's that?" she asked, after another blast and more screams.

Byzarien slipped his tunic over his head and peeked outside. His jaw dropped; multi-colored fires rimmed the outer edge of the camp while soldiers ran all around. There was another blast, loud enough to make Byzarien grab Myravelle and duck with her behind the bed while the ground rumbled.

"What's happening?" she shouted over the cacophony.

"Something's wrong. An attack, maybe." He pushed himself up and threw on his jacket. "I'm going to check on the infirmary."

"I'll come with you."

"No, stay here. At the center of camp, you're well-protected, but the infirmary could be a target." He dashed away before she could argue.

Dark ashes floated against the backdrop of smoke and rainbow fires. His scars begged him to retreat and hide—like talons, they reached into his muscles and tried to hold him hostage. The screams of his family roared in his ears, and he bit his tongue hard to focus on the present. He jogged toward the commotion, unsure whether the shivers running through his body were caused by adrenaline from the attacks or by the echoes of his past trying to break free. *Focus.*

Somewhere beyond the haze, Captain Abelard shouted, "Get to the outer edge! Defend the camp!"

Byzarien peered through the crowd of soldiers, but couldn't see any fairies. If he did, he hoped he would be brave enough to fight them. A dozen or so soldiers dashed toward the stables, where the thrashing horses were trying to escape.

Byzarien found a pile of crates near the mess and climbed them. From the slightly better vantage point, he saw soldiers dousing the flames with buckets of water and snow. He was then certain the fairies had attacked and run, for there was no one in the fields on either side of camp.

Just like the attack on his village so many years ago, the fairies were quick and moved like shadows. He helped smother the flames, trying to fight the memories that would no longer remain silent...

Byzarien was twelve the morning his life changed forever. He stirred, coughing in his bed. Eyes still closed, he coughed and coughed until the smoke in his lungs fully woke him. His family's screams blended together, and he sprang from bed and rushed to the corridor, which was ablaze in multicolored fire.

The roaring flames rolled toward the ceiling, and the blackened walls crackled. All at once, Byzarien was slick with sweat. The intense heat made it hard to open his eyes, but he followed his mother's voice. She called all her children's names. *Byzarien. Beatryz. Bryda. Benoix.* He found her collapsed in the narrow corridor. Cradling his frail mother, he carried her outside. With wide eyes, he stared at the cottage—small, but theirs. His father had destroyed his lungs in the mine, and his mother had developed early arthritis from sewing to pay for it. It *couldn't* be gone. His mother's arms shook as she wrapped them around his shoulders.

"Where's Pa?"

She pointed toward the house with a trembling hand, coughing too hard to speak. Byzarien sprinted back into the inferno. The heat was all-consuming and stung his eyes. He found his father and sister, Bryda, unconscious in the den. His other siblings screamed from somewhere deeper in. With impossible strength, Byzarien dragged both his father and sister outside.

Ignoring his mother's protests, he went back for Beatryz and Benoix. A wall of fire had formed and burning pieces of the thatched roof fell like rain, but the screams of his siblings still reached his ears. The little ones were stuck in the kitchen. They needed him. Byzarien jumped through the flames. His bedclothes ignited.

The entire right side of his body burned. The flames licked up toward his face, and the scent of burnt hair stung his nose. Gritting his teeth, he rolled on the ground until they went out. There was pain, but he had no time for it. He couldn't look at the damage done. It didn't matter.

Through the smoke and dome of flames, he found his siblings. They cried out for him. He couldn't risk dragging them through the wall of fire, so Byzarien chucked a chair through the window. The fresh air made the flames flare even hotter, and his skin seared with intense pain.

Curtains of darkness wavered around the edges of his vision. His siblings' cries helped him refocus, and he scooped them up. As he climbed out the window, a broken shard of glass sliced his back. He heaved ragged breaths while sprinting with the children in his arms. It wasn't until they had met up with their family that Byzarien truly saw the damage to his body. It was impossible to discern cloth from skin along his right side. Head to toe, the agony consumed his focus, making him sway on his feet before collapsing into a dark, dark dream. But the nightmare was far from over.

When Byzarien awoke, his mother barely had the words to tell him Benoix didn't make it. His little brother had succumbed to smoke inhalation. A weight pressed on Byzarien's chest and he howled, wanting nothing more than to hear his brother giggle again. He had just started teaching him how to ride a horse and play knucklebones, little Benny couldn't be gone. The salty tears stung Byzarien's burns, but what hurt even worse was that no one could hug him. His own life hung in the balance. Painful infections and delirious fevers held him in their grip. Bedridden and often unconscious, Byzarien was unable to attend Benoix's funeral.

Though many people had had prejudices and suspicions well before their banishment from the kingdom years prior, the attacks prompted King Zylvain to make statements about the true dangers of the fairies. Byzarien's family recited the warnings from images pasted on the village's walls and repeated lectures from the temples to him while he laid in bed for weeks with wet bandages covering his burns. Every time his mother and sisters changed the wrappings, more skin peeled like shredded paper from his body. But the pain mattered none, for little Benny was dead. An ember of hate had settled in his chest with that fire and grew with every royal statement about the fairies...

Byzarien shook his head and pulled himself into the present:

another fairy attack. He reached the infirmary and, dodging injured soldiers and frantic nurses, he found his friends. A cool rush of relief washed over him when he realized they were unharmed. Xavier and Dezlan were still in their cots while Zelyx, Lana, and a few other women stood guard, their hands on their weapons.

"Are you all right?" Byzarien asked.

Zelyx nodded. "We came to protect the infirmary in case it was targeted."

He looked around to absorb the situation in the infirmary. Nearly all the cots had occupants. Nurses stitched bleeding soldiers and wrapped broken limbs. There were at least a dozen sleeping soldiers.

"Was it the fairies?" Byzarien growled through his clenched teeth, already knowing the answer.

Zelyx looked at him with tears in her eyes, and he knew. Her brows rose as she glanced at the infirmary's entrance. Byzarien followed her gaze, and there was Myravelle, gliding past the carnage. Her eyes, usually full of moonlight and magic, were empty as she stared at the rows of sleeping soldiers.

Byzarien's brow furrowed at an odd prickle at the back of his mind. *Where had Myravelle been this morning? Did she have something to do with this?* He studied her face and movements as she approached.

"What happened?" she asked.

Byzarien's throat was clogged by fear and suspicion, so Zelyx stepped close to the witch before he could say anything. "Fairy attacks." She gestured to all the occupied cots. "Will you be able to wake them all?"

Myravelle frowned, and her jaw quivered. She shook her head and looked around at all the damage. "Fairies?" she asked, voice like broken glass.

Byzarien glared at her. "Yes, *fairies*."

"Did anyone see them?" Myravelle asked.

"I didn't." Zelyx turned to Lana and the other guards. "Did anyone see what happened?"

The women muttered amongst themselves for a moment as their voices blended with the commotion around them.

"No." Lana, the petite woman, grabbed Zelyx's hand. "We all woke up to explosions and screams. They vanished before we reached the outer edge."

"What does it matter?" Byzarien narrowed his eyes at the witch. "It was certainly the fairies."

"It's just," she began, shaking her head, "I didn't feel them."

"*Feel* them?" he asked. "As in, you can sense other fairies?"

Myravelle's cheeks grew pink as she glanced at everyone listening. She rounded her shoulders before turning toward all the sleeping soldiers. Byzarien grabbed her shoulder. When she turned around, her gray eyes shined like quicksilver as they brimmed with tears.

"What do you mean?"

"It's nothing."

"*Nothing?*" Zelyx stepped closer. "Are you sure you can feel them?"

Lana and the other soldiers formed a semi-circle around Myravelle. Byzarien's heart raced, but he hesitated to step in. "Was it the fairies or not?" Lana asked.

"Can you wake them or not?" Xavier shouted from his cot.

With a shiver, Myravelle took a step back. "I don't know," she whispered and dashed away.

Like in the Sleepy Wood, she slipped around every obstacle, fluttering like a moth, and was gone before he could stop her.

Zelyx looked at Byzarien, whose jaw was set hard. "Byz, what are we going to do? She could barely heal my leg. How is she going to help all the sleepers?"

Chills pulsed through his limbs as he thought about the soldiers trapped in an endless nightmare. Filoux, he thought, certainly had his work cut out for him now. Would this finally be enough for the god of nightmares? Enough payment for humans of Eglantyne Kingdom having killed his fairy love?

"And what in Guerrix's name did she mean by *feeling the fairies*?" Lana asked so loudly it was nearly a shout. "If she can feel them, why doesn't the captain use her to prevent things like this?"

Use her. Byzarien's stomach soured as he recalled what Myravelle had said about her mother. Her magic abilities were something she had never wanted the king to exploit...but what if she'd had something to do with the attack? His head swam with waves of pain and confusion. All at once, everyone hurled questions at him.

He waved his arms to silence them. "I'll talk to her," he said, and then took Zelyx to the side. "Keep an eye on the infirmary."

"I will," she said. "These men and women have no way of protecting themselves if the fairies attack again. You need to find out what's going on with the witch."

He cringed at the word *witch* and headed through the chaos toward Myravelle's tent, where she had collapsed onto her bed.

"You need to tell me where you were this morning."

"Why?" Myravelle sat up, dark brows stitched together. "You think *I* had something to do with this?"

"It is oddly suspicious, isn't it?" He stepped to the edge of the bed, towering over her. "Did you lead them here?"

"How can you suggest such a thing?" She shook her head. "I would never put anyone in danger, trust me on that."

He huffed and paced around the tent. "Will you just tell me where you were?"

Myravelle's face hardened, and she crossed her arms. "No."

"Then I cannot trust you." A bubble of pain rose in his throat, but he managed to squeak out, "I can't trust any of *your kind*."

"You're blinded by prejudice," she said, which inflamed Byzarien's cheeks.

"Excuse me?" He stooped close and tugged the neckline of his tunic to show his scars. "More like *burned* with prejudice. You have no idea the pain the fairies have caused."

To his surprise, Myravelle didn't shrink away from his nearness, but tilted her head to gaze into his eyes. "Did you ever *see* them?" she asked, pointing to his scars, "that night or this morning?"

"What does that matter?" he snarled.

"Then you have no proof."

"*Proof?* Who else would have done this?"

"I, myself, would love to know," Myravelle, whose lips were dangerously close to his own, said in a steady voice.

Using the mattress to push himself away, he stepped toward the tent flap. "Can you heal them?"

"I don't know."

He turned and was about to shout at her when he noticed she was trembling. All of her outward confidence had melted away by his question, and she looked more exhausted now than ever. He softened his tone. "Will you try?"

She nodded and touched the hilt of her dagger on the bedside table. "We still need to perform the enchantment."

Byzarien shuddered. His body burned with the desire to let her carve him, but his head screamed at him to run. He looked at her weary eyes and knew she wasn't ready for so many sleeping soldiers, anyway. *Why would she still be here*, he asked himself, *if she had something to do with the attacks?* Maybe he had been too hard on her.

"Later," he said. "After you get some rest. Otherwise, you won't be able to heal anyone in your condition."

Myravelle curled up into a fetal position on her bed without a word.

"I, uh, I'm going to help clean up the damage," he said, unsure whether she was still listening. "Then I'll go to the infirmary."

Outside, ash and snow swirled through the air as Byzarien walked through the empty rows of tents. All the soldiers were on the outer rim of the encampment, either standing guard or clearing debris. Byzarien's head and heart were battling, and the headache nauseated him, so he stopped into the infirmary for some relief. After gulping down pain medicine, which Myravelle had probably made, he jogged to the outskirts of camp to help the cleanup crew.

Though he was the *canvas* and shouldn't have been working, he buried himself in hours and hours of physical labor. Others took regular breaks for water, food, and rest, but not Byzarien. He hoped shoveling rubble and rebuilding tents would keep his mind occupied.

No matter what, though, Myravelle kept resurfacing in his thoughts. *Was she right?* Her words made Byzarien doubt. And doubt was a dangerous thing. One ember of it could burn down a life's worth of morals, duty, and beliefs.

What if the fairies weren't responsible for the attacks?

The more he worked, the angrier he grew. But not even anger could break Myravelle's spellbinding presence in his mind.

10

Myravelle

D*raft. Pinch. Spin. Park.* Myravelle spun away her worries into the night. Her fingers tugged at the roving, and she admired how the loose fibers resembled cobwebs until she released her pinch, and the spin twisted up the yarn. *You are a spider.* Byzarien's words haunted her mind. *In more ways than one,* she thought as tears pricked her eyes.

Hatred dripped from nearly every word he spoke to her, yet she missed his presence. Maybe her fondness for him was an unfair and one-sided result of the sweet pea. Myravelle had slept for a few hours after the 'fairy' attacks, but her anxiety had not waned. No, it cinched her chest up tight, as if her nerves were twisted by a spindle.

Byzarien was still away, either helping with the damage or visiting his friends. He was such a good, caring, and loyal person; she hoped to someday be on the receiving end of his kindness. When Myravelle's mind wandered to how many soldiers she would have to heal, she shuddered and began spinning again. The shuffle of footsteps approaching caught her attention as she twisted the spindle.

"The king is here," Byzarien said when he entered. "He wants to meet with us." *The king.* The spindle in Myravelle's chest twisted tighter, and she closed her eyes to focus on breathing. "Myravelle, did you hear me?"

"He's going to wonder why Dezlan isn't awake yet, isn't he?" she asked, parking the spindle beneath her arm to draft and pinch more roving. "And why I couldn't help the soldiers today?"

"Probably."

Myravelle stared into Byzarien's dark eyes. "I beg you, please don't mention how weak I've been. I'm sure Abelard has done enough damage to my reputation."

"Do you truly believe the king would hurt your mother?" he asked.

She clenched her jaw, biting back the prodding pain in her throat. A flash of her mother's empty gaze and branded skin burned in her mind. "Yes."

"Fine," Byzarien said, leaning against the worktable. "I'll say your strength is improving, as long as you promise to try healing Dezlan again."

"I will." She wrapped the spun yarn around the shaft of the spindle, leaving enough length to sink it into the notch and secure it around the hook. "I cannot tell you where I was this morning, but I promise it had nothing to do with the attacks. The only other fairy I know is my mother."

Although his mind seemed far away, he nodded. Myravelle stood when a dark, weightless rush passed through her head, and she grabbed the worktable to hold herself steady.

"Are you able to go?" Byzarien's concern came through his deep voice and made Myravelle's heart flutter. "You're still weak."

He was right. Myravelle's muscles and bones felt like whispers, and all she wanted to do was crawl back into bed. But her nightmares had been composed of nothing but her mother's screams. Every time she'd floated out of sleep's embrace, Myravelle worried the king and captain's threats had come true.

She knew she had to face the king for her mother's sake.

"Yes."

Stepping behind the privacy screen, Myravelle rummaged through her clothes to find something fit for a royal occasion. Everything she owned was black with intricate beadwork she had done herself. Rumors within the army encampment said she had stitched spells into the folds of her gowns, but it simply wasn't true.

Xylina had been a storyteller, spinning tales while spinning gold. Myths about healing waters, enchanted shoes, and merciful gods—Myravelle had desperately wanted to believe. Growing up, with only spiders and her mother's stories to keep her company, she'd always imagined herself in gowns like those in *Tale of Reverie*. The goddess of dreams cloaked herself in midnight while spiders spun gossamer stars into the skirts. This allowed the goddess to float, undetected, into bedrooms to weave tales for sleeping minds. Reverie once wandered into the bedroom of Enferrix, god of the underworld, but her deep, dark beauty couldn't hide from his eyes, so well-adjusted to the night. They fell in love and had a child: Filoux. It was Reverie's gown, though, that had inspired Myravelle's love of fiber arts.

For the *royal* occasion, Myravelle slipped into a dark gown with sprawling white briar roses on the hem and bodice, moonstones glittering at the center of the flowers. The gown fit snug to her body and revealed ample amounts of cleavage, which she hoped would distract from her tired eyes.

She moved from behind the divider to find a mirror. As she pinned her dark hair into an updo, she caught Byzarien staring in the reflection.

"Shouldn't you be getting dressed?" she asked, quirking a brow.

He cleared his throat. "Your, um, gown is...pretty."

His deep voice threaded heat through Myravelle's veins, and she blushed at the compliment. "I made it myself."

"Really?" He tilted his head, then turned to dig through his own trunk.

"Yes, my mother taught me to spin and to sew—mostly to keep

me occupied while we were locked away, so I wouldn't get into mischief."

He cradled a bundle of clothes in his arms as he turned to her. "Well, Reverie must bless you with wonderful dreams to create such lovely things."

"No," Myravelle said, staring at the floor. "I don't think I've ever been visited by Reverie. It has always been Filoux, and his nightmares often spill into reality."

She looked back up at Byzarien, whose face was strained as he nodded. "*That*, I understand." He disappeared behind the privacy screen to change.

Soldiers didn't own many clothes, but they had all been issued a dress uniform in the rare event of a formal occasion. When Byzarien came out and waited by the tent flap, Myravelle couldn't help but admire how well his tall and muscular frame filled out the dark gray uniform. He coaxed his wavy hair to cover his scars; Myravelle truly wished he wouldn't.

They left for the captain's quarters, stepping out into the frigid night. Glowing fires crackled against the darkness and the King's Guards, the highest-ranking soldiers in the kingdom, stood at attention all around the encampment. Myravelle should have felt safe, but the king's presence never meant good things for her. Acid sloshed in her stomach more and more with every step.

Outside the large tent, she took a few cleansing breaths which bloomed into white clouds around her head.

"Are you all right?" Byzarien asked, leaning down to peer at her face.

She squeezed her eyes shut. "I don't know."

"If it helps, I'm nervous to dine with the king as well." Byzarien touched her arm, but retracted his hand just as quickly. "I've only seen His Majesty King Zylvain in person twice."

Myravelle had the unfortunate *pleasure* of being in the king's presence far too many times to count. She wished to disappear in a cloud of smoke and hide somewhere far, far away.

Straightening her posture, Myravelle entered the tent with Byzarien trailing behind. Servants had transformed the inside of Abelard's dank and sterile quarters. Lavish tables of wines, breads, and meats hugged the walls, with a crescent moon of velvet loungers arranged around them. Myravelle's stomach grumbled at the intoxicating aromas, for she had never eaten such rich foods. Oil lamps flickered warm shadows all around the canvas, creating an illusion that one was not in the middle of an eternal winter or that a brutal attack hadn't recently occurred.

When King Zylvain rose from his lounger, everyone in the room stood with him. The thin and pale man with mousy-brown hair wore a plush fur cloak, which dragged along the ground as he walked. While twirling golden rings on his fingers, he approached Myravelle and Byzarien, who knelt before him at once.

"Your Majesty," they said in unison.

King Zylvain grabbed Myravelle's chin and forced her gaze to meet his. She clenched her teeth, and her heartbeat pounded in her ears. *Would he kiss her? Slap her?* She never knew what to expect from the man. His dull gray eyes roved around Myravelle's face in a way that made bile burn in her throat.

"Looking rather tired, are we, Myravelle?" He cocked an eyebrow and clicked his tongue. "I need you to be in peak performance, darling. Are you unhappy with your newest canvas?"

She swallowed her needling fears. "Very happy, sir."

"Good," the king said, letting his mouth hang open as he studied Byzarien for a moment. "Sit with us as we discuss our plans."

When he released Myravelle's chin, she nearly fell over. Byzarien took her by the elbow to help her stand and escorted her to the only empty lounger. They sat on the plush velvet, which should have been comforting, but only set her nerves ablaze.

Across from them, the king sat next to a woman Myravelle assumed to be a concubine, for she was certainly not the queen. Queen Lya, originally from Basenfort Kingdom, had once been proclaimed as golden as a summer's day, but rumors of depression and melancholy tarnished her persona. The poor woman had yet to provide the king with a child. Myravelle mused that if he wanted a legitimate heir, Zylvain should spend less time with concubines and more time with his queen.

Also seated on the semi-circle of loungers were Captain Abelard and Lieutenant Eryck. The lieutenant, whose tan skin appeared a bit yellow and sickly, adjusted his uniform over and over again, refusing any food or drink from the servants.

"Tell me about the attack," the king said, raising his glass for a servant to refill with wine.

Abelard gestured for Eryck to speak. The lieutenant's blond brows shot up, and he adjusted his clothes again before speaking. "My king, the fairies attacked us this morning before dawn, while many soldiers were still asleep. The attacks came from the north side of the encampment. We raced outside to defend ourselves, and there was already a wall of smoke from the brightly colored flames."

"Did you see these fairies?"

"No, sir," Eryck said. "The smoke blocked our vision, and the other explosions distracted us while they got away."

"Tell me about these explosions," the king said before popping a cube of cheese into his mouth and rubbing the concubine's thigh.

"They were nothing like I have ever seen, sir," Eryck said, wide-eyed. "The flames burned with every color, and one explosive was laced with Dormrya splinters."

"Dormrya splinters?" King Zylvain took a sip of his wine. "Clever."

A fire burned in Myravelle's chest at the thought of such horrible weapons being considered *clever*.

"Yes, sir. The shards blasted outward and struck many of our men and women."

"And they're asleep?" the king asked, glancing at Myravelle. "How many?"

Staring blankly at the floor, Eryck nodded. "Eighteen, sir."

The king clutched his chest and dropped his jaw. "We must retaliate! We must get through their defenses and attack their village. I've been there once before, but the damned Dormryas and the disorienting spells of the fairies have made it difficult to find again. How are the plans for the next expedition, Captain?"

Abelard sat up straight. "Sir, we have a plan in place and a new area to cover, thanks to Byzarien here."

The king narrowed his eyes at Byzarien. "Myravelle's new canvas? How so?"

"He and a small group of brave soldiers explored on their own," Abelard said with a proud grin. "Unfortunately, his friends were harmed, but Byzarien was able to tell us where an enchanted Dormrya was located. Using that as a guide, we might find our way to their village."

"Well, thank you, Byzarien, for your discovery and for your *services*," the king said, tilting his head toward Myravelle.

Her cheeks flushed, and when she glanced at Byzarien, red splotches had bloomed on his face and neck.

"You are most welcome, sir," he said, tugging his hair to hide his scars.

King Zylvain encouraged everyone to eat while the captain and lieutenant explained the expedition. Myravelle picked at her food like a bird. She didn't want to hear about an expedition that would place more sleeping soldiers in her path. When the men finished their detailed plan, the room fell into a lazy silence. The king stared at the maps of the Sleepy Wood on the table, twirling his rings.

"I like it," he said at last, then glanced at Myravelle. "How strong are your healing powers, my darling?"

Before she could speak, Captain Abelard jumped in, "She may look tired, my king, but this often happens with a new canvas."

"Should I be concerned? There are already eighteen sleeping soldiers," King Zylvain asked. "The soldiers could rebel if they fear for their safety."

"Not at all, my king," Abelard said, gesturing to Myravelle. "Right?"

She nodded, but couldn't form words due to the lump in her throat. *What if the king catches our lie?*

"As our bond strengthens," Byzarien began, taking her hand, "so does her magic."

Myravelle looked at him, wishing she could thank him. She managed a weak smile, which he returned with a gentle squeeze of her hand.

"Good," said the king. "Then I do believe we will be prepared to retaliate against the fairies. We'll have the full support of the nobles and the High Priest, as announcements about the attack have already been dispersed throughout the kingdom."

Propaganda, Myravelle thought.

After the king enjoyed a few more glasses of wine and some non-business conversation with the captain, he dismissed everyone. Myravelle's feet itched to race outside, but she remained calm and knelt before the king.

Taking her chin once more, King Zylvain stared at Myravelle. The gold rings on his fingers pressed like ice against her skin, and the smug grin on his face was stained red with wine. He yanked her up to his level and wrapped his arms around her shoulders.

The embrace was merely for show, because he growled into her ear, "Your magic better work, my darling, or it *will* be Xylina's life."

Myravelle stifled a sob as the king kissed her cheek and stepped away to speak to the others. Keeping her head high, she left the captain's quarters and turned a corner before bending to catch her breath. When Byzarien caught up to her, he helped her stand and let her lean against him as they walked through the rows of tents.

"You're shaking. What's wrong?"

"I must heal them tomorrow," she said, clutching Byzarien's arm. "I'm worried for my mother's safety, now more than ever."

II

Byzarien

Nightmares of the fire made Byzarien toss and turn all night, but it was Lazaire, all mangled and gray, that made him lurch from sleep. Pressing a palm to his chest, he felt his heart slamming against his ribs. The echoes of his siblings' screams, shadows of the flames, and the rot of Lazaire's skin still seeped into the edges of his mind.

Rubbing his temples, he stared at Myravelle, who may also have been having a nightmare, for her eyes danced wildly behind her lids, and her dark lashes fluttered. Byzarien wanted to understand her, to know her, to *believe* her. But he also didn't. She was dangerous, for she made the ember of doubt set his once firm beliefs on fire.

Why would King Zylvain have done the things she claimed? Enslaving a fairy? Myravelle had clearly been shaken after the meeting with the king. *But why?* He had defended her for Dezlan's sake, but a splinter of his soul had wished to tell the truth—wished to be rid of her. Byzarien cursed himself for even considering that level of selfishness. The truth would have damned not only Dezlan, but eighteen other soldiers forever to the web of Filoux's tortures.

Even after a full night's sleep, Myravelle had dark circles under her eyes, and her skin somehow looked paler than before. Pushing his tall frame from the floor, Byzarien shuffled to the worktable and stove to make some tea. When he poured the hot water into the mugs, the scent of botanicals from Myravelle's tea concoction wafted into the air—herbal with a touch of sweetness.

She stirred and sat up before running her fingers through her wild hair. "Good morning." He nodded as he brought her a cup. "Thank you."

He watched Myravelle's hands wrap around the steaming mug while goosebumps climbed up her arms. Her loose locks fell in waves down to her hip, and he enjoyed the way her dark hair nearly swallowed all the morning light. *Stop it.* He looked down at his mug, but Myravelle's beauty still crept into his peripheral vision, the way Filoux's nightmares still edged their way into reality. After drinking her tea, she swung her legs over the edge of the bed.

"I suppose it's time to get to work," she said, lifting her dagger.

Heat flooded Byzarien's body at the mere thought. Why did he enjoy being carved up so much? *This is for Dezlan*, he reminded himself as he removed his nightshirt and reclined on her bed. The mattress, pillows, and blankets all smelled like her: sandalwood, rose, and vanilla.

She rested the cold dagger against his bare skin. "Are you ready?"

"Yes."

She sunk the blade into the fresh wound on his chest, and rivers of bliss spread through his body. The pillow helped hide the erection he had before Myravelle's rune was even complete. He took deep breaths, trying to compose himself, and watched with wide eyes as Myravelle licked the blade. He wanted her tongue on his skin and, with an involuntary movement, he gripped her thigh.

Myravelle flinched but continued to carve into her palm. Byzarien's hips squirmed as he waited, and the pillow gave him no reprieve from his arousal. When she pressed her palm to his chest and their blood swirled together, every muscle in his body went rigid. Wave after wave and pulse after pulse, the shocks of pleasure made his body arch. He moaned and didn't care if anyone outside of the tent could hear. Through his euphoria, Byzarien caught sight of Myravelle's lips—rose red and beckoning.

He sprang up and kissed her, tangling his fingers in her soft hair. Myravelle stiffened at first, but then eased into the kiss. The dance of their tongues only fanned the fire within, and he lowered her to the bed.

"Byzarien," she whispered, pushing against his shoulders before he could kiss her again. "Stop."

He leaned back and tilted his head.

Myravelle took a deep breath and said, "You don't want this, remember?"

"Oh, but I do." He caressed her bottom lip with his thumb and pressed kisses against the adorable freckles on her cheeks.

"Shh, you'll hate me again soon," she said, and her eyes glistened with tears.

Though his lips still burned for her, Byzarien began to filter through his fuzzy mind. A sourness rose within his stomach, and he shuffled away from the bed. *Did he actually kiss her? Again?* He touched his lips, tender and raw.

Myravelle disappeared behind the privacy screen to clean up and change.

His body refused to cool down, but his mind screamed at him. *You just kissed a fairy.*

When she emerged, Byzarien glared at her. "Did you...make me do that?" he asked, not believing he could be physically attracted to a fairy.

She smoothed her embroidered gown before looking him in the eyes. "I don't control you, if that's what you're asking."

"Why did I do that then?" He stepped forward and towered over her. "You did something. Was it a spell?"

She shook her head, keeping her stormy eyes locked on his. "I simply gave you pleasure, and you wanted more."

"From you?" he asked as he pulled a tunic over his head. "Never."

Wiping her bloody hand on a cloth, Myravelle's brows dropped low over squinting eyes. "Ready?"

"Give me a moment."

She wrapped herself in a crushed velvet cloak and slipped out of the tent. Byzarien was thankful for the privacy, grabbing his jacket and waiting a few moments for his body to calm down. He stepped outside, where the air seemed ready to disappear with the wind, for the cold struck his nose and throat with such force it was difficult to breathe.

From afar, he watched Myravelle's hips sway for a brief moment before snapping his gaze to the gray sky, which was the same shade as her eyes. He clenched his fists. *Stop it.* His friends were injured, but all his mind wanted to do was think about Myravelle. *Xavier and Dezlan, Xavier and Dezlan, Xavier and Dezlan,* he thought to himself.

When they got to the infirmary, Byzarien passed rows of sleeping soldiers and many busy nurses before reaching his friends and Myravelle. Zelyx was asleep on the cot next to Xavier, who was wide awake and stroking Dezlan's hand. He looked up with a weak smile at their arrival.

Byzarien gestured to Zelyx. "Is she hurt again?"

"No," Xavier said. "She stayed up late to sit with Dezlan so I could get some sleep. We decided to take...turns." He could barely finish his sentence before tears welled in his big brown eyes.

Byzarien patted his friend's shoulder. "Myravelle can fix this. Dezlan will be good as new once she builds up her strength."

"Ready?" Myravelle stepped to the side of his cot.

With a nod, Xavier pushed his blanket down. Myravelle rested one hand on each of his legs and closed her eyes. Byzarien focused on Myravelle's lips as they moved with whispers of magic. He was enchanted by her, fully and deeply, and he hated it. Static crackled through the dry tent air and rushed toward her hands. Just as before, Myravelle trembled and winced. Byzarien rushed to her side, worried she would collapse again.

While Myravelle shrieked, the gleaming lights moved from her hands into Xavier's legs. She gasped and fell slack into Byzarien's arms.

Zelyx sprung up in her cot. "What happened?" Myravelle's screams had also caught the attention of the nurses, who erupted into chatter.

"She healed me." With wide eyes, Xavier bent and stretched both of his legs. "It worked."

Byzarien adjusted Myravelle in his arms. "I better get her to bed... again. I'll come back to check on you."

"Thanks, Byz," Xavier said, placing an arm around Zelyx as he stood. He nodded to Myravelle. "And thanks to her, too. I hope she'll be all right."

"Me too."

During the trek back to the tent, Byzarien admired Myravelle's sleep-softened features. While awake, she always appeared so...*haunted*. Her past was written across her stoic and cold façade, if only one took the time to read it. He knew she only remained the healer in order to protect her mother. In that moment, he promised to be a little kinder, for she had never asked to become a monster.

When they reached the tent, he placed Myravelle on the bed and wrapped her in blankets and furs. Before stepping away, he brushed a lock of hair from her face. His eyes caught on her lips, and he recalled how they had felt like home. *Stop. I can be civil, but she is still a fairy and the spider who drained Lazaire.* These repetitive thoughts, though, like a banal litany, no longer held the same power over Byzarien.

He returned to the infirmary, where Xavier was shuffling around with Zelyx's help. The three friends hardly had time to speak before Captain Abelard strode into the tent.

"I see her magic is working," he said with an odd grin on his face.

"Good. Our expedition...and *retaliation* against the fairies will begin soon."

Acid dripped in Byzarien's stomach, for many more soldiers would certainly be harmed during this expedition. If Myravelle had collapsed while healing legs, would she truly be able to wake an infirmary full of sleeping soldiers? Why wasn't the captain taking more precautions?

"Where is she, by the way?" Abelard asked, gesturing to Dezlan and all the other sleepers. "She needs to take care of them."

Zelyx opened her mouth, but Byzarien jumped in first. "She's back at her tent, cleaning herself up, sir," he lied, and lifted his tunic to reveal all the blood.

"Fine, fine, fine," Captain Abelard said, scanning the beds. "We need this place empty before the expedition."

After the captain left the infirmary, Byzarien turned to his friends. "Don't say anything about Myravelle's state, please? Her mother's life may be in danger."

Both Zelyx's and Xavier's eyes grew wide.

"Is that true?" Xavier asked.

"I believe so," Byzarien said. "Her mother has been the king's slave for years. Myravelle only does all of this in hopes of freeing her mother."

"Slave?" Zelyx's gaze dropped to the floor, and she shifted her weight. "Now I feel terrible for calling her a witch."

Shame clawed at Byzarien's insides for not believing Myravelle's story as quickly as Zelyx had. He cursed himself for being so stubborn. "Me too," he barely breathed, wanting to change the subject. "Will you be staying here with Dezlan still?"

Xavier walked to his lover's side and stroked his cheek. "I can't let him sleep here alone."

"I'll stay, too," Zelyx said before a naughty grin crept across her face. "But I might disappear for stretches of time. I think Lana is quite smitten with me now."

Byzarien and Xavier chuckled and wished her luck with her

newest affair. When he returned to the tent, Myravelle was not in her bed. In a quick study of the cluttered area, he noticed her cloak was missing too, and he cursed under his breath. He hoped she hadn't fainted somewhere, for if the captain and king discovered how weak she truly was...

He shook his head against the nagging worries that had crept into his skull like spiders. *You don't care about her,* he reminded himself. Though, with a quick touch of his lips, he knew that was a lie. She was wonderful. After everything the king had put her through, she still remained strong. He truly didn't want anything to happen to her mother, no matter his conflicted feelings. So, he set off to the only location he assumed she would go.

The Sleepy Wood was a mysterious thing. In one moment, a man would brush through thickets and squelch through mud then, all at once, be surrounded by ancient, towering trees. Byzarien knew the way to Myravelle's graveyard, but visions of Dezlan, Xavier, and Zelyx blasting through the air startled him and made him tremble. He focused on the frost-covered earth and swept his hair over his scars again and again until he spotted a paper flower dusted with snow.

When he glanced up, she was sitting next to Lazaire's grave, folding little sheets of paper. Myravelle was an ethereal creature amid the bleak and wintry forest. Byzarien's lips burned once again, and he remembered he was supposed to hate her. Hate should have been easy enough, but it slipped from his skin with the breeze.

"They're quite beautiful," he said.

Myravelle slid her eyes to him, and he waited for a response, but she simply returned to her craft. After being so terribly unkind to her, Byzarien supposed he deserved to be ignored. He tiptoed forward, so as not to disturb the graves, and squatted to watch her work. She folded a delicate white rose, and an ache thrummed in his chest as he recalled the one he had crushed.

"I'm sorry," he whispered, "for ruining that flower before and for...well, for being cruel to you all this time."

Myravelle nodded and drew a small pair of gilded scissors from her cloak. She trimmed the edges of the paper to add details to each petal, leaf, and thorn. Once she'd inspected her artwork, she placed the gift on Lazaire's grave and stood.

"Where are you going?" Byzarien had to stop himself from grabbing her wrist.

"Where else am I to go?" Myravelle's eyes drooped, and he caught sight of the broken and brittle soul hidden beneath her reserved exterior.

Under her eyes were dark quarter-moons; the magic was destroying her. There was no way she could wake Dezlan in that state. He had already lost Lazaire, he couldn't bear to lose another friend. *Bond.* She said they could bond by opening up to one another. He scratched at the scars on his neck, not ready to talk about those quite yet.

He gestured back to Lazaire's grave before they walked too far away. "You know, he used to make me laugh more than anyone."

"Me too."

"Really?"

Myravelle nodded. "Once, I was making some paper flowers, and he tried to help."

Byzarien grinned, imagining Lazaire attempting such delicate art.

"He snipped his monstrosity into a million tiny pieces and tossed them at me; it was a mess. *He* was often a mess."

At that, he chuckled. "Sounds like him," he said. "But your flowers truly are beautiful."

"Thank you," she said. "My mother has always loved roses. I started making these for her when they would no longer grow because of the winter."

"That's lovely, Myravelle, truly." After clearing his throat, he said, "My mother used to tend to a small flower garden. White roses were her favorite."

Myravelle tilted her ear up to him with a slight smile curling the edge of her lip, and Byzarien decided to keep speaking.

"When the plants began to die, my mother clipped a white rose for each of us. My younger sisters played with theirs or plucked the petals, but I kept mine in a jar of water for weeks. After it had fully bloomed, I pressed it into a book. I would often look at it to find some remaining beauty in the world."

"Do you still have it?"

Ghosts of flames danced around Byzarien, setting his scars on fire. Like many belongings, they'd had to pawn their books. He shook his head.

They walked in silence through the Sleepy Wood. Myravelle effortlessly glided through nature's obstacles like the fairy she was, while Byzarien stumbled over brambles to keep up. He was thinking about a new question to ask her when they heard a shrill caw.

They came across a crow on the ground, crying and flapping a dislocated wing. A rustling of feathers created a shadow overhead as its murder settled in the branches, watching their fallen soldier. They all cried for the injured bird, and their melancholy song echoed through the woods.

Myravelle fell to her knees and made soft kissing sounds, as one would do to coax a cat.

Byzarien knelt and watched her stroke the shiny black feathers. The wing bent at an odd and horrifying angle, and the crow cawed with such deep anguish that pity coursed through Byzarien's veins. He drew his knife from his belt. "I'll put it out of its misery."

"No!" she shrieked, removing her cloak. "Don't!"

She rested her cloak on the ground until the midnight bird hopped onto the inviting fabric. Then she swaddled the poor creature and cradled it in her arms. "I can fix it," she said.

Byzarien followed her from the crow-infested grove to her tent, receiving odd stares from soldiers. Once inside, Myravelle handed the bundled-up crow to Byzarien. He shifted the cawing nightmare in his arms and watched with wide eyes as Myravelle set up a basket with a blanket next to her bed.

He was thankful when she took the crow from him. Instead of

resting the bird in the little bed she had made for it, she took it to her worktable and removed the cloak. It bounced around, cawing and screeching so loud, Byzarien covered his ears. Myravelle gently pushed at the dislocated wing and snapped it into place with a small crack. The crow fell silent when she twirled her finger above its head. Byzarien dropped his arms and watched the magic shimmering in the air dance toward the crow. Myravelle trembled as the crackling sparkles disappeared.

"Is it...dead?" Byzarien asked.

"Only asleep." Myravelle grabbed two sticks, some twine, and a bundle of dried herbs. She stroked the crow's wing straight and created a splint. "I couldn't fully heal the wing."

"What are the herbs for?"

"To help the poor thing stay calm," she said, tying the bundle to the splint, "and to provide a bit of cushion."

Stumbling, Myravelle approached the little basket and rested the crow inside. Byzarien stepped close, worried she was going to faint. Without a word, she collapsed onto her bed and closed her eyes. He sat next to her on the mattress and drew a blanket up to her shoulders. What would possess this woman to have such compassion for an injured bird? A cawing little nightmare of a bird? *Maybe*, he thought, *she was much more than she appeared.*

12

Myravelle

That night, Myravelle settled into bed early, for she could never seem to get enough rest. Fatigue had burrowed into her every bone. Snuggling against her pillows, she watched Byzarien pet Little Nightmare. He had called the crow that when it first awoke from its magic-induced sleep, screeching and cawing, and the name had stuck. He cradled the injured bird and placed it into its basket. Byzarien's eyes widened when he noticed Myravelle looking.

"He's growing on me." He shrugged before blowing out the candle and resting on his floor palette.

"Thank you," she whispered.

He rolled toward the bed and gazed up into her eyes. "For what?"

"For not telling the captain I collapsed...again."

One side of his mouth lifted. "I know what it's like to want to protect your family."

"Is that how you got your scars?"

Nodding, he gave her a pained stare before rolling over and going to sleep. Despite her weariness, it took Myravelle a while to fall asleep, but listening to the rhythm of Byzarien's breaths helped calm her soul.

In the morning, Myravelle didn't need to ask Byzarien whether he was ready for her. As soon as they finished their tea and fed Little Nightmare breadcrumbs, he removed his tunic and reclined on the bed. Myravelle grabbed her dagger and sat next to him.

"I'm going to cut you now," she whispered and trailed her finger over the wound on his chest before her touch found its way to the scars on his abdomen. They flared over his skin in the pattern of licking flames. She lightly traced a few more before Byzarien grabbed her hand, eyes strained. "Sorry," she said as a blush crept up her neck and onto her cheeks. "You should know, your scars aren't as monstrous as you think."

Byzarien's deep, dark eyes connected with hers for a long moment, and she watched as they glistened in the pale morning light. *What horrors had they seen?* Myravelle lifted her dagger and rested it against his chest. He covered his groin with a pillow, and she wished he wouldn't. For a brief moment, she imagined herself going completely feral with him: becoming one with a man who hid as much pain as she did.

She touched her lips, which still burned from his kiss. Byzarien made her feel things no other canvas had since Pazcal—*no*. Myravelle tore away from her thoughts. She couldn't think about him. She couldn't think about romance. The sweet pea had been nothing but a reckless mistake.

The sparkling golden rune hovered above Byzarien's heart—the exact place she had carved twice before. That had never happened before, but she forced herself not to worry about what it meant. She traced the swirling pattern with her dagger, and heat bloomed within her as his muscular body writhed with every turn of the blade. Myravelle licked his sweet blood from the dagger, sending rushes of pleasure through her body. She let herself enjoy the moment, for she knew what would happen next.

After slicing her own palm, Myravelle rested it against his chest to let their blood swirl together. While his body thrashed and squirmed with bliss, she absorbed his every pain and misery to harvest into healing power. Closing her eyes, she let it wash through her.

Over the years, she had become accustomed to her torturous brand of enchantments. It was a price she was willing to pay for her mother's security. She wasn't sure what was scarier: the sheer agony she endured with her early canvases or the dull, barely noticeable ache she felt with Lazaire. She would often ask herself, *what kind of monster doesn't feel pain?*

With Byzarien, however, her feelings had returned with full force. And his pain—his deep, traumatic anguish—surged through her like black lightning. Her muscles trembled, and she had to clench her teeth to keep from screaming. After the final wave, Myravelle gladly pulled her hand away from his chest.

Byzarien grabbed her wrist and said, "More."

He sat up and pressed his lips against hers, taking her by surprise once again. All the pain she had harnessed melted away with the warmth of his lips. His tongue slid against hers, drawing her closer. She surrendered to the pleasure. What started as soft and sweet turned into passionate lust as Byzarien's hands wandered around her body. She moaned and let her head fall back when his lips met her neck, drawing away her sorrows.

With a growl, Byzarien pushed Myravelle down to the bed and gripped the neckline of her dress. With one tug, he ripped the fabric apart, sending beads flying. At once, his hands and mouth were on her skin, and Myravelle wanted everything Byzarien could give her. In that moment, she was certain Amyor, goddess of love, had never swum in seas of such lust before. Something needled her mind through the veil of pleasure, though. She had to stop him. She had to do the right thing.

"Byzarien," she whispered, putting her fingers to his beautiful mouth. "You don't want this."

He blinked and scrubbed his face with one hand, while the other still had a firm grip on her breast. His mouth and eyes widened when he realized what he had done. He took his hand off of her at once.

"Wh-What happened?" he asked, shoving a blanket over her bare and bloody chest.

She remained silent, still trying to slow her breathing, for her body had yet to catch up with her mind.

"No, no, no." He tugged his hair and groaned before he stood up from the bed.

Myravelle's weak fingers circled his wrist. "What would we be if you didn't hate me so?"

"I don't want to think about that." He yanked his arm from her grasp and slipped his tunic back on. "Let's wake Dezlan."

"You ripped my gown," Myravelle said, touching the frayed pieces of the top.

He disappeared behind the privacy screen. The creak of Myravelle's trunk made Little Nightmare caw, though the bird had been politely quiet during the ritual, too busy with a beak full of seeds.

Byzarien stepped out and tossed her a new dress. "I'll meet you there," he said before hurrying from the tent.

Myravelle wanted to cry. In fact, for a moment, she tried, burying her face into the pillows. But, deep in her moonless soul, she knew it was her fault for changing the canvas ritual. Byzarien still hated her, and rightfully so. Her heart melted into her stomach like dripping candle wax, settling into a pit of loneliness. She swirled the drops of Byzarien's blood around her chest and turned to Little Nightmare, who was hobbling about on the floor beside her bed.

"Am I a monster?" she whispered and outstretched her clean hand to the bird, who nuzzled his head into her palm. If such a sweet and innocent creature could love her, maybe she wasn't a monster...at least, she hoped. "Thank you, my pet."

Myravelle washed herself up, changed into another Reverie-inspired gown, glinting with spider webs and stars, and set out to the infirmary. Along the blustery walk there, she crossed her arms and bit her lip. She had hardly been able to harvest any new magic. Byzarien's pain had faded with his passionate kiss. That had also never happened. *How could he take the pain away so? What did it all mean?*

She was running out of time and would soon have to draw from her own pain, the dark cavernous place she had never allowed herself to touch. *Where the real monster lay hidden.*

A storm was already brewing within, ready to seep through her emotional armor, cracked just like the porcelain plate her mother had once broken. It had slipped, just like that, from Xylina's fingers, weak from hours of spinning. Myravelle had studied the sharp edges and how the stark white shards contrasted with the stone floor up in their tower. She could have fixed it, for a glowing circle with stars connecting a jagged line appeared in her mind, but her mother had forbidden her. When the guard had arrived, he'd torn open the back of Xylina's dress and hit her with a switch. That was when a new and dangerous rune had glowed in Myravelle's eyesight.

"Please don't," her mother had cried. "No!"

She had not been speaking to the guard, though. *No.* Xylina had stared at Myravelle, begging her not to attempt magic. Her mother had always seen the monster within. Now, holding it back was a daily struggle.

As Myravelle walked down the familiar path toward the infirmary, she hardly paid attention to anyone around her.

"Well, she finally graces us with her presence," Abelard said, stepping before Myravelle, making her flinch. "Are we feeling better?"

"Yes, sir."

"Good," he said. "I don't know what game you're playing, but I guarantee the king will always win."

"What? I'm playing no game whatsoever," she said, shaking her head.

Abelard stepped so close, his sour odor stung Myravelle's nose. "You're letting these soldiers rot inside a death-like sleep. You're trying to make a point to the king—but he has the upper hand. He can *make* you heal them if need be." Myravelle opened her mouth to argue, but Abelard held up his hand in front of her face. "This conversation's over," he said and walked away.

The whistling breeze between the tents clawed at Myravelle with its icy fingers as she stood there in shock. *This is all just a game to the king*, she thought and picked up her heavy feet to move.

She took a few cleansing breaths before entering the infirmary, where Byzarien and his friends waited. Busy nurses hopped out of the way to avoid Myravelle as she glided past sleeping soldiers. *Would she ever be able to wake them? What tortures were these men and women suffering in their death-like sleep? How was Filoux exacting revenge for his only love?*

Byzarien avoided eye contact, staring at the plank-wood floor when Myravelle stepped next to Dezlan's cot.

"Can you wake him?" Xavier asked, his large brown eyes drooping.

"I'll try my best."

Myravelle placed her hands over Dezlan's eyes and shuddered as shadows of his nightmares filtered into her mind. She focused on waking the sleeping soldier, something that should have been easy—something that had taken very little effort in the past.

Tingles coursed through her veins like embers and ash as she focused. Something malevolent churned deep within. An inky, oily flow of her own pain, heartache, and rage beckoned her to use it. It whispered. It slithered. It showed her power. She recoiled from its temptation and scraped out what little healing magic she had left, scratching remnants from every bone, muscle, and vein. Energy crackled in the air like static, and she focused on waking Dezlan.

As her entire body trembled, Myravelle's strength fled along with the magic. Without Byzarien behind her this time, she crashed to the floor. With great effort, she propped herself onto her elbows and kept her heavy eyes open to watch Dezlan twitch.

Xavier gasped and leaned over his writhing boyfriend. "He's waking up!"

Dezlan's body contorted into unnatural angles as he screamed, back arched and arms twisted into the air while his hands bent into claws. Xavier grabbed his shoulders while Byzarien and Zelyx hugged one another. Myravelle covered her ears as his screams turned to high-pitched screeches. His entire body seized.

"No, no, no," Xavier cried out. "Wake up, Dez! Please wake up!"

Pulling herself up to the side of the cot, Myravelle knelt and watched the small man struggle against a cursed sleep. Dezlan's cries turned into whimpers, which turned into gasps for air. His body settled down with small twitches until he was sound asleep once more.

Xavier glared at Myravelle. "Why didn't it work? Why didn't you wake him?"

Her lips trembled, and she could only shake her head as the sour shame swelled in her. *What will the king do if he knows I failed again?* She tried to stand, but the room spun, and her body went cold. Byzarien rushed to her side as she collapsed, weak, to the floor. Darkness tunneled her vision as Xavier's cries echoed in her ears.

13

Byzarien

On a borrowed horse, Byzarien rode toward the hot springs with Myravelle slumped in his arms. After failing to wake Dezlan, she had gone in and out of consciousness, growing colder and colder with every passing moment. No number of blankets or coal in the stove could keep her warm.

Zelyx suggested Byzarien take her to the hot springs in the shadow of the Forbidden Mountain. Apparently, it was a choice location for Zelyx's romantic trysts, but it was also renowned for its healing powers. It took nearly an hour uphill on horseback but, at last, they reached the rocky location, where clear pools of water reflected the mountains and steam curled toward the sky with the acrid scent of sulfur.

When Byzarien tugged on the reins to slow the horse, Myravelle's eyes fluttered open. "Where...are...we?" she asked weakly.

"At the Enferrix Springs," he said, concerned with the dull shade of her eyes, like the passing clouds above. "You collapsed again."

Myravelle shivered. "I'm so sorry," she said before her eyes rolled back and her muscles went slack.

"Myravelle," he said, feeling her icy skin. "Stay with me."

When she opened her eyes, Byzarien eased her from the horse and helped her shuffle toward springs that time and nature had carved into rocky basins.

"Being here makes me feel better already." She stood with her toes in the steaming water and sighed.

He followed suit and kicked off his boots, and the stones were warm under his feet.

Myravelle stepped toward a shelf-like outcropping, and Byzarien's eyes darted to her as she let her cloak fall to the ground and raised her trembling fingers to the buttons on her gown.

"What are you doing?" he asked, snapping his gaze back to the water.

"Did you bring spare clothes?" Myravelle folded her garments and placed them on a dry rock.

"I was in a hurry." He tried to avoid looking at her, but his curious eyes betrayed him. "I think Zelyx packed towels from the infirmary."

"Well, it is either *this* or you can ride back with me in nothing but a towel," she said with a smirk rising in her voice. She slipped into the cloudy turquoise water, and he thought she looked like a goddess. "The waters will feel good on your scars."

"Well, it would be the safest thing—in case you faint again, that is. I wouldn't want you to drown before you save Dezlan," he said, voice wavering as he removed his cloak. His heart raced at the idea of soaking in the warm basin with her. "Would you mind...um, looking away?"

Myravelle turned toward the rising rocks of the cliff as he undressed. He stepped into the water, which burned at his toes. It took a moment for his skin to adapt to the temperature but, once it did, he let the water envelop his entire body like a warm hug. "How are you feeling?" he asked.

Her cheeks were pink when she turned. "Much warmer."

"Good." He studied her face, trying to think of something to say. "Zelyx claims the waters have magical powers infused by Enferrix."

"It's true."

His face scrunched. "Really?"

"You believe in Guerrix, but not Enferrix?" she asked, gesturing to his crossed-sword pendant. "There certainly are places where the gods' magic slips into our mortal realm. I can sense these places—with the same shiver in my bones when other fairies or enchantments are near."

Byzarien's eyes slid to the clear, steaming basins of water. "And this is one of those places?"

"Indeed."

When Myravelle's eyes danced along the scars on his shoulder and torso, Byzarien slunk deeper into the water and found a rock to sit on. She floated over and sat next to him, still staring at his shoulder. To his surprise, she brushed her fingers over the wound on his chest. Wisps of pleasure emanated from the cut. Byzarien gasped.

"I'm sorry to carve the same place each time," she whispered, withdrawing her hand. "My magic likes your heart."

Byzarien's heart thrummed against the rune scar, and he wished Myravelle would touch him again. She rested against the rocks, but he couldn't relax at all. *What did she mean?* If her magic liked his heart so much, why didn't it work? What was wrong with him? Despite the steaming-hot water, a chill curled around Byzarien's spine and across his shoulders like a thorny vine.

He sat back and closed his eyes, trying to relax. The soothing sounds of water trickling over the rocks in the distance and Myravelle's little movements rippling nearby did nothing to calm him. The anguishing thoughts kept stewing in his mind.

"What happened back there?" he asked, turning to Myravelle.

"In my tent?"

He shook his head. "In the infirmary. Why can't you wake Dezlan?"

"I only harnessed a small bit of magic from you," she said, dropping her chin to her chest, pink with heat.

He coaxed his hair to cover his scars. "Am I...am I not good enough to be your canvas?"

"That's not it. My magic works with your pain." She touched his chest again, and her hand felt like home against his skin. "During our ritual, I harvested a sea of pain from you, more than all of my previous canvases combined. It's just..."

"Just what?"

"When you kissed me, all of it melted away." She touched her lips, and Byzarien's tingled. "That has never happened before."

"Why isn't it working?" He searched her face, leaning close enough to kiss her.

"Why do you *reject* me?" she asked. The inflection in her voice told him she was talking about sex.

He dragged his fingers through the steamy surface of the water, avoiding Myravelle's intensely silver eyes. "I, uh...I've never been with anyone before."

Silence spread over the water like the steam, and Byzarien's insides curled in on themselves, his confidence collapsing further. He closed his eyes and prayed to Enferrix that the water would boil him down to his bones. *Why did I tell her that? Why hadn't I just thought up a lie?*

"Are you celibate for religious purposes?" she asked, running her finger along Byzarien's crossed-sword pendant.

"No. Guerrix makes no such demands," he said with a humorless laugh, then looked up at her with his brows pressed hard over his eyes. "Isn't it obvious?"

"Your scars?"

He nodded as a painful lump in his throat prevented him from speaking.

"Byzarien, we live in an army encampment," Myravelle said. "Scars aren't stopping anyone from having sex, and there are plenty of prostitutes you could pay."

"I don't think I could give myself to someone in that way," he whispered, his voice barely audible over the trickling waters. "I want it to mean something. I've suffered so much pain, what I crave more than sex is *love*."

Myravelle was silent, but her eyes pierced into his. He waited for her to laugh at or mock him. But she didn't. She touched his hand under the water. "Me too," she finally said, with tears brimming against her eyelids.

"*You* crave love?" He pulled his hand away, but immediately winced, regretting the cruelty in his tone. Those tears rolled down her cheeks before she silently floated to the other side of the basin, a wake of ripples flowing from her inky black hair. "You're like a painting," he said, watching her. "Beautiful, yet unreachable. You hide somewhere under layers and layers of brushstrokes."

"You are one to talk."

"What does that mean?" he grumbled and coaxed his hair over his cheek.

"That," she said, pointing to his face. "You hide, too."

"At least you are pretty," he said. "I can't hide this."

Byzarien glided forward in the water, pausing only inches away from Myravelle. He pushed his hair back and raised his body to show her his full torso. His scars burned hotter than the Enferrix Springs under her eyes' exploration. To his surprise, her face softened as she studied his skin. Myravelle's silvery gaze slithered upward to eventually lock with his eyes. "Beautiful."

He lowered himself into the water. "How can you say that?"

"Like tree roots, knotted and wild, your scars tell a story." She traced his cheek, sending shivers across his skin. "A story you won't say aloud."

"Fine." Gritting his teeth, he sat next to her, close enough for his arm to graze against hers. "Do you really want to know? When I was twelve years old, the fairies attacked and burned down my house." After taking a deep breath, he told her the story about the flames, screams, and pain. The deep, deep pain of losing his brother.

"What was his name?"

Byzarien cleared the thickness in his throat. "Benoix...I called him Benny."

His muscles trembled, and Myravelle took his hand while tears sparkled in her eyes. Part of Byzarien wanted to let her comfort him, but instinctual anger took over instead. He tugged his hand away and waded to the opposite side of the pool.

"You still hate me," she stated, with no hint of emotion in her voice.

"You're still a fairy," he said, "and you are still the reason Lazaire is gone."

Myravelle didn't say another word as she stepped out of the hot water and found one of the towels in the horse's pack.

Byzarien turned his back to her while she dressed, not for modesty's sake, for Myravelle didn't seem to care about that, but for the sake of his own heart. He knew he didn't hate her, which only made him angrier with himself.

"I'm dressed," she said after a few moments of rustling into her garments. Byzarien went to step out of the small tufa basin, and she turned away for him as well. *Was it for modesty or her heart?* He cursed himself for wondering.

After he was dressed, Byzarien helped Myravelle climb onto the horse and looked up at her. Guilt over his words twisted his stomach, and he had to make it right. "For what it's worth, I spoke earlier out of grief and...pain. But the truth is, I don't hate you, Myravelle. Not at all."

Keeping hold of his hand, Myravelle made a pinched expression as if holding back tears. "Thank you."

The ride back to the army encampment was silent, save for the trotting hooves of the horse and the whoosh of the wind biting at Byzarien's ears. The pair dismounted on opposite sides. As Byzarien led the horse to the stable, Myravelle walked in the direction of her tent without a word.

His chest tugged at him with the same unspooling yarn sensation from the night of the ritual, yearning to follow her, but he didn't. His head pounded with every beat of his heart as he forced himself to walk to the infirmary. He hoped she believed him and bit his tongue for ever speaking those horrible words to her. She couldn't help her ancestry, and she didn't choose to become a healer. And she was the only person capable of helping Dezlan. Byzarien needed her.

Before he reached the infirmary, he spotted the messenger trudging through the filth and snow of the encampment, heading straight for him. "Byzarien Dumont?" the smaller man said, holding out an envelope. "Myravelle said you'd be at the infirmary."

He accepted it and thanked the messenger, who dashed away to his next delivery. He opened the envelope, and the letter rustled in the wind. The curls of his mother's script made Byzarien's pulse quicken, for he couldn't handle any more bad news.

My dearest Byz,

Words cannot express our gratitude for what you did. There will never be enough words, kisses, or hugs to thank you. We don't know what you had to do to help us, but we are forever thankful. I know you were adamant in your letter not to say a word about it, but how could I not? You are the best son a mother could ask for!

When the skein of gilded thread arrived, we were amazed. With this fortune you provided us, we were able to purchase a home on Lord Riccard's estate near our old cottage. It comes with a parcel of land to farm should the eternal winter ever wane. We even had money left over to put toward Bryda's education.

You'll be happy to know Beatryz is about to be engaged to a dashing young baker!

From the bottom of our hearts, thank you. We look forward to the next time you can take leave and visit us. We miss you every day.

All my love,
Ma

. . .

Byzarien wiped tears from his cheeks as his mother's words settled in his mind. It took him a moment to wade through the sheer joy bursting through his soul to make the connection.

The gilded thread.

Myravelle.

Why would she do that for him? Why hadn't she told him?

Instead of entering the infirmary, he changed his course and headed straight for Myravelle's tent to thank her. When he arrived outside the dark, greenish-brown tent, the captain's voice echoed from within. Byzarien paused just outside the flap to listen.

"...infirmary full of sleeping soldiers, and you are *resting*?"

"I will heal them—"

"Yes, you will," the captain said, voice chillingly calm, "or Xylina will be terminated."

"No," she squeaked. "Please."

Little Nightmare cawed, which made Byzarien glad that the pet was defending Myravelle. Byzarien himself bristled at the venom in Abelard's tone.

"King Zylvain and I are done with your games," the captain said. "This is your final chance, or she dies."

The blood drained from Byzarien's face. Myravelle had told the truth about the king and her mother all along. He still hadn't wanted to believe the king had been capable of such behavior, but the captain's words were like a spear through his heart. Footsteps shuffled his way, so Byzarien hopped a few steps back and pretended to be engrossed in his letter.

"Ah, morning, Byzarien," the captain said as he stepped outside.

"Good morning, Captain Abelard."

"See to it that she gets rest and wakes those soldiers. We need the infirmary cleared before the expedition next week." Abelard crossed his fists over his chest. "Serve him."

"And he will serve you," he said, copying the gesture.

The captain walked away, and Byzarien inched toward the tent flap, where he heard Myravelle's sobs and Little Nightmare's caws.

His legs turned into deeply rooted tree trunks—heavy and unmoving. He had no idea how to comfort Myravelle. Growing up, when his sisters had been upset, he would simply make them laugh or sneak them sweets. This was different. Myravelle was a woman with a grave problem.

His head tugged at him to leave and go to the infirmary like he'd planned, but the letter in his hands grew heavy. Myravelle had helped him. *Beyond* helped him. She had rescued his family from poverty without a word or any expectations—and Byzarien had accused her of inciting the fairy attacks instead.

Her cries fell silent, piercing his heart even further. He took a deep breath to gather his courage when Myravelle's voice filtered from the tent. It was a song about spinning, and her low, ethereal voice ribboned through his ears and into his soul.

Draft and pinch. Draft and pinch.
Spin. Spin. Spin.
Draft and pinch. Draft and pinch.
Again. Again. Again.

Simple yet haunting, her voice sent goosebumps across his skin and made his rune scar emanate wisps of pleasure.

14

Myravelle

Myravelle spun to settle her nerves and quell the *thing* churning within. The dark place she had almost touched, which felt like a sea of stars calling her home. As she recalled her mother's words about the night she was born, her weak fingers dropped the spindle, and the yarn loosened on the ground. *Had the stars truly fallen for her?* The fibers were never quite the same, though, when they came undone, as if there was no return from the damage the spinning had caused.

Once spun, forever changed.

She reached for the spindle, and her head grew heavy while dark spots bloomed in her vision. When she leaned against the worktable, a stream of frosty air woke her senses. Byzarien stood in the opening of the tent with a letter in his hands. Her heart raced at his appearance. *I don't hate you, Myravelle. Not at all.* His words looped through her mind over and over while Little Nightmare waddled from his bed and pecked at the soldier's boots.

He strode forward, searching her face. "Did you have something to do with this?"

Myravelle's eyes narrowed at the parchment. *Who else would it be from besides his family?* When Byzarien held the letter toward her, the signature was a short and sweet *Ma*. She bit her tongue and cursed herself for thinking his mother would listen to straightforward directions.

"Did you?" he asked slowly, as if he were angry about the good fortune.

"What?" she asked, but her scorching cheeks certainly revealed the truth.

"You did, didn't you?" he whispered, closing the distance between them. "Why?"

"You cannot tell anyone." Eyes strained, she gazed up at him. "Please."

Byzarien's brow furrowed, and he looked down at the ground. "Because you'll be locked away like your mother?"

Myravelle shivered at the thought. "Yes."

"Well, thank you," he said, sighing, the harsh edges of his face and body softening. "Thank you for taking care of my family."

"Thank you for taking care of me."

"I think I still owe you." A slight grin tugged at the corner of his mouth. "I haven't been very kind."

Myravelle sat on her stool like a wilting flower and shook her head. "I haven't healed Dezlan."

"You were really close." Byzarien leaned onto the worktable to meet her eye-level and touched her hand. "We can try again tomorrow. I want you to free your mother."

She stared at their joined hands until Byzarien removed his.

"I suppose I'll leave you alone to get more rest." He turned toward the flap but looked back at her.

"Byzarien," she whispered.

He held her gaze, as if waiting for her to say more. She had never been so emotionally tangled with a canvas since Pazcal, and the feelings spun tightly around her heart. Everything was new and raw and dangerous. Myravelle worried that, if she were to admit how much she enjoyed having Byzarien around, he would call her a *spider* again.

Little Nightmare cawed, flapping his good wing. Byzarien stroked the bird's dark feathers and fed it seeds, which brought a grin to Myravelle's lips. She wished she could be as open and honest as Little Nightmare, who was able to make Byzarien stay with one caw.

"You want *more* seeds?" He laughed as he sat on the ground with the crow. "If you keep eating this way, you'll be too big to fly." Myravelle giggled as she ground peppermint with her pestle and mortar. The sharp aroma wafted into the air. "Speaking of eating," Byzarien said, glancing up at her. "Uh, would you like me to bring back some food from the mess hall?"

"Thank you," she said with a nod. "I'd rather not show my face there."

"I'll check on Zelyx and Xavier first."

After he left, Myravelle should have napped, but she mixed ingredients instead. She added the oil from the peppermint, ground oatmeal, honey, oil from seeds, and olive oil to a bowl and stirred. It created a thick, creamy substance. She funneled the mixture into a bottle and stared at it. *Another gift for a man who doesn't want you*, she thought. *What is wrong with you?*

Her head knew he was only being kind because of his family and because she was the only one who could save Dezlan. But her heart, *oh her damned and reckless heart*, dared to wish for more. Though there was none left in her stash and it should have been impossible, the scent of sweet pea overwhelmed her senses.

Byzarien returned just as Myravelle had corked the bottle. She jumped, not expecting him to return so soon. Her breath hitched in her chest when she spotted the two trays in his hands. She assumed he would eat with his friends and bring her something later...not dine *with her*.

He held the trays out and gestured to each. "Mush or mush?"

"Mush."

He set the trays down and stood on the other side of the table. They ate in silence for a few moments, catching one another's gazes but never looking for too long. After chewing on the 'mush' made of grains, fish, and mushrooms, Myravelle needed something to wash the flavor down. She rifled through one of her cabinets and retrieved a dusty bottle of wine. Byzarien's thick brows shot up.

"Care for a glass?"

"Anything to get this taste out of my mouth," he said, wiping his lips with his sleeve. "I think they're trying to poison us."

Myravelle dumped the water from their mugs into a potted plant and refilled them with the deep red wine. The smooth, almost chocolaty notes coated the inside of her nose, and the taste that slid over her tongue was even better.

"Where did you get this?" Byzarien asked. "It's delicious."

She swallowed and hung her head. "Lazaire."

He stared at the bottle for a long moment before raising his cup. "To Lazaire."

"To Lazaire, he was a good man," she said, clinking her cup with Byzarien's. "For what it's worth, I did care for him."

"I know."

After they sipped in silence for a few minutes, Myravelle slid the bottle of ointment she'd made toward Byzarien. "What's this? More alcohol?" he asked. "Are you trying to get me drunk?"

She giggled. "No, it will help with your itching."

His dark eyes searched her face as a half-smile tugged on his lips. "Thank you."

"Do you want to try it?"

"What, now?"

"Now." Myravelle reached for the bottle, toying with the cork as she stared at him.

Byzarien thumbed the hem of his tunic and avoided eye contact. "Fine."

She uncorked the bottle, drizzling the creamy oil onto her fingertips. "I've seen them," she said, massaging his cheek, "and I like them."

He closed his eyes as she applied more ointment to his face and neck. One scar swirled toward his lips, and Myravelle licked hers, wanting to kiss him.

"Why?" he asked.

"Why do I like your scars?" He nodded as she continued to trace the warm, fiery patterns. "They're proof of your deep pain, which you cannot hide," she said. "Your history, written across your skin. I want to read it all."

Byzarien opened his eyes and caught her in his gaze. Something melted across that stoic face of his, and Myravelle leaned forward and grabbed the hem of his tunic. Without protest, he raised his arms to let her remove it.

Myravelle's heart thrummed as she poured more oil into her palms. Her fingers burned to touch every part of him. Starting at his shoulder, she massaged the ointment into his scars. Some large and raised, others small and wiry. With one hand on his chest and the other on his back, she pressed calming circles into his muscles before tracing every line. Byzarien's chest rose and fell with deep breaths as he watched. Soon, though, his breathing slowed, and his muscles melted with every motion of Myravelle's hands.

When she finished applying the oil to his arm, Myravelle moved her hands to Byzarien's lower back and abdomen. Her chest, cheeks, and torso were on fire, as if she could feel the flames rolling around him. She should have felt embarrassed, but Byzarien was flushed as well. She circled her fingers around his hip, just above his pants, desiring to dip them even lower.

He took her oily hands in his. "Thank you. I can do the rest."

After re-corking the bottle, Byzarien drained his glass of wine and pulled his tunic on. Myravelle watched him amble toward his palette area and decided to step outside to cool down in the wintry air. If anything, she thought she could give Byzarien a few moments of privacy by taking a nighttime walk around the encampment.

Glancing at the cloudy and ash-filled sky, she was barely able to discern where the moon lay hidden. She rubbed her hands together, recalling the patterns of his skin: every scar now rooted within her. Byzarien had burned himself right into her soul.

When she returned later, he was in a deep, deep sleep with Little Nightmare on his chest.

※

In the early morning, Myravelle woke to find Byzarien rubbing the new ointment into his skin. His scars glistened in the hazy dawn stretching through the tent. She sat up and swung her legs over the side of the bed. Little Nightmare waddled over to her.

"You like it?" she asked as she lifted the crow onto her lap.

"Good…morning," he said, holding his tunic to cover his torso. "I like it very much. Thank you."

Myravelle removed the splint from the crow's wing. "I thought he would have attempted to escape or fly away by now. His wing should be fine."

"Self-preservation," Byzarien said. "Maybe he was injured while flying, and now he's afraid. Fear often keeps us from living."

"Well, I hope he can overcome those fears; he deserves a life." She sighed and patted the mattress. "Are you ready?"

"Yes, but…" he cleared his throat, words stuck somewhere deep within.

"What?" she asked, stroking Little Nightmare's dark feathers.

"What if I, uh, try to…" his words faded away, and his cheeks grew rosy.

"Have sex with me?" She knew her bluntness would turn his cheeks an even deeper shade of scarlet. Avoiding eye contact, he nodded. Myravelle chewed on her bottom lip as she thought. "I may have an idea."

After setting Little Nightmare next to a pile of seeds and breadcrumbs, she rushed to her trunk and rifled through the accessories to draw out two silk scarves. "What are those for?"

She smirked. "To keep your wandering hands still. Lay down with your head toward the stove."

Byzarien did as she commanded, so she took his hands and raised them above his head. His skin was warm and smelled of the peppermint ointment she'd made. He breathed deeply and rapidly, but let her bind his wrists together. She then used the other scarf to secure him to the curled feet of the small iron stove. "Ready?"

"Yes."

When Myravelle grabbed her dagger, the golden rune again glowed upon Byzarien's chest. Again, right over his heart. The heart she wanted to know better. She swallowed and got to work.

Carving into his skin, she released ruby drops of blood. He moaned and writhed in pleasure with every mark of the dagger. Myravelle licked the sweet delights from the blade as she locked eyes with Byzarien, who tugged at the scarves and groaned. After slicing her palm, she rested her hand against his chest and focused on harnessing his pain.

Without the threat of him kissing her and taking it all away, she was able to draw healing magic. Their unconventional bonding had worked: as Myravelle searched inside of him, she dove into Byzarien's vast well of misery. *The fire. The burns. The screams. The loss of his brother. The weeks of wet bandages tearing his flesh away.* What was worse than all of that, though, were his years of shame. The deep shame filled every corner of his life. She wanted to take it all. She wanted to ease his every agony, so she held on longer than usual as the pain swept through her trembling limbs.

Byzarien's body thrashed and bucked, nearly knocking Myravelle off the bed. He tugged at the scarves, and a rip scratched through the air. All at once, he swung his arms, still bound at the wrist, over Myravelle's head. Before she could think, he pulled her onto his lap and pressed his lips to hers. Their frantic and eager lips slowed as their bodies grew desperate to be closer. Myravelle wanted to sink into his skin and become part of him forever. That needling reminder pricked through the veil of pleasure, though.

He does not want this.

Myravelle broke the kiss, though she was still trapped by his embrace. "Byzarien, stop."

He blinked until his lust-clouded eyes cleared. Instead of recoiling in disgust like he had after their previous kisses, he slumped against her shoulder with his wrists still bound behind her back. Their heads rested neatly in the crooks of one another's necks. Myravelle dared to slide her arms around him and give a squeeze. She caught a sob in her throat and had no control over the tears that fell onto Byzarien's bare skin.

"Are you all right?" he asked, leaning back to look at her.

"It's just…I, um, I haven't been hugged in a long time." She looked down at the mattress and cringed over saying those words.

Tugging her with his bound hands, Byzarien wrapped her back up in his arms. "I'm sorry," he whispered, breath tickling her ear.

They stayed in the embrace while she enjoyed his warmth and the scent of peppermint. Before she was ready, Byzarien lifted his arms from around her and held out his wrists. Myravelle worked to unknot the silk scarf, careful to avoid his eyes.

When she finished, she used the torn scarf to soak the blood from her palm and Byzarien's chest. He got up and dressed in his tunic and leather jacket with his back to her. She threw her cloak on and followed him into the cold, where they walked side-by-side in silence. She froze just outside the infirmary.

"What is it?"

"The kiss melted away most of the healing power I drew from you. I don't know if it's enough," she said, toying with the beaded skirt of her dress. "There's something, a raw magic, deep within…but I'm afraid."

"I'm here for you." He held open the flap to the large tent. "I'll be right by your side."

When they entered the infirmary, the sight of the sleeping

soldiers sent a chill spinning in Myravelle's bones. Zelyx and Xavier were there watching over Dezlan. In a matter of days, Xavier had grown thin and had dark hollows under his eyes.

"I'm sorry for how I reacted last time, Myravelle. You were only trying to help." He said, sitting on the edge of Dezlan's cot. "Will you try again?"

Myravelle nodded and studied Xavier's slumped form, knowing he was nearly out of hope. Though Dezlan looked peaceful, with his soft features and calm breaths, how many more days could a man hang on while suffering in his mind? Would he be the same when he woke up? Would any of the sleeping soldiers? Stepping beside Dezlan, she rested her hands over his eyes and took a deep breath.

"You can do this," Byzarien said as he placed a hand on her back.

She closed her eyes and focused on the magic swirling like a painful galaxy inside. It swam through her veins like oil and fire. Stars of heat churned within her chest, eager for her touch. She reached for the magic as it seduced her with its ancient whispers. It felt too large. Too monstrous to control. With one flash of Xylina's battered and pleading face, Myravelle closed it off. *I can't.*

Once again, she was forced to scrape the meager amounts of magic clinging to her insides like a layer of grime. *Scratch. Scratch. Scratch.* Every corner of her flesh became inflamed. Static crackled through the air as Myravelle's arms and legs went weak. The dark magic reared back like a serpent, but she denied it and held on. She transferred as much magic into Dezlan as she could bear, but it was too much. It was much more pain than she had ever felt before, and she collapsed into Byzarien's arms.

Dezlan's eyes bounced around behind his lids while his body twitched and limbs snapped. Xavier held onto his lover's shoulders and shouted, "Dez, wake up! It's me!"

Through weary eyes, Myravelle watched Dezlan continue to writhe in unnatural positions. She knew he was fighting inside Filoux's nightmare.

"Why isn't he waking?" Xavier shouted.

"He's been asleep far too long. We must tether him to reality." Myravelle's mind raced. "Xavier, kiss him. Let him feel that you are here."

Xavier needed no more persuasion; he pressed his full lips against Dezlan's and caressed his pale, hollow cheek. The smaller man stopped twitching, and his hand met Xavier's face. When Xavier pulled away, he watched Dezlan and whispered, "Please, please, please."

Dezlan's eyes fluttered open, and he shuddered. He scrambled to the back of the cot and stared back and forth at the four of them with wide eyes. Byzarien and Xavier tried to reach for him, but he flinched each time. Though he looked like a frightened animal in a trap, Myravelle was relieved to have finally woken him up after all this time suffering Filoux's nightmares. She drew deep breaths, trying to stay lucid while her body grew weak.

"It's me, Dez," Xavier said. "Are you all right?"

Shivering, Dezlan whispered in a croaky voice, "Is this real?"

Losing grip on her final bit of strength, Myravelle sunk completely into Byzarien's arms. Her eyes refused to stay open for longer than a few seconds at a time. She was still far too weak to help the rest of the soldiers.

Byzarien hoisted her into a cradle-carry, and the pair left the infirmary. While resting in his arms, darkness consumed Myravelle yet again.

15

Byzarien

Snowflakes swirled through the air, never daring to touch the earth, while Byzarien walked around the exercise field with his friends. Dezlan's muscles had been unsure like a newborn fawn after so many days in bed, so Xavier and Byzarien guided him around the track to gain strength. Xavier's long fingers wrapped tightly around Dezlan's arm as if he would never let him go again.

"You're doing great," Xavier said, before kissing a patch of freckles on his cheek. Dezlan ducked down, throwing his arms over his head while humming and shaking. Byzarien and Xavier knelt beside him. "It's just us, Dez," Xavier said, soft and sweet.

A stone settled in Byzarien's chest. *What if he's never the same?* The nightmares had burrowed so deeply into Dezlan's mind that he still saw them while awake. The man's eyes bounced around until they locked onto Xavier's. "Is this real?"

"Yes." Xavier stroked his cheek and helped him stand. "It's real."

"Ready to keep walking?" Byzarien asked, desperate for his friend to be healthy again. Dezlan nodded, and the group continued around the track.

It was early enough that the only other person exercising was Zelyx. Having spotted the commotion, she jogged over. "What happened?" she asked as she bounced to a stop and swept her fingers through her blonde hair, wet from sweat and snow.

"He lost track of reality again," Xavier said, tightening his grip on Dezlan's arm. "We just have to keep him tethered is all."

"How did he sleep last night?" she asked.

Xavier gave a barely noticeable shake of his head as they all kept walking.

Zelyx leaned toward Byzarien and whispered, "Has he said anything about what it was like, you know, the sleep?"

"No," he whispered. "He loses control if we bring it up."

As the morning grew later, a few more soldiers arrived to exercise, led by Lieutenant Eryck. The men and women must have been the lieutenant's candidates for leading the expedition to push into a wood that clearly did not want them there. *Those poor soldiers*, Byzarien thought. Eryck caught Byzarien staring and made his way over to the small group.

"Morning, soldiers," the lieutenant said, crossing his arms in the Geurrix salute.

They returned the gesture and continued their walk, while Eryck stopped Byzarien. "How are you holding up? Are you suffering from any infections yet?"

"No." He touched the rune on his chest, still amazed at how good it felt, and watched his friends continue around the track.

"Good." Eryck scratched at the golden stubble on his chin. "I want you to know, Byzarien, I am petitioning His Majesty and Captain Abelard to ask for full body armor of leather and chainmail."

Curiosity tugging his brows, Byzarien studied the lieutenant. "For?"

"For the entire Sleepy Wood Company," he said, clapping

Byzarien's shoulder. "If we were outfitted properly like other companies, we would be much safer against the Dormrya wood. More often than not, our soldiers are put to sleep by mere splinters. *Splinters.*"

Byzarien's heart raced, for if less soldiers fell into a death-like sleep, maybe he wouldn't have to die. "And?"

Eryck leaned close. "I know it's expensive, but I'm trying to make them see how many lives it would save."

A sinking sensation filled Byzarien's gut, for he was doubtful that much money would be spent on the Sleepy Wood Company. Especially if the only lives truly lost were those of Myravelle's canvases.

"There's always a chance," Eryck said, lowering his voice to a whisper. "Please don't mention this to anyone, I don't want to get hopes up until the king gives an official answer...but, I figured *you* were someone who needs a little hope at this time."

"Thank you."

"Well, I better get back to my platoon," he said, giving Byzarien the Guerrix salute. "Good day, soldier."

Byzarien copied the gesture and walked the track at a slow pace while his mind reeled with this new, yet slight possibility that he could survive being the canvas. But what if the Sleepy Wood Company didn't need Myravelle any longer, though? What would the king do with her?

"Byz," Xavier's deep voice broke through Byzarien's spiraling thoughts.

He looked up to find his friends had made their way back to him, and he joined their walk. Dezlan's eyes had grown even duller, the poor man was exhausted and haunted.

"What was that about?" Xavier asked.

"Oh, Eryck was asking about my well-being and trying to offer some hope," he whispered, staring off to think about what the lieutenant's plan might mean for him...and Myravelle.

"Hey," Zelyx said, shaking him back to reality. "What's wrong?"

"I'm concerned about Myravelle," he blurted, then tried to think of a lie for his reasoning...which wasn't entirely a lie. "She isn't feeling well."

Zelyx gave him a look. "What's wrong with her, Byz? You must know why her magic is weak."

"It's all my fault."

She punched his shoulder. "Don't say that."

"It's true," he said, face scrunching as if in pain. "She can't harness enough healing power from me, so she ekes out what she can. The magic is..."

"What?" Xavier asked.

"The magic is draining her," he said, hanging his head. "All she does is sleep and spin. Speaking of spinning..."

Byzarien told his friends about Myravelle's gift to his family, making them promise to never tell a soul.

"Gold?" Xavier's brown eyes grew the size of coins. "That's wonderful, Byz."

"So, she's not as *bad* as you first thought?" Zelyx asked, a smirk tugging at her lips. He cleared his throat but remained silent, focusing on the muddy tips of his boots.

"You *like* her?" Dezlan said in a weak, scratchy voice.

Byzarien's eyes widened as a flush flared across his entire body. Why did Dezlan's first semi-coherent thought have to be hurled at him? Despite his embarrassment, the truth struck him like a spear: he liked Myravelle. He liked her silent grace and unselfish kindness. He liked her wisdom and calming presence. He *really* liked the way her hands felt against his skin.

Xavier smiled at Dezlan, and the look in their eyes no longer made Byzarien jealous. Had he found the person to make him smile? Every time he was away from Myravelle, he wanted to return—a vast difference from the night of the ritual. *What had changed?* It had happened so slowly, Byzarien didn't know where his hatred ended and his fondness began. The hug they shared was real and something they both desperately needed. *Were his feelings real or just part of the magic?*

When he blinked away from his thoughts, Byzarien's friends were all staring at him.

"Wow," Zelyx said, smacking his back. "I would say something salacious or humorous, but I'm, for once, speechless. I'm happy for you, Byz."

"We have to be careful with what we say around Captain Abelard," Byzarien said. "Especially with what I told you about the gold...Myravelle fears if the king finds out she can spin gold; he'll lock her away like her mother."

"That's sad," Dezlan said, staring up at the sky.

"It's true what I told you about her mother—I overheard Captain Abelard threaten her life." Byzarien shook his head. "Promise me you won't say anything."

"Promise," his friends said in unison.

"Do any of you remember seeing the fairies the night of the Fairy Raids?" Shadows of flames licked around Byzarien's body, and he loosened the collar of his jacket to let in the cool breeze.

"Well," Zelyx began, then tilted her head. "No, actually. I remember being afraid. There was panic in the streets, but I never saw anything."

Byzarien looked to Xavier and Dezlan. "What about you two?" The glaze over Dezlan's eyes had returned, and he stared at nothing while they walked around the track.

"No, there weren't any raids in the Verte Quarter. My parents talked about it the following day," Xavier said. "Why?"

"It was just something Myravelle said," Byzarien answered. "Did any of you see any fairies the morning of the attack here?"

Zelyx sucked in a deep breath and stitched her eyebrows. "We already told you we didn't."

"What did you see?"

"I was with Lana, her tent's near where it happened," Zelyx began, tucking a short lock of hair behind her ear. "We woke up to the sounds of screams but, by the time we ran out, we only saw our soldiers fighting the flames. Then the blast happened." Her eyes were far away in thought, and she shuddered.

"What are you saying, Byz?" Xavier asked. "Do you think there were never any—"

"Good morning, soldiers," Captain Abelard called from behind, making them all flinch and turn.

"Good morning, Captain," all but Dezlan said.

Byzarien stared into Abelard's yellow-brown eyes, wondering how long he had been following them. The captain breathed heavily, for he had not properly exercised in years. Relief washed over Byzarien, knowing the round man with a bad leg couldn't have kept up with them for long.

"I'm glad our sleeping soldier is awake at last," he said, gesturing to Dezlan then turning to Byzarien. "How long before Myravelle wakes the rest of them?"

He cleared his throat. "Very soon, Captain Abelard."

Abelard squinted his beady eyes while staring at him for a moment. Byzarien kept his face calm and posture straight, hoping the captain would not catch him in a lie. "Not soon enough," Abelard began with a smirk on his face, "but the king is sending a special gift for our healer today that will certainly encourage her to work faster." Stones rolled in Byzarien's stomach as he pondered what type of *gift* the king would send. "Good day, soldiers," Abelard said and crossed his fists over his chest. "Serve him."

"And he will serve you," they replied in unison as the portly man walked over to Lieutenant Eryck's group.

"Shit," Byzarien whispered.

Zelyx jogged in place and rubbed her hands together. "What?"

"I don't like the sound of that at all."

"Well, she's clearly getting stronger," Xavier said, sounding hopeful. "She woke Dezlan. She can heal the rest of them."

Byzarien nodded as they kept walking. Lana sprinted across the field toward them, and Zelyx greeted her with a smile. "How is he?" Lana asked, gesturing to Dezlan. Zelyx shook her head. "I know it's not the same but, one time, my cousin was attacked in an alleyway. He had a terrible head injury," Lana said. "He only started talking again after my aunt took him horseback riding. It was *therapeutic* for him."

Byzarien rubbed Xavier's back. "It might be worth trying?"

The group headed for the small stables. Xavier took Dezlan to rest on a bench while Byzarien, Zelyx, and Lana prepared the horse. When it was saddled, they led the animal from its stall while Xavier guided Dezlan toward it. The horse flicked its tail and shook its haunches, as if flies were biting it. Dezlan reached his hand to the horse's snout, and the animal grunted. The horse kicked up and whinnied, thrashing around as if it were too close to a Dormrya tree. Byzarien grabbed the reins and led the horse away from Dezlan. *Was there still too much poison in him?*

Xavier, Zelyx, and Lana all helped pull Dezlan out of the barn while Byzarien shushed the horse. It at last stopped flinching, and he was able to return it to the stall. He brushed it down, hoping to help calm the animal.

When he finally stepped outside, Dezlan was slouched against Xavier. "Do you want to go back?" Xavier asked, lifting Dezlan's chin.

"I'm really sorry," Lana said.

"You were trying to help," Zelyx said, taking her hand. "There's no way any of us could have known that would happen."

"Don't worry about it," Xavier said to Lana. "I think he just needs rest."

Byzarien helped the pair get to their tent. Dezlan rested on the bed while Xavier and Byzarien played knucklebones into the afternoon. Although the weight of the talus bones felt familiar in his hands as he tossed and caught them, so much had changed, and the game didn't make him nearly as happy as it had before.

He thought of Lazaire. He had been so angry at Myravelle for his death, when in reality the fault wasn't hers. A glimmer of warmth ignited in his chest at the thought of Lazaire spending his final days in Myravelle's arms. He knew, without a doubt now, that Lazaire was truly happy with her. He knew she took care of him. That warmth, though, burned into a sickening jealousy when he thought about the other things Myravelle and Lazaire may have done...things Byzarien was too much of a coward to do. His mind swirled. After rolling a series of dogs and noticing how tired Xavier himself was, Byzarien decided to say goodbye.

Leaving the tent, he headed toward the Guerrix Temple because he needed somewhere to think and to pray. Every step burned through him with anger at himself. He should have felt guilty. He should have felt ashamed for not praying in so long. Had his faith and devotion been so easily swayed by a fairy with silver-dusted eyes?

Ducking into the low cavern, he lit a few candles. They flickered a golden glow through the temple and sent smoke curling towards the stone ceiling, which was dark with soot. He knelt before the icon of Guerrix. The god of war had a haughty and imposing gaze, held two swords across his chest, and wore a gilded crown.

He shifted and turned to make sure no one was inside the small temple with him, then slid his eyes back to the sparkling deity. "Do you know the truth about the attacks?" he asked. "Why would you let us serve in the Sleepy Wood Company under false pretenses? None of this makes sense.

"My head tells me not to question the king and captain, but my heart is tugged in another direction," he said. "Myravelle has spun herself right into my soul, and I can't help but want to believe her. Is it magic or is it...*love*?"

Did Guerrix ever know true love? Certainly, he knew something if Amyor, the goddess of love and fertility, was his wife. But there were no tales of their yearning or romance or heartache...the couple had always just *existed*. Byzarien wondered whether the gods even fell in love the way mortals did. The only god to have possibly known the heart-crushing feeling was Filoux, who had once been the apprentice of his mother Reverie, goddess of dreams.

Filoux himself fell for a fairy named Scarlytt, who had lived in an orphanage in Eglantyne Kingdom. Once she had grown, like many orphaned fairies, she had nowhere else to go. Though the priestesses let her remain there as a maid, they mistreated her for being a fairy and wouldn't even supply her with shoes. Filoux once peeked up through a well and watched Scarlytt dance barefoot with a bucket as her partner while fetching water. Startled at first, the fairy grew fond of Filoux and the beautiful dreams he could spin in her head. He gave her a pair of red shoes, fit for her name, and enchanted them to make her dance gracefully wherever she roamed.

The priestesses at her orphanage despised those red shoes, calling them vile and sinful. But, when they tried to remove them from Scarlytt's feet, the shoes would not budge. That, and her constant dancing, made the humans condemn her as a witch. After they stoned Scarlytt to death, her broken body rose and continued to dance through the streets, like a puppet controlled by the red shoes. She danced until Filoux's rage burst with the explosion of the Forbidden Mountain near the Eglantyne Kingdom. He gave Scarlytt a proper burial and vowed to torture humans for all eternity by never allowing them peaceful rest.

Love had made even a god change to his core.

In all his life, Byzarien had never felt ridiculous praying—but he did there in the temple before images of cold and unfeeling gods. The fibers that held his principles together were tattered and moth-eaten due to a fairy. He was no longer worshiping an all-powerful god before him, no. It was simply a piece of wood, painted and gilded. What good could Guerrix or any other god do for him? It was Myravelle who had plucked his family from poverty. It was Myravelle who had saved Dezlan from the darkness. It was Myravelle who made his soul sing. And Byzarien was too ashamed of his body to be with her.

He reclined onto the chilly stone floor, smooth from the ages, and closed his eyes to meditate on everything he had been through in recent days. His name glittering in the sky during the ritual. The cursed Dormrya tree harming his friends. The meeting with the king, which shook Myravelle to her core. The fairy attacks. The gilded thread. Myravelle's enchantments. The things that had changed him completely all spun together in his mind.

Byzarien emerged from the Guerrix Temple with no new answers or insights. The sky had given way to darkness, and the rumble in his stomach reminded him to eat. He slipped into the mess hall without speaking to anyone—not that he needed to try avoiding conversation, for the soldiers were eerily silent as they ate their fish, mushrooms, and root vegetables. On his way out, he overheard two women discussing the lieutenant's plans. He realized why everyone was silent, the king and captain were ready for the next expedition, and all the soldiers were afraid. He couldn't blame them. Eighteen men and women were still trapped in a death-like sleep. *Would all of their minds be as damaged as Dezlan's?*

With his food, Byzarien hurried through the winding rows of tents as it began to snow. Standing just outside Myravelle's tent, he could smell the herbs and incense filtering through the tent flap. Sandalwood and vanilla. The scents he had begun to associate with Myravelle. The scents that eased the ache in his chest and cleared the fogginess of his mind. The scents he had grown to love.

His legs refused to budge. He thought about her lips, her eyes, and especially her warm hug. What would he tell her? And what would it matter? Was she only kind to him because he was her canvas? Was she simply trying to *bond* for magic's sake? Either way, the moment he surrendered to his feelings, they rose like a tide and threatened to spill over his armor of stone, steel, and scars.

When he finally gathered his courage to enter the tent, Myravelle was already fast asleep with Little Nightmare tucked against her chest. He smiled at the sight and ate silently, so as not to disturb her slumber. When he finally rested on his palette, Byzarien stared at the paper constellations on the ceiling until sleep swept him into its starless arms.

16

Myravelle

Before daybreak, when the night still clung to the sky like a child to her mother's leg, Myravelle vanished into the woods to forage. She had woken up much too early, haunted by another nightmare. Filoux certainly had it out for her. *My life is already a nightmare, why torture me during my sleep too?* Rolling over to watch Byzarien sleep only made her chest grow tight, for she desperately wanted to hold him close again, so she decided to go gleaning through the forest.

It was the most peaceful time of day in the most peaceful place in all the land. In the Sleepy Wood, Myravelle could be herself. Her breath could become one with the breeze. Her toes could sink into the earth and connect with the roots. Her body could sway with the branches. Her voice could harmonize with the birds.

It was a place with no one to judge her.

Myravelle had it all planned out: one day, she and her mother would live in a small cottage in the woods. If the seasons ever returned, they would fill their gardens with honeysuckle, lavender, and roses. They would be free. And whenever they wanted, they could travel to the black sand beaches in the north to enjoy leisurely walks in the sun and watch the moon twinkle upon the Sombry Sea. Myravelle's chest tore in two, frayed and threadbare, as she thought of Xylina.

"Someday, Mother," she whispered in the direction of the Eglantyne Kingdom. "Someday, you'll be free."

Dawn turned the sky a lighter shade of gray, so Myravelle gathered her basket and returned to camp, where people were starting their days. Every step closer to the tent made her head swim with thoughts of waking the soldiers. She couldn't do it. She would die before they all woke up. She would die and her mother would rot in the tower.

When Myravelle entered her tent, Byzarien was doing pushups wearing only a light pair of shorts. He jumped up at the sight of her and reached for his tunic.

"Don't let me interrupt." She took slow steps toward him, her beaded gown brushing over the floor in metallic whispers.

The sweat on Byzarien's temples and chest glistened in the candlelight as he clutched the tunic to cover his scars.

"I told you." Myravelle reached for his shoulder and traced a river of fire. "They are so beautiful."

Byzarien swallowed. "Myravelle—"

"...Spinner?" a voice boomed from outside. "Myravelle Spinner?"

They both turned toward the sound. "It's a little early for the messenger," Byzarien said, throwing on his clothes.

They lifted the flap to find a royal messenger holding an ornate wooden box. It appeared to be made of polished Dormrya. A valuable piece, indeed. "Myravelle Spinner?" the man asked, wearing gloves to protect himself from not only the cold, but from the wood itself.

"I'm Myravelle."

"A gift from His Royal Majesty."

The blood drained from her face as she accepted the box, and the man marched away. She stepped back into the tent, showing the box to Byzarien.

"Is that Dormrya wood?" he asked.

"Yes." The box was a lead weight in her hands.

Byzarien's face, which had been red from exercising, paled to a ghostly white. "Abelard mentioned you'd be receiving a gift from the king."

After taking a few deep breaths to gather her courage, Myravelle opened the box. She shrieked at the contents. A long, thin finger rested inside, the extreme paleness of which was a harsh juxtaposition against the dark wood.

"What is it?"

Myravelle's weak arms could barely hold the box as she trembled.

Byzarien guided her to sit on the edge of the bed before he peered inside.

Studying the grotesque gift further, Myravelle's world spun, and she clutched her sheets. When her eyesight focused once again, she recognized the moonstone ring on the *gift*.

"It's mother's," she whispered as she slid the ring from the finger. "This is hers."

Byzarien wrapped his arm around her as she lifted the dainty finger from the box. It had a puncture wound, about the size of a spindle's tip. Myravelle's heart sank when she recalled the time her mother had pricked her finger, and their lives were upended. At the bottom of the box was a bloodstained letter on royal stationery with the briar rose emblem.

"Will you read it for me?" Myravelle said, placing the finger and the box on her nightstand and crashing to the bed.

Byzarien opened the stationary and read aloud,

"Dearest Myravelle,
I regret to inform you of your mother's unfortunate accident.

While spinning gold, she somehow pricked her finger on the spindle and fell into a death-like sleep.

It would be to your advantage to wake these soldiers. Such a shame it would be for an accident to befall you as well.

Sincerely,

His Royal Majesty King Zylvain"

Myravelle could not move. The king's words built up like frost in her mind, making the world blurry and obscure. Little Nightmare cawed and cried from his bed, but he sounded far, far away.

Byzarien cradled her face in his large hands. "Myravelle?" She stared at him as the edges of reality flickered with the dance of the candlelight. "Myravelle?" he asked again.

The ice holding her hostage began to thaw, replaced by a scraping hollowness within her chest. Myravelle's breaths hitched in her throat, not allowing her to cry or fully inhale, as she sat up and leaned into his warm touch.

"I am so sorry," Byzarien said. "Is there anything I can do?"

"Hold me." Her words escaped in a mere breath rather than a whisper.

Byzarien did, and his warm pressure kept Myravelle from crumbling. She cried, and her tears soaked the fabric of Byzarien's tunic. She didn't know how long he held her, but he didn't let go. She didn't know how many tears fell from her eyes. Her mother was gone. Gone. Gone before they could build a cottage in the Sleepy Wood. Gone before they could visit the black sand beaches. Gone before she could truly live a life.

It had been so many years since she had seen her, Myravelle had difficulty recalling her mother's features. Her face was like her own, she thought, but with subtle differences. Xylina had rounder cheeks and a softer brow. But it was their eyes—yes, their eyes held the starkest difference. Myravelle's were gray, nearly devoid of color, while Xylina's were the brown of rich soil. Now, her beautiful mother was likely at the bottom of the Enferrix Pix, a sulfur-smelling crevice where Eglantyne's most despicable criminals were sent, never to rest, but to linger forever along the Darkened Path. Xylina did not deserve such a fate. When someone wasn't properly buried, their souls would wander for eternity in a place darker than midnight and colder than the longest winter's night.

Myravelle broke the embrace to slip the moonstone ring onto her index finger. "Do you think she's lost along the Darkened Path?"

Byzarien stroked her hair. "No, I don't believe so."

Though she wanted him to hold her again, fatigue won out, and Myravelle reclined on the bed. He covered her with blankets and furs and tucked Little Nightmare in with her. "I'll give you some time alone and let you rest," he said. "Will you be all right?"

She didn't want him to go, but she didn't want to beg him to stay either. Her life was a disaster, it was best for Byzarien to get far away. She closed her eyes so she wouldn't have to watch him leave. "Sure."

Myravelle snuggled deeper into bed, where sleep wrapped her up in dreams of stone walls, spindles, and spiders in her lonely, twisted tower while her mother's voice echoed through the darkness.

Draft and pinch. Draft and pinch.
Spin. Spin. Spin.
Draft and pinch. Draft and pinch.
Again. Again. Again.

She stirred at the sound of Byzarien returning. Reality washed over her with a cold sweat, causing her to scramble to the waste basket to vomit. Byzarien dashed toward her and helped her sit on a stool by the worktable.

He offered a glass of water. "Drink this."

The water tasted like acid in her mouth and scraped against her sore throat the entire way down. She chewed on a few leftover peppermint leaves to rid her mouth of the flavor.

"I...um, I had an idea," Byzarien said, holding out her cloak. "For your mother, if you are up for it?"

His eyes locked onto hers with none of the former hatred or disgust. *Maybe,* she thought, *he really wanted to do something nice.* She agreed and let him wrap the cloak around her shoulders.

He grabbed an empty jar from the worktable and the Dormrya box containing the morbid gift. "Why don't you bring her spindle?"

With the spindle in hand, Myravelle followed Byzarien outside. As they entered the woods, he even threaded his fingers with hers. A fog settled into her mind as she let him guide her through the forest. It wasn't until they passed a few familiar trees and rocks that she realized he was leading her in the direction of the secret graveyard.

When they reached the location, Byzarien stepped aside to show her his *idea*. There, in the clearing, was a miniature pyre of elder wood, just the right size to fit the Dormrya box.

"No one knows how much of a person needs to be cremated for a proper burial," he said, resting the box atop the pyre. "I personally believe it is about the spirit. And you cared so much for your mother, I'm sure enough of her spirit is here with us."

Myravelle's eyes stung with tears. "Thank you."

Withdrawing matches from his pocket, he knelt to light the kindling beneath the miniature pyre. Myravelle toyed with the moonstone ring, hoping Byzarien was right. The flames sparked to life and ignited the elder wood. Soon, the Dormrya box burned brightly in every color imaginable. Flashes of blue, yellow, purple, green, orange, and red danced in a magical display just for Xylina. Byzarien tossed a few coins into the blaze, and Myravelle stepped close to rest the drop spindle on top.

"Mother, it's me, your spiderling," she whispered. "I miss you more every day. I love you."

She returned to Byzarien and leaned against his side while they watched the fire eat away at the small pyre and offerings. Myravelle hoped the drop spindle, her most cherished possession, would provide her mother with some comfort in the Underworld.

The box and spindle charred and flaked from the crackling flames. All the while, Myravelle felt her insides do the same. Xylina had been the one thing standing between Myravelle and the vast well of power within. Her mother's safety had been a dam holding back the flow.

Now, the arcane magic wanted to break free. It smoldered through her veins, threatening to consume her entirely.

She welcomed it with open arms.

17

Byzarien

Byzarien watched the funeral pyre's flames dance in Myravelle's eyes. Those silver eyes, which had cried countless tears, burned with something that made his veins run cold. For she was far too still and calm. *Was she in shock?* He wrapped his arms around her in an attempt to keep her warm.

When the miniature funeral pyre smoked and turned to dust, Myravelle remained a statue staring at the ashes. Byzarien released her and knelt to sweep the ashes and tiny bone fragments into the ceramic jar.

After settling the jar between some tree roots, he stood and turned to Myravelle, who didn't blink. He reached to touch her shoulder, stroking the soft crushed velvet of her cloak but, still, she didn't move.

"Myravelle?" he asked gently. "Are you ready to walk back?"

Her eyes slid to meet his, but there was something different about them. They usually sparkled with a dusting of magic, but now it was as if something had opened up and flooded them with incendiary starlight.

He touched her cheek. "Or we can stay a little longer if you like?"

"No," she whispered, deep and throaty, raising her hand to meet the scars on his cheek. "I must heal the sleeping soldiers."

"That's probably not a good idea right now," he said, leaning down until their foreheads touched. "You're in mourning, and you still need rest."

"There's no rest for *wicked ones* like me."

Myravelle raised up onto her tiptoes and pressed her lips to Byzarien's. He stood in shock for a moment, not expecting a kiss. Her lips, like always, were soft and laced with botanicals, but there was something new—a sweet fire that crackled from her soul into his. The first four times they had kissed, he was able to blame the ritual. Now, as his tongue grew thick and his head fizzed over like a boiling cauldron, he knew without a doubt it was Myravelle who was all-enchanting. He gladly slipped under her spell.

He wrapped her in his arms, gently kissing her back. Their fragmented souls fit together just right, and their pain—mirror images of one another's—finally crashed together. He wanted to comfort her with sweetness, but Myravelle kissed hard and tugged his hair before shoving him against a tree. She slid the collar of his jacket open and licked the scars on his neck, which sent rushes of tingling delight over Byzarien's skin. A moan rumbled through his chest and broke past his lips.

Although he enjoyed what was happening, it was wrong to take advantage of her in this state of grief. When he made love to Myravelle, he wanted it to be right—not rushed and in a graveyard. "What are you doing?" he asked, holding her back enough to look into her eyes.

She licked her lips and grinned. "I'm going to wake those soldiers."

In a twirl of her cloak and gown, Myravelle set off toward camp. Byzarien scrambled to get the ceramic container and rush after her.

His boots and pants snagged on the thorns, while Myravelle moved through the forest like smoke. She was so fast, he had to jog to keep her in sight. He shouted her name, but she didn't stop.

She stormed through the army encampment with her arms spread wide like a soaring crow. Byzarien's stomach lurched in fear for anyone who dared get in her way. That change in her eyes. That change in her kiss. She was brimming with something dangerous. He ran to follow her, unsure what she was planning. Her once graceful glide of a walk now made her appear to fly, and her formidable appearance sent soldiers into a frenzy.

Byzarien turned the corner to follow as she disappeared into the infirmary. He entered and found her standing between rows of sleeping soldiers. The nurses all huddled together, off to the side, while a few curious soldiers began to shuffle in with their hands on their weapons.

"What are you doing?" Byzarien asked, reaching for her.

"Waiting."

Captain Abelard entered, followed by an entourage of guards with their swords drawn. Byzarien stood tall, holding his place between her and them. "You've stirred quite the commotion, Myravelle," Abelard said. "We had to see you weren't going to harm these soldiers."

"Why would *I* do something like that?" she asked, head held high. "Is that not *your* job?"

Abelard laughed. "Did you enjoy your gift from the king?"

Myravelle's eyes narrowed, and the air in the infirmary grew dry and itchy with static. A few people gasped at the change. The enchantment carved over Byzarien's heart burned, and he fell to his knees clutching his chest. No one seemed to notice; all eyes were on Myravelle.

Abelard strode forward, a haughty grin on his face as he leaned to whisper in Myravelle's ear. Byzarien strained to hear him. "I'm glad you've come to your senses. You know what you must do, unless you wish to suffer Xylina's fate."

"*Fate*," Myravelle said, as if she were tasting the word for the first time, "is a funny thing, is it not?"

Abelard rolled his eyes. "What do you mean?"

"It seems I control the fate of all these sleeping soldiers," she said, "and you *think* you control my fate."

Both Abelard's voice and face hardened. "Because I do, Myravelle. One word from me, and my guards will make sure there's nothing left of you to burn."

What began as a slight melodic giggle erupted into a fit of laughter from Myravelle. Byzarien managed to stand and drag himself a few steps closer, wishing he had a weapon.

"You don't understand, Captain," Myravelle began, lifting her finger to hover near his sweaty forehead. "I am already burning."

When she touched his skin, it singed beneath her finger, steam curling from boiling blisters.

Abelard groaned and stumbled back. "Seize her!"

With a lift of her arms, the air crackled with gold and black sparks, setting parts of the canvas tent on fire. Byzarien tensed at the sight of flames, and his scars tingled for him to run. As Myravelle stretched and twirled her fingers, dark tendrils of smoke escaped, lifting the sleeping soldiers above their beds. Byzarien tried to move toward her, but shock and fear locked him in place.

"Stop this wicked magic!" Abelard shouted.

Myravelle's eyes glowed with moonlight as she traced circular patterns in the air. The ground shook with such force that Abelard and his men fell to the ground. Byzarien held on to the cot nearest to him, unable to take his eyes off Myravelle. She was haunting and eerie, enchanting and beguiling. He no longer wanted to make her stop—he wanted to see what she was capable of. The excitement made his heart thrum against the rune on his chest.

Abelard managed to push himself from the unstable ground and shout, "Arrest her!"

Myravelle twirled her fingers in the air, releasing more of her crackling power. All at once, a rush of hot air burst through the infirmary. Everyone shielded their faces. The sleeping soldiers fell to their beds, the fires went out, and the air went still.

The soldiers opened their eyes and sat up in their cots. Byzarien sighed in relief as he made his way to Myravelle, who had grown pale. He held her in his arms as a sweat broke across her forehead and her lips turned blue.

While some of the witnesses began to clap and cheer, Abelard's voice carried through the tent, "She fucking did it."

Nurses rushed to the sides of the freshly awakened men and women, and Byzarien grinned at the scene. He looked to Myravelle to congratulate her but gasped at her appearance. The dark quarter-moons had reappeared under her eyes as she shivered, from cold or shock, he didn't know. She looked nothing like the woman who had just demonstrated such raw and arcane magic—nothing like the woman who kissed him in the woods. Byzarien nestled her into his arms and left the infirmary.

"Where do you think you're going?" Abelard said, following him outside.

"She did exactly what you asked her to do," Byzarien said, glaring at the captain. "She woke the sleeping soldiers, and now she needs rest." Though Byzarien didn't quite understand what had just happened with Myravelle and her magic, he knew it wasn't good. *I must protect her.*

18

Myravelle

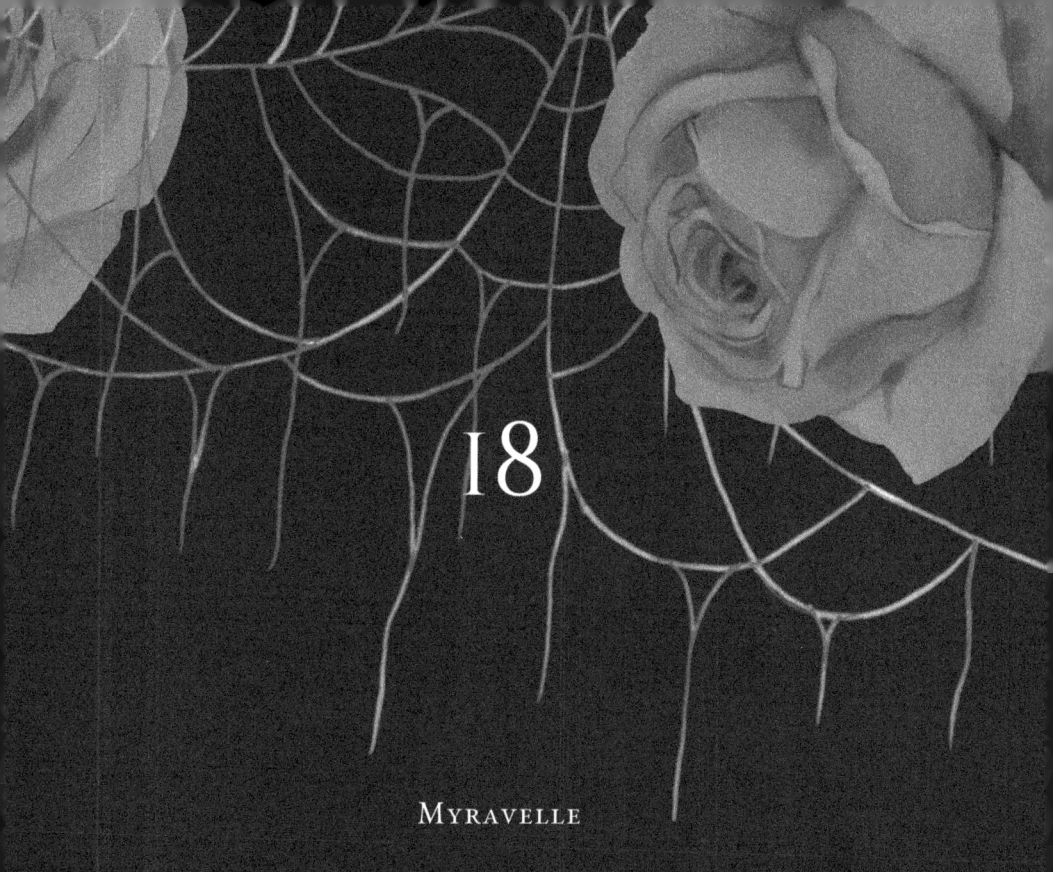

A warm, damp cloth was covering Myravelle's eyes when she stirred. Little Nightmare cawed to her left and herbal scents clung to the air, so she knew she was in her tent. The mattress sank as a warm body sat next to her. Myravelle removed the cloth to find Byzarien holding a bowl of broth, its steam curling into the air.

Myravelle sat up and rubbed her aching temples. "What happened?"

"After our ceremony for your mother, you woke *all* of the sleeping soldiers," he said, handing her the broth. "Drink this."

Memories swirled, making Myravelle shudder. One in particular broke her more than the rest: her mother's death. Her mother was gone. *Gone.* She glanced at the ceramic container on her table and let the sadness slide down her face. *I failed you, Mother.* Only the warmth of the bowl and Byzarien's presence kept her from shattering like glass.

He wiped her tears and leaned in to kiss her cheek. "I'm here for you."

Studying Byzarien's face, Myravelle remembered all too well how she had kissed him—*really* kissed him, in the forest. What if his affections right now weren't sincere and merely an extension of the new and wild magic? She didn't know what it meant that she could wake the entire tent of sleeping soldiers in her state...what if she had done something to Byzarien too? Had a twirl of her tongue caused him to fall in love? She was cursed to lose everyone she loved. Stones spilled into her stomach, and her chest grew tight. She sat back and drank the broth, deep in thought.

"Do you need anything?" Byzarien asked.

She shook her head and set the empty bowl down as a thought crossed her mind. "But you...you should stay far away from me. I am worse than a spider. I am worse than a witch. I am a monster."

"That's not true," he said, taking her hands. "I'm sorry for ever calling you those things. I was blinded by duty to the king, my grief over Lazaire, and my misguided hatred of fairies. You are wonderful." His cheeks flared with fiery patches as he opened and closed his mouth a few times. He finally took a deep breath and squeezed her hands. "I want to help you, Myravelle, because I'm falling for you."

He leaned in and kissed her, ever so gently. When his fingers caressed her hair, tingles coursed over her body, and Myravelle believed she was happy at that moment. That was until the dark, oily magic pricked her with memories of her mother and Pazcal.

She broke the kiss and rested her hand over Byzarien's heart, as if to protect it from herself. "We can't. Terrible things happen to those close to me. Just look at what happened to my mother...and to Pazcal."

"Wait, who's Pazcal?"

"My first love, innocent and sweet." She strained to fight rising emotion. "He was a castle steward, and he made the mistake of meeting me. You see, Mother would never let me attempt magic, so I planted a garden with all sorts of herbs and botanicals I could use to heal her after punishments. And the guards punished her all of the time..." She looked away.

"I had always been lonely, so I stitched sachets of vanilla and sandalwood into my dresses and braided sweet pea into my hair, hoping to find love like I'd read about in fairy tales," she continued, brushing fingers through her wavy locks. "When Pazcal showed up—all golden hair, freckles, and lopsided grin, I thought my innocent little spells had worked. One night, he and I had spent hours on the rooftop only to return to find my mother slumped in her chair. She had pricked her finger on a spindle."

Byzarien's dark brows fell hard over wide eyes as he studied her. Myravelle continued to tell him about how she had used Pazcal to heal her mother, not knowing what she was doing, not knowing what the glowing runes meant, and not knowing it would change things forever.

"When the king discovered I could help with his Dormrya obsession, he forced Pazcal and me to go to the hospital wing filled with my very first sleeping soldiers. I never saw my mother again, and I was forced to use Pazcal over and over...until nothing was left of him. It didn't take long before King Zylvain made me work with another canvas. Essentially, he built this encampment and created the Sleepy Wood Company because of me. It's all my fault."

A coil of grief and shame cinched Myravelle's stomach as she closed her eyes.

To her surprise, Byzarien wrapped his arms around her. His embrace was like a home, but one she had to leave. "I'm sorry," he whispered.

She pushed him back. "That's why you should stay away from me. I no longer need to drain your life with this violent magic taking over, but the king will certainly use you against me. Only death comes to those I love."

Byzarien's eyes clung to hers, as if the word *love* was holding his sight hostage—as if an inkling of hope had overpowered Myravelle's entire argument. She wanted him, but a hard knot formed in her throat when she realized she would have to hurt him to protect him.

"They broke me, and I feel different inside," she said. "I am wicked. I am cursed. I am dangerous."

He took her hand and pressed his lips to her wrist. "No, Myravelle, you are lovely."

"You don't mean that." She took a deep breath to fill her body with courage and thought up a lie. "Everything you feel for me is simply the magic; it will wear off soon."

She slipped from the bed, not wanting to see the pain on his face, but a shiver passed over her skin with the abrupt separation from Byzarien's warmth and an empty hollow broke open in her chest. Magic slithered into the void and filled the space, preventing any tears from falling. Little Nightmare hopped from his bed and pecked at her ankle, so she lifted the bird and let him rest on her shoulder.

A shuffling sound caught her attention, but she dared not turn. In her peripheral vision, she saw Byzarien step toward the tent flap and look back at her. "Myravelle," he whispered.

"You need to leave now." Clenching her fists, she steeled her nerves to say the largest lie she would ever tell: "I don't love you."

With that, Byzarien stormed out.

She collapsed into her chair, left alone with her terrible thoughts. What could she have done? Confess her feelings to him? Make love to him? No, not if that meant putting him in danger.

She stepped to the worktable and swept her finger over the jar of her mother's ashes. Byzarien had been nothing short of amazing that morning, helping her honor Xylina. He was a good man who never deserved any of the horrible things life had heaved at him. Myravelle considered herself equal to the fire—a horrific tragedy. Not only had she left scars on his skin, but on his heart.

Had she become what the king and captain had always called her? After breaking Byzarien's heart, she certainly felt it was true.

She was indeed the wicked fairy.

19

Byzarien

For the next few nights, Byzarien drank and played knucklebones with Dezlan, Xavier, Zelyx, and Lana. With them, he always felt like the fifth wheel of a cart, unpaired and useless. Taking another swig of ale, he tried to wash away the taste of Myravelle on his lips. But no matter how inebriated he became, he still burned for her.

It had been three days since he—or anyone—had seen her, but Byzarien didn't dare try. For she had lied to him; it wasn't magic that had made him fall for her. Even being away from her for several days, his heart still yearned. But she didn't love him.

"What's with him?" Lana asked, twirling one of her braids and bumping her shoulder with Zelyx.

"I think he's in *love*," the blonde said, smirking.

The rune scar above his heart ached, and his feet itched for him to walk out of the tent at once.

Xavier glared at Zelyx. "Leave him alone."

That was why Byzarien had first felt drawn to and comfortable with Xavier and Dezlan. Unlike his other friends, including Lazaire, they had never pressured him to talk about romance or sex. It was a nice change, since Lazaire had always been trying to set him up with women. He had simply thought he'd been *helping* him, even though it made Byzarien uncomfortable.

As self-proclaimed soulmates, Xavier and Dezlan understood Byzarien's need for something more than a physical relationship. Usually, Zelyx didn't give him too much grief, but there were often times when she acted like Lazaire by trying to help him meet women or by teasing him. He supposed she was correct this time; he was falling for Myravelle, but it didn't matter.

Byzarien shook his head, tossed the knucklebones into the air, and caught them on the back of his hand. His shoulders slumped when he saw he had rolled yet another dog. Xavier, Dezlan, Zelyx, and Lana all laughed when Byzarien tossed his silver dynar into the pot. When it was Zelyx's turn, she rolled an Amyor, the highest number, named after the goddess of love.

She held her hand steady and smirked at Lana. "*Amyor*," she whispered. "Does this mean I'll get lucky tonight?"

"You wish," Lana said, knocking the talus bones from Zelyx's hand.

The group continued to play the game, and Byzarien continued to have bad luck.

Zelyx eventually steered the conversation back to Myravelle. "But you do like her? Right?"

"She is beautiful," Lana said, sticking her tongue out at Zelyx.

Xavier and Zelyx both giggled until they were cut off by Dezlan. "And powerful," he said, eyes peeled wide. "She saved me from that horrible and dark place."

Smiling, Xavier rubbed his back. Dezlan hardly spoke, so it was good to be reminded he was alive—alive because of Myravelle.

"She is both of those things," Byzarien admitted, taking another swig of ale. "But she doesn't need me, nor does she love me—*that*, she made very clear."

The tent fell silent, and he counted the seconds until someone would try to offer him a useless piece of advice or comforting word. His rigid muscles and burning scars were like a shield against their pity.

Lana spoke up, scooping the knucklebones into her palm. "I don't know you very well, Byzarien. But, from how Z talks about you, I think you have a heart worth loving. Give her some space, but don't give up. I'm glad Z didn't."

Zelyx gazed into her girlfriend's eyes with a beaming smile. Though both her words and sentiment were nice, they twisted Byzarien's insides even further.

"I need some air," he said and stumbled from the tent. With his hands in his pockets, he walked aimlessly between the rows of tents, where only small fires and a few torches cut through the starless sky. *Don't give up.* He chuckled humorlessly at the thought. What, was he supposed to kneel outside Myravelle's tent and beg? *Pathetic.* He had been just fine before meeting her and had only started to care for her. He would be fine.

Right?

Could his heart return to its previous shape after being twisted by Myravelle's spindle?

Scratching the ridges on his neck, he wondered whether Myravelle really liked his scars—*or had she only said that to lure him into her web?* Bile rose in his throat at the thought of Lazaire and all the other canvases. Turns out, he meant nothing more to Myravelle than any of them. Maybe less, actually, since he had never even slept with her.

He released a heavy breath, clouding the air around him. *Was he being unfair?* Myravelle was more damaged than he was, and her mother had just died. He glanced in the direction of her tent, and a deep pain welled in his chest. He missed the scent of dried botanicals. He missed Little Nightmare. He missed *her*. He wanted to comfort her. But her words cut him deeper than her blade ever had.

I don't love you.

From all the drinking, his bladder needed attention, so Byzarien zigzagged through two rows of tents to the outer edge of camp to relieve himself. From afar, he saw some of the King's Guards near Captain Abelard's quarters. His brow furrowed, and he headed in that direction only because his fuzzy, drunken mind told him it was necessary. He saluted the guard near the back corner of the tent, who went rigid upon Byzarien's approach.

"What's going on?" he asked.

The guard's eyes narrowed. "Return to your quarters, soldier."

"I just want to know why the king's here," he asked, a little louder.

The guard grabbed his collar as Lieutenant Eryck walked from around the tent. "What are you doing, Byzarien?" he asked, gesturing for the guard to release him.

"I was just asking why the king is here."

"Oh," he said with a chuckle. "It's great news for you, actually. Captain Abelard wants to arrest the witch for her display the other day. They'll lock her up and only bring her out when we have soldiers to wake."

Although a sharp breath hitched in his throat, Byzarien tried to appear calm. "Oh, good."

"You could say Captain Abelard has saved your life," Eryck said and poked Byzarien's chest right where Myravelle's rune burned.

"Thank you for informing me, Lieutenant." Byzarien crossed his fists over his chest, which he exaggerated to make himself appear even drunker.

Eryck returned the salute and began speaking with the guard as Byzarien shuffled away. He tried to keep his feet from taking off into a sprint. He needed help first. Picking up his pace, he turned down the row back to his old tent.

When he entered, his friends all stood and muttered a cacophony of apologies, but Byzarien couldn't make out what anyone was saying.

"Stop!" He held out his hands until they hushed. "I need your help; it's about Myravelle."

"Whatever you need, Byz," Xavier said.

"They're going to lock her up and only use her when they need her magic," he said. "She needs to escape tonight."

"Where?" Dezlan asked. "You'll have to be careful."

Byzarien swept his hair over his scars, deep in thought. "I'll hide out with her in the Sleepy Wood for now, until they stop looking for us. Then, go south to Basenfort Kingdom for sanctuary."

"You could be arrested for treason," Zelyx said. "This could start a war."

"I must do something," he said, shaking his head. "I can't let them exploit her for the rest of her days. What if the person you loved was going through this?"

Xavier and Dezlan looked at one another, as did Zelyx and Lana. "I wouldn't give up," Dezlan said. "Just like Xavier never gave up on me."

Everyone nodded in agreement.

"First," Lana said, stepping forward and taking charge. "You must quietly go to Myravelle and pack only what you need. *Only* the essentials. The four of us will take care of supplies and provisions."

Overwhelmed by their support, Byzarien fought against his tears and managed to whisper, "Thank you."

"Now go," Zelyx said. "We'll meet you near the Guerrix Temple."

Byzarien set off to Myravelle's tent, hoping the escape would work...and hoping she would agree to it. He entered the tent to find her spinning, and his eyebrows shot up at the sight of gilded thread. Though she had sent a skein of it to his family, seeing the roving twirl into gold as she spun was incredible. As the fibers twisted, the glint of the candlelight sparkled against them like little stars.

Myravelle's eyes swept to Byzarien, but her blank expression didn't change.

"The king's going to arrest you." He stepped to her side of the table and held out his hand. "Come with me, we'll escape together."

She continued spinning and sang,

*"Draft and pinch. Draft and pinch.
Spin. Spin. Spin—"*

"Did you hear me?" He touched her cheek. "Myravelle."

She leaned into his hand, pain pinching her face. "No matter what I do, whether I save a thousand lives or more, I am always a fairy. Always a witch. Always a spider. Always a monster. Let them lock me away."

"No." He knelt beside her. "The only thing you are is wonderful."

Tears glistened in Myravelle's eyes, but she continued spinning. "Why do you want to help me?"

"You know why," he said, heat consuming his cheeks. "We'll hide out in the Sleepy Wood until we can get help from a neighboring kingdom, Basenfort or Riviere, even. This is the right thing to do, the king must be stopped before he hurts any more of his own people."

Myravelle shook her head and wound the gold thread around the shaft of the drop spindle. "Another human kingdom will exploit me just the same."

"What are you saying?" Byzarien's heart thrummed with such pain, he thought it would break in two. "Are you giving up?"

"No," Myravelle said as she stood. "I stayed in this kingdom and in the king's army for one reason: my mother. Now, I must find other fairies like me."

Byzarien rose and threaded his fingers with hers. "Let's go, my friends will be waiting with supplies and provisions for us."

"You'll help me find the fairy realm?" she asked, her dark brows stitched together.

"Yes." Byzarien leaned in to kiss her cheek but recoiled. "Sorry, I shouldn't have done that. Let's take only what we need."

They packed the drop spindle, the small cauldron, some flax seeds for Little Nightmare, medicinal herbs, oils for Byzarien, fresh candles, and the jar of Xylina's ashes. Myravelle donned her cloak, and they left the tent without even snuffing the candles. Byzarien didn't want it to be obvious she had escaped.

They stuck to the shadows and moved between rows of tents until they reached the field near the Guerrix Temple, the Sleepy Wood looming in the distance. Byzarien would be labeled a traitor for aiding in her escape but, at that moment, he didn't care. In his heart, he knew it was the right thing to do. In the entrance to the temple, they huddled together and waited.

After twenty minutes or so, the sound of hooves echoed in the darkness. Byzarien's pulse went wild. The king's cavalry galloped into view, surrounding them on all sides. Their torches burned bright against the night. The standard-bearers held the insignia, rippling in the wind, of the Eglantyne Kingdom: a white briar rose.

They were surrounded. Through the crowd, Byzarien spotted his friends near Lana's tent, their arms full of provisions. He made a small gesture for them to leave, but they stayed and watched. Byzarien's stomach sank when he saw who was riding forward through the parting cavalry: King Zylvain. The Guerrix Priest was at his side; he must have seen them approach the temple.

Byzarien hyperventilated, but Myravelle stood tall as an ancient fortress, her eyes glowing like stardust.

Sneering, King Zylvain called, "Going somewhere, my darling?"

20

Myravelle

The sight of the king sent waves of dark magic crashing through her chest. It didn't whisper or seduce this time— no, it raged, begging to be released. Everything hurt, and her fingers itched to trace the dangerous runes glowing in the air. She took steady breaths, trying to assess the situation.

Byzarien inched closer to her as the king signaled to his men. All at once, soldiers drew their swords and archers nocked their arrows. Little Nightmare cawed and took off from Myravelle's shoulder, flying for the very first time since his injury. She watched her pet soar toward the Sleepy Wood, thankful he wouldn't get hurt.

"Well," King Zylvain called, "our priest's old eyes were correct: the *witch* and her canvas really were trying to escape. How sad."

"I've paid my price," she said. "I'm leaving."

"I cannot let you leave my kingdom, darling." King Zylvain shook his head and pursed his lips. "We need your magic now more than ever."

"You killed my mother," she said, her voice smoky and low.

"And she was a *fairy*."

The king's nonchalant admission and the laughter from the surrounding soldiers grated at Myravelle's patience. She trembled, and Byzarien took her hand.

The king toyed with the rings on his fingers. "Xylina could no longer earn her keep," he said. "Such a shame, really. Let's hope your magic doesn't fade as well."

"Murderer," she growled while her magic blazed like an inferno inside.

"Now, let's not call each other names," he said, clicking his tongue. "Come with me, and we won't have to execute your newest canvas."

As if having been struck in the chest, Myravelle gasped. She glanced at Byzarien's sweet brown eyes before turning back to the king. "Leave him alone."

"The choice is yours, darling. Either surrender peacefully, or the man dies."

Her magic waned from the heartache like a flower wilting in the wake of a frost. No one else she loved could die. There was only one thing she could do. She kissed his hand. "Goodbye, Byzarien."

"No," he said and tried to grab her, but she slipped away toward the king.

Two soldiers gripped her arms as the king dismounted and stood before her. He made a twirling gesture and the soldiers promptly jerked Myravelle around to face Byzarien. The king's men had him on his knees. Captain Abelard stood behind them, spear in hand.

Myravelle shook her head and fought her captors. "What are you doing?"

"Oh, I apologize, darling," King Zylvain said, leaning so close, his wiry facial hair scraped her ear. "I almost forgot; I've charged Byzarien Dumont with treason. Do you know what the captain does to traitors?"

Myravelle seethed through her clenched teeth. "No!"

Everything inside hurt again. The thunderstorm of inky magic churned through her body with crackling heat as she stared at Byzarien. He remained too still and stoic for the situation. Myravelle thrashed against the soldiers, their grip tearing through her gown and into her flesh.

The king waved a hand. Abelard raised the spear. Myravelle froze when Byzarien looked at her with tears in his hopeless eyes. They had been so close to freedom. In a swift motion, the captain plunged the spear into Byzarien's chest.

Abelard removed the weapon, and Byzarien slumped to the ground. The sound Myravelle made was inhuman, and time stood still. They were responsible for killing her sweet Pazcal. Jon. Henri. Olivier. Lazaire. Every innocent canvas. Her mother. And now Byzarien. Something wild broke inside her, and the dark magic—a mix of lifelong pain, agony, and rage—flooded through her. Her fingers traced over burning runes, allowing her to tap into the arcane power of the galaxy within.

The soldiers holding her screamed as the flesh of their hands melted off bone. They released her and scrambled away.

"Seize her!" the king shouted, backing toward his horse.

All at once, hundreds of runes flashed gold in her eyes, making it difficult to choose as the soldiers raced toward her. Myravelle's gaze locked on one that matched her own darkness. She traced the circular design with rays extending from the central star, not knowing or caring what it meant. When her finger reached the last ray, an explosion shook the field.

Horse and man alike fell, unconscious. The dead grasses of the field had been scorched. Steam curled from the remains of snow along the edge. Embers sparkled against the sky like stars.

Myravelle sprinted to Byzarien and rested her head on his chest. *Thump. Thump.* She sobbed in relief when she touched his bloody chest and discovered that the spear had missed his heart. His sweet, sweet heart.

"Wake up," she cried, shaking him.

Myravelle found a knife on Byzarien's belt and carved her palm.

She placed it on his chest and focused on healing him, giving him all the magic she had. It renewed and filled her with ease, and she hoped there was enough. The warmth between them intensified as their blood swirled together. Heartbeat by heartbeat, she let her magic flow into him like a star-speckled river. Though it sapped her energy, though she trembled and felt lightheaded, she would not give up. With one final push, Byzarien blinked and looked around before he sprung up, embracing her.

"Am I alive?"

"Yes."

He looked around at the soldiers and fires. "What did you do?"

"It doesn't matter," she said, touching his cheek. "We must go."

As they helped one another stand, Myravelle prepared her free hand to fight off the soldiers running toward them from the encampment. Though exhausted, she began tracing another rune.

"Byz, wait!" Xavier shouted, waving his long arms. She lowered her hand when she realized it was his friends.

"Here," Zelyx said, tossing Byzarien a rolled tent.

Dezlan then handed him a sack. "Here's food."

"Now, go!" Xavier said.

"Wait." Myravelle twirled her finger toward the ground in concentric circles with a small star at the center. With a rumble of the earth, the soil lowered into a pit which she then set on fire. Drained, she slumped against Byzarien and closed her eyes.

"Why'd you do that?" he asked, wrapping his arms around her.

"Everyone saw you die," she said, her eyes fluttering open to glance at the unconscious king and captain. "We must keep that illusion intact to protect your friends and family."

With his eyes narrowed, Byzarien bit his lip and nodded.

"You all," Myravelle addressed the group. "For your safety, you must pretend to be on the king's side. Once we're gone, the four of you should begin helping everyone, starting with the king. They'll wake soon. Tell everyone that I burned Byzarien's body in this pit as a makeshift pyre."

With pinched faces, they all agreed before wrapping the pair in a final hug.

Taking Byzarien's face in his hands, Dezlan said, "Go."

Byzarien grabbed Myravelle's hand, and they sprinted into the night and the Sleepy Wood. Her energy had been sapped, but tingles crept through her skin and filled her—as if the dark magic could replenish itself with ease. With the new strength, Myravelle guided them deeper and deeper through the thick and tangled forest.

"I'll make a torch," Byzarien said.

She shook her head. "Not yet. They'll see us. I can lead, trust me."

As they ran, Myravelle's body crackled with magic, and she navigated the woods faster than ever. Her feet knew every stump, root, and vine before she reached it. Her skin sensed every wicked thorn to avoid. Her bones forewarned each fairy curse carved upon the trees. Byzarien stumbled and caught his clothing on branches a few times, but Myravelle tightened her grip and focused on leading him.

"How are you doing this?" he asked, mimicking her every step. "I can't see a thing."

She didn't know how to answer. She didn't know how the new magic would affect her or those around her. The king and captain had broken whatever dam was holding her magic back. White-hot stars burned in the churning blackness inside, begging to be released again, and her mother's words bloomed in her mind. *The stars fell for you.*

After two hours of running, Byzarien clutched his chest. Myravelle's eyes had adjusted to the darkness, so she stopped to check on him, fatigue finally outweighing the magic. He reached inside his jacket and, when he pulled out his hand, it was slick with blood.

"The wound was deep, and I didn't have time to heal it properly," she realized. "I need to stitch you."

"Do you think we're far enough away to make camp?"

"We'll never be far enough away," she whispered as she unfurled the tent roll. "But this will do."

Byzarien tried to help with the tent, but Myravelle guided him to sit.

"Rest now, I'll take care of it." She set up the tent, barely large enough for two. After she drove the last stake into the ground with a mere swirl of her finger, she led Byzarien to lie inside.

He removed his jacket and tunic, wincing, and reclined on the bedroll. "I didn't believe I'd ever be doing this again."

Myravelle retrieved a small candle and jar of matches from her pack. With an acrid snap of sulfur, she lit a match and held it to the wick. The flame flickered across their faces, highlighting just how alone they truly were. Alone in the deep, dark Sleepy Wood. Sliding a needle through the flame to sanitize the tool, Myravelle then threaded it and leaned over Byzarien. He made no effort to cover his scars.

"This won't hurt," she said. "I promise."

Stitching Byzarien's flesh, Myravelle released a little magic into the thread and drew away his every ache with her needle. This magic was once unbearable, but Myravelle and pain had become close friends. Byzarien shut his eyes as a few pleasured moans slipped past his lips. After she knotted the thread, Myravelle snipped it with her small sewing scissors.

When it was over, Byzarien sat up to study his chest. The scar from Myravelle's rune now had stitches above it.

"How did you do it?" he asked. "From the sleeping soldiers to the king's cavalry—how did you manage to do it when you had been so weak before?"

Myravelle swallowed and stared at her bloody fingers. "They broke something inside of me—something that was always there. I only kept it pushed down for my mother's sake. Between them killing her and attempting to kill you, I lost control. Everything feels...different."

Byzarien studied her features, a frown forming on his. "The fairies will surely be able to help you."

She looked at him, tears flooding her vision. "Thank you for helping me."

Their nearness made her heart tremble and skin grow hot. She reached for his cheek, their lips but a dagger's width apart. Byzarien closed the distance with a kiss and slid his large hands around her waist. The wind rattled against the tent, but Myravelle was warm with desire. Moving to straddle his lap, she traced the scars on his neck, chest, and abdomen with the tip of her finger.

Byzarien broke the kiss and leaned back. "Wait," he said, catching his breath. "I'm sorry."

"What?"

"I don't want this as a *thank you*," he said. "You are not a reward, Myravelle. I love you, and this will be too painful if you don't love me in return."

She bit her lip as her ears and cheeks burned. Sourness coursed through her stomach because she didn't want to say it back—couldn't say it back. To give him her heart would be an added vulnerability the king could use to manipulate her. They had gotten away that night by the sheer force of her anger—but, if they were caught, what could the king make her do for Byzarien? In that moment, she regretted the sweet pea. *Was love a weakness?*

She was silent for too long, and Byzarien gently moved her from his lap and rolled to his side. "Why won't you love me?"

Caressing his shoulder, Myravelle whispered, "I can't."

"Then I *can't* do this."

A sharp pain formed in her throat, and, afraid of bursting into tears in front of Byzarien, she left the tent. The cold breeze swept any heat from her body as she roamed the woods, foraging for mushrooms and bark to give herself purpose.

She knelt, placing her palms to the frosty earth, and wept for her mother. The cryptic woman who had protected her by never telling her about her magic or her father. Though her eyes produced tears, Myravelle realized she had been in an agonizingly slow state of mourning for *years*. The idea of ever seeing her mother again had always been a dream, a wish, a fairy tale.

"Goodbye, Mother." The words were white plumes rising in the darkness.

A thread wrapped around her heart and tugged toward the tent. Myravelle had been alone for far too long, letting the king dictate her life. Her thoughts returned to Byzarien—the man who burned himself into her soul, the man she felt alive with, the man she cared for deeply, the man just as scarred as she.

"What is wrong with me?" she whispered to herself.

For so long, the king had narrated Myravelle's life of heartache. He had denied her a life with Pazcal, separated her from her mother, forced her to do things with soldiers, but never fall in love. She suffered a life of numbness and pain, for what? Maybe love was a strength.

What was a heart for, if not to be stitched to another?

21

Byzarien

The tent flap opened with an icy gust, and Byzarien peeked over his shoulder to discover Myravelle had returned. He quickly pretended to sleep, for the deep ache in his chest hurt worse than his burns ever had. Myravelle shuffled around and, by the sounds, he knew she was right in front of him. He squinted one eye open while she snuggled next to him on the bedroll. Byzarien opened his mouth to protest, but she placed a finger to his lips.

She hushed him, gazing into his eyes. "Did you know that I wished for you? I slipped sweet pea into my cauldron for the ritual to find both a lover and a friend. I never expected it to work—I never expected to find my soulmate."

"Soulmate?"

"Yes. I do love you, Byzarien. I love you despite myself—despite the fact that loving you could consume me entirely. I never want to be apart from you."

Byzarien's pulse quickened as he grinned at her, unable to breathe. When he realized his tongue wouldn't let him speak, he wrapped his hand behind her back, drawing her hips against his, and nodded.

"Do you want me still?"

"Of course, Myravelle," Byzarien said, breathing deeply. "I'm a little nervous, though."

She caressed his cheek. "It will be perfect."

With a sultry grin, Myravelle stood and untied her dress. Keeping eye-contact, she peeled the torn, sparkling fabric away to reveal more of her moonlight skin. When the dress pooled around her knees on the ground, Byzarien's eyes widened to drink in her full breasts, the curves of her waist, her graceful thighs—and the special place between.

Kicking her dress off completely, Myravelle straddled him, which gave Byzarien the perfect view of her beauty. When she leaned down for a kiss, the tightness that had coiled around Byzarien's heart unraveled and he turned to clay in her hands. She pulled her lips away, and desperation shot through every piece of him.

He pressed his fingers against the rune scar on his chest. "Cut me."

"Are you sure?" Myravelle's hand teased him through the fabric of his trousers, making his hips writhe. "I no longer need to harvest magic from you."

"Please."

Myravelle grabbed her dagger, staring into Byzarien's eyes. She rested the blade flat against his throat and licked the scars on his cheek. Instead of cutting him, she dragged the dagger lightly over his skin and flatly raked it down the front of his trousers. Byzarien clenched his teeth, seething heavy breaths, as she trailed the chilling metal back toward his chest.

"I love you," she whispered, the blade hovering above his heart. "I am yours, and you are mine."

Waves of pleasure coursed through Byzarien's body as she slipped the blade into his skin and carved the special rune, letting more magic than ever spill into him. He gripped her thighs to contain his energy as a stream of blood slid down his ribs. When she finished, Myravelle licked it from the blade. Byzarien watched with wide eyes, wanting her tongue on his skin.

She tossed the dagger aside, and her eyes danced over Byzarien's body. "Are you ready for me?"

"Please."

She leaned down and kissed him ever-so-sweetly before moving to his scars. Her tongue traced the peaks and valleys of his burns, bewitching him with tingling delight. Every inch of his body flushed with delirious heat. Her fingers teased rivers of euphoria into his skin until they reached the place where he needed her most. At last, Myravelle untied and removed his pants.

Byzarien tangled his fingers into her dark hair and gasped with bliss while Myravelle satisfied him with her lips. Her silver eyes sparkled in his direction while she performed her magic, and he thought his heart would explode. When Myravelle straddled him again and guided him inside her warmth, Byzarien was completely lost to erotic delight.

She showed him where to touch her, and he was eager to learn. With his thumb, he coaxed the most beautiful sounds in the world from her. His body arched with pleasure when she circled her hips above him. He gazed upon Myravelle like a gilded icon of a goddess he desired to worship again and again and again. He was hers. Truly and completely.

Between the stitches and carvings, blood drenched the room. When Byzarien touched Myravelle's breasts, he left red marks on her flawless skin, but she didn't seem to mind. She leaned forward, which slicked even more blood onto her chest, and kissed him hard.

Her lips brushed against his ear. "I want you on top of me."

He guided her to the bedroll with a kiss.

Myravelle raised her hands above her head, crossed at the wrists. "Hold me down."

He grabbed her wrists, and their two bodies moved like waves in the sea. He kissed and nibbled her neck, and the sounds escaping

Myravelle's lips were a seductive song just for him. The pleasure moved beyond physical as their souls swam together in the sea of Myravelle's magic, until they both collapsed with ecstasy.

Sucking in deep breaths, Byzarien relaxed fully and completely.

Myravelle lifted herself to rest against his blood-smeared chest, and he was sure she could hear his pounding heart.

She turned her head to gaze into his eyes. "You are mine, Byzarien Dumont."

Her words made his heart brim with love. "And you are mine, Myravelle Spinner."

The pair decided to leave before sunrise to place more distance between themselves and the army, but not before Myravelle traced a rune into the soil where their tent had been. "Should the eternal winter ever cease, white roses and sweet pea will grow here," she said.

Byzarien brushed his lips against hers again, for he couldn't seem to get enough of her taste.

They held hands as they walked through the woods. Even when gray light filtered from the cloudy sky, he still needed Myravelle's guidance between thickets and low branches. She walked barefoot and brushed her fingers against trees to find the way. He tripped and snagged his clothes. It didn't help that his mind constantly returned to the night before, time and time again. Myravelle would often catch him staring and give a knowing grin, and he thought his chest would burst from happiness.

"How do you know where we're going?" He pulled her close to share a bit of warmth. "This all looks the same to me."

"With the roots at my feet and the bark at my fingertips, the forest guides me," she said. "The closer we get, the more the fairy magic rattles my bones."

A sharp caw pinged through the air, and they looked up to find

Little Nightmare soaring toward them. Myravelle sobbed in joy and extended her arm, where the crow perched.

Byzarien stroked the bird's shiny feathers. "We missed you, Little Nightmare."

They continued on, and Byzarien studied Myravelle as she walked. He loved how at ease she was in the woods with her pet on her shoulder. She had been through so much heartache recently, he wanted her to be happy. Memories of the night before swarmed yet again. The kisses. The way their bodies moved together. Myravelle declaring her love.

Her brows furrowed. "What's so funny?"

"What do you mean?"

"You're smirking."

Byzarien laughed and leaned toward her ear. "I was thinking about last night...again." They pressed their lips together, but Myravelle broke the kiss and looked around.

"What is it?" he asked, concerned.

Myravelle held her finger up to hush him and whipped her head to the side. "Show yourself."

From behind a wide Dormrya, two archers appeared with their bows drawn. The woman and man were both wearing embroidered tunics with feathers covering their shoulders and braided into their hair. Despite the frost on the ground, they were barefoot just like Myravelle. *Fairies.*

"Who are you?" the woman demanded.

Myravelle's fingers twitched and traced the air. "Lower your weapons."

Byzarien grabbed her hands and shook his head.

"She's a fairy, I think, but he isn't," the man said. "*Eglantyne scum,*" he added under his breath.

Myravelle's cheeks grew scarlet. "What did you call him?"

Byzarien held his hands up in surrender. "We're not your enemy," he told them. "We seek sanctuary."

"Who are you and why do you seek sanctuary?" the woman asked, the wind rustling the feathers in her hair.

"I'm Byzarien Dumont, and she is Myravelle Spinner. We are on the run from King Zylvain," he said. "He exploited Myravelle and her mother for their magic for years. And...we believe the king was behind many of the tragic events in the kingdom which have been blamed on the fairies."

The fairy jerked her chin at Byzarien. "Why are *you* here then, if the king wants her?"

"Fortunately, at the moment, the king believes I'm dead," he said. "But if he finds out I'm alive, I'll certainly be put to death for treason."

The woman leaned over and whispered in the man's ear. He nodded, lowered his weapon, and sprinted into the woods.

"He's on his way to alert Queen Sebira of your presence," the woman gestured with the tip of her arrow and stepped around them. "I'll walk behind you...and I have a lethal aim. So, don't even think about attacking me."

They walked through the forest, following the directions of the archer at their backs, until they reached a path worn from foot-traffic. Byzarien's palm was sweaty, but he dared not let go of Myravelle's hand. Soon, they passed cottages made of earth, logs, and vines. Many were covered with moss and lichens, and some had smoke rising from stone chimneys. Colorful stained glass windows added to the charm. Bells hanging from the rooftops and fence posts chimed around them. Byzarien, bristling with fear at the alarms, inched toward Myravelle.

"It's just the morning bells, *Eglantyne scum*," the archer said with a chuckle.

As if on signal, the fairy men, women, and children exited their homes and gaped at Myravelle and Byzarien as they passed through the village. Like the archers, many wore light-colored tunics covered with beading and feathers. Woven leather belts held tools of their various trades, but everyone clenched a wooden stick in their fists.

When Byzarien got a closer look, he realized the sticks were made of Dormrya wood. He didn't understand their purpose until he noticed a fairy woman in her garden, which was dead and barren from the eternal winter. She waved the stick in the air above the soil. When she dug into the ground with a spade, out came a large sweet potato. Byzarien's stomach grumbled at the sight. He had survived on fish, imported grains, and mushrooms for months.

Though they were stuck in the eternal winter as well, being so close to the Forbidden Mountain just like Eglantyne Kingdom, the fairy realm smelled of sweet florals and fruits that he hadn't enjoyed in a very long time. He was so busy studying the fairies and the homes, he had forgotten to watch Myravelle's reaction. He turned to find her staring straight ahead with a scowl, as if the magical scenery was not only commonplace, but angering.

Byzarien tugged her close. "Are you all right?"

"I'll let you know."

The cottages grew closer and closer together the further they walked and, down the lane was a massive structure built around the base of the largest Dormrya tree Byzarien had ever seen. It was nearly as tall as the Temple of the Gods in Eglantyne City. Circular in shape, the building around the tree consisted of uneven stonework at the base with wattle and daub walls rising toward the steep pitched, mossy roof. Despite the size of this temple or grand hall before him, Byzarien judged the size of the village, estimating a little less than one thousand fairies in total. *Less than one thousand.*

An ache of guilt and shame washed through his veins and churned in his stomach. Though he already believed Myravelle's accusations against the king, now he was struck by how correct she had been. There was no way, even with magic on their side, that the fairies had a large enough army to attack the Eglantyne Kingdom.

The king was behind the attacks.

The king was behind the fires.

The fairy who had gone ahead to give the warning returned, light on his feet and not breathless at all from the journey. "Queen Sebira said to let them rest in a cottage and that she would summon them later."

"Thank you." The archer stepped in front of the pair and lowered her weapon. "Come with me."

They followed the fairy to a moss-covered cottage near the massive central structure. Byzarien had to duck to get through the low and uneven door frame. Inside was a wash basin, a table and chairs, a mirror, and a bed with a patchwork quilt. His shoulders ached from the pack, and he sighed with relief upon setting it down. On the wall hung various decorations of vine wreaths and baskets. Little Nightmare flapped over to perch on the sill of the stained-glass window, where a spiderweb hung in the corner.

Byzarien and Myravelle studied their travel-worn appearances in the mirror framed by wrought-iron with real ivy snaking through the whorls. He needed a shave, for thick and dark stubble covered the left side of his face, making his scars even more prominent. Myravelle still looked beautiful, of course, but her hair was in tangles and her dress was filthy.

"Someone will bring you food and clothing," the fairy said. "You have time to rest and wash up before meeting the queen."

"Thank you," Byzarien said as the archer closed the door.

Myravelle plucked one of the many decorative pillows from the bed and placed it on the windowsill for Little Nightmare. The crow hopped on and snuggled in deep. Myravelle stared at the window, shoulders rounded.

Byzarien strode over and cupped her cheeks. "Now will you tell me how you're feeling?"

"I don't know what to think," she said and gestured around them. "Mother would never talk to me about this place. I half-hoped it didn't exist." She slumped onto the bed, and Byzarien joined to hold her in his arms as they sank into the plush mattress.

"I don't know if my father is here." she continued. "I don't know if I have other family here. I don't even know whether my mother was taken or if she left willingly," Myravelle nuzzled into Byzarien's chest. "Either way, these fairies seem like a quaint, close-knit community. I'm not sure I should trust them. Why didn't they go after her? Why did no one care for her? She was pregnant and alone."

"These are all questions you need to ask the queen." He traced the curve of Myravelle's neck and pressed a delicate kiss upon her lips. "We're here for our safety and for answers."

She nodded while rubbing her hand up and down Byzarien's thigh. "How long do you think we have to rest?"

"I don't know..." Byzarien trailed off when his eyes locked onto the smirk tugging at Myravelle's lips. "What?"

"Want to make love to me on a proper bed?" she asked, quirking an eyebrow.

22

Myravelle

Despite the bed, Myravelle still ended up on the hard floor beneath Byzarien, kissing lazily, enjoying their post-love bliss. She had let her magic run wild, spilling not only into Byzarien, but all around them. She was certain traces of it still clung to their skin and the corners of the small room. The blood made their bodies slide together. Little Nightmare cawed from the windowsill, but they ignored the bird for a few moments, fully entangled in one another.

The door to their cottage swung open, and two fairies carrying folded clothing and trays screamed. Their eyes widened at the blood and the dagger on the floor. Myravelle and Byzarien froze in place. Little Nightmare continued to screech.

"The human attacked her!" the young woman shrieked and dropped the garments on the floor. The second fairy, a young man, set the trays on the table, and they both lunged forward to grab Byzarien, while Myravelle was bewildered by shock.

"This behavior is not accepted here, *Eglantyne scum*," the first fairy said as she tugged Byzarien's arm. "You will be put to death."

"No, no, no! You don't understand," Byzarien blurted. He had turned bright red. "I-I d-didn't!"

Little Nightmare set flight and flapped around the small space, adding to the chaos. Byzarien shoved both fairies to the ground. They both jumped up and drew their wands, pointing them at him.

"Stop." Myravelle finally found her voice and positioned herself before the fairies. The young man turned toward the door to avoid her nakedness. "He did not attack me."

"Miss, please." The young woman grabbed a sheet from the bed and tossed it to Myravelle. "I don't know how things are in the kingdom, but you do not need to protect your attacker."

The glittering ink of darkness swirled in Myravelle's chest and itched toward her fingertips. Runes glowed over the faces of fairies, and she knew she could obliterate them with a mere twirl of her finger. Little Nightmare landed on her shoulder and nuzzled her cheek. She took a cleansing breath and blinked the runes away; she was not there to make enemies.

"Listen well," Myravelle stepped forward and ripped the fairies' arms away from Byzarien, who grabbed a handful of his clothing from the floor to cover himself. "He is my lover, not an attacker."

"But, but," the male fairy said, gesturing to the dagger and the blood.

Myravelle snatched the dagger and placed it against his cheek, making the fairy's smooth brown skin pale a shade. "What if I told you, I am the one who used the blade because he likes it?"

The two fairies scuttled toward the door, noses wrinkled. "The queen expects you at the Hollow when the bells chime at midday," the young woman muttered before she pulled the door open, and the two servants vanished.

Byzarien placed his hand over his chest and took a few deep breaths. "That was intense," he said and reached for Myravelle, who dropped her sheet and embraced him.

"I would never have let them hurt you," she said, rising on her toes to kiss him.

The fear and adrenaline were washed away by the dance of Byzarien's lips and tongue. They pulled away and gazed at one another. She watched the light shining through the stained-glass window sparkle in his dark eyes. Her heart cracked at the mere threat of harm coming to Byzarien. She finally had him—someone to pour her love into, someone to share a life with. She needed him.

"I hate that they think I attacked you," he said, crimson flaring up his neck and cheeks. He drew her closer and nuzzled her neck. "I would never."

"That was amazing before they interrupted."

"What if I make it up to you later?"

"I'd enjoy that very much." She kissed him again, raking her nails over his chest as if she could climb right into him.

With a pitcher of rosewater, they washed the blood and dirt from their skin. Byzarien shaved while Myravelle combed out her long hair. They dressed in the clean clothes the fairies had provided, but Myravelle scowled when she caught her reflection in the mirror. The white gown sparkled with snow-like crystal beads, and the heart-shaped bodice was covered with soft, white feathers. Her dark hair and brows were shocking compared to the pure-white gown. She turned to Byzarien, who gaped at her with wide eyes.

"What do you think?" she asked and twirled around.

"You," he said, grinning, "look lovely...but it isn't your style, is it?"

Myravelle shook her head and rummaged through the pack for her small sewing kit. Byzarien fed Little Nightmare some bread as he watched her work. Following the shape of a golden rune, she embroidered a midnight-black circle around a curving stitched line, which led to a star.

When she stepped before the mirror again, the thread bled blooms of darkness that licked upwards with inky tendrils. The dye reached the feathered bodice, and a burst of sparkles spilled down the skirts like the night sky of years gone by. Satisfied, she turned to Byzarien. "Do you like it?"

"Very much." He took her hand and spun her around. "You are otherworldly."

Myravelle's fingers twitched with the same stitches and star rune, stirring a metamorphosis of Byzarien's white tunic until it matched her starry sky ensemble. "We could be king and queen of the night," she whispered with a playful smile.

Byzarien guided her to the table and pulled out a chair for her. They removed the lids of the trays, expecting a grand feast, only to find tiny cakes of various colors and shapes.

"Is this what fairies eat?" Byzarien asked.

Myravelle shrugged. She lifted a green one decorated with turquoise piping and sugar pearls and nibbled it, while Byzarien did the same with his. The sweetness melted in her mouth, sending a saccharine chill through her teeth.

"Mmm," Byzarien said and popped the entire cube into his mouth. "This is delicious."

Myravelle took one more bite of the cake before her stomach twisted and she gulped down some water. She wasn't sure whether the food was too sweet or she was simply nervous about meeting the queen. Her bones vibrated, and her veins buzzed beneath her skin. *What answers could the fairy queen provide? Could I learn about my father? Could I learn about the magic runes? Could I finally have a home? Would Byzarien be allowed to stay? Would he want to return to his family in Eglantyne Kingdom?*

Even though she hadn't met the queen, Myravelle already didn't trust her. She allowed one of her own to be trapped in a tower for over two decades. It was all too much, and it made her head spin.

"Are you not hungry?" Byzarien asked, pulling her from her thoughts. He had already finished his entire plate while she still hadn't touched any more of her cakes.

"They aren't all sickeningly sweet," he said, pointing at the variations. "This one is savory, this one spicy, and, yes, these two are sweet."

Bile churned in her stomach, and she pushed her dish toward him. "You take mine. I'm too nervous about meeting the queen."

Before eating, he caressed her hand. "It will be fine."

She nodded and opened her mouth to reply, but Little Nightmare's caw cut her off as the bird hopped over toward their feet.

From the plate, Byzarien plucked the sunshine-yellow confection with flower petals and a dollop of meringue on top and placed it on the ground. Little Nightmare pecked at it until it was gone, aside from the meringue stuck on his beak.

Myravelle laughed and wiped it off with a cloth napkin.

The bells chimed from outside, their tinny melody scraping Myravelle's ears.

Byzarien stood and extended his hand. "Ready, my love?"

The pair left the cottage hand-in-hand and, again, all eyes were on them as they headed to the Hollow. Though it was made of sticks, vines, and moss, the building around the tree was utterly charming, and Myravelle could feel in her bones that it was a sacred space. Two fairies in feathery white uniforms stood at the doors to the Hollow with large Dormrya staffs rather than the smaller wands others carried.

As the pair approached, the guards opened the double doors. Inside, light filtered through gaps in the roof, creating a watery effect through the wide hallway leading into the base of the tree. It was dim and cool like a cave and a chill climbed Myravelle's arms. There were no signs of people aside from the music echoing from the actual hollow of the Dormrya tree. The massive tree opened for them, and their every step pressed into ground bumpy with roots older than the gods.

They passed a few storerooms of supplies built into the vaulted spaces of the ancient tree. Most held bags of grains or jars of preserves, but one had heaps of gold thread. With a sharp inhalation, Myravelle's chest filled with a tingling lightness. Byzarien looked down at her with a question pulling at his brows, possibly the same question she had: *Are there other spinners here?* She bit her lip against the grin creeping across her face.

When they reached the largest room in the Hollow, guards opened the double doors thick with ancient bark, and the music stopped. Myravelle gripped Byzarien's arm, her heart thrumming like a hummingbird. Out of the room strode a woman with hair whiter than snow and braided with feathers, whose milky-white eyes focused on nothing. Candles ignited in the niches, sparkling against her shimmery gown as she glided to stand before them in silence. She reached up with bone-pale fingers to adjust the silver circlet on her head.

Myravelle and Byzarien knelt before the queen. The woman circled them with delicate steps and only a whisper of rustling from her feathered gown. When she stood before them once more, she stopped and folded her hands together. "Rise," she said in a soft, velvety voice.

They did.

"My faithful servants informed me that you seek sanctuary."

"That is correct, Queen Sebira," Myravelle answered.

The queen tilted her head, the crease in her brow cracking her porcelain features for a mere second before returning to her soft, serene visage. Myravelle's bones rattled as she felt the full breadth of the queen's magic.

"I shall begin with an apology for my servants," Queen Sebira said. "Although, in their defense, they would have never suspected such *behavior*."

"Behavior?" Myravelle's face twisted, hot defensiveness creeping into her chest. "We are two adults. Your servants could simply learn to knock."

"Ah, well," Queen Sebira began with a whispery chuckle, "it seems my servants have much to learn about *human* culture. You see, we fairies have very specific mating rituals at certain times of the year. It is only human to desire sex as...*recreation*. My servants would never have expected to open the door and discover what they saw."

An odd prickling sensation swept over the back of Myravelle's mind at the queen's words, though she wasn't sure why. She should have felt angry or embarrassed, but she felt neither.

"They will be much more careful now," Queen Sebira said. "I guarantee your safety during your stay. Come and let us discuss matters in a more comfortable setting."

They followed her deeper into the dark Hollow. Myravelle led Byzarien by the arm, guiding him around every slope of uneven ground and rising tree root. Further inside, the soft glow of candlelight flickered but could not reach the vast expanse of shadows overhead. They turned into a wide room where fairies sat on the ground or on boulders. Moss covered the floor and even crept onto the dais at the back of the room.

When the fairies took notice of Queen Sebira, everyone rose. Myravelle studied their bright and ornate gowns and tunics, many glimmering in the candlelight from the antler chandeliers above. The queen waved her hands, and the fairies returned to their seats. In the corner, a quartet wearing silver-beaded outfits began playing soft music.

The queen gestured to a boulder, and Myravelle and Byzarien sat. Three young women walked over and stood beside Queen Sebira, who reclined in the silver throne on the mossy dais.

"These are my daughters," she said. "The Three Good Fairies: Fleur, Faune, and Sola."

Fleur wore her red curls pinned up, and her blush-colored gown seemed to be made with real flowers. Next to her was Faune, whose blonde hair cascaded over her fur shrug. Her green gown rattled with intricate patterns of decorative wooden beads. The shortest was Sola, whose brunette braids trailed down to her blue gown stitched with golden suns. They each nodded to Myravelle and Byzarien before retreating to seats behind their mother.

"Now, tell me who you are and what you *really* want."

Myravelle looked to Byzarien, who patted her hand. "I am Byzarien Dumont, a soldier—well, *former* soldier, in King Zylvain's army," he said. "The king believes me to be dead, and I seek sanctuary here with Myravelle."

"Welcome, Byzarien Dumont," the fairies around the room said in unison, their voices echoing up into the massive tree.

The queen shifted her pearly eyes to Myravelle, who swallowed before saying, "I am Myravelle Spinner, a former healer in the king's army. I also seek sanctuary from the king, who has exploited my and my mother's magic for years and wishes now to imprison me."

"Welcome, Myravelle Spinner," the fairies said.

The queen rose from her throne and took two steps forward. "Your mother?"

"Yes. Her name was Xylina Spinner."

The music paused, the chatter about the room fell dead silent, and Myravelle was sure she could hear the ancient tree growing.

The queen took a deep breath as if trying to mimic a gasp. "What happened to Xylina?"

"She was *executed*," Myravelle said, voice cracking. "In an attempt to protect me, my mother was often cryptic about her past. I wish to find out how she ended up at the Eglantyne Castle in the first place. Did you know her?"

The queen tucked her chin to her chest for a long moment. "Yes."

"You did? How did she end up in the king's custody?" she asked. "Why didn't anyone try to rescue her? Does my father live here?"

The more questions that poured out, the more Myravelle trembled against the growing darkness inside. It reared its serpentine head, wishing to lash out at the queen—the queen who hadn't rescued her mother. Byzarien wrapped his arm around her to hold her steady.

"You do not know who your father is?" Queen Sebira asked.

"No. She was pregnant, and no one came after her," she growled as golden runes nearly filled her eyesight, no matter how much she tried to blink them away.

"Hmm." The queen tilted her head. "What is your gift, Myravelle?"

"What do you mean?" she asked, voice lowering with impatience.

"We all have a special *gift*, each fairy does," Queen Sebira said, gesturing to her daughters. "Fleur works with plants, Faune with animals, Sola with temperature, and I can see different paths to the future. Being of royal blood, my daughters and I have extra *touches*, but every other fairy you meet has one rune they can master. So, what is your gift?"

"Well, I was a healer. Although I could heal normal injuries, the king used me to wake those under Filoux's curse," Myravelle said and thought for a moment. "But I don't know, I can also spin gold like my mother and...before we arrived here, my magic exploded and nearly killed the king's entire cavalry."

The queen's mouth gaped ever so slightly, and her shoulders jerked as if a chill had swept through the Hollow. Whispers rose from the other fairies, and Myravelle's brows furrowed. *Were fairies really only supposed to master one type of magic rune? How did it work? Why are my powers so explosive when I'm angry?*

Hushing the crowd, the queen stepped forward and reached out. "Take my hands, sweet Myravelle."

"Why?" she asked.

"I must see your path," she began, tilting her head, "your *fate*."

When Myravelle rested her hands, which had dark fingernails and rings on nearly every finger, into the queen's clean and cold ones, a spark jolted her. She caught a flash of a young Sebira: her eyes seeing and blue while she gifted young Xylina a drop spindle.

A shudder pulsed through Queen Sebira's paper-thin body. She ripped her hands from Myravelle's and stumbled back. Her daughters rushed to help her sit upon the throne.

"What was that?" Myravelle asked. "What did I just see?"

"Please, take a seat," the queen said, lowering her head again.

Myravelle looked around, staring at all the fairies who had never cared about her mother—never cared that she'd gone missing.

Byzarien took her hand and rubbed calming circles into her palm as they sat on a boulder.

Queen Sebira took a deep breath and tightened her features. "I will tell you all you wish to know if you agree to two things."

Myravelle narrowed her eyes at the queen. "And those are?"

"Attend a celebration tomorrow, in honor of your homecoming," she said with a smile, "and take lessons from me and my daughters."

"Lessons?" Myravelle tilted her head. "Why?"

"Your magic is...*tempestuous*," she said. "We must set it right and find your true gift."

A bubble of pain rose in her throat. An insult to Myravelle's magic was an insult to her. She didn't want to trust the judgmental fairies...but deep, deep down, all she wanted was to belong. "If I do these things, you will tell me how my mother ended up a prisoner of the king and why no one attempted to rescue her?"

The queen gave a single, slow nod. "Yes, darling."

Myravelle turned and met Byzarien's eyes.

He squeezed her hand and leaned to whisper in her ear. "I'm with you, whatever you decide."

Her gaze returned to the queen. "I need your word that Byzarien will be safe here."

"Of course," the queen said.

"How long may we stay?"

Sebira's lips stretched into a thin smile. "Oh darling, as long as you like," she said, gesturing all around. "This is your home, now."

Home. Myravelle twirled her rings and stared at the floor in thought. She wanted a home. She wanted to learn. She wanted this, right?

"Do we have a deal?" the queen prodded.

"We do."

"Argus," the queen called, and a fairy with short wavy hair and a glittery tunic stepped forward and knelt before the dais. "Escort my new guests back to their cottage for some rest."

"Yes, my queen." He stood and gestured to them. "Come with me."

Following Argus, Myravelle left the Hollow with Byzarien at her side and thought back to the odd vision she'd had when she'd touched the queen's hands. Her magic danced with delight, for it somehow knew that, should the queen break their bargain, Myravelle could *take* the information she needed.

The only thing keeping the wild magic tame was her love for Byzarien and desire to keep him safe. She trailed her finger along the scars on his cheek and smiled as they walked.

23

Byzarien

In a whirl of fabric, ribbons, scissors, and thread, the queen's daughters swept into the cottage to dress the newcomers for the ball. Though Byzarien anxiously brushed hair over his scars at the idea of them being the center of attention, he reassured himself knowing at least Myravelle would be by his side. He bit his lip when he thought about dancing with her.

While the three fairies fussed over his ensemble, he caught her smirking from her chair where she played with Little Nightmare. Byzarien exaggerated a scowl, only making her smile crack further. Myravelle had not slept well during the night, so he was glad to see her happy.

A needle pricked his back, making him jump.

"Sorry!" Sola squeaked.

"Enough," Fleur, the eldest, said. "More flowers!"

With a special flourish of her Dormrya wand, petals rippled their way from Byzarien's shoulder to the back of his hip. He sighed, for the blue tunic looked more like a wedding cake than proper clothing.

In the mirror's reflection, he glared at Myravelle whose shoulders shook while she covered her mouth.

"Hmm." The quite petite Fleur stared up at Byzarien's chest, then aimed her wand and said, "More!"

Faune shook her head, making the wooden beads in her braids clink. "No, no, no! We must add feathers and furs to make it right!" The middle sister then added large feather plumes to Byzarien's shoulders, making them appear even broader. Around the wrists and hemline, she added fur.

Fleur scoffed as she circled Byzarien. "That looks ridiculous."

"That's because there are too many flowers!"

As they bickered over flowers and furs, Sola hid behind the mirror and gave her wand a flick. Starbursts of glittering embroidery cascaded all over the fabric, which only added to the overall gaudiness.

Byzarien narrowed his eyes at Myravelle, who covered her red face with her hands. He recalled how proud Queen Sebira was that her daughters had multiple fairy *gifts*. He wasn't so sure that fashion was among them.

Fleur and Faune had hardly noticed Sola's addition to the outfit when Fleur held up her hands and said, "I have an idea! Perhaps we'll be inspired by Myravelle's gown, then we can fix Byzarien's to match."

A slow grin crept across Byzarien's face and he turned toward Myravelle, whose silver eyes dimmed as she stared at the sisters. He walked to her and leaned close. "Your turn, my love," he whispered. "No matter what they do to you, I'll still think you're beautiful."

As he laughed, Myravelle pinched his sides. Before she could stand of her own volition, the sisters grabbed her by the arms and tugged her toward the mirror. Byzarien sat and placed Little Nightmare on his lap, so they could both enjoy the show. Without rhyme or reason, the sisters cut various fabrics and draped them about Myravelle's thin frame. Sola wrapped bright blue velvet around her straight from the bolt, trapping Myravelle's arms.

"Why are you helping us prepare for the ball and not the servants?" Myravelle asked, her voice rising high when Sola tugged the velvet tight.

"Mother wants you to look your very best tonight," Fleur answered, "and we wanted to get to know you."

Byzarien tilted his head and wondered if she was telling the truth. It seemed more likely that the queen didn't trust Myravelle and wanted her daughters to keep a close eye on her. Myravelle had been rattled after her meeting with the queen and mentioned the vision she had upon touching her hands. Sebira had clearly been friends with her mother, but never tried to rescue her. It had been enough to water the seed of untrustworthiness already planted in Myravelle's mind.

"She needs a place for her arms." Faune cut holes in the velvet, helping Myravelle poke her arms out. She stitched scraps of mismatched cloth around them and tapped them with her wand, producing feathers at her shoulders to match Byzarien's. "Yes, that's it."

Fleur shook her head and added ribbons and flowers to Myravelle's waist and skirts. Sola kept adding sparkles and embroidery every chance she could. It was as if they were competing over who could add the most embellishments. Myravelle had her own unique style, and Byzarien was sure she would hate the *thing* the sisters draped her in.

"There," Faune said, spinning Myravelle toward the mirror. "Perfect."

Horror flashed over Myravelle's strained face as she gazed at the monstrosity. Byzarien brought his fist to his mouth and coughed to hide his laughter. He couldn't believe the once serene and otherworldly healer had been reduced to a gaudy fairy cake.

"Don't you just love it?" Sola said, sneaking another pop of sparkling embroidery down the skirts.

"I'm...speechless," Myravelle said in a low flat voice.

"What did you wear to your first ball?" Fleur asked, fluffing the fabric.

"*This*, apparently."

"What?" all three asked in unison, their heads whipping toward her.

"I grew up locked in a tower," she said. "My only friends were spiders, spindles, and stone walls. I've never been to a ball before."

The sisters' faces paled as they stared at Myravelle as if she were some pitiful creature who'd clawed its way up from the Darkened Path. Byzarien's heart broke for her, but he was proud to be her date for their first ball.

"Well, that's *unfortunate*," Fleur said in a high-pitched voice. "Have we decided on a color?"

"I say blue," Sola said, touching the dress with her wand and creating a shade to match Byzarien's outfit. "Won't they look perfect?" Although they looked *perfectly* absurd, Byzarien didn't mind the idea of matching her. Everyone would know they were a couple, even if he was itchy and sweaty.

"No, no, no," Fleur said. "Her skin is so fair, the blue washes her out! She needs something brighter to bring out her cheeks." With a flick of her wand, Myravelle's dress bloomed into a bright shade of pink. Not a dusty rose nor a pale blush—but *pink*. Byzarien's jaw dropped at the gaudy color.

"Blue!" Sola said again, turning the dress a bright turquoise this time. "This shade looks beautiful with her skin!"

"I don't know," Faune said, pressing her wand to the corner of her mouth as she shook her head. "Maybe we should try green."

"Don't be ridiculous!" Fleur stuck out her tongue and pushed her sister back while waving her wand. "Pink."

This time, as if the dress could no longer choose a color, it bloomed with patches of pink across the blue fabric, turning purple in many areas. Myravelle grimaced.

"Oooh, let me try," Sola said, raising her wand.

"No," Myravelle said in a smoky voice and held up her hand, stopping Sola.

The sisters stared at Myravelle with wide eyes, and even Byzarien's skin buzzed, unsure of what she was about to do. She plucked a needle and black thread from Fleur's sewing kit and sat in the chair across from him, her voluminous gown puffing up all around. Needle and thread in hand, she embroidered the small circle with stitches and a star onto the fabric, as she had the day before. He grinned, eager to see what she would create. Taking the needle, Myravelle pricked her fingertip, and the fairies gasped. She let a drop of blood hit the star.

"Oh, no!" Fleur cried in horror.

Myravelle stood and walked to the mirror, twitching and twirling her finger in the air. Blackness bled from the stitched rune, devouring the flowers, feathers, and embroidery with fire and smoke until the entire dress was dark as midnight. The drop of blood sparkled and spilled scarlet rubies down the skirt. Myravelle swirled her finger over her chest, creating an onyx and ruby necklace, which dripped down toward her cleavage, over her shoulders, and across her exposed back like a spider's web.

"I-I didn't know you had the gift for *fashion* too," Fleur said as she and her sisters slowly stepped toward the door. "How curious."

"I think it's pretty," Sola said.

Fleur snapped toward her with a scowl on her face.

"Your mother talked of these *gifts* as if they are some limited resource," Myravelle said. "How many gifts can one fairy have? How many runes are possible to master?"

"Usually, a fairy is only capable of mastering one," Faune said. "We have each mastered more only because our mother is queen."

Myravelle looked down and lifted her fingers as if counting. Byzarien counted in his head, knowing she could heal, spin gold, change fabrics...and take down armies. It seemed like she could do anything she tried and was not limited to a single rune or enchantment.

"I don't know what they mean," Myravelle said. "My mother would never teach me about the runes, but...there's a stirring inside of magic and the runes glow when I need them."

The sisters looked at one another and shrugged. Sola and Faune inched behind their eldest sister. "We'll begin your proper training tomorrow," Fleur said, folding her hands together. "For now, let us enjoy the celebration."

Myravelle nodded, though her brow remained furrowed as if she was deep in thought. Her bottom lip trembled.

"See you at the Hollow!" Sola said before the fairies left the hut, murmuring to one another.

Stepping forward, Byzarien took her hands in his. "What is it?"

"I thought coming here would be exactly what I needed," she said, tears sparkling in her eyes. "But I'm not like them. Did you see their faces? They're afraid of me."

Byzarien swallowed the lump in his throat, for he knew exactly how she felt. Being half-covered with scars always gave people a reason to pity him or, worse, fear him. He wrapped her in a hug. "They grew up in the Sleepy Wood surrounded by other fairies. Your life was unfairly different from theirs. Yes, they fear your magic, but they want to train you. Let's enjoy the evening together, and you'll have your answers soon."

She nodded. "Thank you."

They turned to the mirror, and Little Nightmare cawed. Myravelle giggled at Byzarien's ridiculous outfit.

He tickled her side when she kept laughing. "I look like a giant bird."

After she twitched her finger in the air, Myravelle lifted her skirt to touch Byzarien's tunic. From the fabric of her dress, an ink-like darkness spilled into his outfit and bled all the way around. The flowers, feathers, and sparkles disappeared in its wake. She pinched her fingertip, creating another droplet of blood, and traced a rune on Byzarien's chest, making rubies trickle into a swirling pattern on the tunic.

Myravelle admired their reflections as Byzarien pushed her midnight hair behind her shoulder and kissed the bare skin between strands of beads. With her eyelids fluttering, she hummed a moan. His heart raced from the sound, only encouraging him to kiss more of her exposed skin.

Bells chimed outside, signaling that it was time for the ball.

"I wish we could stay in tonight," Byzarien whispered, losing himself in Myravelle's silvery gaze. "I've never been to a ball—I don't even know how to dance, but I certainly want to dance with you."

"We shall learn how to dance together then," she said, extending a hand.

Byzarien laced their fingers together, and they stepped out into the night, headed to the Hollow. Fairies gathered along the path, either holding candles or twirling their wands in the air. Confusion swirled in Byzarien until they passed through a warm and toasty patch of air. Some of the fairies must have had the same gift as Sola.

They followed groups of fairies to the Hollow, and Byzarien and Myravelle were the only ones in black. Fleur, Faune, and Sola had been correct with their gaudy ideas of fashion, for all of the fairies wore bright ballgowns and dress tunics decorated with flashy beading, embroidery, feathers, and furs.

In the Hollow, candles and twinkle lights sparkled high into the tree. They followed the procession into a large opening. The ballroom was circular with boulders along the edges of the room, leaving an empty floor at the center for dancing. Vines and flowers hung from the ceiling, brushing their shoulders with sweet scents as they walked. The orchestra played their melodic and enchanting music low while servants offered beverages and hors d'oeuvres. All the guests sipped drinks and chatted around the edges of the wide space. Byzarien itched to dance with Myravelle, but it seemed it wasn't yet time.

The queen sat on boulders at the back of the room with her daughters. When the sisters spotted the pair, they flinched. The oldest, Fleur, immediately whispered into her mother's ear. Myravelle tightened her hold on Byzarien's hand as the queen rose. The entire room fell silent as Queen Sebira glided to the center of the room.

The queen wore a voluminous white gown that twinkled in the candlelight, as did the iridescent makeup on her cheeks. Her white hair was in an updo held in place with sparkling feathers.

"Welcome, everyone," she said, her soft voice somehow reaching the far spaces of the Hollow. "We gather tonight to celebrate the homecoming of Myravelle Spinner."

The crowd applauded and turned to study their odd clothing while the queen paused. If Byzarien's skin crawled from their exploring gazes, he couldn't imagine how Myravelle felt. Instead of covering his scars, he rubbed circles down her back.

"Unfortunately, she did not grow up here with us," the queen said. "We owe it to Myravelle to make her feel welcome and comfortable in her new home."

The word *home* echoed in Byzarien's mind. *Would Myravelle want to stay? What would that mean for him?* He glanced to see if she was smiling, but she scowled at the queen instead.

"Now," Sebira began, raising her hands, "let the celebration begin."

The crowd cheered and the orchestra began playing at full volume. The queen glided toward her daughters and spoke to them once more. Each sister kept glancing their way and nodding. Myravelle's breaths grew short and quick, and Byzarien wished he could take her every concern away.

He stepped in front of her and extended his hand. "May I have this dance, my lady?"

Her silver eyes glowed as they locked onto his, and her entire face relaxed. "Yes," she said, taking his hand.

They weren't the only couple to step out onto the dance floor: fairy couples wearing all styles of matching clothes twirled around them.

He held her close and whispered in her ear, "You are the most beautiful creature in this room."

"I couldn't have done this without you." She planted a lingering kiss on his cheek, making his desire flare. "My distrust of the fairies makes my magic flare. I'm so glad you're here to keep me grounded."

"I'm here for you," he said. "Always."

Although they didn't waltz with ease about the floor like the fairies, he enjoyed swaying with her. Their bodies fit together with precision, and their souls twisted into each other. Myravelle's eyes reflected the twinkling lights and, mixed with the delicate spray of freckles across her cheeks and nose, it was as if she was his own starry sky.

"My girl of stars," he said, leaning down to brush his lips against her freckles.

Although everything was so uncertain, and they were still in danger, he knew one thing was right: her—the woman who'd enchanted his soul and spun herself into his heart. He imagined introducing Myravelle to his family, even though he had no idea how long it would be before they could return to the kingdom, and the hope lightened his steps as they danced.

Someone tapped his shoulder, tugging Byzarien from his daydreams. It was a short fairy with red curls piled on top of her head and green leaves adorning her dress. Her overall appearance was that of a tomato plant.

"May I cut in?" she asked in a squeaky voice.

Byzarien tightened his grip on Myravelle. He looked around the room and, as the music changed, so did many of the partners. A tall fairy with a midnight-blue tunic embroidered with stars and gems tapped Myravelle's shoulder and asked her the same thing. She stiffened and glanced at Byzarien with the same apprehension he had.

"It's customary to dance with others," the man said in a smooth voice, hand still stretched toward Myravelle.

She turned to Byzarien, swallowed, and said, "I suppose we should follow customs. Will you meet me here in an hour?"

He nodded and kissed her cheek before taking the tomato fairy's hand. She kept trying to press her body close, but Byzarien held her at arm's length. He twirled her around to get a view of Myravelle, whose partner held her tight to his body with his hand dangerously low on her back. Heat built in his chest.

"Byzarien, is it?" the tomato fairy asked, tilting her head. "I'm Iva."

"Hello, Ivy," he said, standing on his toes to find Myravelle, who had been whisked off into the crowd.

"It's *Iva*," the fairy said, touching his cheek to turn his face back to her. "And your partner will be fine."

Byzarien lowered his gaze and swayed on his feet a little in an attempt to dance.

Iva pointed to a fairy wearing a green tunic covered with the same leaves as those on her gown. The man danced with a woman in a billowing lilac gown of flowers and silk ribbons. "My partner is over there. We dance with everyone. It's not romantic...it builds community."

Community. That sounded nice, and Byzarien did want to help Myravelle fit in. "Um...so, Iva." He relaxed a little, thinking of something to ask. "What is your *gift*?"

"Plants, of course," she said and then frowned. "The eternal winter has made it more difficult, but my partner and I do help out at the greenhouse to feed our neighbors."

"Oh! Myravelle is good with plants and medicinal herbs too," he said, thinking about the endless gifts she possessed.

One of Iva's red brows shot up. "I heard she was a *healer*. She has more than one gift, like the Three Good Fairies? How is that possible? Is she royalty as well?"

Before Byzarien could answer, the music changed, and another fairy was at his side. He said goodbye to Iva and began dancing with a fairy in a blindingly yellow dress with flames embroidered on the hem. She swept her blonde braid, adorned with orange gems, over a tan shoulder.

"I'm Flavia." The flame fairy pressed her body close to his and looked up with a grin. "How are you enjoying the ball, Byzarien?"

"Fine," he said, creating distance between them and glancing around to look for Myravelle.

"You seem tense," Flavia trailed her fingers across Byzarien's arm, to the bare skin where his tunic exposed his chest. "Want to go to my cottage to *relax*?"

He froze. "No, thank you. I thought you fairies, um..."

"Only mated at certain times of the year?" Flavia finished for him.

He nodded.

"It's true, but I'm interested in learning what being with a *human* is like," she said, nearly choking on the word.

Byzarien studied her strained features, nearly hidden by her obnoxious outfit and makeup. "Is someone making you do this?"

Flavia's smirk fell, and her yellow eyes darted about the room as her breaths grew quick and shallow. "We were supposed to seduce you. Maybe Ignatius succeeded—I don't see him or Myravelle."

"What?" Byzarien tried to release her, but her grip tightened.

"Now, don't act jealous—"

"*Jealous?*" He scowled at her. "No! I'm worried someone will harm her. Who put you up to this?"

Flavia darted away from him. He searched the crowd, which was an array of bright colors and shiny embellishments. The fairies were beautiful, true, but they paled in comparison to Myravelle. Her enchanting presence and deep shadows had caught him like a willing insect in a beautiful web. Not seeing her black dress anywhere, he jogged around the edge of the room where fairies reclined on the moss-covered boulders and sipped bubbling beverages.

In a darkened corner, a fiery fairy who matched Flavia pressed Myravelle against the wall. Byzarien's pace quickened as he hurried toward them, only to skid to a halt when Myravelle slapped the man.

He held his cheek and shouted in her face. "You're not even a fairy!"

She tilted her head and twitched her finger in the air. Byzarien took a deep breath, unsure what she was about to do. The man stopped shouting, holding his throat as his eyes bulged. Myravelle stood still, eyes aglow with a look of pleasure on her face. The man fell to his knees, gurgles escaped his gaping mouth.

Byzarien rushed forward and touched her shoulder. "What happened?"

Her eyes dimmed, her hand dropped. The fairy fell to the floor, gasping for air. She growled at him through clenched teeth, "Touch me again, and you die."

Byzarien took her hand and guided her out of the Hollow, rushing into the crisp night air. "Are you all right?"

"He tried to kiss me," she said, smokiness scratching her voice. "So much for feeling welcome here in *fairyland*."

"This was all a plan," he said as they wandered into the woods, the breeze rustling the snowy branches. "A fairy named Flavia tried to take me to her cottage. She said they were told to seduce us."

"Why?"

"I don't know, she ran off before I could get any more answers."

Myravelle bit her bottom lip. "You weren't tempted, were you?"

"Nothing could pry my heart away from you." He pulled her into an embrace before searching her eyes. "Are you sure you're all right? Did he hurt you?"

"My magic wanted to kill him—kill *all* of them." She squeezed his hand. "If not for you, I would have let it. And what did he mean I'm not a fairy?"

"It's not true." He wrapped an arm around her. "Let's keep walking. The woods always bring you comfort."

She nodded and kissed his cheek.

They walked along a creek bubbling over rocks, playing its own delicate music in the night. "This is much better than the ball," Byzarien thought aloud.

Myravelle frowned. "I can't figure out why they would try to separate and seduce us. It makes no sense."

"I don't know." As Byzarien rubbed Myravelle's back, he felt her rigid muscles through the fabric of her gown. In the distance, water rushed and splashed louder than the creek tumbling over the rocks. "Do you hear that?" he asked.

She still trembled, so he guided her toward the sound. The slope of the frost-hardened earth rose steadily as they followed the icy brook. Byzarien gripped Myravelle's hand to help her climb crumbling boulders as the terrain grew even steeper. They ducked below pine branches, sagging with snow, and discovered the source of the water's song. Spilling from the crest of a towering bluff, a waterfall splashed onto the rocks below forming a round pool. Byzarien turned to watch Myravelle's sparkling eyes as they reflected the rushing water. He smiled and gave her hand a slight tug, and they kept walking toward it.

"This must be a sacred space," she said, gesturing to the piles of offerings around the basin: rocks, wood carvings, and other trinkets were left stacked with care along the bank.

They listened to the waterfall's enchanting melody for a few moments before Byzarien noticed a tiny cave behind it. Helping Myravelle over slippery stones, they made it behind the curtain of water. Inside was cool and damp, so he wrapped his arms around her.

"I thought being here would feel different," Myravelle said, resting her head on his chest as they swayed, her voice echoing against the rocks of the hollow space.

"You are supposed to start your lessons tomorrow. Regardless of the fairies' intentions, perhaps you can still learn from them. You'll be safe—not only can you handle any man who comes near you, but I will keep you safe."

She smiled, burrowing into his chest. Alone behind the roar of the waterfall, Byzarien felt as if nothing existed but Myravelle and he.

"I just don't understand why," she sighed. "Why the secrecy? Why is the queen withholding answers about my life? Why did the fairies try to separate us tonight?"

The phrase *Eglantyne scum* echoed in Byzarien's ears.

"Maybe it's because I'm human," he said, heart cracking a little. "Maybe the queen doesn't *approve* of me."

"She promised you were safe here," she said. "But if that changes, I will protect you."

They danced to the waterfall's music, but Myravelle's brows were still stitched tightly together. Byzarien touched her chin, tilting her gaze to meet his.

"I just want to belong." She sighed and snuggled deeper against his chest.

He stroked her hair and wished he knew what to say to make her feel better. "You belong with me."

She looked up at him with a smirk tugging her lips as she drew the dagger from the folds of her dress. Confused, Byzarien squinted and followed her out of the waterfall and watched her scour the edges of the little pool and creek. She waded into the water, soaking her dress, and selected a dark, smooth stone. Sitting on the bank, she carved into the rock with her dagger.

Byzarien knelt next to her. "What are you doing?"

"Leaving our own offering."

When her work was complete, she handed it to him. She had etched a sword crossed with a sprig of sweet pea onto the stone.

Byzarien smiled and placed it on the edge of the water with the others before kissing her cheek. "I love it."

24

Myravelle

Myravelle awoke to morning bells and Little Nightmare's caws, while Byzarien stirred next to her in bed. She snuggled against his warm chest and sleepily massaged his arm, thinking about the night before. After an abrupt knock on the door, though, they both shuffled from bed and got dressed. Myravelle opened the door to find one of the queen's servants.

"Queen Sebira requests your presence in the Hollow at once."

"This early?" she asked, stretching her arms.

"I'm just the messenger," he said. "The queen is waiting."

"Thank you," she said, closing the door.

Byzarien fed Little Nightmare more of the fairy cakes, for the picky bird no longer tolerated plain seeds, then stood to embrace Myravelle.

She grinned at the delightful pressure of his arms. "Shall we see what the queen wants so early?"

He kissed the top of her head. "Must be important."

When they set out to the Hollow, the village was silent even though the morning bells rang loud and clear. The fairies had danced into the wee hours of the morning and were probably catching up on sleep—just as Myravelle had wanted to.

Their footsteps echoed in the Hollow as they made their way to the throne room. Passing the storerooms, the one containing gilded thread yet again caught Myravelle's eyes. She wanted to ask the queen who had spun the gold, as it would be delightful to meet a fairy with the same gift as her mother. Their guide stopped outside the throne room's double doors, uneven to fit the natural whorls of the tree and adorned with carved stars. He knocked on the wood and waited.

Two guards opened the doors, and the servant gestured for them to follow him inside, where the queen sat upon her throne. The Three Good Fairies stood behind her on the mossy dais. Fleur wore a gown of blush-colored petals with large green leaves curling from the hem and neckline. Faune was in all tans and furs while Sola wore a blue dress with fluffy cotton clouds and glittering suns. The sisters all glared at Myravelle's ensemble: a black dress glistening with spider webs she had created that morning. They could hardly contain their disgust, so Myravelle focused on the queen. She appeared fresh and rested for such an early hour. This time, the skirts of her gown glistened with dewdrops and the bodice was covered with white moth wings.

"Good morning," Sebira said.

Myravelle and Byzarien knelt before her. "Good morning, Queen Sebira."

The queen's white eyes stared at nothing in particular, but a tingle crept through Myravelle's bones. She knew the queen was trying to read her. Myravelle was growing tired of the secrecy and games. Runes burned at her fingertips, wanting to take the queen's knowledge, but she held her magic back.

"Are you ready for your training?"

"My queen," she began, doing the best curtsy she could muster, while the darkness danced inside of her, wanting to strike. "I would first like to know why two fairies tried to separate and seduce my lover and I last night."

Byzarien took her hand and gave it a squeeze. His pressure reined in her destructive desires. She felt guilty for making him nervous, but the question nonetheless needed to be asked.

"What?" The queen rose and shook her head. "I haven't the slightest idea what you're talking about."

"You made it clear to us that fairies only *mate* at certain times of year," Myravelle said through gritted teeth. "Then why did a fairy couple separate us and offer sex? A male fairy even attempted to assault me." Next to the throne, Myravelle caught sight of Fleur shifting and avoiding eye contact. In fact, she looked quite sickly. Fire flared in Myravelle's veins. *Why would Fleur do that?*

The queen folded her hands together and lowered her head, tilting in the direction of Fleur before sighing. "I assure you, no one shall bother you again. But that's not the only issue."

"No?"

"Our water fairies were leaving offerings at the sacred spring before sunrise and found *something* at the site."

"Yes, my queen," Myravelle said. "We were there and left a carved stone."

"Your *carved stone* desecrated the area." The queen cleared her throat. "Not only is it a large source of water for us, but all water is connected. Now our water fairies will have to work day and night until it is purified once more."

Myravelle darkened, but kept calm. "I'm sorry," she said. "I didn't know I couldn't leave my own offering."

"You have much to learn." Sebira brushed her hands over the shimmering skirt of her dress. "Starting today, we will give you lessons. We must find your true gift."

"Thank you, Queen Sebira."

Byzarien patted her back, and she looked up at him. Mirror grins spread across their faces. His kind supportive heart, made hers swell with love.

"You will come with me first," the queen said, stealing Myravelle's attention. She gestured to her daughters. "Later, Fleur will introduce you to plant magic. Tomorrow, Faune and Sola will introduce you to animal and weather magic, respectively."

The sisters touched their mother's shoulder as they each passed her throne and descended the dais. Lifting her extravagant pink gown a rose petal's length off the floor, Fleur held her head high and gracefully made her way over to stand before Myravelle.

"I will meet you in the library after my mother's lesson," she said with a strained look on her face, as if she were but a porcelain doll ready to crack.

Myravelle nodded and watched Fleur leave the throne room with her sisters trailing in her shadow.

"Ready?" Sebira asked.

"Yes, my queen, but," Myravelle trailed off and looked toward Byzarien. "What about—"

"Argus," Sebira called, and he entered the throne room wearing a new shimmering tunic. "Put this *soldier* to good use today chopping firewood with the group."

"Yes, my queen," Argus said with a bow.

Myravelle gripped Byzarien's arm. "Wait."

"It's all right. You'll do great, I know it," he said, leaning to kiss her cheek. "Good luck."

She wished he could be by her side all day. Though no one had outright said it, she was certain the fairy queen didn't want a *human* to witness magic lessons. She took a deep breath and reminded herself how much she wanted answers. Plus, a small part of her still longed to fit in.

Once everyone, aside from a few guards, had left, Sebira rose from her throne and descended the dais, her gossamer gown meandering over lichens and moss. Myravelle stiffened when the queen touched her face.

"I wish I could see you," Sebira breathed, icy fingers tickling Myravelle's cheeks and nose. "You sound so much like her."

"My mother?" Tears welled in Myravelle's eyes in an instant. "What can you tell me about her?"

"She is difficult for me to talk about, but I will try when the time is right." The queen pulled back her hands and adjusted her posture. "Come."

Following Queen Sebira through the Hollow, Myravelle eyed the storerooms once again. The tangled heaps of gold thread glimmered, piquing Myravelle's curiosity.

"Where did the gold come from?" she asked.

"A fairy made it," Sebira said, continuing her graceful steps over the knobby roots.

Another spinner? Her pulse quickened at the thought. The cauldron of Myravelle's curiosity was bubbling over, and she could no longer contain her questions. "How do the gifts work? How can I learn more about the runes?"

A muscular guard with a red mop of hair opened the door for Sebira and Myravelle, who stepped out into the crisp breeze.

"I will explain everything, but first I have a surprise." The queen gestured to a little lane east of the Hollow. "This way."

Myravelle scrunched her brows and held her tongue, ambling next to the queen down a small dirt road. Trees lined the lane and stretched their empty boughs overhead, creating a skeletal canopy. Only the thick pines offered a source of color in the bleak, eternal winter. A little workshop emerged between the tree trunks and the sounds of chopping, sawing, and sanding permeated the frosty air. A carved and painted sign hung above the door with the words *Sleepy Wood Wandery & Woodworks*. The queen tugged Myravelle's sleeve, and they approached the door engraved with Dormrya trees and stars.

A lanky fairy with leather gloves opened the door and immediately dropped to her knees. "My queen," she said, bowing her head.

"Good morning, Gilly. Would you show Myravelle how a wand is made?" she asked, touching Gilly's shoulder.

"Yes, indeed, Queen Sebira," the woodworking fairy said, holding the door open for them. "Please, come in."

Stepping inside, the scent of wood and lacquer overwhelmed Myravelle's senses. Half a dozen woodworking fairies knelt as the queen glided past.

"Rise," she whispered and gestured all around. "Please, continue your work."

Myravelle watched one fairy slowly saw a piece of wood, while another fairy used his wand to spray a dome of mist overtop.

"To keep the dust down," the ruggish fairy with the saw said, winking at Myravelle.

She nodded in understanding. If a splinter could place someone in a death-like sleep, she imagined breathing the dust would too. Horror strained her features though and she turned her scarred palm up, wondering if the fairies had anyone stuck in a death-like sleep.

"My queen," she began. "If there are any *sleepers*, I could wake them."

Sebira tilted her head. "That is quite thoughtful of you, darling, but it won't be necessary. The poison in fairy dust isn't nearly as potent. Those who inhale it may sleep for hours or days at most, but we haven't had an accident in a long time."

"Knock on wood!" chanted the woodworking fairies as they rapped their knuckles against the tables.

Myravelle moved on to a table of fairies whittling and sanding the wood down further into wands while more water fairies helped keep dust out of the air. It was enchanting to watch the master woodworkers, for everything was as natural as breathing to them. The queen waited for Myravelle near the final fairy who brushed lacquer on the completed wand.

"When a young fairy shows signs of a burgeoning gift, they are presented with a wand to help them harness the magic within." Sebira plucked the wand from the table and held it out to Myravelle. "Your wand."

It reminded her of the shaft of the drop spindle as she spun it in her fingers to test its weight. A glowing warmth blossomed in her heart, for she felt like one of them: a real fairy. Blinking away her tears, she hugged the wand to her chest. "Thank you."

"You are most welcome." Sebira touched Myravelle's face again, brushing the tears away and tracing her jaw. "So much like her."

After thanking the woodworking fairies, the queen led Myravelle back toward the Hollow. Inside the dim and sacred tree, she followed Sebira down a spiral staircase held up by earth and roots. The further they descended, the darker it became, and she almost lost sight of the queen's bright white gown. Myravelle used the knots on the wooden banister as a guide. The steps eventually gave way to a narrow corridor, lit by wall sconces carved into the tree roots.

The queen opened a door, and Myravelle's breath caught when she stepped into a massive library. Pazcal had once described the famous library in the Eglantyne Castle when he'd delivered gardening books to her, but Myravelle couldn't imagine it was anything like the fairy library. Scrolls encased in ornate metal and leather-bound books were tucked into niches created by the random pattern of the Dormrya roots. Vines with twinkling lights crawled along the natural arches and hung from the ceiling to provide a warm glow throughout.

They passed a fairy older than time itself sleeping behind a desk piled with books.

Sebira gestured to the librarian. "You may borrow books whenever you like, Myravelle. Thea here can locate books and scrolls faster than anything," she said with a snap of her pale fingers. "She's a book fairy."

Myravelle nodded and let her gaze take in the mere mass amounts of knowledge held within one room. The queen lifted a little bell from the desk and gave it a gentle ring. The book fairy shook herself awake and gasped when she looked at the queen.

Thea slid from her chair and knelt. "Good morning, my queen."

"There, there," Sebira tapped the old fairy's shoulder, prompting her to stand. "Good morning to you, Thea. I would like to show Myravelle the *Grimoire of Runes*."

"Yes, my queen," Thea said, twirling her wand as she dashed out of sight amongst the rows and rows of shelves. Before Myravelle could take another breath, the old fairy had returned with a worn book in her hands. "There you are, Queen Sebira."

The queen accepted the massive leather text. "Thank you, Thea. You may return to your slumber."

After bowing, Thea did indeed snuggle into her cushiony chair surrounded by piles of books and closed her eyes. Myravelle followed Sebira toward a table at the back of the long, arched space. They passed beneath a massive chandelier of antlers at the center of the room. The moss floor absorbed nearly all sound, giving the library a sacred sort of hum.

With a thud, Sebira placed the grimoire onto the table and rested her hands against it. "Do you know about the very first fairy?"

"No, my queen," Myravelle said, stepping closer to study the binding on the thick book.

"Fae was a human who worshiped the earth goddess Terryx more than any other," Sebira said. "As you probably know, Terryx and her husband Cielyx had a volatile relationship: loving and passionate in the summer, and cold and cruel in the winter. Fae would stretch her fingers into the soil of her garden and thank Terryx for her blessings, even when times grew hard and the harvests were low.

"Terryx felt something for this special woman and blessed her with these gifts and the magic runes to harness them," Sebira paused, tapping her finger on the leather book. "Fae became the first fairy, connected with nature in a way no human had ever been. She grew up and had children, who each mastered a rune.

"Though they shared their blessings by helping others, eventually the humans grew wary of their magic." The queen sighed and pinched her fingers together. "Mistrust and misunderstanding grew into hatred, which is why many of Fae's descendants emigrated into the woods in the first place."

"We're not much different, humans and fairies, after all?" Myravelle whispered.

"Oh, but we are, my dear," the queen said. "After many generations, humans and fairies became so different, they could not even procreate."

Myravelle's heart sank, knowing she and Byzarien would never have a child together. What a good father he would have been.

Sebira released a chuckle and shook her head. "So much like your mother, wanting to see the best in humans."

The mention of her mother made Myravelle's throat tighten. "How well did you know her?"

"We were the best of friends," she said with a sniffle. "My visions of Xylina became *shrouded* after she left. Will you tell me what happened to her?"

Myravelle clenched her fists and took a deep breath. "They locked her up in a tower to spin gold and beat her, branded her, and starved her when she didn't produce enough," she said, stifling a sob. "Then, because of me, they executed her."

Tears glistened in Sebira's opalescent eyes only for a moment before she cleared her throat and hardened her face and posture like marble. "I am sorry for your loss," she said and opened the grimoire. "Now, back to your lesson. These are the various fairy runes passed down to us from Fae herself."

Myravelle shook away the unsettling mix of sorrow and anguish churning in her stomach with the queen's swift change of subject. Her eyes widened to take in the beautiful hand-painted illustrations of the fairy runes. The gold paint popped against the deep black pages in the swirling and gleaming runes that often filled her visions. At last, she understood what she saw in her mind's eye: Fae's enchantments. Myravelle's grin widened with every page the queen flipped through. It was beautiful, breathtaking, and absolutely validating.

The door to the library creaked and the hushed sounds of footfall along the moss carpeting stole her attention. Fleur strode toward their table with a small satchel tied around her waist and she narrowed her eyes at the wand in Myravelle's hand.

"Just in time, daughter," Queen Sebira said. "I believe Myravelle is ready for your lesson."

"Wonderful," Fleur snipped the word hard and threw a glance at Myravelle. "You will learn about working with plants."

Bubbles rushed through her chest, for she knew it would be an easy lesson. All of her years cultivating the rooftop garden and foraging through the woods couldn't have been for naught. *Myravelle the plant fairy* had a nice chime to it. Her heart thrummed at the thought of proving herself.

The queen stepped away from the table, but turned, raising her finger to her chin. "Myravelle?" she asked in a melodic voice. "Would you and your *soldier* like to join me this evening for supper?"

"Yes, of course, my queen," Myravelle said. "We would love to."

"I shall have someone fetch you this evening, then. Good day," she said and left the library.

"We fairies are connected with nature, but it is our duty to never control it," Fleur said and drew her wand from her braided leather waist belt. "The humans often believe our magic is some all-powerful weapon, but this is untrue. Our magic is a delicate balance with nature. Everything requires a sacrifice. When the eternal winter began, many fairies nearly went mad trying to fix it. We learned we must do what we can to keep our people comfortable, but nothing more. Do you understand?"

"Yes," she said, though she wasn't sure. Since the barrier on her magic had broken, there were things she could do that did not feel like a *balance*.

"Now, plant fairies like myself help feed our people during this time. We can manipulate plants in exchange for another, but it takes practice and energy." She reached into her satchel and plucked out a mushroom. "Now, I will change this mushroom into a blackberry bush."

Fleur twirled her wand slowly so Myravelle could watch the

design. It was a circle with lines shaped like a tree with a star at the base. Brows furrowing, Fleur stared at the mushroom as it began to sparkle. It elongated in all directions, unfurling with bright green leaves. When she finished, it was indeed a blackberry sapling in her arms.

The fairy sat down and sighed, her shoulders drooping a bit.

Myravelle looked at the blackberries. "How many of these can you do per day?"

"Oh, maybe a few, but they can't thrive with the current weather conditions, which is why we rely on fairies like Sola to create heat and sunlight in the greenhouses," Fleur said. "But, with all of us plant fairies combined, we can create a varied and nutritious diet for the village. Now, it's your turn to try." From her bag, she pulled out another mushroom and tossed it onto the table.

Myravelle took a deep breath and lifted the mushroom cap. She saw the golden circle with a tree and star hovering over the fungus as she held it in her palm. She traced the enchantment with the wand and focused on transforming the fungus into a bush. Sparks and crackles burst into the air, making Fleur jump out of her chair.

The mushroom scorched Myravelle's hand. She dropped it onto the mossy floor. Sprigs shot out in twisted and unnatural directions while a cloud of smoke and ash circled the plant. Fleur gasped and stepped back. As the dark plant grew thick and tangled, even Myravelle was forced to scramble away from the thorns.

When the dark, shimmering cloud evaporated, what was left was a large rosebush, with blooms darker than the deepest night. The plant was wider than two of the library tables combined and taller than Myravelle, making it difficult to walk around.

Although she hadn't produced a blackberry bush, Myravelle gaped at her creation. She plucked one of the black roses and admired her work until she glimpsed the tight and drawn look upon Fleur's face.

"I'm *sorry*," Myravelle said as the warm feeling of belonging drained from her veins, leaving her hollow and cold once again. "What about gold? Can't spinning gold be my gift?"

"What?" Fleur sneered. "No. That's not a real fairy gift."

"Wasn't that my mother's gift?"

Fleur stiffened, shifting her eyes to the grimoire, which she carefully slid out from under the tangle of thorny vines. "I don't...know."

"What is it? Are there any other fairies with that gift I could meet?"

Fleur stepped around the rose bush, avoiding it like a hideous beast, and sighed. "No."

Myravelle's mind went to the storeroom with heaps of gilded thread, knowing someone had to have spun it. The queen had even said so. She opened her mouth to ask when Fleur cut her off with a wave of her hand.

"We'll have someone clean this up," Fleur said, guiding Myravelle with a push on her back toward the exit. She woke Thea with a ring of the bell and handed her the grimoire. The old fairy dashed away to return the ancient text.

Myravelle twirled the Dormrya wand in her fingers, shoulders slumped.

"My sisters will each give you lessons tomorrow," Fleur said. "Maybe you'll be better with animals or weather. Good day."

Fleur exited the library, leaving Myravelle alone with Thea, who settled back to her chair and fell asleep. With all of the new knowledge about fairies and their runes, Myravelle had hoped to feel...well, fulfilled. Instead, Queen Sebira's secrecy only left her with more questions.

On her way to the cottage, Myravelle hugged her wand to her chest and looked forward to Byzarien's arms around her.

25

Byzarien

With his shoulders sore from chopping wood in the forest all day, Byzarien stretched his arms skyward as he trudged down the lane. Once the late afternoon bells had echoed through the village, the fairies dropped their axes and turned in to enjoy time with their families and eat dinner. His heart hurt watching fairies run to hug their families, for he missed his own so terribly. He didn't know when—if ever—it would be safe to return to them.

Waving goodbye to the few fairies who didn't call him things like *monster* or *Eglantyne scum*, the tightness in Byzarien's chest lifted when he saw the cottage edge into view near the enormous Hollow. He had Myravelle, and hoped to someday make her part of his family. He was eager to see her and ask about the magic lessons.

When Byzarien reached the cottage, he opened the door and ducked beneath the unlevel frame only to find Myravelle sitting before the iron and ivy mirror. She seemed lost staring at her reflection while twirling a wand in her hands as if she were holding a spindle. Little Nightmare hopped from his bed and soared to perch on Byzarien's shoulder. He gave Little Nightmare a few pets before the crow flew away to perch on a wooden beam overhead. All the while, Myravelle continued to stare and spin, clearly trapped in her thoughts.

Byzarien knelt beside her and stroked her cheek. "How were your lessons?"

She flinched as if she only just noticed his arrival, then sighed and snuggled against him.

He wrapped her in his arms. "What's wrong?"

"My lesson with Fleur went so dreadfully wrong," she whispered. "I couldn't perform the task."

"It was your first try," he said, adjusting his position to look her in the eyes. "Tomorrow will be better."

A weak smile lifted Myravelle's lips and she looked down at the wand.

Byzarien nudged her a little. "What's that?"

"Queen Sebira showed me the wandery and gave me this." She lifted it, eyes gleaming. "My very own wand."

"If she didn't believe in you, she wouldn't have given you a wand."

Myravelle slid her gaze to Byzarien and stared at him for a long moment, her bottom lip trembling. "Why are you so good to me?"

"Because I love you." He pressed his lips to hers and, when he peeled away, tilted his head. "Can you show me how you use it?"

She took a deep breath and stood before stepping toward the little table. She twirled her new wand above a leftover fairy cake, an extremely sour one that not even Little Nightmare dared to touch. Byzarien stood to watch the little cake glimmer and smoke, changing shape before his eyes. Little Nightmare squawked from his perch, and Byzarien's mouth fell agape as the pastry stretched and unfurled into the delicate blooms and curling vines of a sweetpea flower. Myravelle slumped her shoulders.

"What? It's wonderful," Byzarien said, lifting the beautiful flower and placing it into a glass of water.

She shook her head and shrugged. "It was supposed to turn it into a blackberry bush...well, I think."

"But you made something beautiful." He rubbed her back. "And everything takes practice."

Myravelle drooped into a chair and twirled her wand some more. "The queen would hardly answer any of my questions."

A nervous tingle swept through Byzarien's skull and down his spine, so he sat as well. He didn't like that the queen was continuing to withhold information from Myravelle, but reminded himself that she did give her a wand. She truly wouldn't do that if she didn't want to help Myravelle, right? If she trusted her with a wand, why didn't she trust her with information though?

"Speaking of the queen," Myravelle began, tapping her wand on the table, "she wants us to dine with her this evening."

Byzarien's chest filled with hope, and touched her hand. "That's wonderful. You can get your answers tonight."

Nodding with a blank expression on her face, Myravelle turned her wrist to caress Byzarien's hand. He traced the rune on her palm, knowing that, like him, her scars of distrust ran much deeper than her skin.

After getting cleaned up with rose-scented water from the wash basin, they dressed for the evening in their fine outfits from the fairy ball. Night fell swiftly through the village, so they lit a few candles which set the cottage aglow and twinkled against the mirror and stained-glass window. While Myravelle combed out and plaited her hair, Byzarien tried to feed Little Nightmare some seeds and berries, but the bird was not at all interested.

"You can't live on fairy cakes alone," Byzarien grumbled, holding his hand out to the crow. "You need something healthy."

"He's impossible," Myravelle said, and they both laughed.

Byzarien stood next to her and admired how her intricate and swooping braid cascaded around her head and over her shoulder. "You look lovely."

"Thank you," she said, fingering his dark waves of hair into place. "As do you. Only..."

"Only what?"

She ran her hands down his chest and grinned. "Well, we already wore these outfits."

Byzarien furrowed his brows thinking about how their only other clothes were tattered and bloody, but Myravelle lifted her wand and twirled it toward his tunic. The dark fabric and gleaming rubies melted away and swirled into a pattern of silver stars that swept around their bodies. The beadwork and embroidery sparkled in the dancing candlelight. With an extra flick of her wand, Myravelle made plumes of midnight feathers burst from their shoulders.

Turning toward Little Nightmare, Myravelle asked, "Do you like it, darling? Now, we look like a family."

The bird cawed and flapped its wings in approval just as the dinner bells chimed throughout the village.

Byzarien chuckled, taking Myravelle into his arms. "Are you ready?"

She nodded, and they said goodbye to Little Nightmare before stepping out into the snow-dusted night. Their breath fogged the frosty air, but their entwined fingers were warm. Blankets of white snuggled the roofs and treetops above the welcoming glow of windows. Once inside the embrace of the Hollow, a servant led them along the twisted and knobby hallway into a room with a long table. Hundreds of candles floated through the air, and the table was crowded with tiered trays of fairy cakes and decanters of wine.

Slender and regal, Queen Sebira sat at the head of the table and gestured to the chairs beside her. "Welcome, please sit."

Byzarien pulled out a chair for Myravelle before sitting on the other side of the queen. Servants immediately filled their glasses with an aromatic and heady wine.

"Are you enjoying your wand, Myravelle?" Sebira asked.

"Very much, my queen," she said. "Thank you."

"I did hear about your lesson with Fleur."

As the queen's words settled like snow, Myravelle shifted in her chair and twirled her rings.

Byzarien cleared his throat. "Maybe she was nervous since it was her first try," he said, nodding at Myravelle. "She will get better. In fact, she used her wand to change the design of our outfits tonight."

Thank you, Myravelle mouthed and gave him a slight smile.

"Indeed," Sebira said. "All in good time."

Myravelle perked up and placed her hands on the table. "Would now be a good time to tell me why my mother left the village?"

The queen took a sip of wine. "Your mother was taken from this place."

"Why didn't you go after her?"

"Our queen—my mother—passed away the night Xylina left," she said with a sigh. "Our numbers were small and we couldn't risk invading the Eglantyne Kingdom for one fairy, even if she was my dearest friend. My priority as the new queen was to keep my village safe."

"Why didn't you use your gift to see what would happen to her?" Myravelle asked in a ragged whisper.

Byzarien desperately wanted to hold her.

"You could have done something."

"My gift of premonition was in its infancy at that time," Sebira said. "When I finally had my powers under control, I did try to see her fate, truly I did. But, like I mentioned this morning, Xylina was shrouded by shadow. I...I had assumed she died a long time ago."

Silence grew thick in the dining hall until the servants returned to refill wine and deliver more tiny cakes. The queen sampled a few and hummed her approval while Byzarien tried to take a few bites, but his stomach was in knots. He assumed Myravelle felt the same, for she simply pushed the decorated delights around her plate, not eating at all.

Byzarien cleared his throat before addressing the queen. "What about the gold? Does Myravelle have any relatives she could meet?"

"No, I'm sorry." Sebira shook her head. "Xylina's family died at the hands of humans many years ago. She was alone."

Byzarien held eye contact with Myravelle, and he swore he watched her shatter inside like broken glass. He was about to stand to sweep her away when the queen spoke to him.

"Speaking of humans, *Byzarien*," Sebira said as if his name was sour on her tongue. "What was your role within the Eglantyne Army?"

Caught off-guard, he fumbled with his hands. "Um, I was a soldier in the Sleepy Wood Company. They said our mission was to protect the kingdom from fairies, but it was really to push into the forest and collect Dormrya wood for the king."

Sebira's cheeks flared red, from anger or the strong wine, Byzarien wasn't sure. "And what is Zylvain's plan for all of that poisonous wood, do you know?"

"He is creating dangerous weapons," he said, shaking his head. "I suppose to put all of his enemies to sleep."

"And how—"

"Why are you questioning Byzarien?" Myravelle snapped, slapping her hand against the wooden table. "Why don't you just look into the future to see what the king plans to do?"

Waiting for a beat, Sebira relaxed her face and folded her hands together. "My visions are rather...jumbled. To glimpse the future, I must untangle events and threads of time like combing out a long, twisted braid," she said, twirling her fingers in the air. "For a very long time, my visions were infallible and helped the fairies in all aspects of life. Until recently, that is, when I began hitting more *snags*. Often fates are entangled and dependent on others, while some, like yours, are completely shrouded. When you and I met and we touched hands, you saw something? What was it?"

Myravelle narrowed her eyes at the queen. "You were giving my mother a drop spindle. What does it mean?"

Blinking away tears, Sebira scowled and fidgeted with her gown.

"Please, tell me why I saw that," Myravelle begged. "What aren't you telling me?"

The queen stood so quickly, she knocked over a glass of wine. Two servants rushed to wipe the spill away. It appeared as if the queen was going to leave the room, so Byzarien got up and blocked her path.

"You owe Myravelle answers," he said in a low, calm voice.

"Do I?" Sebira asked, standing tall and turning toward Myravelle. "I believe it is she who owes *me* answers."

"What?" Myravelle scoffed and rose from her chair.

"I've been trying to figure out why my gift began to fade; why you were completely hidden from me," the queen said. "Are you the one casting shadows in my mind? Has it been you this entire time?"

"I have no idea what you're talking about." Myravelle shook her head. "I didn't know you or the fairy realm even existed until we arrived here. I'm as much in the dark as you are."

Trembling, the queen adjusted the silver circlet on her head and folded her hands. "I apologize," she said. "I should not have raised my voice or accused you of wrongdoing, it's just…"

Byzarien glanced at Myravelle then back at the queen. "Just what?"

"I feel like I'm losing my mind, like I'm losing my village," she said. "I want everything to be perfect."

Taking Myravelle's hand in his, Byzarien gave it a squeeze.

"Will you please accept my apology for this outburst and continue your lessons with my daughters tomorrow?" Sebira asked, tilting her head. "Once you find your gift, everything will fall into place. Everything will be perfect."

"Yes, my queen," Myravelle mumbled and offered a lazy curtsy.

"Goodnight then." Sebira twirled around and dashed away, and Byzarien was certain he heard her sobs echoing from the hall.

26

Myravelle

A man—or creature—with greenish-gold skin and stringy dark hair peeked through a window at a fairy sleeping in her bed. With baskets of spindles and roving scattered across the floor, and with wavy black hair tumbling over her pillow, Myravelle recognized Xylina at once. The creature crept into the cottage on all fours and pulled himself onto her straw mattress. His yellow eyes studied her moonlit face as he threaded his claws with her fingers.

"Xylina, Xylina, Xylina," he whispered and kissed her palm. "I bless you with this gift."

Myravelle burst forward in a cold sweat, drawing deep breaths. Little Nightmare cawed from his perch and Byzarien stirred beside her in bed.

"What is it?" he asked, sitting up to stroke her hair.

"I had a strange nightmare...or vision," she whispered, cradling her head in her hands. "It was of my mother with some fearsome creature."

"A creature?" he asked. "I wonder if it has to do with why she was taken?"

"I don't know," she mumbled, trying to recall the fading details of the dream.

Byzarien slid from bed and dressed. "Don't dwell on it too much," he said, offering Myravelle her own clothes. "You have more lessons today. What do you think—will you be an animal fairy or a weather fairy?"

Little Nightmare flapped down to rest on Myravelle's hand, and she smiled from him to Byzarien. "I sure hope I can work with animals, wouldn't that be lovely?"

"It would." Byzarien leaned to kiss her cheek. "Your magic is," he paused, tilting his head as if thinking, "beautiful. I truly don't think there's anything you *can't* do."

Myravelle's heart swelled with his unwavering confidence in her as she followed his lead and got dressed. She looked in the mirror and pouted, a bit bored with her gown. She plucked her wand from the table and gave it a twirl. The stars scattered away from the fabric, chasing Little Nightmare around the small cottage. Myravelle flicked her wand at a spiderweb in the corner, and it floated and stretched through the air before draping the dark fabric of her gown and Byzarien's tunic.

After eating a light breakfast, Myravelle left for her lessons with Faune and Sola while Byzarien once again headed into the forest to chop wood. While waiting for the sisters inside the main corridor of the Hollow, Myravelle stepped toward the storeroom of spun gold, toying with the fibers between her fingers. The soft, enchanting gleam was too familiar. Too perfect. Myravelle clutched her chest, hardly able to breathe. She missed her mother more than ever, and this gold had to be connected to her somehow. A light touch of hand on her shoulder made Myravelle gasp and spin around.

"It's just us, sweetie," Sola said, smiling. "Are you all right?"

"You gave me a fright." Myravelle took a few deep breaths and fluffed out her dress. "Yes, I'm ready."

Faune narrowed her eyes and reached out to trace the spider web on Myravelle's dress. Feeling her insides squirm, she avoided the fairy's scrutinizing gaze.

"Sola," Faune said, tugging her sister closer. "Isn't this lovely? It looks so realistic."

Myravelle stood in shock, with her mouth agape while the sisters admired her handiwork.

"Oh, I think I like this even better than the one for the fairy ball," Sola said, nodding. "If you don't feel like your gift is connected to plants, animals, or weather, I dare say you have a future with fashion."

Myravelle blushed. "Thank you."

Holding out her forest green skirt adorned with furs and wooden beads, Faune gave Myravelle a sheepish look. "Would you mind?"

"You want me to change your outfit?"

"Please," Faune said.

Sola bounced on her toes. "Oh, me too! Me too!"

Nodding, Myravelle couldn't help but smile. "Only if you tell me about this gold. Where does it come from?"

"We don't know," Sola said.

"You don't know?" Myravelle narrowed her eyes. "Aren't you curious?"

"We don't use money like humans do." Faune shrugged. "And Mother is very...*secretive* about many things, we've just learned not to ask."

"Well," Sola said, tilting her head. "We do know one thing."

The sisters stared at one another, having a silent conversation with merely the expressions on their faces. Faune finally nodded.

"Well, we know that Mother's servants bring more of it every month."

Myravelle crossed her arms and thought for a moment. *Every month.* "Like a payment for something?"

"We don't know," Faune said, raising her hands in supplication. "That's the truth."

"Well, a deal is a deal."

Myravelle took out her wand and traced the gleaming rune over Faune's dress. The fur and beads burned away, and the golden fire left in their wake swirled about the gown creating a design of embroidered animals on the skirt. A doe. A rabbit. A fox. A sparrow. A snake. A squirrel and many, many more. Faune cooed as she twirled around, admiring the dress.

"Thank you," she said. "It's positively lovely."

Using her hip, Sola bumped Faune out of the way. "My turn."

With Sola's gown, Myravelle traced a new shape, causing one half of the dress to turn powder blue and the other half midnight blue. On their respective sides, the half-faces of the sun and moon blossomed to life and nestled together side-by-side. As Sola twirled, embroidered clouds and stars bloomed all around.

"Oh, mine is ever better," Sola said. "Thank you."

Myravelle followed the sisters outside into winter's grasp. The three of them twirled their wands, creating warm, furry shrugs to match their gowns.

Once they reached a wide field next to the edge of the forest, Faune stopped them. "This will be perfect."

The overcast gray sky pressed against the bare branches of the trees in the distance while the icy breeze bit at Myravelle's cheeks. She worried what her next two lessons were going to be like after the first had gone so horribly wrong.

"As you know," Faune began, "my gift is animals. Although we fairies do eat meat on occasion, we live harmoniously with nature. We raise small amounts of livestock and, when we hunt, we never take more than we need."

Myravelle took a deep and confidence-building breath. Not only had she always felt connected with nature but, below her feet, she could feel every hibernating insect and snake. She sensed every animal on the ground and bird in the tree. She could do it. She could prove to them that she was an animal fairy like Faune.

"For our lesson today, I will simply show you how to call an animal to you." Faune adjusted the folds of her dress to retrieve her wand. "We'll start with something small, like a rabbit or a squirrel."

Faune's wand danced a circular pattern filled with lines, almost like a net with a star, while silver speckles dripped from the tip. In only a moment, a small white rabbit hopped toward them from the forest and through the field. Faune lifted the fluffy thing and stroked its fur. "Why don't you try, Myravelle?"

She mimicked Faune's wand motion, causing black and gold sparkles to glimmer about the netted shape. The ground rumbled under their feet when she traced the star. The sisters gasped and held one another's arms. Faune dropped the white rabbit, which bounded away into the woods.

From the tree line, hundreds of spiders scuttled toward them, followed by a swarm of moths. The fairies shrieked, hopping in a frantic dance around the arachnids as they swatted at the dark furry moths. From the creek flowing in the distance, snakes slithered toward them. Myravelle tried using her wand to send the creatures back, but she didn't know how. Turning the wand in the reverse pattern over and over, she finally saw a new rune glowing against the overcast sky. She traced the circle with an eye at the center and a star for the pupil, and everything went dark.

She blinked to find herself on the floor of the cottage, but she wasn't herself. There were shiny black feathers where her arms should have been and dark talons where her feet should have been. The taste of sweet meringue coated her mouth. *Little Nightmare?* Her mind connected to his with a shocking sensation, like lightning traveling through a cloud.

Fly.

At once, they were in the air and on the windowsill.

Push.

They nudged the stained glass window with their head.

Fly.

They soared over mossy cottages, through chimney smoke, and over treetops toward the field. Myravelle's body was flat to the ground, while Faune and Sola rushed toward her and lifted her into their arms.

Eat.

On the way down, they swooped through the air, enjoying a mouthful of moths. They landed amidst the chaos, ate the spiders, and pecked at the snakes. They ate and cawed until the creatures retreated.

Wake.

Myravelle opened her eyes to watch Little Nightmare soar overhead. Her pulse quickened with excitement at the new connection with her pet. With a concerned look on her face, Faune helped her sit on the frosty earth.

"What happened?" Sola asked, brushing her dress as if there still might be spiders crawling over it.

Myravelle extended her arm for Little Nightmare to perch. "I connected with my crow," she said, still shaking her head in disbelief. "I was him, or he was me. Together, we fought away the creatures."

"That's...something." Faune's green eyes grew wider than two moons as she stood and took a step back. "I think we're finished with animals for the day."

Sola grabbed Myravelle's hand to help her up. "Ready for your lesson with me?"

She shrugged. "I suppose."

"Don't worry," Faune said. "If we don't find your gift today, we could introduce you to some other fairies. I'm sure we'll find your gift."

Along the walk to a row of greenhouses, where Myravelle was to have her final lesson, Fleur approached, glaring at her sister's ensembles. "What in Fae's name are you wearing?"

"Myravelle made them," Sola said, beaming. "Aren't they lovely?"

Fleur quirked an eyebrow before turning to Faune. "How did the lesson go?"

The Three Good Fairies fell in line, whispering to one another. A sinking sensation filled Myravelle's stomach as she followed. Fleur and Faune quickly glanced back at her. Certain she overheard the word *witch,* Myravelle clenched her teeth. Darkness churned inside, but she cut it off—she still had time to prove herself to the fairies.

She stroked Little Nightmare's feathers. "You were such a good boy today," she whispered. "Don't listen to them."

But Myravelle couldn't follow her own advice. The word *witch* pressed against her temples and seeped into her skull. Even in the fairy village, she was different. Unwanted. Unwelcome. Feared. *Would she ever find a real home?*

"Oh, stop," Sola whispered, smacking the back of her sisters' heads. "She is still learning."

Sola's kindness eased some of Myravelle's worries. If Sola could see her potential, the others could too. When the fairies reached the row of greenhouses, Little Nightmare took to the sky, and Myravelle felt alone once again. Lifting her skirts to avoid a muddy puddle near the threshold, she followed the sisters into the first greenhouse. The structure was composed of oddly-shaped glass with wooden planters lining the walls, and baskets hanging from the ceiling. To Myravelle's surprise, it was cool inside, and many of the plants were dead. She touched a black vine, which crumbled between her fingers.

"My gift is temperature and sunlight," Sola said. "I can adjust the heat and cold of a small space for a short amount of time. I can also create sparks to produce fire or cool water into ice."

"If you can control the weather, why not reverse the eternal winter?" Myravelle asked, making the fairies' jaws drop.

"Oh, no, no, no, dear. No one is powerful enough for that," Sola said. "But some of us take turns keeping the greenhouse warm with faux-sunlight for fairies like Fleur to work with plants. And I can charm fires to burn all night long without the need for new logs."

Fleur placed her arm around Sola. "Yes, that alone has kept us from using the entire forest for firewood."

"So, for our lesson," Sola said, "we shall warm up and brighten this greenhouse."

"Do you mind if I use this time to grow a pumpkin?" Fleur asked, already digging into the soil of a planter.

"Not at all." Sola turned to Myravelle with her wand ready. "Watch my movements, dear."

Her wand traced a circle with a star surrounded by rays, like a sun, while yellow and orange sparks bounced from the tip. A balmy dampness formed on Myravelle's skin, and she flushed with heat right away. Humidity clung to the glass as the radiance from the wand made her squint.

Waving her wand toward the planter, Fleur created thick vines that twisted and coiled from the soil. Leaves sprung from them, along with a bright yellow flower. What started as a small, green orb morphed into an orange pumpkin.

Fleur harvested her gourd with a grin. "This will make delicious fairy cakes!"

Sola lowered her wand; the greenhouse dimmed but maintained some of the warmth and moisture.

"This greenhouse will hold some heat for a while, even without sunshine. I'm sure some plant fairies will be eager to work here for now," Sola said. "We'll move next door for you to try."

They left the greenhouse, exchanging the balmy warmth for a dry, crisp breeze. Sola had been correct: there were fairies waiting outside, gardening tools in hand. Myravelle entered the second greenhouse behind the sisters.

Sola pointed to Myravelle's wand and gave her an encouraging nod.

She copied Sola's wand motions, but nothing happened. She released a deep breath, shoulders slumping.

"Try again," Sola said, patting Myravelle's back. "Go on."

Myravelle spotted a similar golden rune hovering against the glass ceiling of the greenhouse. After taking a deep breath, she traced the rune and thought about heat, warmth, and fire. When her wand reached the end of the shape, it shook, and Myravelle held on tight.

An intense rush of heat burned through the greenhouse, charring any plant remains to a crisp. Sparks and flames erupted from Myravelle's wand, turning the tip black with ash. The three sisters shouted at her to stop, holding their arms over their eyes, unable to get to her through the scorched air. Cracks echoed from the ceiling as spiderweb fractures broke along the panes of glass. The plant boxes blazed in rolling black flames. The intense heat continued to rise.

The wand burned Myravelle and she dropped it. It rattled and sputtered sparks. An odd pressure pulsed against Myravelle's ears. Her heart raced, and fear burrowed deep into her chest like a shard of glass. She rushed to the fairies, pushing them from the greenhouse. Coughing, the sisters stumbled to get fresh air.

A high-pitched squeak, like that of a kettle, rang through the air. Myravelle shoved the fairies to the ground as the greenhouse exploded. A wave of heat and broken glass fanned out, and she covered her head.

When they all sat up, the frame of the greenhouse was on fire, as were the trees and shrubs around it. Fairies rushed to fight the black fire with either magic or buckets of water.

Fleur helped Faune and Sola stand, glaring at Myravelle. "What have you done?"

"I didn't mean to do that." With weak arms, she lifted herself from the ground. She was about to say more, but a sickness swam in her belly, and tendrils of darkness crept into her vision. The shouts of the fairies dissipated with the wind. Myravelle fell into a dark cavernous sleep.

27

Byzarien

The village bells echoed through the wintry forest. Byzarien and the fairies around him dropped their axes to look around. Murmurs and nervous whispers spread through the group collecting firewood until a fairy in a soil-brown cloak with bark on his shoulders ran down the hill toward them

"There's been a situation!" he called out. "We need help!"

All at once, Byzarien and the fairies followed. He thought of Myravelle. *Is she all right? Did the Three Good Fairies do something to her?* Concern fueled his steps.

A fairy with sticks twirled into her golden hair sprinted past him and asked a fairy in all blue what had happened. "It was the witch."

Byzarien's chest tightened. He cursed himself for ever calling her that but, even more, he hated that Myravelle couldn't avoid the term even among peers. The fairies were supposed to be like her, and were supposed to welcome her. She was an outsider yet again, and Byzarien had no idea how to help her.

The intense smell of smoke hit his nose before the group had even made it back to the village, and he came to an abrupt halt. A tingling sensation ran along his scars, and he took a few steps back as fairies ran toward the fire. He leaned against a tree and sucked in deep breaths. His family's screams pierced through his senses. The intense pain of his burns returned fresh and raw as phantom flames licked their way up his body. Benoix's grave scorched his mind.

"Grab water and bring it to the greenhouses," the turquoise fairy shouted, but the words swirled in Byzarien's ears. "It's magic fire!"

Hyperventilating, his feet became one with the frozen earth. *But Myravelle could be in danger.* With his heart leading the way, he managed to break free of his paralysis and sprint toward the fire, as he had for his family years ago. He had walked through flames for those he loved before and would certainly do it all over again for her. He lost Benoix, but he wouldn't lose anyone else he loved.

When he arrived at the greenhouses, his eyes widened. Black fire devoured everything in sight, sending plumes of smoke skyward. Ash swirled in the air like angry snow until it rested amongst the broken glass scattered upon the earth. Water fairies used their wands to spray the intense fire while others poured their buckets of water and snow to douse the flames. It all turned to steam upon contact. No matter what, they could not extinguish the fire laced with ebony flames. Magic fire. *What had Myravelle done?*

He rushed toward the burning remains of one of the greenhouses to find her, but Faune darted in front of him. "Stop!"

"Where's Myravelle?"

"She collapsed after creating this mess," Fleur said through gritted teeth as she lugged a pail of water. "Someone carried her to the cottage to rest."

Byzarien sighed with relief and gestured to the water. "The flames won't go out."

"Sola is fetching our mother," she said. "If anyone can put out these wicked flames, it's her."

He realized the fairies could only keep the flames at bay, not snuff them completely. At last, the queen emerged. Led by Sola,

Queen Sebira strode toward the chaos and twirled her wand toward the sky. The clouds above the greenhouses churned in response. Thunder roared, and they released their waters. Droplets singed against the hot wood, metal, and glass until all the flames were gone.

The queen melted into her daughter's arms. "Now, let me rest."

Fleur, Faune, and Sola guided their weak mother toward the Hollow. Byzarien planned to help the other fairies clean up, but he jogged toward the cottage to check on Myravelle first.

When he entered through the low, uneven door, she was asleep in bed with the quilt up to her shoulders. Her lips were tinted blue. Little Nightmare perched on the bedpost, watching over her. Byzarien sat on the edge of the mattress and stroked her hair. Her dark lashes fluttered as she opened her eyes.

"How are you feeling?"

She rose slowly, and draped her arms around him. "Weak."

"What happened with your lessons?" he asked, holding her ever-so-gently, for she seemed brittle in his arms. "Did you cause the fire?"

"I didn't mean to," she said. "Every time, something went wrong. Well...not *everything*."

He massaged circles down her back. "What do you mean?"

"During Faune's lesson about animals, I connected with Little Nightmare somehow," she said, turning to stroke the crow's dark feathers. "I could see what he saw and control what he did."

"Really?" Byzarien also reached to pet Little Nightmare, who nuzzled into his palm. "That's incredible."

"Well," she said with a scowl. "The *Three Good Fairies* didn't think so."

"I certainly do." He rested his forehead against hers. "It could be useful."

"What?"

"This connection with Little Nightmare," he said. "We could see what's happening in the kingdom. We could find my friends."

"If the king plans to bring the army here, we could warn the fairies. Maybe then, they would think of me as one of their own." Myravelle attempted a half-smile. "Let's try sending a message now."

"Are you sure you're strong enough?"

"I want to try."

After rummaging through their few belongings, he retrieved a bit of parchment and a quill. He wrote a message to his friends, careful not to reveal their location should Little Nightmare be caught, asking for any news from the kingdom...and his family. A painful lump formed in his throat at the thought of them. After rolling the parchment, he tied the message to Little Nightmare's leg with a piece of twine.

Myravelle shook as she rose from the bed, and Byzarien guided her to the chair. "I lost my wand," she said with a frown.

"You never needed one before."

She closed her eyes, her finger twitching in the air, and Little Nightmare tilted his head, watching her. Then, the crow hopped toward the stained-glass window and flew away.

Once he was gone, Myravelle slumped into the chair. "He knows what to do."

Byzarien guided her back to bed. "I'm going to help the fairies clean up the mess. You should stay here and sleep."

After tucking her in with a kiss to her cold forehead, Byzarien left. Back at the greenhouses, he moved debris and swept broken glass. Some of the fairies used magic to help clear the area, while others used their hands.

"Why don't you just use your magic?" he asked one of the fairies sweeping glass who wore a light brown tunic covered in leaves and acorns.

"We all have different gifts," the fairy said as he swept. "Did you see the queen?"

Byzarien nodded.

"Even she is not all-powerful. Using magic often drains our energy. We are not dangerous and evil like your king says we are."

Sour hate churned in Byzarien's stomach at the thought of the king. He swept in silence until he came upon a charred, black stick. As he tilted it in the air to study it, the ash flaked away with the breeze to reveal a bit of Dormrya wood beneath. It must have been Myravelle's wand.

The fairy stepped beside him. "Oh, that looks bad. Take it to the wandery, they can repair it."

Thanking the acorn fairy for the advice, Byzarien tucked the wand into his pocket and made a mental note to get it fixed for Myravelle. After the mess surrounding the greenhouses was cleared away, and only a small group remained to begin repairs, Byzarien decided to head into the forest, where they had all dropped their axes. Between the fires and his adrenaline, Byzarien had managed to stay quite warm in the village, but now winter's chill settled around him once more, seeping into his bones. He shivered while picking up axes and storing them in a neat row.

Adrenaline gave way to anxiety. What if he had lost Myravelle? If her status among the fairies was precarious, his was certainly unwelcome. *Eglantyne scum. Fairykiller. Monster.* He was only safe in this village because of one weak queen's promise. Despite Myravelle's desire to fit in, Byzarien realized they might have to leave earlier than she would like. He wiped his cheeks with the back of his gloved hands, and eyed the row of axes. He needed a weapon.

Byzarien attached an ax to his belt and hurried through the forest to meet the main lane of the village. Grown fairies stared at him. Children stared at him. He didn't have to hear their whispers to know what they were saying. He dragged his hair over his cheek and marched on. When he entered the cottage, Myravelle was already awake.

With Little Nightmare on her shoulder, she held a scroll and scowled at her reflection in the mirror. "Myravelle?" Byzarien shut the door behind him and studied her. "What is it?"

"Xavier wrote back." She slid her eyes to him and held out the scroll. "The king not only has the soldiers looking for me in the

Sleepy Wood, but he has spread propaganda about me throughout the kingdom."

He took the parchment, and his eyes bounced between phrases such as 'The Wicked Fairy' and 'The Mistress of All Evil.'

"If I wasn't already an outcast, I would certainly never be welcome in the kingdom again," she whispered.

"*We*," Byzarien said, taking Myravelle's hand. "We're in this together."

She gazed into his eyes and nodded. "Maybe we should inform the queen about what's going on."

"That's a good idea; you could earn her trust with this information." Byzarien nodded and extended his hand to her. "Let's go now."

Standing up, Myravelle eyed the burnt wand on his belt. "What's that?"

"It's your wand." He shrugged and handed it to her. "I heard the fairies at the wandery can fix it."

She stared at the wand for a long moment. "Why can't I—"

A knock at the door interrupted Myravelle, and Byzarien answered it. Sola slipped inside and shut the door quickly. She was red in the face and breathing heavily.

Myravelle stepped toward her and tilted her head. "Sola, what's wrong?"

"I...I had to tell you," she said. "My mother and sisters are planning something."

"What?" Byzarien asked.

"To hand you over to the king."

The hair on Byzarien's neck bristled like an angry wolf, and he wrapped his arm around Myravelle. "No."

Sola nodded. "Mother thinks your magic is wicked."

Myravelle wilted against him. As he bit his tongue to remain silent, heat crept into his temples. *They were supposed to be helping her.* He touched the ax on his belt, realizing that his gut instincts were correct.

"I'm still learning," Myravelle said in a small voice, looking down at her destroyed wand.

"I know, dear," Sola said, reaching out to stroke Myravelle's hand. "But there's another thing."

"What?" Myravelle whispered as if she couldn't take any more bad news.

"Mother said the reason your magic is...*different*," she began and shrugged, "is because you are only a half-fairy."

"Half-fairy?" Byzarien asked, as the words rattled around his mind like knucklebones. He held on a little tighter to Myravelle as she more heavily slumped against him. "What does that even mean?"

"I don't know," Sola said. "Mother wouldn't say who your father is, only that he was indeed not a fairy. Whoever he is, he is the reason your magic is, well, different."

Silence fell. The only sound was Byzarien's pulse, which he was certain echoed through the cottage. Myravelle shook her head and sniffled.

"I'm sorry, I truly am." Sola strained her face as if holding back tears. "I don't think Mother or even Fleur wanted to give you a fair chance to become one of us. But I still believe in you."

"Thank you."

"I had to warn you," Sola said. "They plan to broker a peace treaty with the king in exchange for you."

"We need to leave now," Byzarien said, heart pounding. "Can you distract them long enough for us to get away?"

"I'll try my best," the Good Fairy said, wrapping her arms around Myravelle. "Goodbye. I wish you luck and hope to see you again someday."

As Sola left the cottage, Myravelle's silver eyes darkened into storm clouds, and her entire body shook.

"Myravelle?" Byzarien asked, lifting Xavier's note.

"What?" she asked, her voice bladed with anger.

He pointed at certain lines of the letter, which made the tight lump form in his throat again, but this time it was with excitement to see his family. "Xavier says we should be safe at my parent's house since everyone already thinks I'm dead. He and Dezlan visited my family and told them the truth."

Tears fell from Myravelle's eyes as she nodded.

"We'll be fine," he said, dropping the note to take her hand. "You can lead us through the woods."

"If I'm a half-fairy, then it's true," she said. "I don't belong anywhere."

"You belong with me." He pressed kisses against the freckles on her cheeks. "Now, let's leave before the fairies enact their plan."

28

Myravelle

I am not welcome anywhere. The voice in Myravelle's head sang the words over and over again like a haunting lullaby. Her mind spun while Byzarien packed items to venture into the woods once again. Little Nightmare scarfed down fairy cakes as if he also knew they were leaving.

"We should send word to my family," Byzarien said, scribbling on some parchment. "I've also written Xavier to let him know the plan, if you think Little Nightmare can handle two letters."

The crow cawed and returned to eating. Myravelle stared through the swirling imperfections and bubbles in the stained glass window, barely making out the shapes of the fairies outside.

When Little Nightmare finished his meal, Byzarien tied one letter to each of the bird's legs. Without looking at either of them, Myravelle twisted her finger in the air and connected with Little Nightmare. He hopped to the windowsill and took off toward the Dumont's house near Pezit Quarter with the knowledge to find Xavier after getting some rest.

"I'm only half-fairy," she said, perching herself on the edge of the mattress. "That is supposed to be impossible."

Byzarien sat next to her and combed his fingers through her hair. "You are a miracle."

"A *miracle* they want to lock away."

She lifted her charred wand, which left soot and ash on her fingers. She stared at it for a long time while Byzarien gathered the remainder of their things. She should have helped him, but she couldn't move. Not frozen in place, but on fire. Flames coursed through her body, scorching her nerves in crackling bursts. Her hands trembled around the burnt wand. Like her, it was dark, damaged, and unwanted by the fairies. Surely it still had value. Surely it deserved to live.

"Ready?" Byzarien asked, his deep voice pulling Myravelle from her thoughts.

"Not yet." She plucked a needle from the sewing kit and pricked her finger before drawing a tiny rune in her blood on the charred wood: a circle with one large loop curling in toward a star. The wand melted, molten and dark, and slithered like a snake around her hands and wrists. Sparks and dark glitter escaped the pliable material, which dripped from her fingers to the ground. With each drip, a staff grew taller and taller until it reached her outstretched hand. It took the shape of a branch, irregular and twisted, but gleaming like slick oil. Lightning passed from Myravelle to the staff. She grinned, for it was more powerful than any fairy wand, simply because she had made it so. *They don't hate me because I'm different—they fear me because I'm powerful.*

With the staff complete, she caught sight of Byzarien, who had been staring at her. There was a slight smile on his lips, and her heart melted for him even more. "Thank you," she said, reaching to trace his scars.

He leaned into her touch. "For what?"

"For not being afraid of me like everyone else."

Byzarien stepped closer, trailing a finger up the staff until his hand rested atop hers. "I used to be but somewhere along the way, that fear faded, and my love grew."

She kissed him, love spinning from her heart into his as if tethered to one another by threads weaving between bone and vein. "I'm ready," she said.

They peeked out the door to make sure they were alone, then set off toward the woods. Byzarien's heavy boots could not match the silence of Myravelle's shadowy steps, but night had fallen, giving them the advantage. Still, they hurried to put more distance between themselves and the fairies.

As they came upon a grove of Dormrya trees, something tingled in Myravelle's bones. She held out her arm, hitting Byzarien in the chest. "These trees," she began, looking around, "won't let us pass."

"What do—"

"Stop," Queen Sebira said from behind them in the woods as bells rang out through the night.

They whirled around to find the queen, escorted by Fleur and Faune with a large group of fairies all around. The men and women advanced with either their wands or arrows raised.

"Let us pass," Byzarien said, raising the ax. "You have no right to keep us here."

The sisters helped Sebira move closer on weak legs. The queen trembled and had dark circles under her milky-white eyes. Myravelle knew the signs all too well; the queen's magic was draining.

"I couldn't see your shadowy future," the queen said with a small smirk lifting her lips. "But I know my daughter all too well."

"Daughter?" Myravelle asked.

With slumped shoulders and a downcast face, Sola stepped forward next to Faune. "I'm sorry," she whispered.

It was a trap. Myravelle scowled at the queen for using her daughter as a pawn.

"She only wanted to help you. We *all* wanted to help you," Sebira said, "but you are too dangerous, Myravelle."

"*Dangerous*?" she asked. "To whom?"

The queen blinked slowly, as if a silent conversation was enough to justify her actions.

"Why are you so weak, Queen Sebira?" Myravelle asked.

"I think you already know why."

Fleur, Faune, and Sola gasped when Myravelle glided forward and stood nose-to-nose with the queen. Sebira's guards flinched, but she gestured for them to remain still.

"Why don't you tell us anyway?" Myravelle asked.

It had begun to snow, but she could barely feel the flakes melting on her inflamed skin; the magic in her veins burned hotter than the lava within the Forbidden Mountain.

The queen sighed. "In each fairy realm, there can be but one queen," she began. "She is the most powerful fairy in the land until a new queen comes along. When this new queen grows into her full powers, the old queen fades away. I had hoped one of my daughters would be the next queen of the Sleepy Wood, but it is your magic, Myravelle, that is threatening mine."

"That's not my fault," she said, standing tall. "I don't want to be a queen; I just want to be accepted."

"It is not that simple," Sebira said. "We also desire peace with the Eglantyne Kingdom—and you must be locked away for everyone's safety."

"It wasn't me who created problems between fairies and humans." She winced as a sharp pain struck her temples with the image of Sebira and Xylina—as if she was reading the queen's mind. *Was it a power she had drained from her?* "And you know it."

She traced a rune against Sebira's temple, making the queen's eyes roll, gurgling sounds leaving her lips. The image of Sebira and Xylina grew clearer and clearer, until it flashed bright like a memory...

When her mother's powers and life faded, Sebira expected her own talents to grow. She was the Good Fairy, after all, the daughter of the queen—the queen who enjoyed mental games and belittling Sebira at every opportunity. Though the dying woman was now confined to her bed, she had somehow become Sebira's inner voice. *You're not even fit to be queen of an anthill.* Sebira sniffed back her tears and clenched her fists. She had to prove herself.

Stress hung like a yoke over her shoulders, for Prince Zylvain of Eglantyne Kingdom would be arriving for a diplomatic meeting that very evening. Moreover, it was Xylina's birthday—and Sebira had forgotten to give her best friend a gift. She felt sorry for Xylina, for her parents had died by the hands of Eglantyne soldiers after the fairies had provided aid to the kingdom of O'Leaux after the Shore Wars.

She paced the mossy floor of her room, high within the Hollow, thinking about Xylina while her mother moaned from the chambers next door. *Think. Think.* Xylina had so many interests, making it difficult to choose. She loved working with her sheep, spinning the sheared wool into the most beautiful yarn. She also enjoyed collecting botanicals from the Sleepy Wood, especially stinging nettle, which she spun into thread.

That was it. It wasn't about animals or plants—Xylina loved to spin. And a magnificent spindle she would receive. Sebira danced with excitement when she came up with the idea. In a rustle of white feathers and furs, she bounded down the spiral stairs and out into the village, toward the woodworking shop where wands were created. Instead of purchasing a wand, Sebira ordered a spindle of Dormrya wood. Since she was the Good Fairy, no one could refuse.

Later that day, when the polished spindle arrived in a silk-lined box, Sebira paid Xylina a visit. She greeted her friend with a kiss on the cheek. "Happy birthday."

Standing next to one another, the two were like shadow and light, Xylina with deep, dark hair while Sebira's was nearly white. When Xylina opened the gift, she grinned and rushed to the spinning chair by the stone fireplace. Sebira sat next to her on the floor while Xylina prepared the roving. She paused, frowning as she stared at the whorl of the spindle.

"What is it?" Sebira asked. "Is it not a good spindle?" Her friend went to the cupboard for a knife and carved into the wood. "What are you doing?" Sebira gasped.

"I honestly don't know," Xylina said, returning to her chair. "But I had a funny dream about this rune I've never seen before."

She finally began spinning, and Sebira's mouth hung open. As the fibers twisted, they became gold. *Gold.* Tingles spread over Sebira's skin at her friend's magnificent power...then that receded into a hard knot at the center of her chest. *What if Xylina is the reason Mother is fading?*

She wished Xylina goodbye and left in a hurry, before her friend could see the tears in her eyes. The Good Fairy knew she needed to impress Prince Zylvain now more than ever—she needed to secure her role as the next queen. Back in her chambers, she paced, thinking of ways to prove her powers or to even *seduce* the prince. She grimaced at the thought.

When Prince Zylvain arrived, Sebira met with him in the throne room, already taking her rightful place upon the dais during her mother's illness. Zylvain's men sat on boulders around the room while the prince and princess discussed their realms.

Things grew heated. Zylvain had said one too many prejudiced things about the fairies, and it was clear he would never accept peace terms. The kingdom wanted Dormrya wood, but the fairies would never allow that. Sebira felt like she was falling over a cliff, grasping at rocks, roots, or anything that would make the prince listen. Something gleamed in the corner of her mind—something she knew the prince desired, for his precious mountains and streams had run dry of the valuable metal.

"Gold," she said. "I can provide you with gold if you let us fairies live in peace."

Zylvain laughed and ran his fingers through his wavy, brown hair. "You have no gold out here in these woods."

Sebira adjusted her posture. "I can make it for you."

"How?"

"I can spin gold with a magic spindle."

The prince's gray eyes glittered as he stared at her, a grin turning up the corners of his lips. "Perhaps we could come to an agreement," he said, twirling the thin beginnings of a beard.

"I'll spin gold every night you are here," she said, rising from her throne and extending a hand to him. "And you will have your gold every morning if you would be willing to work toward a peace treaty."

Prince Zylvain took her hand. "Deal."

Outside, by the water well in the flower gardens, Sebira crouched down and tugged her hair. Feathers and crystals fell from her fingers when she removed her updo. If she did nothing, Zylvain would certainly go to war and take everything from them. If she asked Xylina to spin the gold, then her friend would have saved everyone and become the next queen.

"What am I to do?"

A shrill giggle echoed up the stones of the well. "Is someone in there?" she asked, peering into darkness.

"Only someone who can give you everything you desire."

Sebira looked around, making sure it wasn't some sort of trick. "Are you stuck down there? What's your name?"

"A name is much too powerful a weapon to hand over so easily."

She released a puff of air, shoulders dropping. "Do you need help?"

"*You* are the one who needs help."

"What?"

"You have a dilemma, do you not, Good Fairy Sebira?"

"Yes."

"Then send down that bucket, and let's make a deal."

Sebira turned the crank to lower the bucket, which grew heavy before it even hit the water. She strained to reel it in, until a greenish-gold claw of a hand grasped the side of the well. Recoiling with disgust, Sebira fell to the ground.

When the grotesque man with black hair to match his teeth

swung himself over the well, his yellow eyes turned to Sebira. "I can ensure you become queen."

Unable to swallow against her dry throat, Sebira stared at the monster in silence.

"Is that not what you desire?" He shrugged and turned toward the well as if to hop back in.

Sebira found her voice. "Wait! Yes, that is what I desire."

"Good. You shall trick Xylina into spinning gold for three days while you entertain Prince Zylvain," he said, "then accept any peace treaty the prince offers you."

"*Any* peace treaty?"

"Yes. Oh, and just one other simple, little thing," he began, scraping his claws along the stones of the well, "you must promise me a firstborn child. Only then will I give you a special gift to ensure you become queen."

"My firstborn child?"

"Listen well." The creature clicked his tongue against his black teeth. "*A* firstborn child."

While Sebira thought, the creature crossed his arms.

"*Any* firstborn child?"

"Any of *my* choosing." He stepped closer, reeking of mildew. "And you shall become queen."

"Fine," she said. "I agree."

"I will see you in three days." He jumped back into the well, giggling all the way down.

Sebira rushed to Xylina and, being a good friend, she agreed to spin gold without question. The very next day, Sebira proudly went to Prince Zylvain with a heaping armful of gilded thread. The prince twirled a piece of it around his finger and asked if he could see how she made it. Sebira refused, saying she could only work alone.

The second day, Sebira took more gold to the prince. Once again, he asked to see how she made it. Again, she declined.

Early on the last morning of the prince's visit, Sebira snuck into

Xylina's cottage. Her friend had fallen asleep in her chair, with only half the amount of gold spun.

Xylina sat up straight and began spinning. "I'll get right to work! I'm sorry." When she released her pinch on the roving, the fibers twisted into sparkling gold.

"Good gods," Prince Zylvain said from the shadowy doorway.

Sebira jumped, not knowing that he had followed her. Excuses and apologies stormed through her mind but none were able to leave her lips.

He sauntered into the center of the room, his wide gray eyes were two mirrors reflecting the gold. "This is impossible."

"The prince." Xylina gasped and slid from her chair to kneel before him. "Welcome to my home."

"As you were." Zylvain gingerly touched her chin. "Spin, please."

Xylina settled back into her chair and worked her magic with the drop spindle. Sebira pressed her hands to her mouth, unsure what to say as the prince circled her friend. His eyes followed the gleaming thread toward Xylina's hand.

Shaking her head, Sebira stepped forward. "I can explain."

"You lied to me?" Zylvain rested his hand on the back of Xylina's chair. "Is this the fairy who spins gold?"

"I'm sorry, I—"

"Why? It doesn't matter," he said with a grin. "Gold is gold."

"So, we still have our deal, for peace?"

He narrowed his eyes. "Only if I can take her with me to my castle."

"What?" Xylina asked, looking back and forth between Zylvain and Sebira.

"As long as this fairy returns to the castle with me, I promise my men will not venture past the Dormrya trees." He touched the gilded thread and rubbed it between his fingers.

Sebira thought back to the creature from the well. He said to become queen, she had to accept *any deal* the prince offered. "For how long?" she asked.

"Until we run out of wool." He slid his hand to Xylina's shoulder and laughed. "She shall provide me with gold for the rest of her days."

Xylina shook her head. "Sebby, please," she whispered.

Sebira looked away from her pleading eyes. If she denied Zylvain's request, Xylina's powers would certainly warrant her becoming queen. Jealousy clawed at her chest, shredding the love she had once felt for her friend. "Deal."

"Sebby, no!"

With a twirl of her wand, Sebira made Xylina fall asleep. At last, a benefit for having mastered the most useless rune of the entire grimoire: a sleep spell.

Zylvain called for his guards to carry Xylina out and thanked Sebira for being so understanding. He was so pleased with his never-ending supply of gold, he had no qualms about the fairies placing disorienting spells on him and his soldiers so they couldn't locate the fairy realm again. After the prince and his entourage left with Xylina and her spun gold, Sebira stumbled toward the garden well. Her limbs shook as the blood drained from her face. *What had she done?* Xylina was her dearest friend. She lowered the bucket into the well and drew out the wicked creature. "Can I take it back?" she asked. "Can I bring Xylina back?"

"You want to go back on our bargain?" he growled, somehow growing taller with every word. "Once you make a deal with me, there is no return."

Sebira fell to her knees, tarnishing her pure-white gown with grass stains and soil. "What am I going to do?"

"Take my gift and become queen, like you always wanted."

The creature placed his clammy hands around Sebira's head, his thumbs over her eyes. Scorching pain flared through her head and she shrieked, trying to pull away from the monster. He was much too strong to be human or fairy. The agony ebbed and flowed, each wave nauseating her more and more.

When he released her, the pain faded. She sucked in a breath and opened her eyes. All was dark, and she reached around, waving her arms. "Where did you take me?" she asked, feeling around for the creature. "I can't see!"

"You will never see through your eyes again," he said. "Yet, you will see paths to the future. A great queen must meddle in fate now and again."

He pressed a hand to her forehead. Images and voices and feelings flooded her mind. She shook her head against them, unable to sort through the tangled heaps of information. She laid upon the earth, writhing and flailing against the new power.

"I suppose I can reveal to you my name now: I am Filoux, god of nightmares and trickery," the creature said, cackling. "I shall claim Xylina's firstborn child. There is power in names, and hers will be Myravelle. She will be my greatest creation."

The queen ripped her head away, shrieking and breaking the connection. Myravelle stumbled back. Sebira had willingly given her mother to Zylvain? *She will pay*. A group of fairies approached while she was caught off-guard by the rage interfering with her magic. Towering over them, Byzarien took on a fighting stance with his ax while Myravelle raised her staff.

"You don't want to do this," Sebira said.

With a twirl of her staff, Myravelle knocked the wands and bows from the fairies' hands and turned back to the queen, who trembled in her daughters' arms.

Sola looked at Myravelle with wide eyes. "What are you doing?"

Runes glowed in her mind, and she wanted nothing more than to hurt the queen.

"Look at you, your magic is destructive," Sebira said. "Although I can't untangle every path to the future, I know that, should you not be imprisoned, your fate will lead to chaos. That is why I cursed these trees to stop you."

"And what exactly will happen if we cross your line of curses?" Myrabelle growled.

"I created a special enchantment for you: should you try to cross the Dormrya's without holding my hand, you will fall into a death-like sleep with no one left to wake you. You see, I must be the one to escort you across the enchanted barrier so I can personally hand you over to the king."

"Just like you personally handed over my mother to the king?"

"What?" Sola asked, staring sidelong at her mother.

Other fairies muttered amongst themselves before turning toward Sebira.

"Is that true?" Argus asked.

"Because she was to be the next fairy queen and not you," Myravelle ground out through clenched teeth.

The queen shook her head. "She's lying! I've told you the truth all along: the king kidnapped her without my knowledge."

"That's not true!"

"You all saw her magic and the destruction it brought in only a matter of days," Sebira said.

Fleur nodded and turned toward the fairies. "She made a mess in the library and destroyed a greenhouse with magic fire," she said. "She's not even a real fairy!"

The fairies agreed with her in a chilling harmony of voices.

"We must turn her over to the king," Sebira insisted.

The chatter amongst the fairies died down, and they hardened their stances toward Myravelle. Only Sola seemingly remained uncertain, rounding her shoulders and shaking her head. With the fairies clearly on her side, the queen smiled at Myravelle.

An ember of rage ignited in her chest, and she turned to Byzarien. "Will you still love me if I do something awful?"

He met her eyes. "I will."

Turning back toward the queen, she twisted her staff in the shape of a new rune, sending Byzarien's ax flying. With a slice of flesh and bone, the queen's hand fell from her wrist. Sebira screamed as her daughters wrapped her arm in their cloaks.

"Myravelle, what did you do? You're proving them right!" Sola cried while aiding her mother. "Why would you do this?"

"Because she's wicked, you idiot," Fleur scolded her. "I told you not to fall for her charms."

The queen's corpse-pale hand floated toward Myravelle, who snatched it from the air. She glared at the other fairies, who hesitated to reach for their weapons and attack her.

"Stop her!" Fleur shouted at them.

With Byzarien at her side, Myravelle marched on as the fairies, too stunned or frightened to react, simply let them pass. With each of them holding on to the queen's bloody hand, they crossed the line of the tall, cursed trees unscathed.

29

Byzarien

Once they disposed of the queen's hand, Byzarien and Myravelle headed in the direction of the kingdom, where they would wait at the Dumont's house near the Pezit Quarter. During the trek, Myravelle was quiet—too quiet even for her introverted nature.

Byzarien placed his arm around her and kissed her head. "Are you all right?"

She toyed with the rings on her fingers, particularly the moonstone which had belonged to Xylina.

"What's wrong? You can tell me."

"It's just...when I touched Sebira, I had another vision."

She told him everything—from her mother and Sebira once being friends, to Filoux making his bargain, to Zylvain taking Xylina.

"What does it mean?" he asked. "What would the god of nightmares and chaos want with you?"

She shook her head, jaw trembling.

"Whatever it is, I think he failed," he said, tilting his head to look into Myravelle's eyes. "You wake those he puts under a death-like sleep. You're *good*, Myravelle."

"I don't know. I have done such horrible things."

"Under the threat of imprisonment." He rubbed her shoulder. "I'm proud of you for standing up for yourself."

"My magic," she began, "has become its own creature. It's so dark, and sometimes I feel out of control."

"You don't scare me."

"But you're...you're risking everything for me," she whispered, brows stitching. "It's not too late, you could return home and tell everyone I took you by force. Tell them I had you under a spell or something. Everyone would believe you."

He studied Myravelle's quick breaths, fidgeting fingers, and avoidance of eye contact. He had assumed he was the insecure one in their relationship, but she needed assurance. She needed his love.

"You certainly have me under a spell, that's true," he said with a grin. "You and I, our souls fit together. I promise, as long as we have one another, you won't lose control."

"Do you truly think your family will accept me?"

"Yes, I do."

She shook her head and looked away, but he threaded their fingers and forced her to look at him.

"We're in this together," he said. "We'll meet with our friends and head to either Basenfort or O'Leaux."

"Do you really think they'll help us?"

"Well, Queen Lya is from Basenfort, so her family would have interest in protecting her from Zylvain's madness," he said. "On the other hand, the relationship between Eglantyne and O'Leaux has been tumultuous for decades. This could be their chance to strike."

Myravelle bit at her bottom lip. "It's illegal for your family to house traitors," she said. "No matter your feelings toward me, they might not be willing to accept the risk."

"They will love you." He swallowed against the lump in his

throat, hating to see his powerful lover so unsure. "You're the reason their lives are better."

Rising on her toes, Myravelle planted a kiss on Byzarien's lips. "Thank you," she said. "I promise to spin more gold for your family, so they never suffer again."

They walked through the tangled forest side-by-side. As snow fell in drifts and the night grew dark, Byzarien did his best to mimic Myravelle's graceful steps but slipped on a patch of ice and fell. Giggling, she dropped onto him and kissed his lips. When she pulled back, they studied one another.

"The snowflakes made a starry sky in your hair." Byzarien brushed his fingers through her midnight locks. "My girl of stars."

She beamed and touched his cheek. "Well, the cold has inflamed your cheeks. My boy of scars."

After a few warm kisses, Myravelle looked around. "This will be a fine place to rest."

With a motion of her staff, she pitched a tent, and the pair huddled inside. She carved an enchantment into a log to burn with magic flames, which immediately warmed the tent. They both stared into the fire, losing themselves to the stories told by crackles and flickers.

"I sure hope Little Nightmare found a warm place to sleep tonight," Byzarien said as he held Myravelle.

"I'll find out."

She closed her eyes, twirled her finger, and went slack in his embrace. He traced her relaxed features and stroked her hair until she stirred.

"He's fine," she said. "He's on a rooftop, snuggled up warm and toasty by a chimney."

"Good."

When the snow stopped beating against the top of their tent, Byzarien's stomach grumbled. Myravelle rummaged through their pack only to find a few fairy cakes left. "We should save these for

Little Nightmare," she said, taking out her small cauldron and pulling on her cloak.

"Where are you going?"

"To find us something to eat."

"It's too dark and cold to be wandering around right now."

"I won't have to go very far—at least, I don't think so," she said, tilting her head.

"What do you mean?"

"Another rune is glowing in my eyesight," she said. "So much has changed inside me, I don't even know what I'm capable of."

He followed her out of the tent, where she lifted her staff and swept it through the chilled air. Byzarien watched wide-eyed as the snow blew away like powdered sugar, clearing a large semi-circle before them.

She grinned to herself and turned to him. "Will you collect more firewood?"

When he returned with the wood, Myravelle had set her small cauldron filled with snow over the enchanted log. Byzarien added the wood, and a strong fire crackled against the silent night. Turning to the forest, Myravelle twirled her staff and drew it back, as if tugging it away from an invisible foe. Cracking and snapping sounds echoed from the darkness, rumbling toward them as the earth shook. Roots and mushrooms and herbs came floating toward them and dove into the pot, which was now boiling.

Myravelle took a deep breath and leaned against her staff, hanging her head.

Byzarien moved toward her and let her relax into his embrace. "What's wrong?"

"I think maybe I did too much after all of our walking," she said. "I need to learn my limits."

"I'll watch over the soup," he said, guiding her to the tent. "You should rest while it cooks."

Before entering the tent, Myravelle's silver eyes caught Byzarien in their spell as easily as ever. She stroked his cheek, sending shivers down his spine. "I love you."

Though she had said it before, it still made his heart soar. He never wanted to be apart from her, and a certain question tingled on the tip of his tongue. Biting back the impulse, he leaned down to brush his lips against hers. With each declaration of love, his entire body was set alight with a fiery glow—like drinking hot tea on a snowy day.

He spoke against her ear as he nuzzled it. "I love you, too."

Alone with the pot of soup and the forest, Byzarien ruminated over the question he wanted to ask Myravelle. *Should he do it? Was it too soon? What would she say? He had no ring. How could he make it special for her?*

He touched the silver crossed swords of Guerrix on his pendant. Although he was no longer sure he worshiped the god, he suddenly knew what to do. He was sure about Myravelle.

Removing the pendant from the chain and slipping on his leather gloves, he warmed the silver against the edge of the pot, making the metal more pliable. He used a piece of wood as a mallet to hammer the silver against the rounded lip of the cauldron, twisting it into a ring. He slipped it onto the top knuckle of his pinky to check the fit for Myravelle's long and slender fingers.

It wasn't the most beautiful or luxurious piece of jewelry, but it would work as a placeholder. The flames danced in the reflection on the hammered silver, and Byzarien's stomach dropped. There was no turning back. She would wonder what happened to the pendant he had never once taken off the entire time she had known him.

After tucking the ring into his pocket, he stirred the contents of the cauldron. He spooned a taste into his mouth, and the savory liquid melted against his tongue, bursting with flavor and warming his throat. The soup Myravelle had literally dragged from the forest was ready. He drew the bowls and spoons from their pack and placed mugs of snow near the flames for drinking water.

When he looked into the tent to wake Myravelle, his voice nearly caught in his throat with nervousness. "It's ready," he said, caressing her shoulder.

Her eyes were bright when she sat up, and Byzarien hoped the soup would make her feel even better. They huddled together near the enchanted flames and ate the soup while the ring sat in his pocket like a stone. The warmth from the fire and food at last brought the color back to Myravelle's cheeks.

"How are you feeling?" he asked, leg bouncing.

Myravelle swallowed her last bite. "Much better. I just need to remember that I'm not *all-powerful*," she said with a grin.

"You are to me." Byzarien set down his bowl and extended his hand toward her. "Would you, um, would you like to dance?"

She bit her lip, a grin creeping across her face, and took his hand. With the crackling flames and whistling breeze as their music, they swayed. Myravelle pressed herself so tightly against Byzarien's body, he thought they might become one person.

He kissed the top of her head. "This is perfect."

"Not yet." Myravelle looked around, lips pursed in thought. She broke their warm embrace and plucked her staff from the ground. Waving it above her head, she blew the clouds away.

Byzarien gaped with heart-racing anticipation to see the stars. The gray sky of eternal winter rolled back and stars, brighter than he had remembered, twinkled down. The moon peeked from behind the clouds, glowing with such brilliance that it made him squint. Myravelle circled her staff toward that section of the sky, and the clouds peeled away to expose the entire crescent moon in all its smiling glory.

"Now this is perfect," she said, dropping her staff and returning to Byzarien.

They gazed at the sky as if to memorize every constellation, for fear they would never see them again. The beautiful weight of the heavens pressed on Byzarien's chest, making it difficult to breathe. Overwhelmed, his eyes slid to the woman who made that beauty possible, and his heart nearly burst. The way her hair shone in the glow of the moon and the way her eyes sparkled with the stars was almost too much.

Reaching into his pocket, he knelt before her. She looked down at him, questions pulling her brows together. With a shaking hand, Byzarien extended the crossed sword ring. "Myravelle Spinner," he began and cleared his throat. "You have bewitched me, not with spells or enchantments, but with your love. I want to be with you for the rest of my life, no matter what that may look like. Will you marry me?"

Myravelle fell to her knees, tears sparkling in her eyes. "Byzarien Dumont, you have bewitched me with your love too. I absolutely do not deserve you, but I will take you for as long as you love me. I promise to love you for the rest of this life and the next."

A smile, wider than the crescent moon, spread across Byzarien's cheeks as he slid the ring onto her finger. He leaned in for a kiss, and Myravelle threw her arms around him, making Byzarien feel perfectly at home even in the deep, dark wood. She pressed her hips against his and ran her hands over his body, then under his tunic. The touch of her skin stirred a sensation of stars twinkling in his veins.

When she stroked him in a certain place, his head fell back. Myravelle stood and grabbed Byzarien's arms to pull him into the tent. Though his stomach was full of soup, he grew hungry for her. He tore off her clothes as she did his. When there was nothing left to separate their bodies, his fingers explored smooth skin while her tongue traced roving scars.

"Should I get the dagger?" she asked, touching the rune on his chest.

"No," he said, trailing a finger from her sternum to navel. "I just want it to be you and me tonight."

30

Myravelle

As Myravelle spun gold, the glisten of her engagement ring in the morning light made her giddy. *Engagement. Marriage. Love.* They had all been foolish dreams under the king's thumb. Her fingers drafted and pinched the fibers then twirled the enchanted spindle, letting the twist of gilded fibers rise into the length. She hummed her mother's song, but not loudly enough to wake Byzarien, who was sprawled out on the floor drawing long, sleepy breaths. She gazed from his bare chest down to his hips, where the blanket barely covered him. Half-smooth. Half-scarred. *All hers.*

She placed two skeins of gold into their pack: one for their journey and one for Byzarien's family. Stones rolled in her stomach at the thought of meeting them. She certainly wasn't good enough for Byzarien, and she was leading him down a dark and dangerous path. What would they think of her? Even if the gold could relieve some of their financial concerns, would they really let Byzarien go to another kingdom to commit treason against King Zylvain?

When he stirred and stretched, Myravelle crawled to him and

draped herself across his warm chest. His heartbeat thrummed against her ear at the same tempo as hers, settling her nerves.

"Good morning." He wrapped his arms around her, planting kisses into her hair. "Are you ready to meet my family?"

"I don't know," she said, voice shaking. "I hope they like me."

"Of course, they will," he said, gesturing to the gilded thread peeking from the pack. "Even without *bribes*, Myravelle."

They laughed, and he rolled on top of her for a kiss. It melted a bit of her anxiety, but some still lingered in the tightness of her back and the cinch around her stomach. Having been feared and hated her entire life made it difficult to believe someone could love her. She wanted Byzarien so badly, though, she decided to let him love her, even for a little while.

After packing up the tent, the pair hiked hand-in-hand through the woods all day, only taking short breaks for food and rest. When they could see the king's road through the trees, Myravelle turned to Byzarien and raised her staff, giving it a twirl. As if melting from their heads, disguises of beige peasant clothes draped over the pair. They pulled up the hoods to help hide their faces. Even Myravelle's staff had transformed into a basic walking stick.

"Kneel for me," she told Byzarien.

He smirked. "Did I not satisfy you enough last night?"

She playfully tapped his cheek. "I need the gold."

When he knelt, Myravelle opened the pack and snipped some of the fiber from the skein. With a swirl of her staff, the thread curled and coiled until it became a handful of small coins. She tucked them into her pocket, and they kept walking. Eventually, they reached the Noire River and crossed a crumbling bridge.

"They aren't taking tolls for this bridge," he said, looking around. "It could use some work, though—this farming village must be in worse shape than I remember. Hopefully someone will be able to take us to the Pezit Quarter."

Past the fields, the village rose around them with boarded up cottages, barren fields, and broken fences. It was growing late, and many of the villagers had turned in for the night. By luck, a man was brushing down horses still hitched to an empty wagon. Myravelle handed Byzarien one of the coins, and he approached the farmer.

"Blessed day," he greeted the man. "Any chance you could take us to the city? My wife and I must get to Lord Riccard's estate on the southwest side."

Myravelle blushed to her bones at the word *wife*. Though it was a lie, it felt good.

"Only just returned." The man tipped his hat and gestured to the horses. "Can't overwork them, or I won't have enough to feed them."

Byzarien held out a coin. "For your troubles?"

The farmer's eyes lit up his wrinkly face as he accepted the gold. "Of course, good sir."

Myravelle and Byzarien huddled into the wagon. The ride was bumpy the closer they got to the mountains, but easier on their bodies than walking the entire distance to the Dumonts' house would have been. The old man told them how the eternal winter had devastated the village; many sold everything they could to get by or had already fled. Fire crept into Myravelle's cheeks—she hated how Filoux created such despair and how King Zylvain refused to help his own people.

Myravelle remained silent and wrapped her arms around her knees as if encasing herself in a shell. She played with her engagement ring and glanced at Byzarien: the sweet, strong, and loyal man with a steel heart forged in flame. She didn't deserve his loyalty, and his family would certainly think as much. What if they convinced him to end things with her?

Or worse: what if they convinced him to turn her over to the king?

Were they as loyal to the crown as Byzarien had been? Would one look at *Myravelle the Wicked Fairy* send them into a frenzy? She scooted closer to him and laced her fingers with his.

He kissed her hand. "What is it? What's wrong?"

"I'm not good enough for you," she said. "Your family will see that."

"Nonsense," he said, leaning his forehead against hers. "They will love you because I do."

"What if they want to hand me over to the king?"

"I won't allow it," he said. "Don't worry, they're good people."

Myravelle let Byzarien wrap his arm around her, and she sank against his side like a moth in her cocoon. They rested until the city walls rose into view, as did the Forbidden Mountain to the north. The volcano continued to spew smoke and ash into the sky—and continued to cause the eternal winter for the kingdom. *Filoux*, she thought, *had made everyone endure a living Darkened Path by day and by night.* He made Sebira betray Xylina. Humans thought fairies meddled with fate, but Filoux was by far the biggest meddler. As night blanketed the land, the Forbidden Mountain appeared even more foreboding.

She will be my greatest creation. Filoux's words to Sebira haunted Myravelle and made her insides grow cold. Was she a *half-fairy* and her magic *tempestuous* because she was Filoux's daughter? *Could it be?* The idea made her head spin.

"This is where I turn," the farmer called, ripping Myravelle from her thoughts. "Or I might fall asleep on my way home."

Byzarien helped Myravelle from the cart and handed the farmer the second gold coin, which the man gladly accepted. "This is more money than I make in a month! Are you sure?" he asked with a gravelly laugh.

"Thank you for your trouble," Byzarien said.

After the farmer clicked his tongue and lifted the reins, Myravelle and Byzarien watched him disappear down the road, swallowed by the night. They turned to the city of Eglantyne, high walls coursed with dead ivy against the backdrop of mountains.

As they walked down the road, the houses grew closer together into a little village. They entered the walls of the city proper through the first Pezit Quarter gate. Byzarien knew the shortcut to Lord

Riccard's estate, but being within the city walls and around so many humans made Myravelle's skin buzz.

She gasped when she saw it: a poster of her face plastered to a stone wall. *Evil. Wicked. Dangerous.* She froze in place, shivering to her bones. Byzarien glanced both ways down the alley before ripping the image down. He guided her away from it while she pulled her hood tighter.

Candles flickered in the windows of tenements and the apartments over closed shops. Rising above the rooftops was the steeple of a temple of dark stone and pointed arches. The stained-glass windows glowed against the night, the gods gazing down upon the peasants in threadbare clothes crowding the market area even at night. The god who caught Myravelle's eyes, though, was Filoux. He smiled at her from afar, with his dark webs of nightmares cradled between his fingers. A terrible, horrible thought crept into her mind.

She pointed to the monstrous image of the god and whispered, "What if Filoux is my father?"

Byzarien studied the stained-glass, then looked at Myravelle as if it were the first time, his eyes wide and swimming with fear or wonder. He took her hand, reassuring her of his love. "That could very well be. I mean, he orchestrated everything."

She gulped, trying to swallow the painful lump in her throat. "Why wouldn't my mother tell me?"

He wrapped her in his arms. "She was probably frightened or confused," he said softly. "And if Filoux has truly done all of these awful things, then she could have been protecting you."

Myravelle nodded before she hopped over a puddle of beer or urine, she didn't want to find out. They continued walking, hand-in-hand, past the taverns which opened up to the streets, spilling the scent of stale beer. Drunks approached them, and Myravelle kept her head down, not wanting anyone with liquid courage to get a glimpse of her.

"*Ish* she for *shale*?" a man slurred as he stumbled over the cobblestones toward them.

"What?" Byzarien asked, picking up their pace.

"How *mush* for an hour with her?"

Searing heat spread through Myravelle's body, and she raised her staff.

"She's not for sale," Byzarien growled and reached into Myravelle's cloak, drawing her dagger. In one swift motion, he raised it to the drunk's throat. "You can't even afford to look at my fiancé, do you understand?" The sharp, acrid scent of urine stung the air as the man trembled. It took him a moment before he scrambled away.

The burning magic rearing up in Myravelle's chest retreated as she pulled Byzarien close. "Thank you," she said. "But you don't have to protect me."

"I know," he said. "Believe me, I was protecting *him*."

Myravelle tilted her head.

"Your eyes glowed, and I knew you were about to do something that would garner much more attention than a drunkard pissing himself."

Eventually, after they left the city walls through the second Pezit Quarter gate, the houses and people thinned, opening to villages and farmland once more. In a juxtaposition to the poor Pezit Quarter, a grand manor stood in the distance.

Byzarien leaned to whisper in Myravelle's ear, "Lord Riccard's estate."

Spaced evenly throughout the fields were the worker's cottages. Night pressed further and, with no stars or moon, it became difficult to see. A few of the small homes were still lit from within by the glow of candles, while smoke puffed from the chimneys. Some rented from Lord Riccard but, because of Myravelle's gold, the Dumonts owned their small parcel of land.

They turned down a lane toward the house where Byzarien's family lived. Something pricked Myravelle's mind, and she thought it was simply her nerves taking over again. But, when the pressure, like a migraine, continued she dropped her staff and leaned against

Byzarien. Her eyes rolled back, and she saw the sky. Forests. Mountains. Fields. All from above. *Little Nightmare? Find us.*

She relayed their location to her pet. When she opened her eyes, she was in Byzarien's arms, his face twisted with concern.

"Are you all right?"

"Little Nightmare." She took deep breaths and clung to his neck to keep herself steady. Her limbs and mind felt empty, as if she were but a paper doll about to blow away with the breeze.

"We'll get you some rest soon," he said, grabbing the staff for her. "We're nearly home."

Home. The word wrapped Myravelle in a hug as they made their way along the road. Past the next field was a small house surrounded by a grove of skeletal trees.

Before they even reached the gate, Byzarien's family rushed from the front door. At first, they stared at him like a creature from the Darkened Path. His mother's jaw trembled, his father caught himself against the doorframe, and his sisters cried. Myravelle hid behind Byzarien, shrinking in on herself and wishing to disappear.

31

Byzarien

Muscles and tendons trembling, Byzarien found himself unable to move as he stared at his family. Overwhelmed with joy, he fell to his knees as they rushed to him. His mother reached him first and wrapped him in her arms. Though much larger than she, he folded himself into her embrace like a little boy. When his father and sisters piled onto the group hug, they all toppled over.

Laughing, Byzarien kissed their cheeks randomly as they all rose from the ground. His sisters were weeping, so he placed his arms around them. Both Bea and Bryda had grown so much taller since he had last been home.

His mother stroked his face. "This is...unbelievable," she whispered. "You're really here."

"We thought we...lost you, too," his father choked out.

"Well, I'm here," he said, squeezing his sisters tight. "And I have much to tell you."

Byzarien's family turned to look at Myravelle, who'd been

hanging back. His sisters, Bryda and Beatriz, smiled at one another with mischievous gleams in their eyes.

"Who's this?" Adelyne asked.

Extending a hand to Myravelle, Byzarien tilted his head toward the door. "Let's all go inside."

They followed his family toward the house, and Byzarien, noticing she trembled, placed both hands around Myravelle's arm. It was difficult to get a good view of the exterior of the cottage at night, but once they stepped through the threshold, Byzarien took it all in with wide eyes. Though different from both his childhood home and the cottage his family had rented in the past, it still smelled like home. Candles illuminated the space and a fire crackled in the hearth. The post-dinner scent of garlic and rosemary still lingered in the air as they entered the kitchen, where Byzarien's mother set a kettle on the stove.

At the table, Byzarien pulled a chair out for Myravelle before his family swarmed on him like bees once again.

"It's really you," Bryda said, squeezing his midsection tight before taking her own seat.

"We thought you died—we had a service and everything." His mother patted his shoulder, prompting him to sit, and toyed with the end of her long dark braid that had one gray streak woven through. She stared off at nothing and shook her head. "Then your friends visited, and we didn't know what to believe."

"I've missed you all so much," Byzarien said and looked at his sisters across the table from him. "Who are these young ladies and what have you done with my sisters?"

They giggled, and his father swooped in for his own hug, clapping his back. The man with salt-and-pepper hair was not so tall as Byzarien, but his wrinkled skin and rough hands showed the life of hard work he had led.

"We love seeing you." His father folded his hands together and swallowed as if fighting tears. "But we have heard of *trouble* at the army encampment and we were told you were dead. What happened, Byz?"

"As you can see, I'm fine," he said, patting his father's hands. "But we won't be able to stay long." With that, everyone melted into their chairs, frowning.

"I'm Emeryk, Byzarien's father, by the way." The man stuck out his hand, which Myravelle shook. "It's a pleasure to meet you."

His mother served teacups to everyone and brought over the kettle. "And I'm Adelyne," she said, pouring Myravelle some tea. "And you are?"

Her silver eyes flickered to Byzarien, and he gave her hand a squeeze and nodded. "I am Myravelle."

A stunned hush held the family captive, until the sound of splashing alerted Byzarien that his mother was pouring the tea all over the wood floor.

"Ma!" Byzarien guided the kettle over the teacup. "She's my fiancé," he added, to which his mother dropped the entire kettle. Everyone's questions and protests swirled as the clamor rose within the small kitchen.

Emeryk stood, glaring at Byzarien. "So, this is the Wicked Fairy everyone has been talking about? The one the king said killed you! You're *with* her?"

Adelyne leaned against the table as if too weak to walk while she made her way to her husband. "The Wicked Fairy?"

Myravelle lowered her gaze.

"The king lied! She clearly didn't kill me," Byzarien said, wrapping his arm around her. "She's not wicked!"

The questions from his parents continued while Bea tried to comfort the scared Bryda during the chaos. Byzarien didn't know what to do or to say.

Myravelle sprung from her chair. With a twirl of her staff, a towel danced its way from the sink and soaked up the tea on the floor. When she turned her staff toward the kettle, it rose into the air and poured tea in each cup. Stunned into silence once more, Byzarien's family stared at her.

"Yes, I'm Myravelle Spinner," she said to them. "And yes, I am part fairy. But I am not wicked like the king would have you believe."

As she sat back down, Byzarien began telling their story—Myravelle growing up locked in a tower, how he became her canvas, the king's visit, the attack, the gold, the finger, the magic, the escape, the fairies. Myravelle's shoulders slumped more and more with every detail.

"The king has been spreading propaganda about Myravelle and the fairies, but all the while, he was responsible for the deaths and hardships." He leaned forward, eyes locked with his father's. "The fairies have but a tiny village deep in the woods, I saw it with my own eyes. And their magic is...complicated and not as powerful as you might think. It would not have been possible for them to attack the kingdom."

After a few moments of quiet reflection, Emeryk turned to Myravelle and tilted his head. "So, the gold was from you, dear?"

She could only nod.

"I want to make it clear," Byzarien began and leaned forward to touch his mother's hand, "the king has exploited Myravelle and her mother for years, and he is up to something with all of that gold and Dormrya wood. We are on our way to Basenfort to seek sanctuary and aid."

His parents paled like ghosts at the heaps of information. Adelyne scurried to the sink and frantically washed dishes, wringing her apron between each one. Myravelle sunk into herself even more.

"We want to believe you, Byz," Emeryk said. "But we are also deeply worried for you."

"I know, but this is the right thing." He looked at Myravelle and brushed a lock of hair behind her ear. She met him with a sad smile. "I love her and must help her in any way I can."

"Girls," Adelyne squeaked out and clapped at her daughters. "Run along to bed."

"Yes, Ma," they said. Chairs squeaking against the floor, they gave Byzarien kisses on the cheek before leaving the kitchen.

Once their bedroom door had shut, Adelyne stepped close to Byzarien. "Son, this is dangerous," she whispered, eyes flitting toward Myravelle. "We could be charged with treason."

"Ma, you always taught me to do what is right, not what is easy," he said, wiping a tear from his mother's cheek. "Believe me: she is innocent."

Myravelle rose from her chair and leaned against her staff. "I understand that harboring the *Wicked Fairy* is a crime. And I don't want to cause any trouble for your family," she said to Byzarien. "I can camp outside."

"No, I won't have it," he said, standing by her side and staring at his parents. "If you make my fiancé sleep outside, then you're making me sleep outside."

Adelyne crossed her arms and shook her head. "Now, what sort of mother would I be if I didn't believe my own son," she said, tears glistening in her big brown eyes.

The tight knot in his stomach dissipated, and he sighed with relief before hugging his mother.

"You two must be exhausted," she said, patting Byzarien's back. "This cottage isn't very large, so I'll gather some blankets and you can sleep in the den. Once we've all had a proper rest, it would be nice to catch up."

When everyone was quiet and in their rooms, and Myravelle was lounging on the couch, Byzarien knelt before his family's altar. *One last prayer, for them.* He lit a red candle and bowed his head. After whispering for a while, he turned to find Myravelle watching him.

"I don't know what to believe anymore," he said. "But I still asked Guerrix to watch over them for me, just in case he's listening."

"I admire your spirituality," she said, a smile lifting the corner of her mouth. "Don't let me bother you."

Grinning, Byzarien returned his focus to the altar until tapping sounds from the window drew him from his prayers. Myravelle turned toward the sound too, so he got up and walked toward the window. Tugging the curtains aside, he found Little Nightmare pecking the glass. Myravelle gasped and rushed over as he opened the window to let the crow in.

Little Nightmare cawed and nibbled at the message tied around his leg. Myravelle scooped up their pet and sat with him on her lap while stroking his black feathers.

"Good boy," she said. "We're glad you found us."

Byzarien sat on the floor and untied the message. "It's from Xavier," he said. "The king and captain are leaving for the fairy realm."

"The fairy realm?"

"To search for you." He shrugged. "We'll meet my friends. They'll linger behind the march and meet us at the graveyard. With Eryck's help, they've gathered a group of twenty soldiers who want to speak to the queen of Basenfort." Myravelle kept her eyes on Little Nightmare and bit at her lip.

"This is a good thing." Byzarien caressed her cheek to coax her gaze to meet his. "We'll have our own platoon. The more help we get, the more legitimate our claims will sound to the queen."

"I think I've had enough of kings and queens."

32

Myravelle

After tucking Little Nightmare in on a pile of cushions, Myravelle squeezed next to Byzarien on the couch and traced the scars on his neck. "I can see why you were willing to sacrifice your life for them. Your family is absolutely lovely."

"You'll soon be a part of this family too, you know."

"Perfect."

They kissed, sweet and slow, before falling asleep in each other's arms. Myravelle had hoped to dream about bridal gowns and vows, but she ended up in a strange dark place that smelled a bit like sulfur and mildew. The hem of her dress was soaked with the stagnant water inside the endless tunnel. Roots hung down through the cracks and hit her head.

"Myravelle," a screechy voice called, echoing against the stones.

She spun around to find the same greenish-gold creature from the visions. "Filoux?" she asked.

"Aha, you already know my name," he said, smiling his black smile. "My smart and powerful girl."

She stepped back and glanced around. "Where are we?"

"Oh, just somewhere between the Darkened Path and dreams."

"Why?"

"It's how I get around." He used his claws to climb the rounded stones until he hung upside-down from the roots at the top and scurried toward a gaping hole in the ceiling. "Wells, springs, and the volcano, of course. My specialty, though, are the Dormrya trees."

"The trees?"

"Their ancient roots reach my lair, and I feed them with nightmares and chaos," he said as his black eyes widened, and he reached for Myravelle. "They were my greatest creation until you, dearie. I have my roots in you, too."

She shivered. "What do you want with me?"

Filoux dropped from the ceiling and onto his gnarly feet with a splash. He circled Myravelle, trailing his long claws through her hair. "Oh, Myravelle," he said. "My special creation—you are almost ready."

"What do you mean?"

"I cannot tell you that." He leaned close and sniffed, scrunching his nose. "For you are not my *full creation*, no, not yet. Something holds you back."

"Holds me back from what?"

Filoux squeezed his arms around himself and squealed. "Oh, I wish I could tell you!"

"What?"

"Let's just say, you are destined for great chaos, Myravelle!" he shouted as he crawled on all fours and splashed her with filthy water. "You are my final revenge on the Eglantyne Kingdom, and you will do marvelous things!"

She shook her head. "I don't want to be your revenge. I only want to live a peaceful life with Byzarien."

Filoux jabbed his talon-like finger at her chest. "There," he said. "That's it. That's what's holding you back from greatness."

She shook her head, brows furrowing. "What?"

"Your reckless heart." Filoux stroked his chin and circled Myravelle like a predator. "Now, how to fix this? I could pay Sebira another visit I suppose...though, she won't be too happy to *see* me. Get it?"

The creature cackled as he fell to the floor and rolled in the revolting water.

Myravelle looked around for a way out and attempted to trace enchantments with her fingers to no avail. Her magic didn't work in Filoux's realm.

"You blinded her."

"Yes, but I gave her the power to glimpse the future!" He sat up on the wet floor and lowered his voice to a whisper. "I had to send shadows into her mind now and again to hide you and Xylina."

"You shrouded her visions?"

"Indeed."

"You're evil."

"Maybe." He hopped up and stepped close, the scent of mildew and sulfur radiating off his scaly skin. "I think I have a plan. Yes, I know exactly how to make you mine."

"Please, just leave me alone."

"What? No love for the god who made the stars fall for you?" Filoux's dark brows shadowed his eyes as he frowned. "No love for the god who gave you your celestial powers?"

Myravelle took a few steps back and shook her head. "I just want a normal life."

"Sorry, dearie," he said, frown flipping into a wide grin. "Goodbye, my work of art."

In a swipe of his hand, everything turned to smoke.

"Wait!" she shouted as she remembered what she wanted to know. "Are you my father?"

Nothing. Not even the echoes of the tunnel reverberated in her ears. She was in a dark and barren place with neither dreams nor nightmares.

In the morning, Byzarien rubbed her back as she stared blankly at the floor. "What is it?"

"I had the strangest dream last night." She told him about meeting Filoux, and the god claiming that she was his greatest creation.

"That had to be frightening," he said, caressing her cheek. "Remember what I told you: Filoux failed. You've healed people under his curse. You are *good*, Myravelle."

"Thank you," she said, leaning against his shoulder.

The bedroom doors opened, and Byzarien's family trickled out from their rooms to begin their day.

He helped Myravelle sit up before stepping into the kitchen. "Need any help, Ma?" he called.

Myravelle tucked her knees up under her chin, debating whether to help or remain as invisible as possible.

"Is that a crow?" Bryda asked, pointing at Little Nightmare and shaking her sister's arm.

"It is," Myravelle said. "His name is Little Nightmare...Byzarien named him."

The girls laughed as they dropped to their knees and stroked the crow's feathers. Myravelle grinned, watching Little Nightmare bask in the attention.

"Is he hungry?" Beatriz asked. "What does he eat?"

"Oats, seeds, berries, and," Myravelle paused, reaching into the pack and unrolling a cloth to reveal several fairy cakes, "these."

Each girl took one and fed them to Little Nightmare in turn.

"He's adorable," Bryda said.

Byzarien chuckled as he walked back into the den. "Ma and I decided that you two should still get ready for school and work," he said, lips turning down. "Act like it's a normal day to draw less attention."

Bryda whined. "I don't want to go, I want to play with Little Nightmare."

"Well, he has work to do too," Myravelle said.

"And I need to speak with Myravelle alone." Byzarien raised a brow at his sisters.

"Fine." Beatriz squeezed Bryda's shoulder. "Let's get ready."

When the girls left the den, and the house filled with savory scents of Adelyne's cooking in the kitchen, Byzarien took out a piece of parchment from the pack. "What should we tell Xavier?"

"Tell him that I'll meet them tonight." Myravelle's gaze fluttered about the house thinking about how much she hated to make Byzarien leave his family. "Maybe you should stay."

He cradled her face in his hands, forcing her to look at him. "I love you, Myravelle. We're in this together."

She swallowed the needles in her throat and nodded. "I love you too."

"Then *we'll* meet Xavier tonight," he said as he wrote a message onto the parchment. "We'll leave under the cover of night."

"You're leaving so soon?" Adelyne asked, wiping her eyes with the corner of her apron. "When you just arrived?"

"I'm sorry, Ma," he said, standing to hug her. "But the faster we get to Basenfort, the less time the king has to prepare."

"Will you stay for dinner, at least?" Emeryk asked, emerging from his room in his tattered mining clothes. Though it was wise of the Dumonts to continue working despite the gold, Myravelle hated it. She wanted to let them retire without a worry in the world.

"Of course." Byzarien tied the note to Little Nightmare's leg and opened the window. "We plan to wait until nightfall anyway."

The crow flapped its wings and perched on Myravelle's shoulder to nuzzle her cheek. She stroked his feathers for a few moments before twirling her finger. The crow took off out the window, heading toward the Sleepy Wood.

For breakfast, Adelyne served potatoes, bread, and cheese. The fact that the Dumonts could afford spices made the simple meal a decadence to Myravelle. While eating, she loved watching Byzarien. He lit up when he joked with his sisters and she could tell he absolutely adored his parents. Myravelle stayed quiet, still worried his family didn't approve of her. Byzarien would touch her leg or her hand, constant reminders of his affection that made her heart swell.

Bryda scooted her chair toward Myravelle and lowered her voice to a near whisper, "Would you braid my hair like yours?"

Reaching up to her hair, Myravelle remembered how the night before she had plaited a few strands on either side before joining all of the hair in the back into a single braid. She smiled, delighted the girl wasn't afraid of her, and nodded. "I would love to."

While she braided Bryda's long black hair, Myravelle listened to Byzarien interrogate his other sister about her forthcoming engagement. "Is he good to you?"

Beatriz blushed and brought her hands up to her cheeks while nodding. "He likes to hold my hand," she said. "And he bakes special lavender cookies just for me."

"Such a sweet young man," Adelyne said, resting her hand on Bea's shoulder. "Respectful and hardworking."

"Good," Byzarien whispered. He strained his face and swallowed, and Myravelle knew he must have felt emotional, getting so little time with the family he loves.

She completed Bryda's braid. "Beautiful."

"Do I look like Myravelle?" the young girl asked, holding out her braid and twirling around.

Byzarien tapped her nose and winked. "Just like her."

Adelyne began clearing the table, but Myravelle stopped her. "You've done so much for us, let me take care of the clean up."

"Why, thank you, darling," Adelyne said. She untied her apron and hung it on the hook before turning to her husband and daughters. "Sadly, it's time to leave for work and school."

With frowns tugging their faces, the family gave Byzarien hugs and said their goodbyes. Before Adelyne and Bryda left, though, the little girl gave Myravelle a hug.

Tears sprung into her eyes at the sweet gesture. "We'll see you this afternoon," Myravelle said, returning the embrace.

Bryda nodded and looked up with her big brown eyes. "Will Little Nightmare be back?"

"I hope so."

Myravelle couldn't stop smiling, even after the last of the Dumonts left.

"I have someone else I'd like you to meet," Byzarien said, taking her hand.

They stepped from the quiet house and out into winter's chill. Worried they would be spotted, Myravelle swirled her staff and draped them in their peasant disguises. Down the way, and surrounded by a grove of snow-laden evergreens, was a quaint cemetery with stone markers and offerings. She followed Byzarien to a grave with little wooden toys around it.

BENOIX EMERYCK DUMONT

"Meet Benny." Tears welled up in his eyes. "My little brother."

Myravelle leaned against him. "Hello, Benny."

While they knelt before the grave, Byzarien traced the letters on the stone. "I miss him every single day," he whispered. "He was such an energetic child, so vibrant. He could make me laugh no matter what my mood was."

"Like Lazaire?"

"Yeah, like Lazaire." Byzarien chuckled and wiped his cheek. "He would have been a lot like him, I imagine."

The breeze brushed through the trees and rustled Myravelle's hair, sending a chill across her skin. "You know, I think Benny's listening."

Byzarien strained his face as if in pain, then the tears fell freely and he relaxed. "I'm sorry, Benny. I'm sorry you were taken from us," he said. "I blamed myself for your death. If only I had been quicker or smarter. I thought my scars were a punishment."

Myravelle rubbed his shoulder and shook her head. "It was not your fault," she said. "You were but a child yourself and rescued everyone, nearly sacrificing your life. The fault lies with King Zylvain alone."

Byzarien swallowed and nodded. "Thank you," he said, looking into her eyes then back at the grave. "I know I shouldn't blame myself. Benny wouldn't want me to hold on to that pain."

In silent support, Myravelle squeezed his arm.

"I want to make sure the king never hurts anyone again," he said. "I love you, Benny. Someday, I will join you in the Underworld and we'll play knucklebones, cards, hide-and-seek, and whatever games you want to play. I promise."

He kissed his fingers and pressed them against the stone. Myravelle glanced at the little offerings and decided to leave something herself. Using her staff to stand, she then twirled it toward the grave. All around, little paper flowers popped out of the earth in all sorts of colors.

Smiling, Byzarien stood next to her and admired the flowers. "He would love them," he said, pressing a kiss to Myravelle's cheek.

"I wish I could have met him."

Byzarien pulled her even closer. "Someday, I truly believe we'll all be reunited. You and your mother, me and Benny—and we'll all be one big family."

Family. Myravelle bubbled with warmth at the thought as she twisted her engagement ring. This wonderful man wanted her to be a part of his family. Rising on her toes, she pecked his lips.

Hand-in-hand, they said goodbye to Benoix and headed back to the house. They had planned to make repairs and tidy up the house as a surprise. Something pricked Myravelle's mind, and her eyes rolled back. From high in the sky, she saw soldiers on horses. The connection broke, and, a moment later, Little Nightmare landed on her shoulder.

"We better hurry back," she said, petting her crow. "He saw someone coming."

Soon enough, the sound of horse hooves got their attention, and Myravelle's heart raced as two horsemen approached. Word could travel quickly through a small village, especially if an alleged dead man and a wanted criminal fairy were spotted. The sooner they left the village, the safer it would be for Byzarien's family.

After sneaking home through the patch of woods, they set to work. Byzarien wanted to make a new bed frame for Bryda, repair the leaky roof, and fix the door to the root cellar, so he kissed Myravelle's forehead and headed out to the shed for some lumber. Myravelle planned to use her magic to dust and sweep.

After tucking Little Nightmare in for a nap on some cushions, she grabbed a broom and feather duster and studied the living space. A fire roared in the stone hearth, warming the room filled with a soft couch and chairs. Needlework sat on a table, wood shavings curled next to a wooden bird and whittling tools, and a chess game waited patiently for the players to return. *This is a home.* At that moment, she decided to tidy up but leave all of the comforting clutter.

With a twitch of her finger and a swirl of her staff, she made the feather duster fly and the broom dance. She watched on for a moment and sighed with a grin tugging her lips, for she truly enjoyed using her magic for domestic bliss rather than bloodshed. She sang a dreamy lullaby and swayed to the tune while she completed her chores.

Once the dishes were clean, Myravelle grabbed the feather duster and broom to return them to the closet when Byzarien bumped into her and she squealed.

"Sorry," he said with a chuckle. "I was putting away my tools."

"I didn't hear you come inside."

"I wouldn't dare interrupt such beautiful singing." He pulled her close and grinned.

Her cheeks flushed. "I don't know about *beautiful*."

"Oh, it most certainly was." He glanced at the kitchen and back to Myravelle. "You know, we're all alone."

The flex of Byzarien's fingers against her back sent a thrilling bloom of heat through her. She wrapped her arms around him and brought her lips to his. He moaned and pushed her against the back of the closet, sending the broom and other items clattering to the floor. They giggled, staring into one another's eyes. Myravelle burned for him.

Lifting her up, he carried her across the kitchen. While their lips and tongues danced, he rested her on the table and shoved up the hem of her dress. Myravelle's head fell back and she closed her eyes when Byzarien's hand slithered up her thigh.

"Well." Adelyne cleared her throat, making the lovers jump. She balanced a pile of folded clothing in her arms.

"Sorry," Myravelle mumbled and slid from the table while Byzarien helped fix her dress.

"No need to be sorry, but there are *rooms*, you know." Adelyne laughed, setting the clothes on the table. "There's always sewing to do," she said and admired the tidy house. "Oh my, I see you two have been quite productive."

"We wanted to help out while we could," Byzarien said.

Adelyne gave her son a hug. "Thank you," she said and turned to Myravelle. "Can you sew too?"

Myravelle and Byzarien grinned at one another.

He set outside to make more repairs while the two women sat down to make their own: darning, hemming, stitching, and tailoring garments. At one point, Myravelle caught Byzarian just outside the window as he dug in the garden. She studied his strong shoulders and the grip of his hands on the shovel, thinking back to how they had felt on her skin.

"So, Myravelle," Adelyne said, shattering her reverie. "Can I ask you something?"

Looking into the woman's eyes, which were warm and sweet like Byzarien's, she nodded.

"Do you love my son?"

Heat radiated from Myravelle's chest and cheeks, and she couldn't help but grin. "More than anything."

"I love hearing that, for he never saw romance in his future due to his scars. But I always had hope—hope that someone would see the real Byzarien."

"I do," she assured her. "I admire his bravery, his loyalty, and his strength."

"I'm so glad he met you. He seems...different now, more complete," Adelyne said, placing her hand on Myravelle's.

The touch was so simple, yet it held so much power. People didn't touch monsters so casually. Her breath faltered, and an involuntary sob escaped.

"When our little Benny died, it was like a part of Byz died too. But I think he has at last found purpose and love." Adelyne blinked a few tears from her eyes. "You brought my son back to life."

33

Byzarien

That evening, Byzarien's sisters danced, feet pitter-pattering on the kitchen floor, while Myravelle helped his mother cook. Bryda tugged on Beatriz's dress, making her bend down. The younger girl whispered something, which made Myravelle stiffen. Byzarien set down his book and leaned forward in the chair to listen.

"Pretty," Bryda whispered rather loudly, and Beatriz nodded.

Grinning, Byzarien sat back. He was certain Myravelle had never been on the receiving end of polite gossip before.

Myravelle relaxed and turned toward the girls. "Well, I think you are both pretty, too," she said and pressed her finger to the side of her mouth. "In fact, would you like dresses to match your beauty?"

"You can do that?" Bea asked.

"I make all of my dresses," Myravelle said, holding out the starry skirt.

Bryda twirled her dark braid around her finger and bounced on her toes. "I want one!"

"Bryda," Adelyne said in a low voice, making Byzarien chuckle.

"Sorry." Bryda folded her hands together and blinked her big doe eyes. "Please?"

"Of course." Myravelle reached for her staff and pointed it at the girls. "What would you like?"

"Can I have butterflies?" his younger sister asked, while Bea pursed her lips and stared at the ceiling.

"Wonderful choice," Myravelle said. "And you, Beatriz?"

"Hmm, I do miss seeing flowers."

When Myravelle twirled her staff, Beatriz and Bryda's dresses melted into new and gleaming gowns. Bryda's looked as if it was made with real butterfly wings, delicate and bright, while Beatriz's had flower petals swirling around the skirt.

"Thank you!" they said, twirling in their new gowns.

Warmth filled Byzarien's chest at how his family was coming around to Myravelle. The front door creaked open, and his father entered with confusion twisting his face.

"Did I enter the wrong house?" Emeryk asked, studying his daughter's new gowns as they spun. He looked down at his own clothes, sooty from the mine. "I certainly don't fit in."

Adelyne set the pot of stew on the table and gestured to her stained apron. "You and me both."

Myravelle smirked at Byzarien, then pointed her staff at his parents as well. Their outfits turned into clean white fabric which bloomed with white roses covered in dewdrops.

"Now, we're fit for a ball," Adelyne said, as she took Emeryk's hands and danced with him.

During dinner, Byzarien marveled at how Myravelle fit in with his family. Although she was usually introverted, she asked them questions about their lives and jobs. He placed his hand on hers and remembered how she had grown up in neither a typical human nor fairy household. He hoped to someday give her a real home.

Without a word, his mother stood from the table and dashed toward her room.

"What are you doing, darling?" Emeryk called out.

"Found it!" She returned to the kitchen with an emerald ring pinched between her fingers and offered it to Byzarien. "This was my grandmother's. I saved it for you to use as an engagement ring. Even in the hardest of times, I couldn't bear to pawn it," she said with a smile creasing her tearful eyes. "Don't think I didn't notice your Guerrix pendant as a makeshift ring."

Like removing a heavy cloak, stress lifted from his shoulders. He took the ring and stared at it gleaming in the candlelight. *They really do approve.*

"Traditionally, the emerald represents *love* and *fidelity*." His mother sat next to his father and rubbed his shoulder. "My grandfather claimed he had purchased the ring from fairies, long before they had been banished from the kingdom. He always told me that this emerald truly holds the gifts of love and fidelity and a good marriage would come to the couple."

"Plus, a pendant of *war* is not a proper engagement ring," Emeryk joked.

Myravelle's eyes welled with tears while she bit at the grin creeping across her face.

Byzarien caught her in his gaze as he knelt to the floor. "I promise you my eternal love and fidelity, Myravelle Spinner," he said, sliding the crossed-sword pendant from her finger. "You have given me your answer once before, is it still the same?"

"Yes," she whispered as he slipped the emerald ring over her knuckle.

The family cheered for the couple, and even Little Nightmare flapped about the kitchen, cawing. Beatriz dug into a cupboard, retrieving a bottle of wine.

"Bea!" Adelyne gasped.

"What?" His sister winked at the engaged couple. "This is cause for celebration...and I'm old enough to drink now!"

"You may partake," Emeryk said. "It truly is a celebration!"

Beatriz poured the adults a glass. "To the happy couple!"

Everyone raised their glasses in toast. Myravelle hummed with happiness as she sipped the wine, and Byzarien kissed her warm cheek.

"Now, for the real question," Beatriz said. "Do I get a piece of secret jewelry?"

Everyone laughed. Byzarien tilted his head with a grin. "Old maids don't get jewelry," he teased.

"*Old maid?*" She stood and playfully shoved his shoulder. "You already know Fyrenz and I are about to be engaged," she said, batting her lashes.

"I know, I know. And it's wonderful, sis," he said, pulling her in for a hug. "You'll be such a gorgeous bride."

When the food and drinks were gone, and the excitement of the evening settled to the floor like dust, Adelyne began clearing dishes. Myravelle twirled her finger and the rest of the bowls floated into the sink. The scrub brush dove into the pail of soapy water and scrubbed them. Everyone gaped.

"Now I truly never want you to leave, Myravelle," Adelyne said. "Thank you."

When Myravelle and Byzarien packed up their things, the family was silent. He knew how upset they were. Leaving the comfort of home was not something he wanted to do—especially when it hurt his parents so.

Adelyne sniffled when Byzarien embraced her. "I know what you must do...but we just got you back."

"I promise to return, Ma," he said. "For now, you must keep pretending as if you think I'm dead."

With that, Adelyne sobbed against her son's shoulder.

Myravelle tried to ease his mother's sorrow by giving her the skein of gold thread.

"By the gods," she said with a gasp. "More gold? I promise to tear down any posters I see about you, my dear." Adelyne took her hands. "You saved us."

"It was nothing," Myravelle insisted. "I just wanted to help the man I love."

Adelyne wrapped her in a tight hug. "This will go toward dowries for the girls," she said. "They'll have good marriages because of you."

Byzarien's chest warmed, and the desire to stay with them intensified. *No.* They would only be placing his family in danger. As much as it pained him to admit, it was best if they pretended he was dead.

"One day, we will all be together again," he said, fighting against the swirling unease in his stomach.

"In this life or the next," Emeryk and Adelyne said in unison.

With more hugs and tears, Byzarien said his goodbyes to his parents and siblings. He slung the pack onto his shoulders, and Myravelle grabbed her staff. Little Nightmare, who had been enjoying himself while Bryda fed him oats, flapped his wings and perched on Myravelle's shoulder.

Once they were on the road, she tied a note to Little Nightmare's foot and sent him to alert Xavier.

"Your family is wonderful," she said, admiring the emerald ring on her finger. "Beyond wonderful."

He grinned as he took her hand. "They loved you."

Before they reached the city walls, Myravelle turned her staff and melted their clothes into peasant disguises. They walked down the road into the filthy and bustling Pezit Quarter. She drew her hood up when they passed a poster of her as 'The Mistress of All Evil' pasted onto a stone wall. Though it was getting dark, children were still out and ran up to the image. They dared each other to touch it, then ran away screaming.

"I've become a monster, even to children."

Byzarien rubbed her back. "We're going to fix all of this." They came to a stall where the merchants were packing up their supplies. "Any chance you can give us a ride?" he asked a couple.

"Where you headed?" the woman asked and raised her arm to cover a yawn.

"Anywhere west."

The merchants kept packing and mumbled to one another. Myravelle held out a gold coin, and the man's eyes shot wide. The woman snatched the coin and pointed to their cart.

Byzarien helped Myravelle into it. It was cramped with all of the rattling crates, but they were able to rest their legs. Again and again, the woman turned to stare at them. When Byzarien caught her, she simply smiled and turned around. Myravelle kept her face shaded by her hood while Byzarien rested his hand on the dagger on his belt.

They reached a sleepy village near the river and stopped at a cottage with fields stretching behind it. Byzarien had hoped they would get to cross the river in the cart, but he and Myravelle would be on foot.

"Thank you," he said to the couple, "for allowing us to ride this far with you."

"Our pleasure," the merchant said. "May the gods bless your journey."

The pair walked through the village toward a wide stone bridge where soldiers collected tolls. Myravelle turned, drawing heavy breaths. Byzarien stroked her cheek.

"It's fine. We have darkness on our side but," he said, dipping down to brush his fingers through a muddy puddle, "here." He swept the mud over his scars and on his nose before wiping the rest on Myravelle's face. Looking down at their peasant clothes, Byzarien decided to splash some mud onto those as well. "See, they won't recognize us."

She nodded and walked alongside him toward the bridge. When they reached the men collecting tolls, she extended a coin.

"You steal this?" the taller of the two guards asked as he scowled at their appearances.

"It's the very last we have," Byzarien answered. "We're on a pilgrimage to the Enferrix Springs to heal my wife's leg."

The second guard stared at Myravelle, who kept her head low as she leaned more heavily onto her walking stick. "You may pass," he said.

They ambled across the bridge, admiring the dark Noire River below. Chunks of ice flowed toward the sea while snow clung to the muddy banks. On the other side, they faced a village filled with boarded-up and decrepit buildings. They hurried through it, keeping their disguises on. In the gathering darkness, they could barely make out the encampment in the distance as they drew closer and closer to the Sleepy Wood. Their legs had grown weary by the time they reached the forest, where they turned south toward the secret graveyard.

After resting against a tree to eat and drink, Myravelle touched her walking stick. Black from her hand crept and twisted around the length until it transformed into its more enchanting appearance. She then twirled the staff in the air, making their outfits bleed into midnight fabric to camouflage with the darkness.

Through the snowy woods, they hiked for a while before setting up camp for the night. Thoughts of his family kept surfacing, and Byzarien found it difficult to sleep, but he enjoyed every moment of holding Myravelle in his arms. He looked at the ring on her finger. She was his family now, too. Whatever was going to happen, he would have her, and that was enough.

While she slept, he rested his head against her chest, where her heart fluttered in sync with his. The push and pull of the blood in her veins mimicked his own—and he knew his love for her was deeper than he could ever have imagined. Something stronger than magic connected their hearts, their souls, their minds. They were so entwined; it was impossible not to be completely changed by their love.

She is my home now.

He wanted a life with her. He wanted a family with her. He wanted everything that he never thought possible for his life with her. As much as he had always hated and felt ashamed of them, Myravelle loved his scars. They were a part of him, just like her magic was a part of her. The things they had each tried to hide from others all their lives, they could lay bare for one another. Byzarien pressed a sleepy kiss against Myravelle's forehead and snuggled in tight against her body.

They set out before daybreak, through the icy breeze that whipped the pines and bit at any of Byzarien's bare skin. He rubbed his hands together and wrapped an arm around Myravelle, who grinned at him. He recalled thinking she never smiled at all, and now felt lucky for every single one he earned.

She moved with silent ease as he crunched through the forest. After hours of hiking, they were finally near the secret graveyard, and Myravelle stopped to look around. Little Nightmare soared above their heads and cawed so loudly, it seemed like a warning.

"What is it, boy?" Byzarien asked.

Myravelle shivered. "Magic."

The air and scenery around them glittered and fell like a curtain. They huddled close and watched as, with rumbling and rustling from the forest, Eglantyne soldiers surrounded them. Byzarien drew the dagger as Myravelle raised her staff.

"I wouldn't do that," a familiar voice scratched through the air. The line parted for Captain Abelard, followed by Queen Sebira and her daughters.

The frail queen leaned against the Three Good Fairies, holding her wrapped stump close to her chest. Behind them, soldiers, being led by Eryck no less, dragged Xavier, Dezlan, Zelyx, and Lana forward. They were bound and gagged. Byzarien glared at Eryck who was supposed to be helping his friends.

"These traitors gathered an entire group of soldiers to commit treason. We executed all twenty," Abelard said. "But I wanted you to witness these deaths."

Fear constricted Byzarien's chest as fire coursed through his limbs. "Don't hurt them!"

"We only want one thing," Abelard said, pointing at Myravelle.

Ignoring him, her gaze snapped to Queen Sebira. "Did you do this? Did you lead them to me?"

"I just about used the last of my power," she said, voice like brittle leaves nearly carried away with the breeze. "The cloaking spell nearly killed me."

"Why?"

Abelard waddled forward. "You know why, Myravelle. You're dangerous. The king will keep you safe."

"Safe?" Byzarien shouted. "He wants to lock her up until she rots away just like her mother!"

"Where is the king?" Myravelle asked, her eyes wickedly wide with taunting amusement. "Hiding in his castle?"

"He's tending to Queen Lya, who is on strict bedrest with his child."

"A child?"

"Yes," Abelard said. "They wanted to keep this pregnancy a secret. The baby should arrive next month."

"What a *blessed* day that will be for the king and queen." Myravelle twisted her staff toward a boulder and it crumbled to dust. "Exactly how does the king intend to keep me as a prisoner? No stone wall will hold me, nor any chain bind me."

"That's where our new allies come in," Abelard said, gesturing to the fairies.

Without looking at Myravelle, Sola plucked a clear crystal from her pocket and pressed it into her mother's only hand. Byzarien tightened his grip on the dagger, muscles vibrating with adrenaline.

"This," Sebira began, holding up the crystal between finger and thumb, "is how we shall contain you."

Abelard gestured, and the soldiers tightened the circle around Byzarien and Myravelle. Sebira shuffled forward with her daughters' help. More fairies marched in front of the queen, forming a shield.

Myravelle raised her staff. Roots and vines wrapped around the fairies' ankles, yanking them to the ground. She swept it toward Xavier, Dezlan, Zelyx, and Lana, releasing them from their binds.

Eryck shouted, "Now!"

A handful of soldiers tossed them weapons. Byzarien glanced around in shock. Eryck was on their side after all. They fought to get to them, but more fairies and soldiers filtered in to stand before the queen, while archers aimed at the couple.

Myravelle twirled her staff, creating an umbrella of sparks.

An archer loosed their arrow, but it bounced off her magic.

"You can't hurt us." She laughed.

"Yes, I can. With this crystal, I bind thee, Myravelle Spinner." Sebira lifted the gem, tracing her finger over it, making it glow brighter with her every word. "May your dark enchantments be forever hidden from this world."

The Three Good Fairies began a low chant, twirling their Dormrya wands in Myravelle's direction. She raised her staff, but crackling smoke streamed from her chest. Her protective shield faded. She fell to her knees, struggling to breathe as the magic was ripped from her body.

"No!" Byzarien lunged for the queen.

A soldier wrestled him away, fighting off his blows. When a fairy raised his wand, Byzarien grabbed and crushed his hand, causing him to drop it. Byzarien turned, slicing through a soldier's shoulder and kicking another in the chest. More men and fairies surrounded him, and he was severely outnumbered. His friends at last made their way through to help. One fairy knocked Lana down with a burst of magic. Roaring, Zelyx charged him. Dezlan and Xavier fought back-to-back, but they could barely hold the attackers off. In the scuffle, Abelard sliced Eryck's throat, and the lieutenant fell to the ground, mouth gurgling with blood.

"No!" Byzarien shouted.

With the distraction, two fairies had shoved him to the ground and raised their wands.

"STOP!" Myravelle shrieked as a beam of magic from her staff knocked the enemies away from Byzarien. Shaking, she rose and glowered at the queen. "I said stop."

Sebira held tight to the crystal, which had grown dark. Lightning crackled inside. Myravelle rotated her staff toward it, and a stream of gold connected to the gem. The Three Good Fairies shrieked while the soldiers took a few steps back. Still out of breath, Byzarien crawled to Myravelle as she strained.

With a loud blast, the jewel exploded, knocking everyone to the ground. The smoky tendrils of magic, which had been trapped within the gem, twirled their way back to Myravelle, soaking into the hem of her dress. While everyone shuffled to stand, the sisters helped their mother rest against a tree trunk.

"Seize the witch," Abelard shouted at his soldiers, along with a string of curses, but no one dared move toward her.

"Her ring, Mother," Fleur said, pointing at the emerald on Myravelle's finger. "Contain her there."

Sebira pointed her finger at the ring, while the sisters twirled their wands. Byzarien watched his great-grandmother's ring glow, and heat surged in him when Myravelle's magic again escaped her chest and she fell. He darted for the fairies, but Abelard himself drew his sword. Byzarien's senses heightened at the chance to kill him, and he growled as he swung his fist. He easily knocked the older man down and raised the dagger, but soldiers rushed to protect the captain. Archers aimed at Byzarien and his friends.

"No!" Myravelle squirmed and shrieked on the ground as the smoke poured from her chest and into the emerald, which had grown into a heavy, greenish-black orb.

Byzarien strained against the pain behind his eyes and forgot all about the captain as he stumbled to kneel at her side. "Myravelle, fight them," he begged. "You can do it. You must."

Her eyes fluttered open, and they were a dull gray—devoid of any magic and moonlight. He caressed her freckles with his thumb and kissed her lips, which grew cold. A pain cinched his heart as he shook his head. He couldn't lose her.

"My girl of stars," Byzarien said, stroking her face. "Where are you?"

She managed to touch his face, tracing the lines of scars. A faint twinkle appeared in her eyes, and Byzarien thought it was a trick of the overcast sky.

"Myravelle," he whispered, threading their fingers. "Don't fade away."

The sisters continued twirling their wands, and the queen said, "We almost have her, Captain."

They approached the pair with soldiers holding ropes and chains, ready to seize Myravelle. His friends continued to fight against soldiers and fairies alike, while Byzarien's breaths grew ragged with rage.

"No," he growled, gripping the dagger. "You cannot have her."

He lunged for Abelard. Sharp jolts sliced through him. He glanced down. Arrows protruded from his shoulders, abdomen, and chest—his heart. The world went silent. A metallic tinge swelled in his mouth as he gurgled blood, unable to breathe. He crashed next to Myravelle, whose eyes sparkled and shimmered with raging passion as she screamed.

"My girl of stars," he whispered before slipping down, down, down into the Darkened Path.

34

Myravelle

Byzarien fell, blood spilling from his mouth. Myravelle's shrieks shredded her throat as she cradled him in her arms, and he closed his eyes with a smile.

A dark, excruciating pain rose like a storm in Myravelle; a storm she no longer controlled—it was Byzarien who had kept her heart good. Tracing a dangerous rune, razor-sharp magic burst from the heavy emerald on her hand. It swept through the crowd, knocking everyone, friend and foe, to the ground and creating a wall of curling smoke, violent with lightning, to keep them out.

Myravelle rested her head on Byzarien's chest, searching for a heartbeat. Agony traveled through her veins, escaping from her mouth in a feral howl. Every whimper and sob carved and scraped at Myravelle until her entire body felt hollow. The air around her sparked with untethered magic.

When she lost her voice, she searched for a rune over Byzarien's body, though she knew there wouldn't be one. He was not asleep. He was dead. The man she loved was dead. Myravelle's heart unspooled and threatened to unravel every stitch that held her frayed edges together. Despite the truth, she pressed her hands to Byzarien's eyes. His skin grew cold. Cold and pale.

She dug deep for a bit of healing magic. She tried over and over again, but there was nothing she could do. She rested her head against him again and wept while her magic waned and the protective wall melted away with her tears. Abelard and the remaining soldiers approached, slow and cautious.

She rose, teeth bared, and watched everyone scramble back, slipping in the snow. The fairies had already begun their retreat, dragging away their limp and unconscious queen. Abelard shouted at his men to arrest Myravelle, but no one dared. While most dashed away, Byzarien's friends rushed toward the middle of the graveyard, where Myravelle stood guard over his body.

"No, Byz." Dezlan's face was strained as he fell to his knees and stroked Byzarien's hair. "My bear. No, no, no."

The rest of them crowded Myravelle, and their cries sliced her soul like broken glass. Everything hurt, and she stumbled to a tree stump to vomit. As she wiped her mouth, something caught her attention. There was Captain Abelard, struggling to flee—his boot laces had snagged on thorns. *An insect in my web.* Myravelle glided toward him over the vines and stones like smoke. Flailing in an attempt to run, the man fell onto his back, thumping his head on a rock, and groaned. A glowing rune circled the repugnant human's neck, and Myravelle's eyes widened with delightful rage. Though her broken magic radiated all around them, she needed the rune to control it. She raised her staff.

"Myravelle, don't!" Zelyx shouted. "Come with us!"

She watched the friends huddle around Byzarien. Her boy of scars was gone. Her eyes slid back to the rune around the captain's neck. A few soldiers had turned to make their way back to help him. Now was her only chance.

"Please," Zelyx said, stealing her attention. "We can make a real difference if you travel to another kingdom with us. We can get justice for Byzarien."

"*Justice*," the word slipped from Myravelle's lips with disgust. "There is no such thing."

The heavy green orb on her hand pulled toward the captain, whose fingers gripped another man's shoulder. She glanced at the orb, which swam with dark and crackling clouds of magic. *Her magic.* Heavy and brutal and arcane. She affixed the sphere to the top of her staff and pointed it at the captain. As she traced the golden rune, power tickled through her veins like stardust, and she cackled, drawing Abelard's attention.

"No!" he shouted and shrieked like a spooked child.

The soldiers had Abelard upright, and they scrambled to get away. When Myravelle completed the rune, a thorned vine snapped from the ground and coiled around the captain's neck. He squirmed and fell, the thorns ripping into his flesh. Myravelle growled as she squeezed the life from the despicable man, enjoying how his eyes bulged and grew bloodshot. The soldiers fled, and Myravelle clung to the magic until Abelard released a final gurgle and went still. She giggled and turned toward Byzarien's friends, who backed away from her.

"Shit! Let's just go," Xavier said, gesturing to Zelyx to help him with Eryck's body.

"What about Byz?" Dezlan asked as he reached for him. "We should take him with us too."

"Get away from him!" Myravelle roared as she charged toward them, her magic tightening the air with static.

They scrambled and dashed away, disappearing into the snowy woods.

Myravelle rested her forehead against the staff and caught her breath, cursing herself for yelling at Byzarien's friends. She'd thought seeing the light leave Abelard's eyes would feel good, but it left her burning with rage, for the true culprit behind her miserable life still breathed. *The king.*

She studied Byzarien, wishing he were merely asleep. If he were asleep, she could heal him and kiss him and make him all better. He would be hers until the end of time.

Little Nightmare cawed as he landed and hopped over to rest inside Byzarien's limp hand. A sharp pain crawled up Myravelle's throat and burst through with silent and shaking wails. She curled up next to Byzarien and cried until she was completely empty, then stared at the snowy branches bent like bones against the darkened sky.

A low growl traveled over the graveyard. Myravelle lifted her stinging and puffy eyes toward the sound. Three sets of glowing eyes appeared through the brush. Her pulse quickened as snarling and mangy wolves approached. They were so starved by eternal winter, she could count their ribs.

"Go," she whispered to Little Nightmare, who soared to safety atop the nearest pine.

Myravelle pushed herself up, arms trembling as much as her lower lip—from the cold or the grief or the fear, she didn't know. Emotions wracked her body like thunderbolts. She watched as the wolves ripped into the captain's corpse and dragged it away into the woods. She could not let the creatures of the night tear Byzarien's body apart. *I am the scariest creature in these woods.*

Myravelle let the darkness, which flowed in the caverns of her soul, burst through like lava from the Forbidden Mountain. She no longer felt *half-fairy*, but something else entirely. Something ancient. Something from nightmares.

Something meddled with by Filoux.

Maybe she was the daughter of a god.

The wolves returned, baring their blood-stained teeth. Myravelle bared her own and roared, making the earth tremble and the trees shiver. The predators came to a halt but didn't back away, their glowing eyes on Byzarien. From Myravelle's twirling fingers, tendrils of smoke coursed into the air and crackled with sparks. A burning, acrid scent chased away the stinging cold of winter.

Myravelle pushed her magic toward the wolves. The dark smoke bounded for them, scorching the frosty earth. They dashed away, yelping like pups, as the magic hunted them into the deep, dark woods.

When the adrenaline slid from her body like a cool rush of water, Myravelle slumped against Byzarien's body. The cold, too cold, seeped into her bones, and she prayed the grief would kill her. She found her dagger next to him and rested it on his chest.

"Once upon a time," she whispered, "there was a girl of stars and a boy of scars. They burned one another in ways only true love can. When the eternal winter snuffed the flames inside of them, they froze together into a beautiful statue. Their love remained eternal as the forest grew all around."

35

Myravelle

For three days and three nights, Myravelle scared animals away and decorated Byzarien's body with feathers, leaves, nuts, and shiny stones. She kept watch from a tree, waiting for predators. To appear more fearsome, she adorned herself with furs, darkened her eyelids with soot, and affixed antlers to her head.

"I am the scariest creature in these woods." She recited the litany over and over, weaving courage with her tongue.

The rustle of footsteps made the hair on her arms and neck rise. When the scouts, who were no doubt searching for her, came upon Byzarien's corpse, one of them kicked some of the decorations away, sparking a wildfire inside Myravelle. With frozen and stiff limbs, she leapt from her tree and roared. Gasping, the men fell and scrambled back. One of them even had a wet stain forming down the front of his pants as they sprinted away, shouting things like "witch," and "evil fairy." Myravelle fixed the stones and acorns around Byzarien and rested her head on his cold, cold chest.

She lay there as the snow began to fall. Time mattered not. Her stomach roiled and rolled, but she couldn't pick herself up. For a moment, she even forgot Byzarien was dead. They were just two lovers resting in the woods. His lack of a heartbeat reminded her, though, for their hearts had danced to the same rhythm. He was dead and wandering the Darkened Path. The gods had never paid Myravelle any kindness, but now she knew for certain they would never help her. Especially Filoux, who only used her to create chaos.

Trembling and weak, she wanted to close her eyes and fall asleep forever. Little Nightmare landed at her side, pecking her hand and cawing in her ear.

"Let me die," she whispered.

The crow screeched and flapped into the air before landing on her head. Her finger twitched involuntarily, and her eyes rolled to see what the crow saw: a sad, weak woman and a dead soldier. A soldier who was loyal. A soldier who was brave. A soldier who deserved a proper burial. A soldier whose death deserved vengeance.

"Thank you, Little Nightmare."

Myravelle frayed at the edges when she tore herself away from Byzarien. Snagged on his soul, her heart ripped in two. She was but a skein of unfinished thread—and he had been the notch and the hook holding her together. Now, her half-fairy fibers were unspooled and unrecognizable. It wasn't about her, though. That moment was about giving Byzarien a proper burial, even if doing so wrecked her completely.

She shivered in the winter air as she lugged logs and branches to the center of the graveyard—elder wood and elm for cleansing and purity. She could have used magic to build the pyre, but she needed to feel the bark against her arms and the splinters in her palms. Constant reminders that this was real. Stacking the wood high, Myravelle built a magnificent funeral pyre for Byzarien. As she set the last log into place, Little Nightmare swooped down with a beakful of kindling. She stroked his feathers and looked toward the man she loved.

Though she felt hollow, scraped empty by the rusty spade of

grief, her magic was its own being, holding her upright like a puppet. She managed to trace a rune over Byzarien's body. The magic lifted him from the ground and, ever-so-gently, rested him atop the pyre. Little Nightmare landed on Byzarien's hand and nuzzled it, making a tear slide down Myravelle's cheek.

The wind whistled through the wood. With slow, agonizing steps, she approached the pyre and rested her hand on his chest, twirling her finger in the shape of the rune she had carved so many times. Tingles pulsed in her hand, as if her magic was nuzzling Byzarien—it always did like his heart.

"I am yours, and you are mine," she whispered before kissing the scars on his cheek one last time, pressing hard to memorize the patterns of his skin.

Myravelle rifled through their pack until she found her scissors. She cut pieces of the green canvas bag to make the stem and leaves. She then trimmed the notes from Byzarien's parents to create the petals of a sweet pea—the flower that had changed their fates, the flower that had brought them together. After wrapping the stem with the last of their gilded thread, she placed the sweet pea on Byzarien's chest, crossed with her dagger, as his tokens for the Underworld, but her hand hovered and hesitated.

She was beyond certain no one would ever do this for her—there would be no funeral, no pyre, no mourners, no tokens—and she would wander the Darkened Path for eternity, alone. She studied the paths of scars on Byzarien's sweet and beautiful face. Though she risked never seeing him in the next life, she couldn't *force* him to wait for her along the Darkened Path. It would have to be his choice.

She left the flower on his chest and crossed her arms. "As in war, now in death, guide our fallen brother, Byzarien." Her voice cracked and jaw trembled as she prayed to Guerrix. "Let him not be lost along the Darkened Path. Serve him as he served you."

With Little Nightmare on her shoulder, Myravelle pointed her staff at the kindling and traced a fiery rune. It first smoked with the wind, but soon erupted into flames. The elder and elm caught fire, making the entire pyre a warm inferno. The flames licked up toward the man of fire, and something stirred in Myravelle's chest.

Not any pain she was accustomed to, no, it was a hot coal burning in her body. The heat caught those frayed and ragged seams of her soul, melting everything into embers of hate, rage, and revenge. It killed anything and everything that made her half-fairy. She clenched her fists so tight, her nails dug deep crescents into her palms, and she held in a scream. The flames coursed through her body and clashed with the dark flow of pain that had always been there.

She fell to her knees and shrieked. A black cloud escaped her lungs and swirled with the smoke rising from the funeral pyre. It crackled and sparked, like a churning galaxy of stars. She could barely breathe. The air coming from inside her was too hot, but the winter air outside scraped against her throat like shards of glass.

She felt everything and nothing at once. Her soul balanced on the sharpened edge of a blade. The cloud of smoke coursed toward Myravelle and coiled around her body, scorching away her clothes. It burned so intensely, she thought it was the end—prayed it was the end, the end of her life as part fairy and never whole, the end of never belonging anywhere.

Something new bloomed in her chest and through her limbs, sending shivers down her spine and across her skin. The earth rumbled beneath her feet and the trees quivered. Swirling in a celestial dance, the clouds and smoke vanished into the Forbidden Mountain, as if the volcano had swallowed the eternal winter. When the ground went still, Myravelle peered at the heavens, which broke apart and rained down on her. The stars soaked into her skin and soothed every ache.

She was no longer part fairy.

She was Myravelle of the Stars.

The constellations swirled and draped her in fabrics of ink and stardust. Magic coursed through her veins with ease, for there was no dam left to hold back the flow. Her grief and rage had broken the eternal winter and brought back the sky and seasons. She wept at the glorious heavens, wishing Byzarien could see them. The bright moon and twinkling stars, though, ensured Byzarien's funeral was fit for the king of a man he was.

Little Nightmare perched on her shoulder and they watched the pyre burn until the wind snuffed the flames, leaving only ash, dust, and fragments.

"I will love you for the rest of my days," she whispered to Byzarien's remains. "And for the rest of my days, I vow to seek our revenge."

With a twirl of her staff, she broke the earth beneath the pyre open and lowered the ashes gently into a grave. She carved Byzarien's name onto a large boulder to mark his resting place. Though the grief, she knew, would continue to stick in her heart like a dagger, around it, embers of fury grew.

She looked toward the kingdom, knowing she would need to hide. More scouts would arrive in the inevitable light of day, and the fairies could bring reinforcements in another attempt to bind her magic. Myravelle needed somewhere to practice with her new, celestial powers. She needed a plan to destroy King Zylvain the way he had destroyed her. She grabbed what remained of Byzarien's pack and glided through the woods like smoke with Little Nightmare soaring overhead.

36

Myravelle

Up in the hills with the kingdom at her back, Myravelle leaned against her cane and heaved ragged breaths. Without ash and dust billowing from the Forbidden Mountain, the sky celebrated its first proper sunrise over Eglantyne Kingdom in years. Oranges and pinks burst to life, and Myravelle squinted against the sun glowing behind the mountains like a crown. She should have been jubilant, but she glared at it instead. *How dare the sun rise without Byzarien to witness it?*

Clinging to the swaths of wooded areas, she felt even more conspicuous in the daylight. She passed a few farms and mills along the river, hiding when the families would walk outside to admire the sun. Some would cry. Some would hoot and holler. Some would simply hug their loved ones and stare at the blue, blue sky. The sheep bleated, pigs squealed, and horses neighed. Even the forest creatures skittered from their hiding places to chirp or squeak.

Myravelle, though, collapsed in on herself, for she did not belong in the world of light. She was a creature of darkness, a spider they would squish without a second thought. Her grief and anger had broken her entirely, and now she was nothing but sharp edges. Magic slithered beneath her skin, ready to lash out at anyone who provoked her. She clenched her fists and remembered that her anger was with the king, and she needed a plan.

She needed to be alone.

"Little Nightmare," she whispered, pointing to the gloomy and cragged Forbidden Mountain. "Find us a dwelling place, dark and secluded."

The crow soared toward Filoux's cursed mountain, and Myravelle searched for food and supplies. While one farming family set out to work in the fields for the day, she crept toward their cottage like a spider and peeked through the windows. A savory scent teased her stomach and made it grumble, and she found a shepherd's pie on the sill. She thought of Byzarien's family, though, and knew she couldn't steal from these people. No, not outright at least. Nearby, she spotted sheep in their pen, and knew what to do.

After unevenly shearing a sheep, Myravelle made frantic work of oiling and carding the wool into decent roving. She prepared the fibers well enough before drawing out the spindle from her pack. Tucking herself near the corner of the barn, she spun and spun. The gleaming gold struck the curiosity of the sheep, who all surrounded her. The repetitive turn of the spindle hushed Myravelle's mind to an awful stillness, allowing grief to rise like a storm. She cried and cried, tears blurring with the gold in her hands. Byzarien was dead, and her every fiber, seam, and stitch hurt.

She fell slack against the house, and her eyes rolled back. She saw a deep, dark cave. Down a long tunnel, glistening with volcanic glass, was an opening, wide enough for a home. *Good boy. It is perfect.*

After telling Little Nightmare to return and completing her skein of gilded thread, she reluctantly entered the cottage. It was someone's home. *What laughter did these walls hold? What warmth burned here that no fire can replace?*

She took only that which she absolutely needed. Furs and a blanket, a sewing kit, a pot and utensils...and the savory pie from the window. Her magic could do the rest, right? She tucked what she could into her pack, nestling them next to her mother's ashes, the little cauldron, and the bedroll she shared with Byzarien. The rest she balanced in her arms, only after leaving the skein of gilded thread on the table, of course.

The family, already fortunate with love and a home, would now want for nothing. She imagined them moving into the city for better jobs and education. She imagined them settling even into a new kingdom, far, far away. They never would, of course. Myravelle finally understood how one's roots could be entangled so deeply with a place...or a person.

Outside, she shifted her supplies and lifted her arm to block the intense sunlight only to find Little Nightmare flying overhead. She followed him high into the rolling hills, which soon turned into rocky terrain and steep slopes of the mountains. With every step, Myravelle leaned more heavily on her staff, but she couldn't stop. Deeper and deeper, she pushed until she was at the Forbidden Mountain. The dark cliffs rose at sharp angles, and Little Nightmare flew high into a hidden cave. Slumping, Myravelle was unsure how she would climb up to it. She wanted to fall asleep and, in fact, when she leaned her head against the staff and closed her eyes, she did so, until Little Nightmare's sharp caw echoed from above. There, a new glittering rune hovered in the air. It was a circle with five swirls connecting to five stars.

Holding tight to her pack and items, she lifted her staff and traced the rune. As she completed the shape, an emptiness shivered through her limbs until she was weightless. Everything disappeared, and Myravelle's soul floated like smoke into the sky. She was elated. Relaxed. Sleepy. She wanted to remain in this peaceful, phantom existence, but it was short lived. Soon, the sting of a thousand needles pricked at her and the heavy pain of gravity pulled her back together.

Screaming, she crashed to a stony ledge and dropped her things. The spindle rolled toward her from the pack.

Tears sprouted from Myravelle's eyes, for in those precious moments on the breeze, life was simple. Now, the pain of reality washed over her. Byzarien was gone. Her mother was gone. Myravelle and Little Nightmare were all alone. She lifted the spindle, and pain ripped through her chest, for in that very moment she knew without a shred of doubt that her mother had pricked her finger on purpose.

"I'm sorry, Mother," she whispered.

Little Nightmare landed by her side and nudged her hand. Gathering her things, Myravelle followed her companion inside the cave. The stone floors were warm on her feet from the volcanic activity below. If she truly was the daughter of Filoux, it was the perfect hideout, for no one would dare visit such an evil place. No, these bleak and jagged walls would never hold the laughter and warmth of family. Myravelle set up her bedroll and blanket, then bunched up the furs for a bed for Little Nightmare.

She cradled the jar of her mother's ashes for a moment, missing Xylina more than ever, and rested it on a rocky ledge. "We're finally home, Mother," she said, choking on tears.

Dropping onto her bed, she wished Little Nightmare sweet dreams and drifted into a tormented sleep filled with death. *Xylina. Byzarien. Lazaire. Pazcal.* And on and on the nightmares went.

The acrid scent of sulfur stung her nose, waking her after only a few restless hours. She sat up in the midnight ink, squinting to study the shadows. The unsettling sensation of someone watching sent goosebumps across her skin. There was only one creature she associated with that odious and musty fetor: Filoux.

"Are you there?" she called out, voice echoing in the darkness. "Filoux?"

No answer came, aside from the quick shift of a shadow and the fading of his stench. Anger corded Myravelle's muscles and the magic raged inside like a feverish pulse beneath her skin. He had done this to her. To her mother. To Byzarien. To her canvases. To everyone. He was the grandmaster. The puppeteer. He may have been her father, but he was just as worthy of her rage as the king.

From that day on, Myravelle used her magic—*had* to use her magic to relieve the intense pressure within while she planned her revenge on both a king and a god. She often traveled into the forest at nightfall to forage for food. One night, deep in the woods, she discovered a lonely Dormrya. So far away from the fairy realm, this poisonous tree felt like it was meant for her. Some nights she hacked away at it by hand, others she used her magic, but carefully she gathered the wood and stored a large collection of it in her cave. During the daytime, she would set up her new home, spin gold, or spy.

The connection with Little Nightmare became easier and easier to control as Myravelle spied to watch everyone's movements. He flew over fertile fields, lush groves, and the tumbling Noire River. When she'd become Myravelle of the Stars and broke the sky apart, she had ended the eternal winter. After the long hibernation, plants and crops grew fast and wild, as if to make up for the lost years. Not that anyone would ever *thank* her for bringing back the stars, the moon, and the sun. No, the king and fairies still searched for her and made plans to bind her magic within a large, raw moonstone.

Xavier, Dezlan, and the rest of Byzarien's friends were much harder to locate, for they were not in Basenfort but in O'Leaux, a kingdom to the west, where they worked for King Louis and Queen Emilie. They had no immediate plans for war but spoke of possible political connections and marriages between royal families before overthrowing Zylvain. *Good, he is still mine to deal with.*

She was glad to know Byzarien's friends were well-received and safe for the time being but was sorry for how she had spooked them in the woods. Her stomach ached every time she recalled how she hadn't let them mourn Byzarien properly.

By sneaking into the open windows of the castle, Little Nightmare was able to discover two important items on the king's schedule: a meeting with the Three Good Fairies and a grand celebration for the birth of his child, to be announced as soon as he or she was born.

One day, while Little Nightmare was flying through the city, he spotted yet another poster of Myravelle's likeness. This particular malicious piece of propaganda claimed that she had killed Byzarien. Her chest tightened and she almost lost her connection with Little Nightmare, but she pressed on.

The Dumonts. She had to see them. She had to know they didn't believe the lies. The crow perched on the windowsill and watched the family. It was early morning, and the Dumonts were eating breakfast with hollow, somber looks tugging all of their faces. Bryda stepped into the other room to do needlework while the others remained at the table.

"Do you think they've plastered more posters around the square?" Adelyne mumbled. "Bea and I tore some down, but they always paste more up overnight."

Her husband patted her hand. "You shouldn't tear them down anymore."

"Why shouldn't we?" Beatriz asked, pushing her bowl of porridge away and crossing her arms. She had a delicate ring on her finger, and Myravelle smiled to herself, assuming Fyrenz had finally asked for her hand. "Myravelle couldn't have done it. She loved him."

"I know that," Emeryck said. Warmth wrapped Myravelle like a shawl knowing the Dumonts believed in her. "But you could get into trouble. The king and his guards are becoming stricter."

"We'll be more careful," Adelyne said. "But I can't just leave those wicked signs up."

Emeryck nodded, tears spilling down his face. "I just miss him so much and I don't want anything else happening to us."

As both Emeryck's wife and eldest daughter tried to comfort him, Bryda glanced at the window and tilted her head. She reached out and stroked Little Nightmare's feathers.

"Hey there, boy, we've missed you. It's been awful around here," she whispered. "There's a headstone for Byzarien next to Benny's and everything. We hoped you and Myravelle were safe, though. Tell her if she needs a place to hide, she can sleep in my bed."

Now, choking on her own tears, Myravelle couldn't take much more. *Come home.*

Shedding the grief was an impossible task, so she wore it like heavy chainmail while making a plan for revenge. All it took was a single rune, glowing above the emerald orb of her staff to swing things into motion. She twirled her finger above the new enchantment and watched as images of the king's misdeeds rose to life as smoke in the air above her. Kidnapping and imprisoning Xylina. The 'Fairy Raids.' The attack on the Sleepy Wood Company. Hoarding heaps of gold while his subjects starved.

She grinned, for she could show the congregation at the infant's presentation every single wrongdoing of the king. She even had the letters from Xavier and Eryck as proof. Oh, how she reveled in the idea of Zylvain being ripped from his wife and child and thrown into a deep dark dungeon. Thoughts of the king being tortured while his precious wife would be forced to marry one of his cousins and his baby would be raised by another man made Myravelle positively giddy.

So, on and on, she spun and spied, weaving her web and waiting to strike.

37

Myravelle

One fine day, Myravelle glanced at her mother's small jar of ashes and had an idea. A better way to honor her. With the jar in the crook of her arm and Little Nightmare on her shoulder, she twirled the staff and transported somewhere her mother always wished to go.

With her toes sinking into black sand, Myravelle released her mother's ashes into the Sombry Sea. The warm breeze rippled through her midnight hair and the starry gown she had created as a final act of respect for her mother. A gown Reverie herself would have envied. Myravelle watched the waves carry her remains, an adventure her mother could never experience in life. Little Nightmare perched on her shoulder and nuzzled the tears from her cheek.

"Shall we go, my pet?" she asked, stroking his feathers. With that, Little Nightmare took to the sky and soared toward the Forbidden Mountain. Myravelle walked the beach, the sunshine burning against her pale skin.

She walked until her skin grew pink from the sun, then twirled her staff in the air. A cloud of magic swept around her and weightlessly transported her to her cave-dwelling within the Forbidden Mountain. Through the tunnel, she glided past storerooms glittering with heaps of gilded thread and piled high with Dormrya logs.

There was more wealth within the Forbidden Mountain than in all of the kingdoms combined. For a slight—extremely slight—moment, she had considered taking it all to another kingdom and securing sanctuary, but her experiences with Queen Sebira and King Zylvain made her distrust royalty. She vowed to never be used for her gifts again. Instead, she hoarded the wealth.

Spinning had become a daily ritual to process the pain of Byzarien's death, which had rooted itself deep in her heart, clinging to every muscle and vein. Spinning also relieved the pressure of the never-ending supply of dark magic that grew inside her like a steaming kettle.

She stepped into the main living space, which had all the charms of an old hag's cottage in many a fairy tale: a pot and kettle warming above a fire, a simple straw bed, and a cluttered worktable. She dragged her fingers over the herbs hanging to dry along the walls, releasing their pleasant aromas. Little Nightmare was already on his pillow, resting before supper.

Myravelle sat on her stool and lifted her drop spindle from the basket overflowing with roving. Admiring the enchantments carved upon the whorl, she turned the spindle. Her eyes swept to the shaft, where she pressed her finger to the sharp end, a gesture she performed every day. And every day, she considered ending her life the way her mother had once tried. She was once unsure, but more and more she remembered how badly Xylina had wanted to die. Myravelle's stomach churned with acid for taking her mother's decision away. For that, she would never forgive herself.

She removed her finger and spun instead, not gold this time, but fibers for dyeing and weaving. Usually, when she was not practicing magic, she wove herself fabrics on a special loom she had built with Dormrya wood. She designed beautiful gowns of stardust, nature, and sleep with her magic twisted into every fiber. Weaving and sewing these enchanted gowns helped relieve the magic pressure inside of Myravelle just as spinning had.

At that particular moment, though, the loom contained a gilded web of her dark enchantments. Runes she had been visualizing in her mind's eye ever since Byzarien's death. Runes of vengeance and terror. She swept her fingers over the fibers, glittering in the candlelight, and grinned. Her magic radiated from it, making her shiver down to the marrow of her bones. Only a few more days of work and her web would be complete. And, if Filoux ever dared to visit again, she would be ready.

After feeding Little Nightmare his oats and seeds, it was time for real work. She rested on the furs next to the fire and closed her eyes while Little Nightmare set to the sky toward the kingdom. Throughout the land, posters lined the walls of shops, temples, and homes depicting her the way the scouts had seen her in the woods: fearsome and feral, with horns upon her head. *The Wicked Fairy. The Evil One. The Mistress of All Evil.* Myravelle found it quite amusing. *They should fear me*, she thought.

Even more amusing was the frenzy the kingdom fell into as they awaited the birth of the king's heir. Everyone was in a tizzy preparing while Queen Lya remained on bedrest.

Any. Day. Now.

The Eglantyne Kingdom bustled once more, with the citizens enjoying the warm weather, merchants haggling in the markets, children playing games, and lovers enjoying picnics under trees.

Little Nightmare flew high toward the castle, where he rested in the throne room's open window. Inside, King Zylvain, in all his silks and gold rings, lazed upon the throne while the 'Three Good Fairies' knelt before him. They all wore their usual gaudy ensembles but, this time, with mourning veils draping from their updos. Fleur also had the raw moonstone hanging on a chain around her neck.

Good boy, Myravelle told Little Nightmare. *Just in time for the meeting.*

Inside, Fleur stood and approached the dais. "King Zylvain, we have come to inform you of our mother's passing." Faune and Sola held one another and wept.

Poor babies. Myravelle sneered to herself.

"It was *her* magic that took Mother away," Sola blubbered.

"My condolences for your loss," he said, looking between the sisters. "Who is the new fairy queen, then?"

They shrugged and looked at the floor.

"You mean to tell me, none of you grew in power upon her death?"

They shook their heads.

Zylvain rose from his throne and stroked his beard. "You know what this means, do you not?"

"Yes," Fleur said. "Myravelle must possess the strength of a fairy queen."

"This will not do," Zylvain said, pacing the dais, the fur-lining of his robe dragging over the marble.

"Your Majesty, we are prepared." Fleur held out the moonstone. "But we are also here to collect what was owed to our mother."

"The child is not yet born, I'm afraid," the king said, returning to his throne.

"I assure you, the baby will be fine," Fleur said. "In fact, the three of us plan to give your child special blessings, should you invite us to the presentation."

"Invite you?" King Zylvain's lip curled in disgust.

"On her deathbed, Mother shared with us your deepest, darkest secret." When the king flinched, Fleur stood tall, as if she had assumed the role of fairy queen herself. "We demand the rest of our gold and peace between humans and fairies."

"*Your* gold?"

Fleur's voice deepened with anger. "Yes, *our* gold. Mother blessed you and Queen Lya with a healthy baby, and for that, you owe the fairies gold."

"Why don't you just spin your own?"

"Xylina was the only fairy capable of such magic." Fleur's eyes narrowed. "You knew that! That's why you kidnapped her and—"

"Fine," the king said, twisting a ring around his finger. "And this *peace* you speak of?"

"We do not appreciate the years of propaganda against us, for we are a gentle people by nature. All we want is for you to pull your soldiers out of our wood and let us do business and trade with you."

The king tilted his head back and scratched his beard, humming.

"*Or,*" Fleur began, her tone threatening, "we will tell everyone, including your dear, sweet, sunshine-of-a-wife Queen Lya, that *you* impregnated the fairy Xylina. That Myravelle, the Wicked Fairy, is actually your daughter, your true heir, your *princess.*"

"Silence!" The king sprang from his throne and clapped his hand over Fleur's mouth. "Never speak of this again!"

The argument between the fairies and the king dissipated like fog as a stone settled onto Myravelle's chest. *No, no, no.* She choked on air and gasped for relief. Curling her fingers into the furs beneath her body, her screams echoed through the cave and tunnels, making the volcano tremble with her pain.

Come back, she weakly told Little Nightmare.

Myravelle stumbled to the table and downed a goblet of wine. *It can't be true.* Her tingling limbs felt light as a feather, and she nearly fell over. Pressing her palms into the wood, she steadied herself, taking deep breaths. In through the nose, out through the mouth. In through the nose, out through the mouth. Zylvain was her father and not Filoux? She was half-fairy and...half-human?

I am an unwanted human princess.

I am an unwanted fairy queen.

Pain and heat spilled down her skull as the knowledge of what the king had done to her mother took root. She shook at the fact that none of the fairies ever attempted to rescue her mother. She was certain Sebira had poisoned them against Xylina the way the king had poisoned the humans against her. Filoux may have meddled with fate, but everyone acted by their own free will.

They will all pay.

The rage in her spread like black fire, until she saw nothing but stars. The pressure was too much. She needed a release from the all-consuming dark magic.

Spinning would not be enough.

38

Myravelle

Grabbing her staff, she stamped it to the ground and disappeared in a galaxy of sparks and smoke. Upon opening her eyes, she stepped into the Sleepy Wood, which was alive with leafy boughs, curling vines, and wildflowers of every color. Bees and butterflies danced about the blooms, squirrels gave chase around the trees, and birds soared through the air singing joyous melodies. Myravelle, herself, was a deep bruise against the bright signs of life.

The king is my father. The muscles in her body shuddered, and she collapsed. Ragged and broken, she dragged herself over thorns, thistles, and stinging nettles to her secret graveyard. These poor men were dead because of a king's insatiable greed for weapons, heirs, and power. Their graves, as if forgotten, were overgrown with grasses, clover, brambles, and saplings. Even Byzarien's large stone marker was barely visible, surrounded by white roses and sweet pea.

Myravelle raked her fingers into the earth through stems and roots as she crawled toward Byzarien's grave. She rested her head against the stone to weep, for she missed him so much her entire being ached from her skin to her soul. As she pressed her palms to the ground, she felt him and all of her canvases there in the soil. Then, a glowing rune danced like a flame in her mind. *Bone fragments and teeth are just enough for rebirth.*

She was not so naïve to think the men would be the same, no. Their souls had all traveled through the Darkened Path and into the Underworld long ago. She only needed soldiers—soldiers built with pure heartache and rage, soldiers even the king's weapons couldn't harm.

Pricking her finger on a thorn of the briar rose bush surrounding Byzarien's grave, she traced the rune onto the marker. In the shape of a circle with a spiral swirling toward a central star, her blood soaked into the stone. She licked her finger and waited. The earth began to rumble, and a cloud of crackling magic escaped from her mouth, relieving the pressure inside and breathing life into the dead.

Bone fragments popped up from the earth like wildflowers, and stacked into place with rattles and creaks. Vines coursed from the ground, snaking their way up the figures of ash, dust, and bone to complete the forms. Leaves, wood, moss, and thorns filled in the missing pieces of Myravelle's soldiers.

The forest men marched, lifting their feet high to snap away vines, and formed rows facing their queen. She stepped forward and, with tears brimming against her eyelids, caressed her favorite face. A delicate array of vines mimicked his scars, and she traced them.

"Come now, my boy of scars," Myravelle whispered. "Let's go home."

She took his rose stem hand, squeezing tight so the thorns punctured her scarred palm. Flinching, she let the blood drip to the earth. As they walked hand-in-hand toward the Forbidden Mountain, the trail of her blood prompted the rest of the undead soldiers to follow.

Once they reached her dwelling, which was much too small for all twenty-one of them, Myravelle pressed her dagger to the tip of her finger and anointed every one of the men with a special rune. When she reached Byzarien, she not only blessed his forehead with her blood, but kissed his soft rose petal lips. He stood ever-so-still.

"I know you can't understand me," she said, gazing into his hollow eye sockets. "But I am yours, and you are mine. Together, we will get our revenge."

When she looked at the forest-soldiers kneeling before her, Myravelle twirled her staff to follow the glowing runes on their foreheads. "Anointed, we are now of one mind. You were used by a king for his own selfish gain, but I give you new purpose. I am your queen and, once our revenge is complete, I promise to return you to your final resting place."

An odd sensation, like twenty-one needles threading through her mind, tugged out toward her soldiers, who moved like marionettes. When she thought, *stand*, they did. When she thought, *march*, they did. She commanded them to *build*, and they set out to carve new rooms into the rock and raise walls and towers along the outside of the mountain. All except for Byzarien, whom Myravelle commanded to *sit*. Little Nightmare cawed and flapped his wings to perch onto Byzarien's shoulder.

The three of them sat side-by-side while Myravelle spun by the fire's light. Spinning, spinning, spinning, she used the rhythmic motions to sift through her new knowledge. She had the power of a fairy queen. She was the unwanted heir of a human king. No, not only unwanted, but *used*. King Zylvain had used and abused her, whoring her out to the soldiers he had damned to misery. All over gold and poison wood.

The king had everything he'd desired because of her: formidable weapons and a thriving kingdom. He and his queen were expecting a child—a *wanted* child, a truly *wished for* child—brought about by fairy magic with promises of blessings from the Three Good Fairies. She could hardly wait to reveal his evil deeds to his subjects.

Day and night, Myravelle's soldiers built her a castle. Not just any castle, but one fit for the Unwanted Queen. With dark, volcanic stones, the towers twisted to the sky while pointed arches adorned the structure like black lace. Her home was no longer a meager hag's cottage, but a massive and imposing palace. *I am the scariest creature in this kingdom.*

In a bubbling cauldron, she melted down heaps of her spun gold. With a twirl of her staff, she formed swords for the soldiers, enchanted with an engraved rune for them to strike true. They trained with their weapons down in the courtyard, which was surrounded by a garden of briar roses and sweet pea that Myravelle tended. She would spend hours in that garden with Byzarien, braiding flowers into his vines. Sitting together, they would watch their soldiers train. Her forest men were strong, deadly and, best of all, horrifying. *We are the scariest creatures in this kingdom.*

Every day, Myravelle sent Little Nightmare to the city to spy on the king and gather news. One bright, nearly sweltering summer evening, the type where the sun refused to set, a herald from the castle announced the birth of a princess.

Pain clenched Myravelle's chest with claws of jealousy, but then she felt a sliver of warmth at the idea of family. *Sister,* she thought, *we shall meet soon and I shall rescue you from our wicked father.* The king and queen sent invitations to the nobility, to royalty of other lands and, of course, to the Three Good Fairies.

When Little Nightmare returned, exhausted from the heat, Myravelle rewarded him with seeds and cool water. "Good boy," she said, stroking his dark feathers. "As the Unwanted Queen, I expect my invitation any moment now."

At that, she laughed and laughed until she could no longer breathe. The stubborn sun finally took rest, and Little Nightmare hopped into his bed. Myravelle, though, went to her window, placed her hands on the sill, and looked down at the soldiers practicing drills in the training yard.

Prepare yourself, men, she told them. *You leave at dawn.*

Myravelle occupied the highest room of the tallest tower, weaving textiles on her Dormrya loom to create the perfect ensemble for the princess's presentation. With the Wicked Fairy propaganda in mind, Myravelle stitched and sewed fabrics dark as midnight to become *exactly* the fairy the kingdom feared.

39

Myravelle

Standing before a polished gold mirror, Myravelle admired her handiwork. She shifted the midnight gown and cloak, enjoying how the starlight sparkles and sickle moons glistened in the soft light of dawn. Her tall, silky headdress glittering with chains reminded her of the horns in the propaganda images strewn about the kingdom. She lined her eyes and contoured the hollows of her cheeks with soot. *I am The Wicked Fairy, indeed.*

She turned to Little Nightmare, perched on the windowsill. *Scout*, she commanded.

The crow set to the sky and soared over the Noir River in the direction of Eglantyne City. Myravelle stepped close to Byzarien, who always stood guard over her bedroom at night. She stroked his cheek and swallowed the painful lump in her throat. Her heartache grew worse every time she looked at that face of charred bones, thorny vines, and leaves. He was more forest than man, but she couldn't bear to let him go. She missed him, she missed his heart, and she missed his touch. Tears needled her nose and the corners of her eyes. She spun away from him to fan her face and gaze out the window. She couldn't let her emotions sabotage their revenge.

March, she commanded him and the rest of her men.

Byzarien marched away, toward the kingdom with the other undead. They twinkled in the sun as they descended the mountain. Myravelle had formed enchanted armor and sewn gilded glamour cloaks to mask their fearsome appearances until the time was right. *It's almost time.*

In her throne room, Myravelle lounged on a seat of volcanic glass, dark and cold with razor-sharp points, it was fit for an Unwanted Queen. With her staff in hand, she rested her eyes and connected with Little Nightmare.

Nobles dressed in bright, summery palettes entered the Temple of the Gods, an imposing structure with stained glass images of the deities in the windows. There was Cielyx with clouds stirring around his head, Terryx with moss and ivy clinging to her soil-covered feet, Enferrix guarding the gates to the Underworld, Reverie in her cloak of midnight and stardust, Amyor with her large breasts and round belly, and Guerrix with his crossed swords—forever reminding Myravelle of Byzarien. Little Nightmare perched near the broken window of Filoux and peeked inside. Royal families from other kingdoms already sat in the pews, awaiting the *precious* baby, paid for with gold Xylina had spun.

The Three Good Fairies sauntered down the aisle led by Fleur, who wore a gown of brilliant white with briar roses swirling about the skirts. The lightning in her chest nearly pulled Myravelle from her connection with Little Nightmare when she noticed Fleur wearing Sebira's silver circlet. *So, she thinks herself a queen, does she?* The humans gasped and whispered to one another at the arrival of the fairies. With their heads held high, the sisters sat in the very front row, ignoring the chatter.

Fly.

Little Nightmare took to the sky and found the cloaked undead soldiers weaving through the crowded streets toward the temple.

When they reached the heart of the city, the forest men, draped in their golden cloaks, took positions along the stone walls of the building. Byzarien and a handful of others climbed the steps to the front doors and waited. Myravelle's pulse quickened. Everything was ready.

Spy.

Little Nightmare returned to his perch near the broken window and observed the scene. Musicians played soft lullabies while the last of the guests took their seats. From behind a scarlet curtain at the center of the wall of icons concealing the apse, the High Priest stepped onto the altar. He wore dark red robes embroidered with symbols of the gods. He raised his hands, and the music and chatter echoing into the tall arched ceilings fell silent.

"Welcome to the presentation of Her Royal Highness Princess Briar Rose of Eglantyne," he announced, and the crowd erupted into applause. "Their Royal Majesties chose her name because the very first briar rose of the castle gardens bloomed the morning of her birth."

"*Briar Rose.*" Myravelle rolled the name of her half-sister around in her mouth. "Her Royal Highness."

"Ladies and gentlemen, I present King Zylvain, Queen Lya, and the blessing of sunshine for our kingdom herself, Princess Briar Rose."

Myravelle bit her tongue. *How dare they think an infant brought sunshine to the land?* Almost every fiber of her being wished to make the Forbidden Mountain erupt, bringing forth a volcanic winter once more. A single thread tugged from her chest, though, reminding her of Byzarien's family and all the other innocent people within the kingdom. *No*, she thought, *my vengeance is with the king.*

Everyone in the temple stood as the royal couple, who held a small bundle, stepped out onto the altar. Servants wearing white gloves presented a cradle of polished wood with carvings of briar roses entwining the headboard and railings.

"We thank the gods for our blessed princess," King Zylvain began, "and thank all of you for celebrating our happiness with us."

The queen rested the baby into the cradle, and the priest announced that it was time to present the gifts. Rows and rows of gentry, nobility, and royalty were ushered past the cradle to peek at the sleeping beauty and deposit various objects upon the altar; gilded rattles, embroidered blankets, silver spoons, a set of icons, velvet bags spilling precious gems, and ornate jewelry boxes were only a few of the gifts the baby received. *Just for being born to the right woman,* Myravelle thought.

When the Three Good Fairies rose from their pew, she watched with wicked anticipation pulsing through her veins. They stood tall and approached the cradle, smiling. They cooed at the infant and gave their congratulations to the king and queen, who beamed with pride. A painful tightness squeezed Myravelle's chest at the sight of the happy family. It was time to join the fairies, for she was their true queen after all.

Good boy, Myravelle told Little Nightmare and pulled her awareness back into the physical reality of her cavernous home.

She brushed her scarred palms over the fabric of her dress to smooth the wrinkles and gave her staff a twirl. From the emerald orb atop it, a blanket of smoke swirled around her body while static sparked through the air. Closing her eyes, she imagined the temple. She imagined the altar. She imagined the cradle.

An overwhelming lightness spread through her limbs, as if she was fading to nothing. Her soul moved through the air like a feather on a breeze until gravity tugged her back together in its painful weight. The smoke dispersed, and gasps and screams echoed around the temple. Giddiness bubbled in her soul at the amusing sounds.

"Guards!" King Zylvain shouted from somewhere nearby.

When the smoke dissipated, Myravelle spun to meet the king's eyes. *Her same gray eyes.* She turned her staff toward the guards rushing at her, making them collapse. The men struggled but could not get up, as if they were pinned to the floor with invisible stakes. The royal and noble guests tried to escape, but were tied to their pews by invisible vines. Myravelle glanced at the Three Good Fairies and the queen, huddling around the cradle.

"No invitation for a Fairy Queen?" Her gaze snapped back to King Zylvain. "Or an unwanted princess?"

"Get out!" His cheeks flared red as he shook his head. "You are not welcome here!"

"Oh, dear." Myravelle clutched her chest and feigned offense. "My, what an awkward situation," she said, spinning around to see fear in everyone's eyes. "I only wish to give a little performance, and I'll be on my merry way." She stepped close to the king and whispered through clenched teeth, "It is the very least that you owe me."

He took a deep breath and stood tall. "Then you will leave and never, ever return?"

"Of course."

Stepping toward his trembling wife, Zylvain looked at his trapped guards and conceded. "If she tries *anything*, do not hesitate," he said to Fleur.

Myravelle smiled wide, turning toward the congregation. "Once upon a time there was a ruthless prince who craved gold, poisonous wood, and power..."

She twirled her finger above her staff, and smoke billowed from the green orb taking the shape of a young Zylvain. Myravelle told the tale of how her mother became his captive, all the while the smoke mirrored her words. *The kidnapping. The beatings. The gold.* She then moved along to stories of the fairy raids and the attack on the Sleepy Wood Company.

"I have proof from a lieutenant." Reaching into the folds of her dress, she produced the letters from Eryck and Xavier. She tossed the letters onto the lap of one of the king's trapped guards so he could read them. "The king betrayed his own men."

She ended her story with how Zylvian used her mother's spun gold to pay for a healthy baby.

"Is that not correct, *Queen* Fleur?" she asked, tilting her head at the fairy.

"I have no idea what you're speaking of," Fleur said and crossed her arms. "Mother never revealed where the gold came from, and she sadly passed away along with her secrets."

"Liar!" Myravelle seethed through her teeth. She turned to address the congregation once more, gesturing at smoke images. "He kidnapped and enslaved my mother, spread propaganda about the fairies, and tested poisonous Dormrya weapons against his own subjects."

When the last word was spoken, the smoke swirled back into the emerald, and Myravelle leaned against her staff.

"You see," she said, pointing to Zylvain. "He is no king."

A thick and choking silence hung in the air, as if the smoke had rendered everyone speechless. Myravelle reveled in it, watching their eyes and waiting for someone to call for his arrest. She wanted to snap that crown of his in two.

"Blasphemy!" a single voice echoed from the rear of the temple, breaking the silence and causing chatter and laughter to rise like a tide.

"Liar!"

"Witch!"

"Traitor!"

"Arrest her!"

"Don't believe the Wicked Fairy!"

"She's the Mistress of All Evil!"

Blinking rapidly, Myravelle furrowed her brows and looked around the temple. She shook her head. *No, no, no.* Reality settled into place as they continued to cackle at her and call her nasty words. The people would never believe her. They would never trust her. The king had poisoned their minds. She snapped her gaze to him, next to his wife as they stood guard over their baby. *His precious heir.*

Right then, a new idea spun in Myravelle's head. A wickedly spectacular idea: as Fairy Queen, she was obligated to give the infant her own *blessing*. It would only be the proper thing to do. If she couldn't cause the king pain, she would cause him fear.

Deep and lingering fear.

"You've had your fun, now leave." Grinning, the king gestured to the fairies who approached Myravelle with their wands ready.

She raised her staff at them, making them pause. "Without blessing the child?" she asked in a faux-saccharine voice while her lips and eyes were tugged wickedly taut with madness.

"We want nothing from you." Queen Lya cradled the princess in her arms and inched her way to a side door.

Myravelle twirled her finger, and her undead soldiers entered, promptly blocking all of the exits. When they removed their hoods, Queen Lya shrieked and retreated to her place next to the king. The trapped congregation began screaming as well.

Fleur stepped forward and raised her wand with one hand while touching the moonstone with the other. "Go now, Myravelle. And take your unnatural creatures with you."

"It would be quite rude of me to leave before blessing the princess, though I do need ideas." Myravelle laughed and, with a twirl of her finger, sent Fleur's stick tumbling across the altar along with her moonstone necklace. "What was your gift for the precious infant, *Queen* Fleur?"

Sucking in sharp breaths, Fleur stepped back with her sisters to help guard the queen and princess. "I-I g-gave her the gift of beauty."

"Beauty, you say? What a vain gift." Myravelle rested her chin on her staff. "What else have you imbeciles blessed her with?"

"F-Faune blessed her with the gift of song," Fleur answered for her sister, who cowered behind her.

"Song?" Myravelle rolled her eyes. "Of what use is song?"

"These are fine gifts," King Zylvain said, nodding to Fleur. "For the princess already has everything she needs."

"Indeed," she said, narrowing her eyes at the king while her blood boiled. "*Everything she needs.* Isn't that how every child should be treated? Especially every child of a king?"

The king glowered at her even as his hands were shaking. "I've asked you to leave. I suggest you do so now, and I will let you go in peace."

"*Peace?* Peace!" Myravelle floated toward him, pinching his bearded chin in her hand. "I've never known a day of peace in my life because of you. I lived in constant fear of what you would do to my mother. I want you to suffer as I have suffered. I want you to know real and long-lasting and terrible fear. I want you to lose *everything*."

"No one wants you here," King Zylvain snarled. "You're a monster."

"I am the monster you created."

The king trembled under her gaze, but kept his jaw set tight.

She studied him, this vile man with whom she shared her very blood, and needed to know one thing. "Answer me this," she began in a near whisper, tears welling in her eyes. "Did you ever even love her? My mother?"

"One cannot love a spider beneath their boot."

Sparks charred the edges of her patience, and the temple filled with static. The crowd gasped and screamed. She wanted to snap his neck right then and there, but he wasn't good enough for a quick death. Taking a deep, cleansing breath, Myravelle composed herself. "Now," she began, releasing him. "I shall bestow a gift upon your child."

The king stumbled back, staring blankly at the marble floor at his feet while his cheeks drained of all color.

"Myravelle," Sola said, eyes wide and pleading. "Don't harm an innocent child, this isn't you."

"It is me." Myravelle spread her arms and twirled around, giggling. "I am the Wicked Fairy, the Mistress of All Evil, and I will get my revenge."

"Please, no," Queen Lya whimpered.

"Listen well, all of you." Myravelle twirled her fingers around the emerald orb, creating another cloud of smoke which rose into the air and formed the shapes of a beautiful blonde girl with a drop spindle.

"The princess shall, in her fifteenth year, prick herself with a Dormrya spindle and fall down dead."

The smoke princess touched her finger to the spindle's end and collapsed. Everyone in the room gasped, some even wailed. As she cackled, Myravelle's flow of magic broke momentarily, and the guards and guests ripped free from their invisible bonds. The smoking images dissipated. Confused, Myravelle glanced at the Three Good Fairies, who had their wands aimed at her, draining her powers into one of the princess's gifted gems. Faune plucked a large black opal, sparkling with Myravelle's powers, from the pile and handed it to Fleur. The fairies ripped smoky magic from her chest and filled the gem with storm clouds. She stumbled, finding it difficult to breathe.

"You may be strong, Myravelle," Fleur shouted. "But the three of us combined are stronger!"

The king's guards rushed Myravelle, who used all of her might to strike them with her staff. Shaking, she collapsed to the cold floor. Her undead army came to her rescue, mindlessly hacking the guards to pieces with their enchanted swords. Blood sprayed in the air and flowed freely across the marble, soaking into Myravelle's dress, and the guests fled the temple.

Led by guards, the king and queen slipped away with the infant princess before Myravelle could stop them. A few of the undead soldiers had cornered the Three Good Fairies, though, Byzarien being one of them. He knocked the black opal from Fleur's hand, stopping the drain of Myravelle's magic. Her limbs felt hollow still, and her eyes grew heavy.

Digging deep to retrieve any magic left inside, Myravelle was about to vanish when she spotted two guards overpowering Byzarien as more reinforcements entered the temple. *Not my boy of scars.* A feral howl escaped her throat. Scrambling in their direction, she tried to pry one of the men away from Byzarien, but she was too weak. The man whipped around and struck Myravelle's jaw.

She fell with the copper tang of blood filling her mouth. She opened her eyes to find a guard raising his sword above her chest.

When he brought the weapon down, Myravelle blocked his blow with her staff, sending shards of the Dormrya wood into the air. The splinters struck two of the men, who crashed to the ground in a death-like sleep. She looked around for the Three Good Fairies, who must have scampered away in fear, and only found more of the king's guards approaching her. Her breaths came shallow and rapid as she formed a plan.

Retreat, she commanded her men.

Clasping Byzarien's viny hand, Myravelle squeezed until the thorns bit into her skin and used pain to create magic, as she had done so often in the past. It was enough to send them home.

With a twirl of her staff, she and Byzarien vanished in a veil of smoke and fell to the rocky floor of Myravelle's castle. Peeling her bloody palm away from his, she wept on the ground for what must have been hours. When night stretched to every corner of the land, she dragged herself up the winding stone stairs to her bedroom and flung herself onto her straw mattress, where she slept for days.

40

The Wicked Fairy

Waves of the Sombry Sea roared and crashed against the midnight sand as Myravelle and Byzarien stood hand-in-hand. They watched Little Nightmare soar over the shimmering water. Myravelle's other fist clenched around a glass vial almost as tightly as the invisible thread spun around her heart. She leaned against Byzarien, even though the thorns on his arm scratched her face and snagged the stars embroidered on her dress. Tears blurred her vision and poured from her eyes, causing second thoughts. She shook them from her mind, though, and wiped her cheeks before taking a deep breath.

"I love you, Byzarien," she said, squinting against the bright sunlight to study the bark and roots, vines and leaves of his face. She imagined once more how handsome he had been in life. "We almost didn't get away at the temple because of my love for you."

Little Nightmare flapped past them like a shadow as he flew toward the distant forest. He had continued to spy on the king and, because of this, Myravelle had discovered that Sola had ruined her curse. *Sola, the most ridiculous of the three sisters.* She had changed the spell so, upon pricking her finger, the princess would be in a deep, dark sleep, only to wake from true love's kiss. Myravelle had hoped she could leave this life behind after the princess's presentation and join Byzarien on the Darkened Path, but now she had to wait. She stroked his face with her bloody hand, nearly shredded and perpetually bleeding from his thorns.

"I need to let you go," she whispered, voice raspy, her throat constricted as if by vines. "My heart breaks every time I look at you, because I know deep in my soul you never moved on to the Underworld. I know you will wait for me along the Darkened Path for eternity, and it kills me. Someday, I hope our souls will be reunited, but until then..."

She raised the vial of thick black liquid before her eyes. It matched the dark sands of the beach and the obsidian blooms of magic in her soul. "I must do this, or we'll never see our revenge." She sniffled and straightened her posture to feign bravery. "Goodbye, my boy of scars."

With one more glance at Byzarien's undead face, Myravelle tipped the vial's contents into her mouth. The acrid poison skimmed across her tongue and burned her throat while doubling her over with nausea and dizziness. Biting back the urge to vomit, she stumbled over to her staff and used it to hold her upright.

Before her eyes, Byzarien melted into the shape of an unknown man—no different nor more special than any of her other soldiers. Memories of kisses and daggers and sweet pea all slipped from her mind and fluttered away like moths. The invisible thread snapped and unspooled from around her heart, allowing the oily and sparkling tide of magic to swarm and swim inside the only part of her that had kept her good. Like dye, it soaked into every fibrous tissue, staining her heart black.

Magic crackled from her very skin, tinted greenish gray from the poison. Myravelle of the Stars was no more, for her entire being churned with galaxies of jealousy and fury. She fell to the sand and shrieked at the pain, the fires raging within as she became exactly the creation Filoux had always wanted. Little Nightmare cawed and landed near her, pecking her hand. The tattered edges of her soul caught fire and burned away Myravelle's essence, then waned and turned to embers of magic.

Taking a deep and rattling breath, The Wicked Fairy rose from the beach and returned to her dark and twisted castle on the Forbidden Mountain. Her army of undead men trained in the courtyard and served her every need. Up in the tallest tower, where she befriended spiders, she completed her gilded web of enchantments and wrapped it around the skirt of her dress.

The Wicked Fairy sat on her stool and spun, staring out the window at the valley below. The lush and green Sleepy Wood seemed to breathe like a living creature. Eglantyne City rested safely behind its walls, tucked in the hills while the Noire River tumbled toward the sea. With eternal winter no longer freezing the lands and starving the people, Eglantyne Kingdom was a peaceful, lush, and enchanting place. As she spun, The Wicked Fairy's mind turned with the same two names over and over. *Zylvain and Filoux. Zylvain and Filoux. Zylvain and Filoux.*

Night eventually blanketed the land, and fires burned throughout the city and villages beyond, even into the Sleepy Wood, which then twisted like an animal in agony. *Curious.*

Spy, she commanded Little Nightmare.

The crow soared over the great expanse of the Sleepy Wood until he came upon a grove of Dormryas, burning with magic fire. He swooped below the smoky canopy to find Fleur and a group of fairies enchanting all of the trees to burn. Even their sacred Hollow. Fairies knelt before the massive fire and wept.

Eglantyne City.

When Little Nightmare reached the center of the kingdom, in the square near the castle and Temple of the Gods, a massive bonfire roared. Guards organized the villagers into lines as they tossed spindles and random items of Dormrya wood into the fire, one by one. Apparently, with the kingdom thriving, the king no longer needed his experimental weapons of poisonous wood.

Move.

Little Nightmare flew to another fire on the outskirts of the city where villagers were also tossing spindles into a fire. Again and again, village after village, there were spindle fires everywhere.

In one village square, a soldier holding a scroll announced to the people in line, "As decreed by His Highness King Zylvain, all spindles and items composed of Dormrya wood shall be burned. It is a crime against the royal family to own such items, and anyone found hoarding them will be executed and disposed of in the Enferrix Pit."

When Little Nightmare flew toward the Pezit Quarter, a family with familiar dark hair cried as guards forced them to toss their spindles into the flames.

The king.

Little Nightmare flew toward the castle and perched in window after window to find the king. At long last, he found the man and his queen crying in one another's arms next to an empty cradle. All the gifts from the princess's presentation sparkled in the room like a magpie's den.

"I do not like this," the queen said. "This isn't fair; I want my baby here with me."

"It's for the best, Lya," Zylvain said, stroking his wife's golden hair.

"What if she finds her anyway?" Lya asked, eyes bloodshot.

"Queen Fleur assured me they would be prepared for her next time," he said, face hardening. "And now, we must prepare as well to make sure her *blessing* doesn't come to fruition. There will be no more spindles or Dormrya wood in all the land. I promise you: no harm will come to Briar Rose."

Home.

What started as a smirk broke into cackling laughter as The Wicked Fairy mulled over the king's idiotic plan, for she had plenty of poisonous wood for the princess. "Sorry, *Father*," she whispered, while twirling a Dormrya spindle with her fingers.

When Little Nightmare returned to her window, she set out fairy cakes, seeds, and water for him. "Good boy," she said, stroking his dark feathers. "Rest now."

The crow ate his fill and hopped into the basket of fluffy pillows next to his shiny trinkets on the floor. The Wicked Fairy glided to the hearth to stoke the fire when the acrid scent of sulfur and mildew filled the air and stung her nose.

"I wondered if you would ever show yourself to me again," she said, straightening.

Filoux approached, his greenish-gold skin glistening in the firelight. "*My creation*, you have made me proud. You have spun the entire kingdom into a tizzy!"

If her heart had still been part human and part fairy, the word *proud* may have made The Wicked Fairy feel...well, pleasant. Instead, bolts of rage and thunder of fury surged in her veins. "You," she began, clutching the gilded webbing of her skirts, "dare visit me in my home?"

"Correction: the Forbidden Mountain is *my* home." Filoux twirled his finger toward her and grinned with his black grin. "I detect a hint of anger."

"You don't say?" she asked between clenched teeth, nails digging deep into her palms.

"Dearie, your rage need not be aimed at me." He giggled with a high-pitched squeal. "The king is your enemy...I merely meddled with fate."

"*My* fate!" She glared down at the hideous creature while black smoke and lightning swirled through the green orb of her staff. "Your days of meddling are over."

"Sorry, but you cannot kill me." He held up his wrist and ripped into it with his teeth. The scaly flesh broke but nothing spilled out. "I do not bleed, for I am a god."

"I do not wish to kill you," she said softly, a rare smile playing on her lips as she pointed her staff in his direction. "I merely wish to torture and use you just like you did to me."

Filoux lunged for her, but she struck him with her staff. He rolled on the ground and laid deadly still. She crept up to him and bent over while clutching her gilded skirt. As quick as a spring, Filoux jerked up and pressed his thumbs into her temples. Little Nightmare's caws faded away, her eyes rolled back, and everything went dark.

The Wicked Fairy awoke, cold and soaked through with the putrid water in Filoux's tunnel. She pushed herself from the ground, hitting her head on roots.

"Filoux?" she shouted, her voice pinging against the stones.

She shuffled down the tunnel, feeling drowsy and dull, and found that more shafts were connected to it. Down one of the paths, something glowed. It drew her in like a moth to a flame. She followed the light into a room with her mother. Turning around, The Wicked Fairy was in the tunnel no longer, but in the tower. Spiders, spindles, stone walls, and all. Her mother, full of beauty and grace, spun gold in her chair. The Wicked Fairy tiptoed around the edge of the room, studying Xylina. Out of nowhere, her mother began sobbing.

"Oh, mother, please stop crying," she whispered, but Xylina did not hear her.

Lifting the spindle to her finger, Xylina pricked her finger and fell slack in her chair.

She screamed and reached for her mother, but the image warped into a new setting. One of the dungeons in the castle, of a moment Myravelle had tried to forget. Guards carried another unconscious man down the dark spiral stairs and plopped him onto a table. A young Myravelle hovered over the decaying and graying Pazcal, who weakly stroked her cheek. He had infected enchantments carved into nearly every inch of his skin.

"It's fine, my love," he said.

She mirrored her own weeping in the nightmare. Knowing it was the last time she would see Pazcal, she tried to step closer and look upon his face once more, but the image wobbled. This time, memories of every canvas who died by her hand flashed in rapid succession. Over and over again. Their rotten and butchered bodies. She tried to close her eyes, but the images remained.

She slunk to the floor like a wilted flower. *He's trying to weaken you*, she reminded herself. *This is Filoux's doing.* Taking a deep breath, she found herself back in the damp tunnels. Screams and cries echoed as nightmare upon nightmare surrounded her. She pressed her hand against the stone wall, wondering if she was where Filoux sent those trapped in a death-like sleep. Gathering her strength, she sprung up and ran, determined to find a way out. Around every corner was nothing but horror.

One dead-end tunnel was piled high with gilded thread. When she reached out to twirl the gold between her fingers, it bled while echoes of her mother's screams filled the air. She backed away into a new room where a cauldron bubbled and boiled. The Wicked Fairy peeked inside, only to find limbs, fingers, and eyeballs churning in the brew. She dashed away into a room which looked eerily like her tent in the Sleepy Wood Company. It had a worktable, a bed, dried herbs, paper stars, and all...but it all felt rotten.

Strong hands grabbed her from behind and shoved her to the bed. When she looked up, it was a giant and monstrous version of herself, grinning with teeth sharper than the dagger in her hands. The monster pinned her down while carving an enchantment over her heart. The Wicked Fairy shrieked and wailed in agony as the dagger sliced into her skin. She couldn't move under the monster's power, so she gave in to the nightmare.

This isn't real. Tether yourself to reality.

The Wicked Fairy closed her eyes. Through the sulfuric stench of the tunnels, she tried to pick out scents from her home. Herbs. Incense. The fire in the hearth. Above the shouts and cries, she listened. *Squawk. Squawk. Squawk.* Past the frigid and damp surroundings, she felt. The Dormrya staff in her hand and a beak pecking her cheek.

I am home.

When she squinted her eyes open, Filoux was still holding his thumbs to her temples with his eyes rolled back. The Wicked Fairy's heart raced while she formulated a plan. In one swift motion, she rolled on top of Filoux and pressed the staff tight against his scaly neck.

His brows scrunched over his yellow eyes as he tilted his head. "How did you—"

"Quiet!" She pushed the staff harder against his throat. Leaning forward, The Wicked Fairy repeated Filoux's words back to him, "*You will be my greatest creation.*" She ripped the gilded web from her skirts and tossed it over the god of nightmares like a net.

He writhed and moaned, suffering what she knew were horrific nightmares while steam billowed from his skin. She stood over him, absorbing his powers just like she had unknowingly done with Sebira's. Breathing in the tingling magic, she exhaled a black smoke that swirled around Filoux. While he struggled on the stone floor, his form began to change: his body stretched out like a serpent, his feet hardened into talons, his black hair twisted into horns, and his bones and scaly skin broke free from his back to create wings.

With every one of his whimpers and cries, The Wicked Fairy's cackling grew louder and louder, until she could not breathe. When she finally collected herself, she leaned over Filoux's shaking body and grabbed his slimy snout through the webbing.

"You shall meddle with fate no more," she whispered in his ear, "my pet."

The Wicked Fairy ordered her soldiers to dump Filoux into the lava of the Forbidden Mountain, where he would suffer her nightmares until he grew large enough to be useful. Only then, after paying for his evil meddling, could he be reborn from the ashes and help her terrorize the kingdom. As he thrashed in the molten lava, Filoux cried and whimpered at all hours.

The Wicked Fairy returned to her wooden stool near the window and prepared her roving onto a distaff. Lifting the spindle against the backdrop of the starry sky with fires dancing in the distance, she smiled at the beauty. Watching King Zylvain fret and listening to Filoux shriek for fifteen years would be such a delight. Something resembling giddiness bubbled in her cold, black heart. If her mother could spin, year after year in a tall, lonely tower, so could she.

Twirling her deadly weapon with her fingers, The Wicked Fairy spun gilded thread into the night, singing her mother's words.

"Draft and pinch. Draft and pinch.
Spin. Spin. Spin.
Draft and pinch. Draft and pinch.
Again. Again. Again."

Spinning was an art form of patience, after all.

ACKNOWLEDGMENTS

The idea for this wickedly delightful tale was inspired by a poem I wrote for a flash fiction and poetry challenge. The characters haunted my mind until I gave them their full story. I am grateful to the writing communities on Instagram and Twitter for inspiring me to see new stories in everything.

I am so incredibly thankful to Shawn, my husband, for not only believing in me, but encouraging me along my writing journey. He is my best friend, my biggest supporter, and my soulmate. He inspires me daily with his work ethic and is truly a prince who inspires many of the love interests in my stories.

I say this a lot, but I would have never started writing had it not been for my girls. As someone who fluttered from one hobby to the next, I always needed a creative outlet. It wasn't until my princesses were born that I needed a "quiet" hobby. I started writing down a story one day while my infant and toddler were napping—and I've never looked back.

Writing may be a lonely activity, but completing a novel takes a team. I am forever grateful to my critique partners, Alaura Filbin and Jenna Streety, along with my wonderful beta readers who all provided helpful feedback to make this story what it is today.

I am very thankful for Cassandra Thompson along with the entire Quill & Crow crew for believing in this tale. I feel so blessed to be a "crow." Thank you to my editors Cassandra Thompson and Eli Hayden Loft for polishing this work and making it shine like the stars. Lastly, thank you to my readers for your support.

About the Author

Rosalyn Briar is a former teacher, a mother to two fearless daughters, and a wife to her soulmate. She loves reading, traveling, and playing board games. More importantly, she believes in fairy tales. When she is not reading or writing, you might find her playing dress-up or gleaning through the woods for wildflowers with her princesses.

Also by Rosalyn Briar:
A Sea of Pearls & Leaves
The Mermaid & the Pearl
The Crown of Bones

THANK YOU FOR READING

Thank you for reading *Her Dark Enchantments*. We deeply appreciate our readers, and are grateful for everyone who takes the time to leave us a review. If you're interested, please visit our website to find review links. Your reviews help small presses and indie authors thrive, and we appreciate your support.

Other Titles by Quill & Crow

The Quiet Stillness of Empty Houses

The Ancient Ones Trilogy

The Blood Bound Series

All the Parts of the Soul